Falling into You

You

A.L. Jackson

NEW YORK TIMES BESTSELLING AUTHOR

A.L. Jackson
www.aljacksonauthor.com
Cover Design by Silver at Bitter Sage Designs
Editing by Susan Staudinger
Proofreading by Julia Griffis, The Romance Bibliophile
Formatting by Mesquite Business Services

Print ISBN: 978-1-946420-77-0
eBook ISBN: 978-1-946420-49-7

Falling into You

More from A.L. Jackson

prologue

Violet

I edged down the narrow staircase that led to the kitchen below.

Shadows danced across the walls and held the air in the steady peace of the night. A breeze blew through the valley and billowed through the trees. The hum of it softly battered at the walls.

Within the old house, the silence was heavy and dense. As heavy and dense as my heart that thundered at a ragged beat.

I inched farther.

Carefully.

Recklessly.

There was no longer anything I could do to stop the draw of the quiet chaos that waited in the darkened room below.

When I made it to the landing, my breath hitched with the gust of energy that suddenly lashed and whipped through the stilled disorder.

The man a storm where he sat like a stone fortress at the small kitchen table.

Protective and fierce.

His big body bristled with a rage that seemed to be waitin' for permission to be unleashed.

A wanderer who'd come home.

Did it make me a fool for wanting to remind him that this was where he belonged? That it was right for him to be adored? That he deserved to be loved?

I stepped deeper into the dancing shadows at the base of the stairs.

I knew when he felt me.

When his spine stiffened and his stony jaw clenched.

He slowly pushed to his full, towering height.

The man a dark avenger.

"Violet." My name rumbled through the air like rolling thunder. "What are you doing down here?"

Fear tumbled through my belly when I saw the lust flare in his eyes.

The greed and possession that curled his hands into fists.

But I would no longer live my life running from what I wanted most.

I could live in fear of what was to come, or I could live my life to its fullest, and I knew I wanted to live like a flower beneath the sun in full bloom.

I lifted my chin when I released the words, "I just need to know one thing right now, Richard Ramsey. Tell me it's true. Tell me you still love me because I'm done pretending like I don't need you."

Maybe I shouldn't have given him that trust.

Maybe I shouldn't have given him the chance to lie.

Maybe I should have known I would regret it all over again when I saw the guilt flash across his stunning face.

But I was finished running.

So, I stepped off the cliff I'd been teetering on for the last six years, straight into a free fall, and prayed he'd be there to catch me at the end...

one

Richard

I'd heard it said the thing about running from your past is it always catches up to you.

I'd heard it said that the demons of every mistake you'd ever made were constantly hunting you from the sidelines. Lurking in the darkness where they waited for the perfect time to attack, salivating at the chance to sink in their teeth.

A dark destiny ready to devour.

And sometimes? Sometimes they messed with the wrong damned person.

Someone who had nothing left to lose and only one sacrifice left to give.

Atonement and retribution their one purpose.

Doing a little hunting of my own, I blew out the back door of the banquet room. It dumped me in a long hall lined with doors.

Antique wall lamps cast a yellowed glow through the narrow space.

My attention jerked from one direction to the other.

Searching through the shadows that filled the corridor of the age-old hotel.

Swore I'd seen something.

Someone.

Someone who didn't belong.

That prickly feeling you got when something was amiss.

Wickedness underfoot.

Felt it slithering across my flesh and sinking into my bones.

The sounds of the party echoed through the wall. Carefree laughter, easy conversation, and the joy of the celebration.

What I should be doing was enjoying it with my family and friends.

With my band.

But no—I'd caught a feeling that I couldn't ignore.

Heart raging in my chest. This thunder that howled and ravaged like a beast.

I swore I saw a shadow dip out at the far end of the hall.

That was right when the door I'd just came out of burst open behind me and my future brother-in-law, Royce, came fuming through it.

"What's going on?" he growled. Dude was nothing but intimidation. Covered in tats and wearing one of those fitted suits that made him look like the reaper had come to collect and you were gonna pay. I darted in the direction of where I was sure the shape had gone. Voice filled with the intimation of the feeling I'd gotten, I shouted over my shoulder, "Someone's here who shouldn't be."

"Shit," Royce wheezed, right behind me.

Our feet pounded the floor, a vibration proclaiming destruction was on its way.

"This way. Think he slipped out the back exit," I shouted.

"Who?" Royce was right at my side, venom in the words, dude feeding off the rage I was throwing.

"Don't know, but I'm going to find out."

Desperation clawed through my chest as I raced down the hall, took the left, and pushed out into the night and into the dingy alley at the back of the old building.

My gaze jumped both directions, trying to catch onto a hunch.

To the intuition that had sent me hunting in the first place.

"This way." My head jerked to the left, and we both took off in that direction.

A heavy fog hung low in the darkened sky, and silvered rays slanted through the night from the muted lights flickering from the hotel.

Vengeance pulsed in my veins, and I gave myself over to the fight.

To the instinct to protect.

I rounded the end of the building just in time to catch sight of a burly shadow in the distance. Barely visible through the haze.

"Right there." I pointed at the lumbering figure that blazed a path down the side of the building.

"See him. Don't let him split."

"Not a fuckin' chance," I gritted, increasing pace as that feeling consumed me. Overwhelming in its pull.

I couldn't mess this up. Couldn't stumble. Couldn't stop.

We gained on him. Getting closer and closer. Close enough that I could taste the vileness that throbbed and slashed through the air as he attempted to flee like a pussy bitch.

Under the haze of dim lights, we could see the shape bolt across the next street up that was pretty much deserted.

Wasn't much of a surprise for a town this size at this time of night. Place was mostly shut down except for the few bars and restaurants that remained open.

"He's going right. Asshole is heading for the park." Royce's words were harsh. His breaths panted from his lungs.

Without slowing, I raced across the street, and my heart that was already beating a motherfucking drum jumped into my throat when a car came out of nowhere, making a quick right from the intersecting street.

"Richard," Royce shouted as the headlights bared down on me.

Tires screeched and a horn blared.

Panic jolting through my being, my hands shot out like that

was gonna make a lick of difference, planting on the hood just when the car came skidding to a stop.

"What the hell?" the driver shouted, honking the horn again.

"Holy shit," raked from my screaming lungs, the air coming in jagged heaves when I realized I'd been one distracted driver away from being toast.

My fault.

But the entirety of this load of bullshit was, wasn't it? I needed not to forget that.

Didn't give myself time to process or apologize, adrenaline the driving force as I shoved off the car and redoubled my efforts.

Frantic.

Desperate to get to whoever this bastard was who had the balls to show up here.

In my hometown.

On the night of my sister's engagement party.

Fact that it was undoubtedly not a coincidence only heated my blood another hundred degrees.

Once I hit the opposite sidewalk, Royce was once again right there, taking up my back.

My attention skated through the gloom. Chasing down vapor.

I rounded the building at the corner, glancing both ways before I raced for the park that sat sleeping on the other side of the street and took up an entire city block.

Lush trees grew up like a living hedge of protection, and playgrounds sat at all four corners. Fields for ballgames were in the middle.

In the daylight, it would be filled with children and laughter.

Families spending time together.

This place meant for everything right.

But in the lapping darkness, it reeked of depravity.

Ominous whispers and foreboding howls.

I dove right into the middle of it.

Footsteps pounded just behind and to my right. "You see him?" Royce panted.

"No. Go right. I'll take the left."

He ducked out, flying through a deserted playground while I

drove deeper toward the fields. Where it would be most secluded.

A frenzy burned inside. I had to find him.

My eyes searched.

My heart manic.

Felt like I fucking looked for days.

For a year.

Finally, I came to a plodding stop when I saw Royce coming out of a row of bushes that lined one of the fields.

"You catch sight of him?" I called, so out of breath I was halfway to bending in two.

Royce's expression was grim.

"Fucker's dust, man. Couldn't even pick up a trace."

"Damn it," I spat at the ground.

I tipped my face toward the night sky and inhaled a couple of long, cleansing breaths, planting my hands on my hips like it might stop me from coming undone.

Royce approached. "You get a look at his face?"

My lips pressed into a thin line. "Nope. Saw about the same thing as you."

His brow twisted in speculation. "Then how did you know someone was at the party?"

"Just...felt it."

He frowned. "You felt it?"

"Yup."

"You working off some psychic shit now?"

I tossed him a scowl. "Nope. Just working off my gut."

And my gut had every single hair on my body lifting on edge.

Awareness tripping my consciousness into high alert. Royce tipped his attention to the side, contemplating before he looked back at me, the words quieted and concealed, like we might have an audience standing around us when we were surrounded by the stifling silence.

"Maybe...maybe you're just gettin' paranoid, man."

My head shook. "No. Asshole ran. Proof enough for me."

His nod was glum because he knew it, too. "Honest, this is about the last thing I want to hear at my engagement party."

"Not what I wanted to hear, either." Terror ridged my spine, and I gulped before I forced myself to speak. "Think someone is picking up a trail."

"Or maybe they're just sniffing around. With the trial coming up, assholes are going to be out in full force, looking for a weakness. Fucker was most likely here for Emily or me, not you."

His teeth ground when he said it, his dark stare making another pass through the vacancy, aching for the kill.

No question, the guy would give it all for my sister.

Royce Reed? He'd been the Mylton Records exec who'd been sent to see to it that our band, Carolina George, signed on the dotted line with the mega record label. At the time, I hadn't known he'd had ulterior motives—he was in it to take down his piece-of-shit stepfather, Karl Fitzgerald, who'd been the record label's CEO.

"You don't actually think my stepfather and Cory Douglas are gonna go down without a fight, do you? After what I took from them?" Anger leaked from the statement.

Royce had undermined his stepfather's entire criminal organization and tossed him from his wicked thrown. Found evidence of the vile and depraved acts Karl Fitzgerald was championing—serving up a lifestyle of sex, drugs & rock 'n' roll.

No surprise there.

Except he'd taken it to whole new levels. Throwing lavish parties, drugs laid out on a silver platter in front of you, women or men there to entertain, naked and ready.

Only they weren't willing.

Not present of their own accord.

Forced into servitude.

Indentured to Karl and his seedy empire.

Too many artists were far too happy to take a slide into his perverted playground.

Little did they know they were being photographed. The images used to manipulate Mylton Records' artists into doing what he wanted. Siphoning from their royalties. Forcing them into amended contracts that completely screwed them. A leash tied around their necks. Call me a judgmental prick, but I knew firsthand most of them deserved it.

Problem was, I'd ended up in some of those pictures, but not because I'd been game to overindulge in what wasn't mine.

When Royce had struck, presenting the evidence that'd had Karl Fitzgerald and one of his top musicians, Cory Douglas, arrested, I'd struck, too.

Desperate to do something right. But it was dangerous and probably would cost me my life.

Because that empire went so much deeper than anyone knew.

But I didn't care. Nothing mattered but setting this one thing right.

I'd already lost everything else that mattered to me.

Royce was the only one who knew. The only one I trusted. Him and Kade.

I angled in closer, my tone a low hiss. "And you think they're not gonna notice what I took from them? You think that's just gonna slide? You and I both know Karl was nothing but a puppet. A fall guy. And you know that monster sitting up there on his throne playing Master of the World is pissed. You know he'll do whatever it takes not to be exposed. And if he's caught onto my trail? Coming back here would be the stupidest thing I could have done."

Might as well have put up a welcome sign with the way I'd invited them to my doorstep. Drawing them close to the people I wanted them farthest from.

Royce set his hand on my shoulder. "Whether they're here for you or me, we're in this together. We just have to play it cool until we make it to trial, you get me?"

I gave him a rigid nod and looked off into the distance when I answered, "Yeah."

Problem was, how we were actually going to get there. How we could pull this off when everything was against us.

Royce straightened his suit jacket. "Good. We need to get back to the party before someone notices we're gone."

"My sister will have your ass."

He grinned as we started back in the direction of the hotel. "Nah. She asked me to watch over you."

My brows rose to the sky. "She thinks I need a babysitter?"

"She thinks you're trouble, that's for sure."

A tumble of light laughter rumbled free. "And she thinks you're gonna be the one to get me out of it? Has she met you?"

He chuckled a dark sound. "Your sister basically told me she supports any and all measures in making sure Karl and Cory go down and go down hard. Think my taking up your back counts."

He spared me a telling glance. The less my sister knew the better. With the baby coming and trying to throw together a wedding before the trial, she didn't need the stress or the worry.

"Want justice for her. For your sister. For all of them," I said.

Karl and Cory had hurt far too many people close to me and it was coming back around.

They say payback is a bitch.

Nah.

She was the motherfucking executioner.

Richard

*S*traightening our suits, Royce and I slipped back through the front doors of the nicest hotel in Dalton, South Carolina.

Dalton was my hometown. Wasn't much more than a speck on the map. Farms for miles and old friends for days. You couldn't go anywhere without someone knowing your name.

Which was the reason when I visited, I typically slipped in and slipped right back out. Staying within the safety of the walls of my childhood house. Doing my best to keep under the radar which was kind of hysterical considering the fame our band, Carolina George, was skyrocketing to.

Yeah, that was fuckin' dangerous, too.

It was no secret I'd been pushing for my band to sign with Mylton Records. What they hadn't known was the real motive.

They hadn't known I'd been trying to get closer. On the inside.

To infiltrate far above Karl Fitzgerald himself.

Honestly, I didn't know how to balance this dangerous maneuver with the actual needs of the band who still didn't know what was going down.

No doubt, now that we were signed with Stone Industries, things were getting ready to change for the band and in a big, big way.

Wanted it.

Fuck.

I wanted it.

For my crew because they deserved it more than any group of people I'd ever met.

Just prayed this mess wasn't going to silence us before we even had the chance to really start.

Wasn't ashamed to say that Carolina George was good.

Hell, I'd go so far as to say great, and that wasn't arrogance rearing its ugly head.

It was just the fact of the matter.

Emily was our lead singer, the girl singing alongside me since she was barely five, always saying wherever I went, she wanted to go, too. Loved that girl to pieces. Thing was, there was zero bias when I said she had the best voice of probably anyone on the scene. Sultry and deep and mesmerizing, and she could write a love song like nobody's business.

Rhys, our bassist, and our drummer, Leif, were every bit as talented.

Throw me into the mix?

Suffice it to say we wrote some epic shit and we played it even better.

I roughed an anxious hand through my hair. Just didn't know how to manage both. Being a band and playing this risky game. Being here in Dalton only made it worse, the memories encroaching, suffocating me in the missteps of the past.

Maybe Royce was right. Maybe I was gettin' paranoid.

Royce shot a pointed glance at my disheveled appearance. "Pull it together, man. You look like you just rumbled with a pit bull in an alley."

"I wish," I grumbled, trying to tame my chaotic hair. As disordered as the rest of me.

Sweat beaded on my brow. Adrenaline still sloshing through my veins.

He laughed and patted me on the back. "Pin a smile on that face. Have a fucking beer. Play it cool. That's your only job from now until the trial. Well, that and standing up at my side when I get married."

He shot me a smirk.

"Only doin' that for my sister, man," I tossed back, teasing the asshole. I'd wanted to rip him a new one when I'd found out he and Emily had been sneaking into each other's rooms while we'd been on tour.

Didn't take long to realize he wasn't using her. That their relationship wasn't some twisted manipulation like I'd feared.

We climbed the steps out front and headed inside, crossing the lobby back toward the engagement party while we did our best to act like nothing had happened.

I glanced at him. Sober and direct. "Thanks for having my back."

He squeezed my shoulder. "Absolutely. We're family now...in every way."

"You good with that?" It was almost a warning.

He laughed a morbid sound that didn't have a thing to do with my sister. "Think it's a little late to turn back now, yeah? We're in this shit together."

Tied in a way that neither of us had expected.

"Nope...no turning back. Think we've climbed a train there's no derailing," I told him.

Voices floated out from the banquet room, lifting above the indie band Royce had organized to play for the event, the party still progressing like not a soul had noticed we'd been gone.

He looked at the watch on his wrist, flashing the ink that twisted out from under the sleeves of his suit jacket. "Shit. Toast is supposed to go down in two minutes."

I followed him through the main doors of the private room, the sound of the party amplified in volume by fifteen the moment we stepped inside. "Going to find Emily."

"Yup. Good luck, man."

He tossed me a look. "Don't need luck when I've got your sister."

He disappeared into the fray while I hung back at the far wall. Eyes scanning through the faces, every cell in my body on edge. Ready to jump in at a second's notice.

Town might have been small, but that meant my family knew everyone. The invitations for this party had stretched far and wide.

Piled on top of that were Royce's guests, the few members of his family he remained close to, plus the members of his band, A Riot of Roses.

Industry people ran amok.

Sebastian Stone, the owner of our new label, Stone Industries. Dude a legend in his own right. The original singer of Sunder who'd retired from the stage to start his own label.

Yeah, Sunder was there, too. All of them and their wives.

Fucking surreal that we were now surrounded by one of the biggest bands in the world, now a part of *their* world once we'd struck pay dirt after playing live at the ACB awards two months ago.

I rubbed at the nerves at the back of my neck.

God. That felt like a lifetime ago.

My gaze kept skipping through the faces. Searching for anything that might feel off while simultaneously trying to cool my fucking jets.

Round tables filled the enormous room, each of them decorated in pinks and whites and extravagant floral arrangements.

To the left, there was a dance floor over near the band, and a podium for the toasts was set up in the front.

Royce was currently making his way toward it, my sister's hand wrapped up in his as he led her that way.

True joy broke their faces in these smiles that would be impossible to deny.

A waiter carrying a tray of champagne was passing by, and I took a flute, drained the entire thing, and grabbed another before he had the chance to walk away.

Falling into You

Anything to dull this disorder that wouldn't settle.

This feeling that something was off.

Something wicked gathering strength in the distance. Encroaching fast.

The band trailed off when Royce got to the podium, and he lifted his glass to the room. "Have a little something I would like to say."

That was all it took for the conversations to die out as everyone turned their attention to him.

He cleared his throat. "First off, I want to say thank you to everyone for being here to celebrate with us tonight. I know some of you traveled great distances to be here, and for that, we are grateful. Means more than you could know to look out on this crowd and see the people who are most important to us. Ones who we love, and the ones who love us back."

A round of cheers went up.

Royce glanced at my sister before he looked back out to the crowd.

"Some of you might have questioned the way I came to know Emily."

His eyes traveled to meet hers, their hands held tight between them.

Royce glanced around. "But I want everyone to know that what I saw in Emily was instant. I saw greatness. I saw beauty. I saw a talent unmeasured."

His words thickened. "I fell in love with her when I probably shouldn't have. But the thing is, not loving this girl would be impossible."

A shock of joy pressed against the anxiety that gripped me by the throat—for my sister—for the fact she'd gotten free. For the truth of what shone in her eyes. It was the only thing I wanted, happiness for those that I loved. The ones I'd do anything for.

Live and die and destroy for.

"You showed me what it was like to live again, Emily," he continued. "What it was like to love again. You gave me a second chance when I'd thought I'd hit a dead end. Because of you, there is music in my life. There is hope in my spirit. There is love in my soul. You are my everything, and I cannot wait to spend my life with you."

Happiness radiating from her, my sister reached out and touched his cheek. "I tried my hardest not to fall in love with you, Royce Reed. It seemed crazy, the way I felt when we met. But the thing was, you were sent to make me remember what it's like to sing. To remind me what it's like to truly feel and how to fully trust. You helped me remember who I am and who I want to be. And I can't wait to be that person with you at my side, raisin' our children together."

I thought maybe he'd planned to say more, but he was setting his flute aside, wrapping her up, and kissin' her in a way that was pretty much inappropriate considering the crowd.

No doubt, my poor great aunt Shirley was going to be scandalized by the way the ominous-looking rocker was feasting on my sister right out in the open.

"Get a room!" This from Rhys, our bassist, who was up close to the front.

Our number one heckler.

Royce pulled himself away with a smug grin on his face. "Already got one. Right upstairs. You know where we'll be if you can't find us."

Everyone laughed and cheered.

While I itched.

That same feeling that something was off burned hot across my flesh. Something sticky making me tug at the neck of my shirt.

Suffocating.

Never should have come to this hotel. Too many ghosts lurked in the shadows. Memories I'd tried to bury that just kept getting dredged with every second that passed.

Wouldn't have shown for anyone else other than Emily and Royce. It wasn't like there were a whole lot of options in Dalton, though.

My eyes searched, roving over the guests from where I remained standing at the back of the room, readying myself for the attack.

My attention kept moving to where these heavy floor-to-ceiling drapes hung behind where the band was set up.

Area nothin' but shadows.

Didn't make a damned difference.

I saw her—saw her hiding at the edge of the crowd, timid and wary, eyes darting around like she wasn't sure if she belonged there or not.

My guts clenched, and the air punched from my lungs, so hard I might as well have been kicked in the stomach.

No question, she absolutely did not.

She shouldn't be there.

She couldn't be.

Uncertainty ran fierce, nothing but a slick of fear that warned this was fucking bad. That I had to get her out of there. Push her far, far away.

What the hell did she think she was doing there?

My teeth gritted, and my feet were moving, unable to stop this frenzy that took me over. I wound through the crowd.

Shouldering through the crush.

Surely I was comin' off a prick.

But I couldn't stop.

I was unable to see.

Unable to feel.

My only sense was the destruction that pounded out from the middle of me.

Knew the second she felt me. The way she went rigid, frozen to the spot before her attention whipped my way.

Girl held in shock, like she hadn't expected to see me there and had expected it all the same.

Guilt and something I didn't want to recognize clouding her face.

This was dangerous. Two planets orbiting too close. A collision seconds from happening.

Hurt poured from her stare, and that body rocked in recognition.

A fireball that blazed, burning through the air and eating up the oxygen.

Wisps of black hair fell out of the twist and caressed her cherub face.

Defined cheeks pinked and glossy lips parted.

And fuck it all, my stomach twisted in a gnarl of lust.

The girl looked like a fairy made of blown glass.

Gorgeous and fragile and so strong you wondered if she was really made of stone.

Raven eyes stared back while I made my way toward the girl with the most mysterious eyes.

Pupils surrounded by a starburst of crystallized violet and splintering out to a darkened eternity.

Two blinding thunderbolts.

It was like looking into a kaleidoscope that sucked me into the past.

That sucked me into regret.

She wore this flowy floral dress that hit her at mid-thigh, nothing but toned legs and tight, gorgeous body.

Temptation.

Destruction.

My ruin.

Still, I moved for her.

Unable to stop.

She fidgeted, wavered, her attention darting everywhere before she finally made a choice and turned to run.

I chased her out into the lobby.

Bright lights shined from glittering tiered chandeliers that hung from the three-story ceiling. Lighting her up in sparkles and dust.

She rushed toward the main doors.

Her name dropped from my lips in a hiss. Problem was, I didn't know if it was in anger or pure desperation. "Violet."

Violet

*W*hat did I think I was gonna achieve, comin' here?

I'd known better. Known so much better, but I'd somehow been delusional enough to convince myself I could slip in, witness the joy without anyone noticing me, partake in it in the only way that I could, and slip right back out.

Delusional enough to think I would manage not to get my heart slaughtered anew from a single, scathing look.

In this stupid hotel I'd avoided like the plague, nonetheless.

From behind, my name hit me like a stone.

"Violet."

Hatred flowed through his voice, as stark as the betrayal in his presence.

I faltered for a moment, trapped by the sound, before I frantically looked around the lobby for the nearest exit. A large group from the engagement party had gathered at the front door, laughing and hugging, blocking my escape.

"Violet. Turn around. I want to talk to you."

He wanted to *talk* to me?

Disbelief had me darting toward the next best thing—the sweeping, curved staircase that the opulent hotel was known for. The massive wooden pillars supporting it were carved in intricate flowers, and the stairs that were at least thirty feet wide were covered in the same lush, maroon and gold carpet as the rest of the floors.

I fumbled up them as quickly as I could, the high heels I rarely wore making the task a whole lot more difficult.

Especially when I could feel him. When I could feel him coming after me.

The heat of him rippled through the dense air and covered me in a thick shroud of treason and deceit.

Chains that threatened to bring me to my knees.

I gasped in relief when I made it to the second floor, and I took off to the right, having no clue where I thought I was going except for someplace safe.

Someplace he couldn't get to me.

Someplace he could never hurt me again.

"Violet."

I only made it about ten steps before a hand latched onto my wrist.

Fire flashed up my arm. A fiery storm that consumed me whole.

A rasp raked from my lungs, and my eyes were widening all over again when he had me backed up to the wall before I even knew what had hit me.

A goner before I'd even known I'd been struck.

Sounded about right when it came to Richard Ramsey.

Intense, green eyes flashed ire and spite, as if he had the right to be angry with me, his chest heaving as he grated the words near my face. "What the fuck are you doing here?"

I jerked my arm free, my teeth grinding and my eyes squeezed shut when I spat, "Don't touch me."

Did a whole lot of good considering it only afforded him the space to edge in an additional inch, a wraith that boxed me in between the shadows of the cavernous, deserted hall.

The man towered over me, and his head dropped closer to mine, his breath a soft caress across my cheek though his words were sharp as razors. "And what? You think I should just let you go? Let you walk away from me?"

"You have plenty of experience with that, don't you? Letting me go?" I shouldn't have opened my eyes, shouldn't have allowed myself to look at that face that glared down at me with this violence and agony that I couldn't process.

That I couldn't understand.

My eyes raced to take it all in, and my mind spun like mad with every question he'd left me with while my hands ached to run across the hard planes of his gorgeous body.

His dark aura hit me like a bad dream that I didn't ever want to wake from. A decadent, smooth chocolate melting on my tongue that hit my bloodstream like a straight shot of poison.

Every angle of his face was carved and chiseled and sharp, except for those full, velvet lips that rested somewhere between loathing and horror.

Hair cropped on the sides and longer on top, darkened to a bronzed brown over the years, like every bit of him had aged and deepened and changed.

Like he'd stepped right into that role of a music god. Harsh and intense.

A dark poet.

The shocking potency of it left me all kinds of foolish.

Impulsive and rash.

The way he always made me.

Unable to stop myself, I reached out and barely brushed my fingertips along the distinct curve of his rugged jaw.

Such a fool.

"God, Richard, what happened to you?"

When did he become a man I didn't recognize? Doing exactly the opposite of what I'd trusted him to do.

He flinched and snatched me by the wrist again, only this time, to stop me from touching him. "Don't."

I lifted my chin in defiance. "You used to like it when I touched you."

A bolt of fury left his nose. No doubt, I was playing with fire.

"That was a long time ago," he grated.

"And what changed?" I didn't mean for my voice to slip into a plea. For the suffering he'd caused to come tumbling out.

His eyes dropped closed, and his jaw clenched. I caressed it, the scruff that coated his face, like I was attempting to dip my fingers into the past and knowing I'd never find my way there.

Knowing it had been nothing but a fallacy.

A fantasy.

I pulled my hand away and pressed closer to the wall like I could disappear into it. Still, the man pinned me.

Trapping me in the gaze that had always hypnotized.

The man had always been nothing but a tornado blowing through.

"What are you doing here, Violet? Told you to stay away. From me. From my family. You think you can just waltz in here like you belong? Because let's be clear…you don't."

Every muscle in his body flexed.

Hard. Rippling with an anger that had come into existence sometime when I hadn't been paying close enough attention. Or maybe I'd just been too lovedrunk on the man to see what was lying in wait.

The cruelty that scorched his spirit and sparked from his mouth.

"Then let me go," I whispered hard. "You're the one who chased after me."

Pain lanced through his expression like it was possible that this was as hard for him as it was for me.

"Goddamn it." He exhaled a breath of dire recklessness, and his forehead dropped to mine, his voice dragging through the guttural rasp, "Goddamn it, Violet, I don't know how."

Confusion churned and spiraled and whipped.

This agony that shouted, *why, why, why?*

How could we be perfect one minute and the next he was

leaving me with some pathetic excuse of a note that said goodbye?

I fought it—the tears that wanted to surface—only for both of us to freeze with the gasp that ripped through the air.

Richard's attention jumped over his shoulder.

Emily stood twenty feet away, shock and disbelief and hope in her eyes. "Violet?"

She said it like a question.

Like she couldn't believe I was there.

I was having a hard time believing it, too.

Richard pushed away from where he had me pinned, freeing my body but there was no chance he could free me from the clutch he had on my soul.

Forcing a bright smile, I swiped at the moisture that leaked down my cheeks. "Emily. Hi."

"You're here," she whispered in that low, sweet voice.

I stumbled away from Richard and toward her. Knees weak and my heart flailing. "I'm…I'm sorry. I-I just wanted to see you. To see your happiness for myself. I didn't mean to overstep."

Richard's sister shook her head. "Why would you say that? I invited you. I wanted you here."

The low rumble of a moan echoed from behind. There was nothing I could do but look toward it.

At the man who now had his back pinned to the wall, like he was hooked there, being tortured, his brow twisted in anguish.

Wearing a fitted suit and looking like the star I'd always known he would be. A few tattoos leaked out from under the sleeves of his jacket, the man standing like mayhem and chaos.

I tore my gaze away because continuing to stare at him was liable to do me in. Rip out the last thread that was holding me together.

"I'm so happy for you," I told Emily, the words barely heard through the emotion that clogged my throat.

She came for me, and she wrapped me in her arms and hugged me tight.

Relief gushed from my lungs, and I squeezed my eyes shut as I hugged her as hard as I could, as if it might make up for the lost time.

"Congratulations," I murmured.

Her arms tightened around me. "I'm happy, Vi. Truly happy."

She pulled back and took me by both hands, swinging our arms between us. "I missed you so much."

"I missed you, too."

Her attention landed on her brother, and it felt as if the two of us had gotten stuck in the middle of a thunderstorm. No place to go but to stand under the ferocity of it.

Their gazes held, and I could feel it when he gave, when he retreated down the hall. Wave after wave of anger hit us in his wake.

She shifted back to look at me, her signature blonde curls bouncing over her shoulders, as pretty as she'd ever been. "I'm so sorry about him, Violet. So sorry that he would act like this."

A feeble smile wobbled at the corner of my mouth. "Please...don't be. He brought us together, didn't he?"

She reached out and played with a lock of my hair. "And he tore us apart."

"He tore a lot of things apart."

Her green eyes that were so much like her brother's searched me, this opalescent sage that made me ache and covered me in warmth. "How have you been?" she asked, studying me for the reaction.

"I'm great."

It was a lie, but that was okay. Sometimes you had to tell them in order to get by.

Sadness darkened Emily's expression, and she squeezed my hands in a show of support. "I heard about your mama. I'm so sorry. How is she doing?"

Affection wavered all over my mouth, sorrow and love swimming through the words. "As feisty as ever except for the fact she hardly has the energy to get out of bed."

"And Daisy?" Emily didn't wait for an answer.

Instead, her confession flooded out in a rush, "I was gonna come by, you know. I'd already decided once I got back...while we're here on this break...that I was coming to you. No more of this. No more of you not in my life. It's not worth living life in regret, and I was hoping you might need me as much as I've needed you."

"I do…I missed you more than I can say."

I fought for a lighter subject. The last thing I wanted to do was put a damper on her party.

I turned my attention to the rock on her finger that was as big as the one rolling around in my throat. I lifted her hand between us, refusing to let her go now that we had the connection. "Wow…that is some kind of statement."

Adoration oozed from her pores. "Royce can be…a little over the top."

"Over the top is just fine as long as he is over the top for you."

Wistfulness fluttered through her expression. "I found my heart, Vi. He might look my opposite, but he is my exact match."

"I'm so happy for you. Truly. And the band…I heard y'all struck it big. Got signed with a major label."

I pinned on the brightest, fakest smile.

"We did. Everything I've ever wanted is coming to be. I'm so blessed."

Another tear slipped free, but this one was nothing but joy. She brought my hand to her flat belly.

"Oh," I murmured on a gasp. "Oh wow, you're gonna be a mama?"

She nodded like crazy. "Yes. I still can hardly believe it."

"Oh goodness, Em."

Happiness tangled with my sorrow.

She glanced around covertly like we were being watched.

"No one else knows yet except for my family and Mel, of course."

I grinned through a sniffle.

Mel, that crazy girl. She was Emily's best friend which meant she'd become one of mine.

"Where is she?"

"Oh, who knows. Probably downstairs knocking some poor, unsuspecting fool down a notch or two."

I laughed, unable to believe that we were like this.

Us.

Like no time had passed.

Except for the fact that everything had changed.

"I didn't mean to cause a hiccup in your party. Honest. I just wanted to tell you congratulations. See for myself that he was good for you. Wish you all the joy in the world."

"Don't say it like I'm not gonna see you again."

Regret trembled my chin. "I'm not sure hanging around is such a good idea."

"Rich made his choice. He doesn't get to make ours."

"What if it hurts too much?" It was out before I thought through the admission, but I'd only ever been up front with Emily.

She caught her bottom lip between her teeth, and her head tilted to the side. "And what if it hurts too much without *us*?"

I warred, chewing at the inside of my cheek, before I suggested, "Lunch?"

She giggled. "I was thinking something a little more along the lines of dress shopping, but I'm sure we could fit lunch in, too."

My brow furrowed.

She squeezed my hands in emphasis. "I want you to be in my weddin', Violet."

"Em."

Distress blazed. Misery over what she was asking and grief over the thought of saying no.

"Please. I miss you. I want you standing beside me when I take the most important step of my life."

I nodded, even though a horrible feeling was taking me over. "I'd be honored."

"Really?"

"Really."

It would have been a whole lot more convincing if the word hadn't cracked.

I angled my head toward the stairs. "Now, you better get back to your party."

"Are you going to be okay? Are you sure you don't want to come down? I'd love to introduce you to Royce."

"Someday soon, but I think I need to call it a night."

She hesitated before she nodded and leaned in for a quick hug.

"Okay. I'll talk to you soon. And I mean that." The last she said with a bolt of carefree laughter, pointing at me as if she had me pegged.

"I'm sure you do." I let lightness weave into the words.

I watched her as she turned and headed back for the stairs, tossing me a soft smile as she went. I waited until she'd gone and then worked to gather myself. To put myself back together.

Then I lifted my chin and headed for the stairs as if the man didn't have the power to affect me. To set me off-kilter.

I had too much to be living for to give him the power.

It was a valiant effort, but it didn't change the fact I could feel the weight of him as I edged down the stairs. It didn't change the potent energy that lashed and flared and chased me into the night.

His eyes daggers as he watched me go.

four

Richard

*T*here's a thing about living a lie.

That lie eats at you. Festers and decays and rots away the good until the only thing that remains is regret.

From where I was hidden below the staircase, I watched her flee across the lobby.

Let her go.

I could have chanted the plea a thousand times and I doubted it would have made a dent in the urge that screamed at me not to let her out of my sight.

To love and to cherish and to protect.

She blew out the hotel doors in a riot of color.

Violet and magenta and teal.

Hair a striking black.

A moonflower in distress.

My guts knotted with the chaos she incited. I might have been the one who'd had her backed against a wall, but she was the one who had me chained.

A motherfucking prisoner.

Possession rose like a storm, a roar that intensified. My hands curled into fists like it might keep me rooted to the spot.

No chance I could ignore the call. Not after I'd been sure some scumbag had come riffling around like a predator cloaked in the night.

I edged out the door, gaze instantly peering to the right where she quickened down the sidewalk, her heels clacking on the pebbled stones.

She ducked into the same old truck she'd driven since I'd met her that she had parked at the curb. Not a second passed before the loud engine rumbled to life like a low roll of thunder in the dense, thick night.

She whipped out of the spot and accelerated down the road.

I jogged to my truck parked on the opposite side, climbed in, pushed the button to the ignition, and pulled out behind her.

My headlights cut through the night, and her taillights were nothing but a haze of red dots up in the distance.

I forced myself not to tail her too close. To give her some semblance of space and respect when the only thing I wanted to do was toss her over my shoulder and carry her away where I could keep her safe.

Was pretty sure she wouldn't be too keen on the idea.

I followed her through town, keeping back a block, slowing even more as she took the two-lane road that led out into the rolling hills outside of Dalton.

Farms on every side.

My pulse skittered in a stagnant beat of loss as I drove the deserted road that was so familiar. A million memories rushing and gathering and screaming their truth.

"I love you. Forever."

"Not ever gonna let you go." My voice a growl as I held her close. As I touched her and adored her.

My fairy girl.

My magic.

My reason.

My insides panged in a want and a loyalty that I'd twisted and mangled so fuckin' bad they were no longer recognizable.

I eased around the sweeping curve that I knew would bring the modest farmhouse into view.

Still, it struck me like it was the first time I was seeing it. Like I was going to meet her parents and confess what their daughter had done to me.

Slayed me with a look.

It was off to the right, perched high on the hill.

Tonight, it was lit in a dreary moonlight.

Quaint and peaceful and *safe*.

It overlooked the rolling planes that went on forever behind it.

Rows and rows of flowers, shrubs, and blossoming trees grew over the acres.

Rolling Wallflowers.

The flower farm that was the heart and soul of who Violet was.

My spirit ached and throbbed like it was looking for its rightful place. So near. So far out of reach.

"You are the light hung in my night sky."

"You are the sun breaking with morning's day," she whispered back.

Like some kind of stalker, I pulled off to the side of the road. Watched.

Watched her truck jostle up the dirt road and come to a stop in front of the wraparound porch. The lights cut off, and a couple seconds later, a shadow of her shape climbed to the porch, wrapped in the glow of the lights hanging on either side of the door.

She disappeared inside, and my stomach clutched when I saw the light flicker on through the window upstairs a moment later.

Sorrow smacked me across the face.

Every dream that we had wished.

But that's what happened when you cast lots.

When you made bad bets.

When you thought for even a second something else might be more important than *this*.

You lost.

Fifteen minutes later, I was driving up the narrow one-lane road that led to my childhood home. No chance could I show face back at Emily and Royce's party tonight.

No doubt, Emily was itching to string me up by the balls.

Would deserve it, but still, I wasn't looking for a fight. She and I had had it out enough as of late. The lies I'd been telling, the dark space I'd been keeping her in, making her question my motives.

Her trust.

When I'd been pushing her to sign with Mylton Records when she didn't understand my reason—my desperation behind it—coming off like a complete prick, like someone who hadn't given a shit about her hopes and dreams and wants when it was the farthest from the truth.

It'd fuckin' sucked.

But I'd tell lies until my mouth rotted off if that's what it took.

My fucking head throbbed. Body aching and spirit moaning. Missing and missing and missing.

The road came to a fork at the top of the hill. Rhys' childhood home was on the left, ours was on the right.

Taking the right, I eased up to park in front of the darkened house. The unassuming two-story was done in natural stained woods, quaint and peaceful and close to plain, the home surrounded by trees.

The stalls and barns were out back, and our younger brother, Lincoln, had a house he'd built out on the farthest section of the property.

I physically cringed when I saw Royce's rental car parked at the side of the house.

"Shit," I mumbled as I put the truck in park and killed the engine.

Wary, I climbed out.

Instantly, I felt the stir in the air. The hostility and anger and confusion.

She had every right to them.

She was sitting on the top step, and Royce was leaning on the railing off to the side.

Two of them waiting.

Royce cut me a glance of apology.

He was doing this for his fiancée.

I pushed out a sigh and roughed a hand through my hair. "Fuck...I messed up your party."

Emily pushed to her feet.

"No. The evenin' was over, anyway. We stayed until everyone left."

"And weren't you supposed to be staying at the hotel tonight?" I hiked a brow.

Royce chuckled. "Don't worry...we're heading back. Doubt very much your parents want to hear what I have planned for Emily tonight."

Emily huffed at him, but it was in pure affection. "Royce."

He shrugged. "What?"

"Do you have to be so crass all the time?"

"Uh...yes?"

A light chuckle fell from my tongue. Two of them this perfect contradiction.

She turned back to focus on me. Even through the lapping darkness, I could see the concern on her face. "I don't understand, Richard. What did I see back there? Why would you treat her that way? She was my guest."

My teeth clamped down on my bottom lip to keep from shouting a thousand curses. To stop myself from giving her information she couldn't have. "What happens between Violet and me is between Violet and me. I told you that before."

"Yeah, and what happens between she and I should be my own business, too, shouldn't it? I invited her—one of my best friends—someone I care about deeply." She touched her chest in a plea. "And you made her feel like an outcast. Like some kind of reject."

My own frustration burned through my blood. "I asked you not to invite her, Emily. That was my one request, coming here and staying here, and you did it, anyway. Imagine my surprise when I saw her standing across the room. Can you not give me that one ounce of respect?"

"It was my engagement party." She looked at me in disbelief.

Yeah, and this was *our* lives.

My head shook in frustration.

"I know that, Emily. But I asked you not to invite one person. One fucking person, and you couldn't give me that."

"I've been asking you to let me in for years. Beggin' you to make me understand why you would do this. What you're going through. I know there's something there, and after everything? After Cory getting arrested and us being signed with Stone Industries instead? After you know what happened to me? And you still keep me in the dark?"

"Fuck," I muttered, looking toward the ground like it would afford me patience. Or maybe I could find a hole and bury myself to escape the guilt that was going to eat me alive.

No atonement for what had been done.

Emily and I had gone round and round for the last few years. Fighting.

Me coming off like a prick at every turn.

But she didn't understand what was at stake.

That I had always been on her side.

That I wanted nothing more than to make this better.

I hadn't known the brutality she'd been subjected to because of me.

What that bastard Cory Douglas had held over her, used as twisted manipulation.

I couldn't wait to see that fucker burn. She wanted answers for those pictures I was in. Problem was, those were answers I still couldn't give her.

That was what happened when your life was made up of lies. When you'd been cut off at the knees, bartered through blackmail and intimidation.

I took a step toward her, my head angled low in a bid to reach her. "You think I keep you in the dark to protect myself, Emily? Because I'm some twisted fuck keepin' deranged secrets? I keep you in the dark because it's the only chance I have of making this right."

"I know that. I just don't understand what it has to do with Violet," she begged. "Why you would treat her that way. She was…"

She trailed off, but I knew.

She was amazing.

Kind and good and genuine.

Every-fucking-thing I'd wanted and had proved I didn't deserve.

Fuck. I wanted to yank every last hair from my head.

Royce moved to stand behind Emily. He set his hands on her shoulders, and his voice turned soothing, "Emily…come on, baby, take a deep breath. You don't know what he might be going through. We talked about this, yeah? About everything needing to run its course before it's revealed. Besides, that's his ex we're talking about."

Emily stared over at me with hurt on her face.

"But this is different. This is Violet we're talking about." Her head shook while Royce continued to support her from behind. "I…I just don't understand you, Richard. She loved you like crazy. Would have done anything for you. You should have offered her the same."

I surged forward. "Please. Just don't, Emily. Don't. She's in the past. I need her to stay there."

She had to.

"I love her like a sister. I want the best for her. She needs us, Rich. Her mama and Daisy…" She trailed off with the implication.

She might as well have finished with the way her declaration smashed through my being.

Grief constricting airflow. Throat closing off. Chest squeezing like a bitch.

The words were haggard when I stumbled forward and urged from two feet away, "If you care about either of us, then let her go."

I climbed the steps, winding around her to head inside.

I had to put an end to this.

Leave that girl in the past where she belonged.

Pretend like it didn't matter.

I had the screen door open when Emily's voice hit me from behind. "What if I can't do that?"

I spoke toward the still closed door, holding onto the handle like it might keep me from getting blown away by this storm I felt brewing. "If you want the best for her then you will."

"I asked her to be in the weddin'. She accepted."

Every word felt like a dagger being stabbed in my back.

My teeth ground.

Anger and dread surged.

Overwhelming.

I punched the wall next to the door, roaring as I did it. Pain shattered from my knuckles to my wrist. Anything to divert the fury.

Emily yelped like she was the innocent one in the situation. But the truth was, she had no clue what she was doing. What she was inciting. Thinking she was fighting for the good when she was only going to ruin me a little more.

I turned around to look at her. "Great, Emily. Just fuckin' great."

Because I didn't know how to be in Violet's space without losin' my damn mind.

Didn't know how to look at her without breaking every damn promise I'd made.

Didn't know how to walk this thin line.

Without looking back, I tossed the door open, stormed inside, and moved into the dining room where I grabbed a bottle of bourbon from my father's stash in the cabinet.

They say you can't drink away your problems.

Well, I sure as fuck was going to try.

Violet

*S*unlight flooded through the sheer drapes in my room and nudged me from the last dregs of the horrible night of sleep I'd had. Tossing and turning, falling asleep only to jolt awake from the dreams that wouldn't leave me alone.

My skin still tingled with the phantom vestiges of his touch. My senses still filled with the aura of the man.

I sat up in bed, my knees drawn to my chest, and I rubbed at my wrist that still burned from his caress while my ears continued to ring with the cruelty of his words.

Standing in his presence had made me feel like I was being ripped to shreds by a tornado. Tossed from one direction to another. Lost somewhere between the torment of his eyes and the rejection that had blazed from his body.

I guessed maybe the hardest part of it was the connection that flamed and lapped underneath it all.

Electricity.

That bolt of intuition I'd forever felt whenever he'd come near.

The man like destiny.

A force that could not be denied.

No matter how hard we tried to dismiss it, it was there. Clear where it held fast to the atmosphere.

And if I wasn't already slugging through the dregs of turmoil, the man had had the audacity to follow me home.

The overwhelming presence steady and unwavering as it'd pulsed through the night.

I'd had to stop myself about fifteen times from pulling over and demanding that he leave me alone. That I couldn't handle whatever game he played. To beg him to stay.

Captivating and repelling. The refusal in the same second it felt as if he had me caught in a snare.

Hunting me for the sole purpose to annihilate.

I blew out a sigh, when I heard the indistinct chatter of voices and the clanking of dishes that drifted up from downstairs. I refused to allow myself to lie there and waste any more time on a man who didn't care about me.

I tossed off the covers and forced myself from bed.

I used the restroom, brushed my teeth, and took the small set of stairs that led down into the kitchen.

I was struck with the scents of a typical Sunday morning.

Coffee and biscuits and bacon.

A soft smile tugged at one side of my mouth as I stopped at the threshold at the landing and peered through the blaze of morning light that speared through the cozy room.

The kitchen filled with so much country warmth that it was impossible not to feel at home.

At peace.

My chest stretched tight as I gazed at my father at the stove where he was whipping up his specialty of eggs, bacon, and pancakes while he sang an old Spanish song under his breath.

Daisy was at the table, trying to sing along.

The only person missing was my mama.

My heart clutched, but I did my best to force it down and not to bring a dark cloud over the sweet scene playing out in front of me.

I edged forward and the old wood floors creaked beneath my bare feet. My father's attention swept toward me, a grin splitting his face. "Ah, mi amor."

Daisy's head popped up, all too eager to parrot her papa. "Mi amor!"

Light laughter slipped passed my lips, and I edged farther into the kitchen, heading for my father and pushing onto my toes so I could press a kiss to his cheek. "Good morning, Daddy."

He eyed me, speculation lifting a single brow. "I hope you're hungry?"

I had a feeling he wanted to ask a whole lot more questions than that one.

I nodded. "I am. It smells delicious."

He grinned. The deep wrinkles around his eyes crinkled, making him look older than fifty-eight. The last few years had come on harder and harder.

"Good. Our Daisy here might have dumped in the whole box of pancake batter." He tossed her a massive smile over his shoulder before he sent me a wink.

"I am starvin' marvin'. We needed the whole big box," she said, not bothering to look up as she focused on coloring in her book, her tongue poked out at the side as she concentrated.

My spirit lifted. Shivered and shook as I crossed the room. I leaned over the chair where she sat on her knees and planted a kiss on the top of her head, lingering as I inhaled, the child smelling like orange juice and bubblegum.

Sunshine.

A single ray of light cast into the darkness.

"Good morning, sweet girl. Were you good for Nana and Papa?"

"Mornin', Mommy. I was the best, right, Papa?" she coaxed.

No doubt, she wouldn't accept a different answer.

"Oh, yes. An angel," he told her in his Spanish accent.

She nodded in fierce agreement. "See. An angel."

Affection tightened my chest, and I gently ran my fingers through her black hair.

"Did you have all the fun last night at the party?" She tipped her head backward to look at me, her sweetness oozing out.

All the fun?

Not so much.

I cleared the roughness from my throat. "I did. I got to see my old friend and tell her congratulations."

"'Cause she's gettin' married?"

"Yep, that's right."

I could almost see the lightbulb go off in her little mind, and her eyes went wide with excitement. "Is the weddin' gonna be here in the special place? Can I go? Remember we got to go to Polly's and I got to be the flowers girl and I was the prettiest princess in the whole world?"

Panic flashed across my flesh, and a stone of dread sank to the pit of my stomach.

God, what had I gotten myself into, agreeing to be a part of the ceremony? This was going to be a nightmare.

I pulled out a chair so I could sit down in front of her. Reaching out, I lovingly tipped up her chin, doin' my best to keep the words from quivering. "I do remember, and you were the prettiest. But I'm not sure of the details yet on this one."

"I sure hopes so! Love weddin's…but only if there's dancin'. Dancin' is my favorite in the whole world. Except for horses. I like horses even better. I'm the best dancer, right?" she prattled on, her chubby cheeks puffed out and her pink cherub lips pursed in question.

Her dark hair was cut in a bob, though it naturally curled out at the shoulders, the child so pretty she looked like a missing piece of the porcelain seraphim collection my mama had inherited from her mother and now had displayed in a case in the formal living room.

"Ooo…ooo…" She raised her hand as if to volunteer. "Do you think I could be the flowers girl for this weddin', too? I got my fancy new shoes. I could go gets 'em real fast."

I would have laughed if I wasn't tied up in a thousand knots.

I blew out an exasperated breath. "I'm sure they have already made plans. You might be getting out ahead of yourself."

Way ahead of herself.

But that was Daisy's way. Running into life head-on. No reservations. No fear.

"Pancakes are almost finished. Can you get the tray ready, Daisy Doolittle?" my father cut in.

"Oh, yes, Papa!" She scrambled down from her chair, ran across the kitchen, and pushed the step stool to the cupboard so she could reach the tray and dishes.

Interrogation forgotten.

I glanced at my father.

He sent me a wink.

Daddy to the rescue, as always.

He plated two pancakes and a small bit of scrambled eggs, and Daisy put the small container of syrup beside it, plus a knife and fork and a napkin.

"One more thing!" She hopped down and ran to her coloring book, ripping out the page and folding it in two. She climbed back onto her perch and placed it on the tray. "There. All ready."

Pride shined from her dark eyes.

I kissed her forehead. "Perfect."

I picked up the tray, and I glanced at my daddy. "I'll take it to her."

His expression faded to somberness. To that weary sadness that he fought to keep contained but would bleed out the second he let down his guard. "I'll be up in a minute. I'm going to clean up a bit."

I sent him a soft smile. "Okay. Take all the time you need."

Daisy raced out the swinging door of the kitchen ahead of me, her little feet pounding on hardwood floors. She darted up the stairs, taking two at a time, and I followed along as quickly as I could.

She hit the top floor landing and burst through the bedroom door to the left, her little voice drifting down as I started up the stairs. "Nana, breakfast is served!" she sang as she banged inside. "You is gonna be so excited!"

I could barely make out the distorted, raspy voice mixed with Daisy's boisterous shout, and my chest tightened and squeezed and panged with each step that I climbed.

I did my best to pin a smile onto my face when I rounded to the door, but I could feel it slipping when I looked inside and found my mama struggling to sit up against the headboard.

Her face ashen, as if she'd aged a thousand days in the last week, the cancer sucking the life right out of her body.

It took everything I had not to drop to my knees and weep.

"Violet," she whispered when she saw me standing there, and even with the pain I could see written on her failing body, she smiled the most brilliant smile.

One wholly directed at me.

Dark eyes the same color as mine brimming with the love she had. That single expression alone left no question of who I was to her. What I'd always meant.

It was something no distance or space or circumstance could ever change, but that didn't mean that made this any easier.

"Good morning, Mama." I tried to keep the warble of emotion from my voice. It still cracked.

Her smile shifted to stark somberness. My mama reading me the way she always could.

In tune with my emotions.

Heck, she'd written the dictionary on them.

And considering those emotions were tugging at me from every direction, there was no question she felt me unraveling.

"Come inside." She patted the bed beside her.

Daisy took that as an invitation and jumped onto the spot on her knees, bouncing all over the place and jostling Mama.

"Daisy," I corrected her.

Mama tsked and waved me off, shifting her attention to the child. "You are my sunshine, aren't you, sweet girl?"

Daisy nodded emphatically. "Yep, I's am!" She started to sing off-key in her voice that should be a balm, "You are my sunshine, my only sunshine, you make me happy, when skies are gray…"

But today, everything was too raw. Too real and wrong and devastating.

I tried not to choke on that clot of grief that always lurked in the recesses, but somehow today, it felt suffocatin'.

Agony so intense it fought to overwhelm.

It left me wondering if I might not make it.

Daisy continued to sing, her innocent joy echoing through the room, while I stood there, frozen to the spot. When she finished their favorite song, she leaned forward and plopped a messy kiss on my mama's cheek.

So sweet.

Mama melted, this puddle of sorrow and joy, her thin, sunken arms wrapping around my child as if she wanted to imprint her embrace on her forever. "Beautiful, my darling Daisy. You keep singing your songs forever."

"I will, Nana. Forever and ever. You'll hear me, right?" she asked, suddenly worried, pulling back to look at my mother.

We'd prepared Daisy. Been as honest as we could in a delicate way.

But I'd learned quickly there was no way to prepare myself.

My knees wobbled, and there I stood, still holding her breakfast tray while I fought the stinging at the back of my eyes.

Mama brushed her fingers through Daisy's hair, solemn affection on her sallow face. "Forever and ever. You keep singin', and I will be listnenin'. Just turn that sweet face to the heavens. I promise. I'll be there."

Mama cast her attention on me, no doubt feeling the waves of torment coming off me.

I sucked it down and forced myself to move farther inside. Carefully, I set the tray on her lap and made sure the legs were adjusted just right.

"My, my, what is this?" she gushed, plucking up the picture and opening it to a squealing Daisy who started bouncing on her knees again.

"It's for you. It's for you." She got up close to Mama's face, hunting for the truth. "Do you likes it? It's got all the colors and all the flowers and the *amor, amor, amor*!"

Love. Love. Love.

It swirled and danced through the room.

She cupped Daisy's face. "All the amor."

Daisy beamed in high voltage.

"Thank you, my darling Daisy."

"You're the welcomest, Nana."

"Why don't you get me a piece of tape and hang it right there so I can look at it all day?"

Mama gestured at the wall that was already covered in the pictures that Daisy colored for her each morning. The display was interspersed with the *get-well* cards that had been coming in at a steady stream since the news had spread around town and the neighboring counties.

Daisy scrambled off the bed. "Be right back," she shouted as she flew out the door, taking all her energy with her.

"Sit with me," Mama said, coaxing me to the spot on the opposite side of where Daisy had been.

Carefully, I sat down on the edge of the bed, drawing up a knee so I could face her. I brushed her matted hair from her sweaty forehead, praying another prayer that I could take it away. Make it better. Do something that would change the brutal reality of this.

She reached out and touched my chin. "Don't be sad, my beautiful daughter."

One of those tears I'd been fighting slipped free. "How could I not be?"

She traced the pad of her thumb over the trembling of my bottom lip. "Because I've lived the best life I could have lived. Have loved and have been loved. Have been given the greatest gifts."

Agony stretched tight.

I'd been wearing an armor of strength for so long, trying to hold everything together for my mama and papa, for Daisy, but I could feel it getting stripped away.

Piece by piece until I was brittle and bare.

Unable to handle the itchy feeling, I pushed to standing and paced toward the window as if I could hide it, hugging my arms across my middle as I stared out on the fields of awestriking color that rambled for acres behind the house.

"You saw him last night." It wasn't even a question.

I glanced back at her with a weary smile. "I did."

"How was it?"

I choked out a laugh. "Horrible. I haven't felt so weak in a long time, Mama. I thought I'd overcome it, and one look at him, and I realized I'm not even close. I shouldn't have gone."

Mama's expression twisted in compassion. "Just because you continue to grieve someone you lost is not the same thing as weakness. It just means you have a soft heart. A good heart. One that continues to beat. And even though it hurts, you get up each day and you live your life beautifully. That's what I call overcoming."

"Mama," I whispered, not sure how to accept her praise when I was feeling this way. I shook my head as if it could toss Richard Ramsey right out of my psyche. "It doesn't matter. Let's just forget him."

Mama blew a huff of air from her nose. "Oh, I'd say it does."

"He left me. That's that."

She stretched out her hand for me, palm up, like she could reach me from there. "Oh, Violeta...there is a very fine line between love and hate. Between condemnation and forgiveness. Between cherishing the memory of a beauty that has faded and hating that it existed in the first place."

I huffed like a petulant child. "I do kind of hate that it existed in the first place."

"But would you take it back?" she pressed. "What does your heart say?"

Mama had always taught me to listen with my heart.

I bit down on my bottom lip, wavered, memories rushing too fast.

His face and those hands and the songs he'd left written on me.

"I don't know." That was about as honest as I could be.

Desperate to change the subject, I pointed at her tray. "You should eat before your food gets cold."

She picked up her fork and pushed her food around, not taking a bite.

"Mama," I begged.

This time, her smile was sad, the look in her tranquil eyes telling.

Knees weak, I moved her way and knelt at the edge of her bed, unable to remain standing. "Mama," I said again, gathering up her hand in a fist and pressing her knuckles to my lips.

"It's okay." She shifted to set that frail hand on my cheek, taking my fingers with her.

I pressed her hand closer.

Desperate to keep her near.

She stared at me, her scratchy voice barely breaking the surface, "It's a good life, Violet. A good, good life. Miss me, but do not despair."

Her thumb stroked my cheekbone, my mama shaking as she murmured, "I am missing only one thing. There is only one thing that I would change."

Grief lashed through her expression, and I saw it for what it was.

She glanced at the empty doorway, at the sound of Daisy bounding back upstairs.

She looked back at me, the truth of her loss flooding out. "Find her, Violet. If there is any way, find her. Bring her home to me. I want to see her one last time."

Anguish squeezed my heart in a fist, completely crushing it when Daisy appeared at the door and came racing in with the tape dispenser lifted over her head. "Got it!"

She ran around me and grabbed the picture, oblivious to the torture that raged inside me.

The fear.

The worry.

I pushed to my feet and pressed a soft kiss to my mama's temple. "I'll try, Mama. I will try."

Knowing her last request might very well be my end.

Peals of laughter floated through my open bedroom window,

a soft breeze blowing through and billowing the sheer drapes.

Fall descending on the hot air.

I glanced out at my father who pushed Daisy on the swing, the child squealing and begging him to push her higher.

Little daredevil.

Affection pulsed through my veins at the same second as my heart trembled in a quiver of dread. Fear glided over my flesh in a sticky flash.

My mouth went dry as I turned back to my laptop that was set on the small white desk under the window. I set my fingers over the keys, and a rush of dizziness canted through my mind.

I was unable to type. Unable to focus. Unable to see.

God, I was terrified.

Terrified of the unknown.

Of what was to come.

Of what I could possibly find.

Of what this might cost.

When she'd first gone, I'd searched for what had felt like forever, desperate to find someone who didn't want to be found. Unable to process the selfishness while I'd reeled with the grief.

I glanced back out the window. Daisy pumped her legs, her sweet face stretched in a brilliant smile as she tipped her head back toward the sky. "Look at me, Papa! Look at me! I'm flyin'."

Emotion clogged my throat, and I squeezed my eyes closed as I forced myself to type the name into the search.

Liliana Marin.

Nausea swept through me when I peeled my eyes back open and I read what the screen had populated. As the same results from all those years ago showed.

Mentions from college where she'd attended in Charlotte.

The restaurant she'd worked at here in town.

The last was a missing person's report that had been written in the paper.

Then nothing. Her Facebook account inactive. Her phone disconnected.

My older sister gone without a trace.

Daisy's precious voice flooded my room. "Higher, Papa.

Higher! I flies so high in the sky. Just like a bird. I'm not even scared. Not even a little bit."

I swallowed hard as I turned back to the computer, typed in a search for a local private investigator, and then inputted the number on my cell.

I clutched it in my hand.

Warring.

Wavering.

Then I pressed send.

And I realized I'd never been so scared in all my life.

Richard

I kissed her like mad in the hallway at the back of the swanky restaurant where we'd just eaten in Hollywood.

I didn't care we were basically right out in the open.

I had my hands on that face as I devoured her mouth. "I love you, Violet."

She grinned beneath that kiss, those lips slipping into one of those smiles I wanted to be responsible for every day of my life. "I think I'm plenty aware of that."

I pressed her farther against the wall, my jean-covered cock rubbing at the floral dress that had been driving me nuts all night. "I think you might need a reminder."

She rumbled a seductive laugh. "We'll have plenty of time for that later."

I groaned. "Don't make me go."

Violet giggled. "This is the whole reason we're here. Go. Enjoy. They want to take you out. Show you what this life is goin' to be like." She leaned up and whispered in my ear, "Superstar. Just wait...everyone in the world is gonna know your name."

I edged back and stared down at her.

Violets and grace and the good.

"Every dream I have is one I want to give to you."

She smiled in sheer adoration. "Together."

"Together."

"Wakey, wakey, asshole."

I jolted awake with the shock of the obnoxious voice ripping me from my dream, and my head jerked from my pillow. I squinted through the bleary light, doin' my best to process the earthquake that shook me awake.

The fucker was jumping on my bed near my feet.

In his boots.

Rhys Manning.

Our bassist.

My best friend for my entire life.

Ex-best friend if he kept pulling stunts like this.

"What the hell?" I threw my pillow at him.

Rhys caught it against his chest. He busted up laughing like he actually thought this shit was funny. "Get up, sunshine. We've got important things to do. Day's almost half done."

With a moan, I slumped back onto my mattress. "You couldn't call or text like a normal human being?"

Rhys jumped off the side of the bed, house quaking as he hit the floor. "Uh, I've texted ten times and called three. And if you lump me in with normal humans, you and I are gonna have a problem. How dare you compare me to a mere mortal when I am a god amongst men. Do you even know me?"

I scrubbed my face.

It was too early for this shit.

"Go away."

He ripped my hands back. "Nope. We have a mission from my mama."

Distress banged through the fucking hangover staging an assault in my head. "I think I'm just fine right here."

Last night was a disaster.

A travesty.

A motherfucking joke.

All of it on me.

"Dude, my mama is making her special homemade chicken pot pie…and she needs a chicken, so we're going to the store. That or she's going to have our asses out at the barn plucking one out of the coop. Your pick, man."

Ugh.

No. Just no. I might have been born in the country, ridden a horse or two, but that's where I drew the line.

Tossing off the covers, I sat up on the side of the bed. "Fine."

A spike of pain pierced my brain. I moaned and rammed the heels of my hands into my eyes.

Shit.

Good fuckin' luck with the whole drowning my problems bit. Only thing taking a swim in a bottle of bourbon had done was double the misery. The gaping hole in the darkest part of me ached and moaned. A blade struck right through my brain, the piercing stab of it a reminder of what I was in the middle of.

Of what I could feel coming closer.

Rhys laughed and patted me on the head. "Aww…did someone have too much to drink last night? Makes me wonder where you disappeared to without sayin' a word. Sketch, baby."

I smacked his hand away. "Fuck off, man."

He laughed harder. "Touchy."

"I'll show you touchy," I warned.

This time he cackled. "You're adorable, Richard. Truly adorable. Keep up with those dreams about taking a stallion like me out. Now get some damn clothes on and let's roll. My mama is downstairs with yours, hatching a plan. Word of warning: favorite topic right now is that surprise guest who showed up last night."

He lifted his brows.

Busted.

Fuck.

No doubt, every busybody in the state knew Violet had shown.

Which undoubtedly meant every single one of those gossip-hounds were currently spreading the word that I'd followed her out. In a town like this, I might as well have set fire to Town Hall.

I really did have to get out of here. Last thing I needed was to face my mother after the stunt I'd pulled last night.

If I'd thought my life was a bad dream, it'd just become a nightmare.

"Fine. I'm coming."

"Meet me downstairs in five."

When he slipped out, I tossed the covers off and groaned as I got out of bed.

No matter which way I cut it, this was gonna suck.

Fifteen minutes later, we were blazing down the road in Rhys' ridiculously over-the-top car at warp speed.

A brand-new GT500.

Lime green and black, of course.

"Would you slow down, asshole?"

"Not a chance, brother!" Rhys drummed on the steering wheel as he shouted out the open window, his dark blond hair blowing all over the place. "Freest I've felt in forever. Home sweet home, baby!"

Rhys blew out a whistle as he dragged his face from the window and faced forward. "Woo wee, is it ever good to be back. Ready for a little R & R. Remind my bones where they came from before I let the limelight go to my head. A country boy could get used to all that glitz and glam."

Dude actually tapped his temple.

I cut him a raised brow. "I'm pretty sure something got to your head, and it doesn't have a thing to do with the limelight."

Rhys busted up and reached over the console in my direction. Asshole patted me on the cheek, action just as condescending as the tone of his voice. "Aww, come on, Richey-Poo, don't be jealous I got double the Gram followers after our big show on the ACB Awards. I know it stings, brother, but there are some of us who are just meant to go down in the history books. Some of us who were meant to love all the ladies. Some of us who are meant to go down in a blaze of glory."

He let his left arm drift out the window, riding on the wind, his grin going double-smug. "No need to get bitter over it. I'm happy to give you a ride on my coattails, and I won't even take credit for it."

I scoffed. "You wish, dude. And would you watch the damn road?"

Rhys was as ridiculous as they came. Loud and obnoxious and wore his heart on his sleeve. He was this thick, brawny, tattooed boy with dust on his boots and country in his soul. He never hesitated to say whatever he was thinking and was glad to throw in a little extra BS, too.

We'd grown up next door to each other, best of friends, two of us nothing but reckless dreams and nonstop trouble. Pretty much drove our poor mamas out of their minds with worry.

I guessed they hadn't been too far off base.

"You know the only reason all those women follow you is because they want to see pictures of you without your shirt?" I goaded him.

After every show, the doucher ripped his shirt from his body and tossed the sweaty, drenched mess out into the crowd. The women who caught it had started a tradition of taking a picture of themselves wearing it with nothing else under and posting it with the hashtag #IGotWetWithRhys.

Dude was a walking STD.

His expression turned wry. "You're saying that like it's an issue."

"Hey, man, all I'm saying is we know who's got talent around here, and it's not you," I teased.

He smacked his hand over his heart. "How dare you! The blasphemy. Stab a boy in the heart, why don't you? I'll just be over here bleeding to death."

He went blazing around a corner, the town coming up fast, words still running nonstop from that flapping mouth. "Words hurt, man. Cut as deep as a knife. Fuck that old saying about sticks and stones. We know the real dagger is the tongue. And here I thought you had my back. I bet you've been trying to get rid of me for years."

"You never know."

Okay, so Rhys Manning was a badass. There was no secret that the ladies loved the hell out of him, boy nothing but charm and charisma, but truth of the matter was he was a fucking beast on the bass. Out of this world talented.

Just like the rest of us.

Unfortunately, Rhys loved to cross every line that had been drawn.

"Don't make me bury you in a shallow grave, man. You know that would hurt me more than it would hurt you," he said, choking back tears.

Pure feigned affliction.

A chuckle rambled around in my chest.

"Do I need to call Melanie to come pick you up?" I raised a brow, waved my phone in the air in warning.

"What? God no. Save me. Mells Bells gets off on cracking the whip."

Melanie was our band manager and my sister's oldest friend. Had grown up across town, the girl as close as family. Was pretty sure we'd be a shitshow if it wasn't for her making us toe the line.

"I'm on vacation, remember? Why would you go and threaten something as horrifyin' as that?" he asked.

"You know you love her bossin' you around."

His head shook. "Nah. Not the way you think, man."

"Sure."

"I am nothing but the speaker of the truth."

He barely slowed as the farms disappeared behind us and the buildings got closer together.

In the daylight, I glanced around at our small hometown of Dalton, South Carolina.

As hard as I tried to keep it down, dread rose.

A searing burn that slugged its warning through my veins.

Nothing but heavy, lethargic beats, heart this slow, hardened drum I could feel in my ears.

Attempting to ignore it, I took in my surroundings.

The place felt so far removed and so familiar at the same time.

Sunshine blazed from above, the sky an endless blue, and a cool breeze swished through the leaves of the trees that grew from the strategically placed planters along the sidewalks. Boughs of colorful flowers grew around them.

Stores lined the narrow streets that had been there for as long as I could remember, old brick buildings that looked like they'd been haphazardly glued together, every color and shape.

Beneath the rays of sunlight, in the brightness of the day, I could almost forget that I'd been chasing down a monster haunting the shadows last night.

Could almost pretend like I didn't feel ghosts prowling for their prey.

My attention scanned, peering into the alleys and coves like the bastard would show his face in the light of day.

Lurking at the fringes of peace.

Fact that some monster was out there had me riding a razor-sharp edge. Butt that up against the thoughts of Violet that swirled and taunted and fought for acclaim?

Had no clue what I was supposed to do. Where I should stand. The lines of my loyalty that should be solid and underscored in black had become grayed.

Right and wrong no longer clear.

Rhys actually accelerated instead of slowed as he took a hard right, tires squealing as we went. I held onto the door handle, leaning with the turn.

Unease shivered beneath my skin when I glanced around.

I was right.

Town wasn't going to be a whole lot safer than facing down my mother.

Every eye on the street shifted our direction as Rhys blazed like a demon down Main Street, speculation and judgement hot on our tail.

Let's just say Rhys and I didn't have the best reputations around here. The bad boys who'd slayed their daughters' hearts and rained havoc on the quaint, quiet streets. Country boys who'd gone rogue, selling our souls for bigger and better things, that dotted line signed in our blood, success and fame and riches at the cost of condemnation.

Sounded about right.

Rhys rammed on the gas, whipping around an old truck that rambled down the road. Dude fucking laughed as he blew by.

I pitched him a glare. "You couldn't possibly buy anything less flashy, could you?"

"Absolutely not," he said, tossing me a grin as he gunned it around a corner.

Asshole was nothing but a bull on a rampage, tearing shit up and being as loud as possible while doing it.

"You compensating for something?" I let the razz out into the air.

He laughed maniacally. "Oh, dear brother. You only wish. Believe me, I don't have a thing to make up for."

He waggled his brows, dude still looking at me when he made a sharp right and skidded into the parking lot of the grocery store.

If the rest of this bullshit wasn't my end, Rhys' driving was bound to do me in.

He rumbled through the lot and pulled into an angled spot at the front. "Hell yes. She is everything I knew she'd be."

He lovingly stroked the steering wheel.

"You're a freak, you know that?" I asked as I unlatched my seat belt and cracked open the door. "And a terrible driver."

"What's the matter? Have your balls gone missin'? You need to borrow some of mine? Mine are big enough to go around."

"Eww and no and what the fuck?" I leaned over the console and punched his shoulder.

"Oww." He rubbed at the spot, throwing me an overexaggerated pout. "Uncalled for, man. Uncalled for. Why you gotta be so violent? I was barely going over the speed limit. It was under control. Calm your tits."

I slipped out, my brow shooting toward the sky as he got out and looked at me from over the top of the car.

"Barely?"

Laughing, he sauntered toward the entrance. "Speed is relative. Fast to one person is another's eternity." He waved his hand for me to follow. "Let's do this. I'm starvin'."

Dude was always starving.

I followed him inside, and he grabbed a cart. Didn't even have it in me to be surprised that he rode it around like he was twelve. He rolled halfway down the cereal aisle, only hopping off to chat with Mrs. Lancaster, a high-school friend's mom, who couldn't help but reach out and touch his tatted arms.

Okay. So, we might have come with reputations but that didn't mean women weren't still all too happy to reach out and brush up on that fame.

Drawn to danger.

Problem was that people didn't get what that really meant. How dark and depraved our worlds got. The sordid, sick corruption that ran rampant.

The greed and the shame and the gluttony.

"Let's go," I told Rhys, not willing to stand around and watch that bullshit going down.

"What's the rush?"

What was the rush?

"Don't want to be here," I told him, point-blank. "And you were the one who just told me you were starving."

This town bled too many memories.

Made me crave and thirst and long.

Her face flashed through my mind.

Violets and dreams and the girl.

Seeing her made me contemplate things I couldn't.

Made me think...*maybe.*

Maybe and what if.

And having thoughts like that would be my ruin.

Utter destruction.

I'd known coming here for Emily and Royce's wedding was going to be an issue. Staying for so long. Unable to slink in to visit my parents and slink right back out without anyone noticing. Knew it was going to leave me riddled with so much regret and loss that it was going to be hard to stand.

What I hadn't known was it would become dangerous in a way that I couldn't have anticipated. Thoughts of who I might be dragging into this town were crushing.

Falling into You

Feeling like I was gonna lose it, I strode the rest of the way down the aisle.

"Sheesh. Come on, man. Can't you feel it? People miss us. They need the life breathed back into them," he shouted at my back. "This town has been on standstill since we left."

I shook my head. "Only thing we would do is suck it out of them," I muttered under my breath.

I couldn't afford it. Couldn't afford wrecking one more life.

I itched, nerves crackling like the threat of a summer storm.

A surge of energy.

Electricity.

Fuck.

I rubbed at the back of my neck.

I was this close to going apeshit.

Awesome. Just what the town needed to witness. A meltdown, too. Needed to get out of there and go back to passing time, playin' the fool, until the trial came to pass.

I moved for the butcher at the back, asked him for the largest, freshest chicken they had, and I had it in the cart by the time Rhys finally weaved his slow ass up to me.

It thudded on the metal like finality.

"Let's go."

I stormed up the side aisle that opened to the bakery to the far side. The smell of sugar and spices and dough wafted through the air.

Leon, who'd baked there for what had to be a million years, still held vigil behind the counter.

But it wasn't the old man who used to sneak me cookies who stopped me in my tracks. What sent dread and need and guilt crashing through my body. So intense I nearly buckled in two.

It was the woman standing at the counter chatting with him. The girl wearing a messy braid that hung over one shoulder, a tank, and short jean shorts, a pair of high-top Chucks on her feet.

Soft and seductive.

A moonflower.

A black-haired angel swayed at her side.

Daisy.

The air punched from my lungs, so hard it left me on a rasping gasp.

Sight of her left me staggered.

Shattered.

A million cracked, splintered pieces on the floor.

My mind shouted to look the fuck away. To turn my back. To run and not return.

But I was edging forward, unable to stop, unable to think.

Only able to go for what I'd been running from for the last six years.

Knew the second Violet felt me, the way her spine went rigid and chills skated across her skin.

Goosebumps rippling.

I wanted to press my hands to it and chase the thrill. Let my tongue follow suit. Get lost in the sea of it.

Collide with destruction.

Since we were ruined, anyway, what more could it hurt than it already did?

That little angel at her side turned like she sensed me, too. Dark eyes the same color as Violet's grew wide, her adorable face breaking out in a curious smile.

Guilt. Guilt. Guilt.

It stabbed and slayed. Cut me open. My guts nothing but a bleeding, mangled mess left like an offering at their feet.

"Hi. Whatcha doin'? You want a cookie? Do you smells that? Mr. Leon makes the yummiest, yummiest cookies in the whole wide world. Well, except for my papa. My papa's are yummy, yum, yum to my tum, tum, tum, but he makes a different kind."

She held one out to me.

Shit.

Someone needed to tell this kid not to talk to strangers.

I roughed a hand through my hair, anxious, but maybe not as anxious as Violet who finally forced herself to turn around and face me.

Fuck.

Didn't matter how many times I looked at this girl. There wouldn't be a time when she didn't knock the breath from my lungs.

She looked like a little bit of magic.

A taste of serendipity.

"Mommy…look…it's the man in your prettiest picture."

Mommy.

My heart spluttered. Failed. Maybe as hard as I had failed them.

And to this kid, I was not a stranger.

She recognized me. Violet had kept a picture of me where she could find it. Would I have thought she wouldn't have, though? Thought she would have purged all evidence of me away?

I knew her better than that, didn't I?

Daisy clung to her hand, swinging around at Violet's side, canting so far toward me that Violet had to hold her so she didn't face-plant onto the floor.

"What's your name?" she asked, her eyes narrowing with keen curiosity. "I asks before but Mommy told me she would tell me when I got big."

She looked up at Violet. "I'm big now, right? I turned five and now I'm almost all the way to six."

The last she directed at me, lifting her hand to show me the evidence with her fingers. Only it was the hand that was holding the cookie. It dropped to the floor and shattered into a million pieces.

Violet looked like she was going to do the same.

Fall apart.

Crumble right there.

I just wished I was strong enough to catch her. Hold all those pieces the way I was meant to do.

"Oops. Sorry," the little thing said, her hand going to her mouth, her chubby fingers splaying over her lips to hide her embarrassment.

Violet's throat trembled and those magnetic eyes filled with moisture. She glanced down at the child. "You're right. You are big. This is Richard, Daisy." Her voice trembled when she said it.

The little girl tugged her hand from Violet's and shoved it toward me. "Nice to meet you, Mr. Richard."

Hand shaking like a bitch, I took it. Felt the warmth. Grief crushed me by the throat. Felt like I was pinned to a wall and being choked out. "It's nice to meet you, Daisy. You have a very pretty name."

A smile split her face. "My papa named me, just like he did my mommy." She leaned forward farther, dropping her voice like it was a secret when she said, "My mommy's name is Violet. Like a pretty flower."

Like I didn't know.

Like I hadn't whispered that name a thousand times.

Moaned it when she'd shown me what heaven really was like.

Shouted it when I'd wake in the middle of the night and realize she really was gone.

Tried to clear the roughness, but the words were raw, "Yeah, her name is very pretty. Just like the rest of her."

Violet shook.

Anger and disbelief.

Could I fuck this up any worse? Stand there like a beggar, a prodigal, and ask her to forgive me?

But I didn't even want that.

Knew I didn't deserve her forgiveness.

Just standing there was breaking every rule I'd given myself.

Nothing but another vulgar betrayal.

But I wished to God she could at least understand.

"We should get going," Violet grated through the emotion clogging her throat.

"Well, who do we have here?" Rhys' voice broke through the disorder.

"Daisy!" Daisy bounced on her toes.

Tiny thing was way too friendly for her own good.

Violet sighed in exasperation. "Rhys."

"Violeta."

He grinned at her before he shifted his attention to the child.

"Daisy? As in Daisy Mae? Holy moly. And are you eatin' my favorite cookies?"

She giggled. "I dropped it. You want it? I'll get it for you, but it's broken."

He laughed. "You offerin' me a cookie from the floor?"

She shrugged. "Hasn't been five seconds yet. Wait, has it?"

She looked at me for the answer to that.

She was a little tornado. A lightning strike. A flare of the brightest sun.

My chest tightened, agony stretched tight, and my gaze shifted to Violet who pulled at Daisy's hand in clear distress.

"We really need to get going. Remember Papa is waiting for things to make dinner?"

"Oh no...we better hurry. Nice to meets you!"

She grinned and waved, and Violet was hauling her toward the registers. Rhys made a beeline behind them, chatting Daisy up the whole way. He got into the lane beside them and paid for our single purchase while I stood there itching.

Violet hefted her two reusable bags up and held out her hand for Daisy with the other. "Come on, sweetheart."

"Need a little help with that?" Rhys asked, back at her side, but he shifted to widen his eyes at me when he said it, the asshole.

This was complete idiocy.

Stupidity on a level that was going to cost everything.

But I shot into motion, anyway, like some kind of knight in shining armor who really was the monster hiding underneath, my hand already on the straps before Violet could refuse.

She attempted to do it anyway. "I have it," she growled. A fierce, ferocious kitten.

"Let me help you."

"I don't need your help."

I tugged it out of her hold.

She held in a high-pitched scream.

"I'm just taking your bags for you. That's all."

She huffed, rambled under her breath, "If that were the only thing you'd taken from me, I'd be just fine."

Still, she gave, and she stomped out the door with Daisy in tow while I followed a couple steps behind.

Basking in her rays like a pathetic fool.

She headed straight for where she was parked a few spots down from Rhys. She opened the back door of the truck and helped Daisy inside.

I opened the opposite door and reluctantly set the bags on the floor.

"Goodbye, Mr. Richard," Daisy sang from her car seat. "I likes meeting you a lot."

"Goodbye, Daisy." My smile was rigid. "I liked meeting you a lot, too."

I wanted to stall. To say something. Fucking explain or apologize or just round them up and carry them away where I could forever keep them safe.

Wishing it was my place and knowing it most definitely was not.

Didn't matter.

I could already feel the fires striking all around me. Getting ready to blaze.

If I wasn't careful, I'd burn this entire thing to ash.

And I was just selfish enough to think it might be worth it.

I closed the door and moved around the back of the truck and onto the sidewalk. Violet hopped into the front seat, rolling down the manual window that whined as she did. She blew her bangs out of her gorgeous face.

Why did she have to affect me this way?

Make me sweat and ache with want?

Why did that sweet body have to be the perfect shape?

The exact outline of what was missing from the middle of me.

She turned over the engine. It rumbled to life, so loud I was sure my mom could hear it from the other side of town.

She started to put it into reverse, and I was moving, unable to watch her go. I rushed to the window and planted my hands on the door, leaning in through the window. "Fuck. Violet."

She scowled. "Kindly let go of my truck."

Except the tone of her voice wasn't so kind.

"I can't."

She scoffed. "I'm fairly sure you can. You just pry those selfish fingers off the metal and step back. And then what you do is stay far, far away."

Those selfish fingers she was referring to curled tighter into the window frame. "I need to know that you two are safe."

She laughed a biting sound. "Oh. That's brilliant. But if you need to know, we've been doing just fine by ourselves. You don't need to concern yourself. I know you're not really, anyway."

The words hitched at the end.

Nothing *fine* about it.

"I'm sorry, Violet. So fuckin' sorry."

She shook her head with a disbelieving laugh. "You're sorry?"

"I am. Sorrier than I can explain."

Would take it back if I could. If there was a single thing I could change. But what I had done had been written in stone.

My penalty carved in the bedrock.

The foundation of who we were forever altered.

"You've got to be kiddin' me," she muttered below her breath.

"You think I wanted it? To hurt you?"

"Don't start givin' excuses now."

"I'm not trying to make excuses, but we need to talk."

What I would tell her, I didn't know. But my guts curled. Instinct kicking. Inciting a rage. The urge to keep them close. Even if it would hurt more in the end.

"Absolutely not," she shot out.

"Need to talk to you. Won't take no for an answer."

"Oh, well you're gonna have to because in case you didn't notice, I don't like you very much."

I roughed one hand through my hair, looking away, still holding on with the other because I didn't know how to let her drive away. "Please, Vi. Need to explain a few things."

What the hell I thought I was going to say, I didn't know.

Only thing I did know was I needed to ensure she was safe. Keep a close eye. Laying low like Royce had told me to do just wasn't gonna work.

Standing there?

That had become a fact.

She angled forward fast, catching me off guard. Her head was outside the window and she had us nose to nose, venom on her breath as she seethed the words, "First you chase me down last night saying you want to talk to me, then you turn around to tell me to stay away from your family, and now you're chasin' me out here? I'm not doing this. Stay away from us, Richard. I don't know what your game is, but I'm tellin' you right now, our plates are full. That child back there?"

Her voice lowered more.

A bear protecting its cub.

Vicious and sure.

"She loves fast and she loves hard. You had your chance with her, and you lost it. So, don't you dare come sniffin' around here. It's too late. My heart can't handle it, and neither can hers."

With that, the truck lurched into reverse, and I stumbled back to get away from the front wheel as she tore out of the spot. Violet refused to look at me as she shifted it into gear and rumbled toward the main road.

But Daisy waved as they passed, and my heart shattered a little more.

Violet made a left out onto the main road, the truck roaring as it accelerated.

I looked to the sky and shouted, "Fuck."

A hand clamped down on my shoulder, and I jumped ten feet in the air.

Rhys cracked up. "You're fucked, man. Always wondered. Guess I should have known."

"You don't know anything."

"Don't know anything?" he challenged as he followed behind me to his car.

"Nope," I told him, shoving around to the passenger side.

He clicked the locks, and I climbed in. Knee bouncing a million miles a minute. Heart frantic. Stomach in knots.

Rhys slipped inside. His cocky demeanor gone. He pushed out a heavy sigh as he gripped the steering wheel. "I know a couple things, man. One, you've been missing something for years. Hiding something. Burdened in a way I didn't quite get." He shifted his attention over to stare at me. "And I know after that right there?" He hooked a thumb toward the spot where Violet had been. "You lied when you said you didn't love her anymore."

He pushed the button to start the powerful engine.

"Now the question is…" He threw it in reverse and glared over at me as he backed out of the parking spot. "...what are you going to do about it?"

Violet

A cool breeze stirred through the mornin' air, and I pulled the collar of Daisy's jacket up higher around her neck as I knelt in front of her. She squished up her nose in the cutest way.

"I hope you have a wonderful day at school today." I brushed back a dark lock of hair that whipped around her face. "Remember, open your heart and your mind to all the beautiful, amazing things out there waiting for you."

She grinned. "And I hope you have the most wonderfulest day at work. Remember to opens your heart and makes sure not to smash *any* flowers."

Affectionate laughter rippled free. "I will definitely try to have a great day, but that's hard to do when I'm missing you so much."

I tapped her nose when I said it.

She giggled and sang, "You not gonna miss me *that* bad."

This time I poked her chubby belly. "Oh, yes, I will," I sang right back.

Her expression turned sly. "Maybe I can just stay here and work with you. It's gonna be my job, anyway, when I'm the boss."

I gave her a stern look that was nothing but a tease.

She giggled more. "Okay. Fine. I got to go to school. Yeah, yeah, yeah."

On light laughter, I pushed to standing when I heard the bus rumbling up the hill. She'd been trying that one on me ever since she started preschool the year before.

The little yellow bus that picked up the kindergarteners came into view as it rounded the curve, and it rambled to a stop in front of our drive. The door whined open, and the driver shouted from his spot, "Good mornin', Miss Daisy and Miss Violet."

I waved at him, Daisy's other hand still in mine. "Good mornin', Mr. Duprea. How are you?"

"Can't complain on this fine Wednesday mornin'."

"I can!" Daisy shouted.

This kid.

"Get on that bus, you silly girl." I dipped down and kissed her cheek.

She threw her arms around my neck and held on like she wasn't about to let go.

It's the only thing I wanted. To hold onto her forever. "I loves you the mostest!" she squealed.

"No way!" I teased back through the rising emotion.

"Uh-huh!"

That was what she left me with when she pulled away and jogged to the bus, her little backpack bouncing all over. She climbed the steps. "All right, take me to school, my mommy says I have to learn all the things."

"That's because you're sharp as a tack," he told her.

"I prefer scotch tape. Much safer," she replied. One-hundred-percent serious.

A bark of a laugh left me, and I hugged my arms over my chest like it could stop the surge of love that wanted to come spilling out.

My sweet, wild girl.

Chuckling, Mr. Duprea gave me a salute as he shut the door, and Daisy slipped into her seat, only to slide over so she could press her face to the window, giving me a distorted grin against the glass.

Nothing but a precious goofball.

I waved, mouthed, "I love you."

"I love you," she mimicked.

I love you the most. Forever and through all eternity.

I watched as the bus rambled away. I finally gave up and headed back up the drive when the tail of it disappeared around the bend. My boots crunched on the gravel, the sounds of the morning floodin' the space with peace and the promise of grace.

I tried to cling to it. To make it my own.

But I couldn't escape the uneasiness that skimmed my flesh with each lick of the cool fall breeze.

Winter coming. Something cold that I couldn't warm.

I trudged up the porch steps, brushed off my soles on the mat, and stepped inside. Daddy was in his chair drinking his morning coffee, TV on to one of those morning news stations.

I went right for him. "Good morning, Daddy."

I pecked a kiss to his head as if he were the child.

He sent me a soft smile. "Good morning, bella. Coffee is ready."

"Thank goodness, I'm goin' to need an entire pot."

I had a ton to do today.

"...the executive director of the..." the reporter on the television droned.

I tsked. "Don't you know starting your day off to bad news is not good for you? It sets a terrible tone for your mood, you know."

He waved me off. "I'm not even listening. It's only background noise, my worry wart."

"If you were sittin' on the porch, the birds would sound a whole lot better."

Sadness softened his expression, and he pointed toward the ceiling. "I think I'll stay right here and listen for her to stir."

My insides twisted in a clutch of pain.

God. I should have realized what he was doing.

Sitting on the porch having coffee had been their routine. Their perfect way to start the day.

"Okay. Just…let me know if you need anything. I need to get to work. There are quite a few orders that need delivered today."

"Business is blooming." He waved an indulgent hand in the air.

Even through the wash of sorrow, I managed a grin. My daddy's belief riding in the air. He'd used that phrase my entire life. Those words inspiring me from such a young age. Inciting the passion to watch beautiful things grow. To cultivate it. The amazement that something could come from next to nothin', just a tiny seed that grew to the fullness of life.

Every flower like the hope of a new day.

A better day.

"It is blooming beautifully," I told him softly, our gazes holding for a minute. In it was the promise that we were in this together. That neither of us were alone.

Finally, I gave him a faint smile. "Have a great mornin', Daddy. I've got my phone if you need me."

I started for the kitchen, only to freeze when I heard the name mentioned in the background.

Carolina George.

My hand shot out to the doorframe, and my heart skipped an erratic beat. I slowly turned around to whatever news story was coming across the airways, knowing I should pay it no mind, pretend it didn't exist, but unable to stop myself from listening.

All of it too close.

Like I could reach out and touch it. Be part of it again.

Richard's face flashed through my mind. The desperation of his plea from three days ago. The look in his eyes that had punched me in the guts and left me questioning everything.

I needed to stay away.

Build a hedge of protection around Daisy and myself. Shun every advance because the man could not be trusted.

Not those seductive words or those knowing eyes or those wicked, magical hands.

I shivered at the thought.

And I'd been the fool who'd accepted Emily's invitation to stand up in her weddin'.

But how could I have said no?

"...Carolina George was to sign with the mega-record label back in August. Karl Fitzgerald, the CEO of Mylton records, was arrested during that fateful meeting. He is facing charges of embezzlement, extortion, obstruction of justice, human trafficking, child endangerment, among other accusations. If convicted, he could face up to 200 years in prison."

A picture of an older man in a suit came up on the screen. Just lookin' at him sent my skin crawling. The man was smarmy and smug. Cocky. Reeking of an arrogance that hadn't been earned but had been stolen.

A second later, the screen flashed to another man.

Royce Reed.

Emily's fiancé.

Shock left me on a lurching breath.

I stumbled forward, completely trapped by the story.

Of course, I'd heard some of the rumors that had spread faster than the plague around town, people whispering about the trouble the members of Carolina George were mixed up in, but I'd ignored it the best that I could.

Now it felt impossible.

"Royce Reed, the stepson and second-in-line to Karl Fitzgerald, is said to be cooperating with the prosecution in the matter. Four weeks after Reed took the top spot at Mylton Records after Karl Fitzgerald's arrest, the company was acquired by Stone Industries, a record label based out of Savannah, Georgia. It's expected members of the bands closest to Fitzgerald will be subpoenaed to testify, including Emily Ramsey of Carolina George who has made allegations against Cory Douglas and Karl Fitzgerald. Adding to the speculation, it is reported Emily Ramsey is now involved with Royce Reed."

It shifted to a reporter shouting at Royce as he walked down the street with his hand wrapped in Emily's.

"Royce, how do you feel about the accusations brought against your stepfather?"

He didn't stop walking, just said over his shoulder, "I wish nothing more than to see justice served, and I'll do everything I can to see that it is."

The clip ended and the reporter was back on the screen with a picture of another man on the screen beside her. "Cory Douglas, the lead singer of the well-known rock band, A Riot of Roses, was also arrested on charges of sexual assault. Studio 4 News has learned Royce Reed used to front A Riot of Roses before a two-year jail sentence for a conviction on an assault of none other than Cory Douglas. It was announced a week ago Royce Reed has reclaimed the spot as the band's lead and is set to hit the studio with A Riot of Roses in the coming months." Sickness slipped across my flesh.

I'd met that man before.

Cory Douglas.

Was it sad to admit this report didn't surprise me?

The way instinct had kicked in the second he'd come into the room?

Megawatt smile and depravity on his face?

One look, and my stomach had curled with an internal warning that had blared for me to stay far away with the volume set to ten.

The lens panned to a second reporter in the main office. He whistled a disbelieving sound as he shuffled the papers on the counter in front of him. "It will be interesting to see how this plays out."

The female reporter nodded. "It seems there are many layers to this complex case. I'll be following the trial closely and will give updates as new details come to light."

"We'll be waiting. Thank you, Nancy."

The screen shifted to focus on the main reporter again.

While I just stood there.

Dumbfounded.

Struck.

Mind racin' to catch up. To piece together the facts when it was clear I was missin' so many of them.

A horrible feeling sank to the pit of my stomach.

Positive that Emily was involved, in deep, but not sure how far it went.

I felt my daddy's gaze on my face. "Oh, bella."

I forced a wobbly smile and a feeble shrug that said more than it should. "I guess I'm a little out of touch."

"For your own well-being," he argued for me.

"She was my best friend. Like a sister to me."

He nodded slow. "Just…be careful, mi amor. Un corazón roto no puede sanar cuando está siendo aplastado."

A broken heart cannot heal when it's being crushed.

"Don't worry, Daddy. It's already scarred over. Hard as a rock."

Sympathy flushed his face, and I dipped through the entryway to the kitchen before I had to face any more questions. Before I had to face what I was feelin'.

This urge to go to Emily and beg her to let me hold some of what she was bearing.

Worse was the urge to go to Richard and ask him for details.

For a way into their lives, when the best thing I could do was stay on the outside.

Heck, even sneaking along the perimeter felt dangerous.

Deciding I would only talk to Emily about it if she chose to confide in me, I shoved the tumult of worry off and focused on what I needed to accomplish today. I filled up a tumbler full of coffee and doused it with cream before I headed out the back door.

The air had warmed a fraction, and I lifted my face to the blue sky that was scattered with wisps of clouds. And I tried not to hear the music written there. Hidden with the stars behind the light.

Where the darkness could so easily drag me back into his arms. *Richard.*

My spirit whispered his name.

My mind was quick to put a lid on it.

That was just reckless thinkin'. Especially with him near. It was a whole ton easier to long for him in the nights when he was so far out of reach. What wasn't so easy was resisting him when he was beggin' me for face-time.

No chance was I going there. No chance was I giving in.

That connection that came alive when he was around didn't mean a thing.

It was just lashes crying out from an old broken dream.

I headed down the path toward the acres and acres of flowers. There was basically every breed that would grow on this land and some we tried to bribe with extra love.

Saul saw me coming, already hard at work, probably there since before dawn.

He took off his hat. "Mornin', Violet."

"Good mornin'. How are you today?" I called as I approached.

"Better than ever."

His attitude managed to pull a slight smile out of me.

"Good. Then I am, too."

Two hours later, I was in the shed arranging the buckets for delivery to the florists we supplied. I had my own stand at a couple farmer's markets as well, but the florists were our bread and butter.

What had kept our flower farm afloat and flourishing through the years.

Business blooming.

That and the select events we hosted on the farm. Weddings and showers and celebrations in the meadow beneath the trees surrounded by flowers.

Daddy had started Rolling Wallflowers from a small flowerbed and three rose bushes in his backyard right after he'd come to Dalton and decided it was home. He'd been passing through from Charlotte on his way to Colorado and had fallen in love with a dream.

It'd probably helped that he'd fallen in love with my mama as he'd been passing through, too.

I carried the first bucket to the trailer hitched to the back of my truck—white lilies, as gorgeous as could be.

I went back and forth, loading everything.

Roses of every color.

Sprigs of greenery.

Baby's breath.

Orchids.

I double-checked my list of orders.

Saul came carrying the two pygmy willows planted in pots.

"Perfect, thank you, Saul." I brushed the dirt from my hands. "I think that's it. If you could prune the palms at the back, we have a big order for those goin' out to Charleston next week. That should be good for the day."

"Already on my list."

"You're always two steps ahead of me, aren't you?" I said with a slight smile as I shut the doors to the trailer and started to work the metal lock into place. "I don't know what I would do without you."

He'd been working here for the last year and had quickly become invaluable.

He reached out to help me get it latched. "Ah, I'd say two steps behind."

I froze when his hand touched mine.

When it lingered.

I stared at his thumb that slowly brushed across the tiny tattoo at the inside of my wrist.

A music note.

Just lookin' at it made me ache. But that was the thing about taking something on as permanent. It was written on you forever. It didn't matter if I had the tiny design removed. It would still be marked on me. Scored on my soul.

"I always wanted to ask you about this. Do you play?" he asked, his head tilting to the side. Handsome in his unassuming way. Dark eyes and dark hair.

A quiet kindness in his demeanor.

I knew where his mind had been going of late. The way he'd been lookin' at me. The way his smile had gotten softer and his stare had grown longer.

Slowly, I tugged my hand away, trying not to be rude, trying not to make a big deal out of him touching me that way, but sure I was doing it, anyway.

An uncomfortable smile wobbled on my mouth.

"No," I mumbled.

"But you have a music note tattooed on your wrist," he asked, half confused, half amused.

My trembling lips pressed into a flat line. "I guess it's just a reminder of how easy it is to get lost in a song."

I thought maybe he felt the undercurrent. That there was so much more to that statement because he frowned.

Searching through my expression as if it might give him the insight to understand.

Awkwardness hovered in the space between. Finally, he stepped back as if he could burst the bubble of it, shoving his hands into the pockets of his jeans. "Well, I guess you better get going."

"Yeah. I should."

I fumbled away and into the truck, and I buckled as I watched Saul wander back up the trail into the rows of flowers, shoulders hanging lower than they normally did.

"Shit," I muttered.

I squeezed my eyes closed as I tried to sort out what had just happened. How I felt about it.

Richard's face flashed behind my lids.

I squeezed my eyes tighter as if it could purge him from my consciousness.

God. It wasn't fair. Wasn't fair that he was still there, haunting me like a flaw stamped on my soul.

I was so lost to thinking about it that I shrieked when my phone went off where it sat on the seat beside me. In my blundering, I knocked it to the floor, and I scrambled to pick it up from where it'd fallen onto the floorboards.

My heart took off at a sprint when I saw it was the private investigator calling. I hurried to accept it, pressing it to my ear. "This is Violet Marin."

"Ms. Marin. It's David Jacobs with Jacobs & Drow. Did I catch you at a good time?"

"Yes…yes, of course."

"Great, I wanted to ask you a few questions about your sister.

I've pulled some basic records, but I need a few more details to really get started."

Grief billowed through my spirit. Part of me wanted to hang up. Tell him to forget it. That I couldn't handle any news he might report.

I looked back at the house. At the window with the drapes parted where I knew my mama was inside. Prayin' for a miracle. I couldn't be the one to stand in the way of that.

"Yes, any information I have, I'm happy to share. Though I'm not sure I have much information that will help. That's why I called you."

I attempted the joke.

It creaked with despair.

"Why don't you start by telling me about her? Her personality. The things she enjoyed. The things she might have been struggling with leading up to the day she disappeared."

Emotions spun a web inside me. Anger and love. Hope and regret. The gift she'd given and the peace that she'd stolen.

Everything in the middle of it.

Every loss.

But I guessed she'd been responsible for my greatest joy.

I cleared the roughness from my voice. "We were close for most of our lives…"

Violet
Eight Years Ago

"I have no interest in goin' to some bar tonight."

Violet's older sister, Liliana, rolled her eyes at her.

"You have no interest?" Lily drawled as if it were the most ridiculous thing she'd ever heard.

"Nope, none," Violet spouted, returning her attention to the book she was reading where she lay sprawled on her bed.

Or at least she attempted to. Vainly, considering her obnoxious big sister ripped the book from her hands like she were twelve and not twenty-five.

"Hey. What is wrong with you? I was reading that, in case you hadn't noticed." Violet scrambled onto her knees in an attempt to grab it.

Her sister dangled it over her head. "What is wrong with me?

What is wrong with you? You're a twenty-two-year-old fuddy-duddy who'd rather sit in her room on a Friday night than go out dancin'. Now that is the real problem. Have I taught you nothing?"

Violet's brows lifted so high they disappeared beneath her bangs. "Fuddy-duddy? I think it's you who has the issue."

Lily waved her off. "It might be the only phrase my boring little sister knows since she's already halfway to bein' a spinster."

Violet scowled at her sister who stalked over to her closet.

Liliana was tall, miles of legs and curves for days. Black hair and eyes the same strange color as Violet and their mother's. A bombshell. So gorgeous she turned heads wherever she went.

But it was the inside that truly made her shine.

Joyful and real and fun.

The one person Violet could always go to, no matter what. The one she'd looked up to her whole life. The one who'd always helped to give her courage to step out and chase down the things that would bring Violet the most joy.

Violet loved that Lily lived her life the same way.

So full of joy and anticipation.

Violet almost smiled at her from behind because when her sister got something into her head, she was a force to be reckoned with.

Violet's closest friend.

That was until she started to dig through Violet's closet and tugged something free. Violet sneered at the short denim skirt that landed next to her on her bed. "You are crazy if you think I'm walkin' out of this house wearing that."

Lily leaned up against the wall with a smug grin. "So that means you're goin'? You know you want to," she sang as she waltzed back across Violet's room and stretched out her hand for Violet to take it.

Violet blew out a sigh. "Ugh. Fine. But you owe me if I have a terrible time."

Forty minutes later, they were ready. Violet's hair was ironed into shiny, sleek sheets that swished down her back. More makeup on her face than she ever wore, shimmering and sparkling thanks to Liliana doing her the favor. Violet had tossed the skirt right back at her and told her to put it on, while she'd pulled on a modest white sundress with tiny pink flowers and paired it with her favorite pink cowgirl boots.

Pink lip gloss to match.

So bars weren't her thing.

But making her sister happy was, so she was giggling right along with her when they rushed out of the house to their daddy shoutin', "You two look too pretty for your own good. Be careful. Call me if you need a ride. Or if one of those cowboys gets too friendly. Better yet, I will chaperone. You know I am the best dancer in town. I will come with you," he called out as he fumbled toward the door behind them.

Lily giggled as she clung to Violet's arm and dragged her down the porch steps. "Not tonight, Daddy. We'll be good. I promise."

They were both laughing at their poor worried father as they ran for Lily's car, and Violet realized she was more excited than she'd thought she should be by the time they hit the road and headed for town.

Anticipation rippled through her bloodstream.

She felt it stronger by the time her sister pulled into the big dirt lot in front of the massive saloon known for the best dancing in town. Violet had only been once or twice, but she'd never been when there'd been a live band.

She could feel the energy of it when she stepped out of the car, feeling anxious and excited and alive as they headed for the double doors with their elbows linked together, laughing as they went.

They showed their IDs to the bouncer and paid the cover, and they stepped into the dimly lit bar that was packed wall to wall. The level of voices and music deafening.

A thunder that thudded to an upbeat country song that was being played over the speakers.

They started to weave through the crush, making their way to the large bar in the middle. They ordered margaritas, and when the bartender slid them across to them, they clinked their glasses together.

"To you being thankful I dragged you out of bed on a Friday night," Lily shouted over the din with a smirk painted over her red lips.

"To *maybe* having a fun night with my big sister," Violet teased.

Lily grinned. "What are you talking about? Any night spent with me is the best night."

Violet shook her head with a laugh, and she let her attention wander over the packs of people gathered around the high-top tables, drinking and letting go of the cares of the day. Her attention drifted to the long line of pool tables on the far side, all the way to the lights flashing around the mechanical bull at the very back.

It was a madhouse.

Freedom flying.

Laughter soaring.

But what really captured her attention was the elevated stage set up to the far right of the cavernous space, a big dance floor surrounded by regular height tables on all sides of it.

Liliana nudged her on the shoulder. "Told you it was gonna be fun. Now come on, Alyssa and Brie have a table up close."

They started in that direction when a squeal of feedback cut through the clamor, and the DJ boomed over the speaker, "Are you ready for this? It's time to put your hands together and get your booty on the dance floor...welcome with me, the ones you've been waiting for—Carolina George!"

The lights flashed to darkness before they came back on to reveal four people climbing the side steps onto the elevated stage.

People shouted. Cheered. Vied to get closer.

Violet's heart skipped in this crazy twist of excitement.

She had the urge to do the same.

To push up onto her toes so she could get a better look.

Lily took her by the hand and led her through the throng. Violet was unable to see over the heads as a sweet voice came through the mic, "Hello, Dalton! It's an honor to be back playin' in our hometown for a very special show. We are Carolina George. Who's ready for a little fun tonight?"

More shouts and cheers and stomps of feet, and drumsticks were counting off a beat before the heavy rhythm of an electric guitar came to life like a sizzle through the air.

A shockwave of intensity.

The woman began to sing.

Violet's spirit lurched, struck by the beauty of what she was hearing.

Unexpected.

Mesmerizing.

Hypnotic.

When she'd heard a local band was playin', she sure hadn't anticipated this.

She and her sister finally broke through to the far side of the dance floor where Lily's friends had a table that had a direct view of the stage.

Violet stumbled in her tracks, coming to a full stop like she'd run face-first into a brick wall.

Gobsmacked.

Her daddy had always taught her to look for the beauty in all things. It was what had sparked her love of growing. Of seeing a seed blooming and unfurling to its full, glorious potential.

But she was sure she hadn't seen anything quite as beautiful as the man standing on the stage with a guitar strapped over his shoulder, and she knew it for certain when he stepped up to his mic and began to sing along to the chorus.

Voice rough and sensuous.

Hair this mess of brown and dark blonds, longer on the top and cropped at the sides, the longer pieces flopping all over the place. When he tilted his head, the locks fell to brush along the most striking, defined jaw she'd ever seen, cheeks cut in the same severe fashion.

But his lips…his lips were full and lush and pink where they caressed up close to the mic like he was whispering to a lover.

Violet's heart went pounding an extra beat, her stomach flutterin' as a rush of butterflies flapped their wings.

He was a little rough and a lot sexy and she was sure she felt her knees knock in a steady drum of want.

A hand was suddenly waving in her face. She jerked her attention to the side to Lily who was laughing at her. "Oh my god. And here I would have thought my baby sister would be the last one to go fangirl on me."

Frowning, Violet fought the overpowering urge to look back at the stage and instead stared down her sister. "What are you talking about?"

"Um…the fact you've got drool running down your chin."

Violet smacked her sister's hand away when she reached out to show proof. "I do not. Don't be ridiculous. I was just checkin' out who we're seeing play tonight."

"Checkin' out, is right."

Violet rolled her eyes. Yeah, her and every other girl in the place.

The man had an aura that flooded the air and seeped to the floor.

Overwhelming.

Captivating.

Entrancing.

He had a way that made every person there feel as if he were looking at them, because Violet was sure she could feel him watching her. Watching as she took a seat at the table with Lily's friends.

As hard as she tried, she couldn't stop herself from watching him back.

Because there was no possible way that he was actually staring at her.

No way his gaze was lingering every time it passed over the crowd.

No way the lyrics from the song he sang about aching to get lost in a beautiful girl were meant for her that night.

No way that she wasn't being completely delusional when she imagined the connection that strung taut between them.

A chord that resonated.

No way.

Their music was this clash of country and rock, an almost-indie vibe that strummed of aching need, a mesh of something seductive and dark mixed with a stunning hope.

She thought it might be the best thing she'd ever heard, and then she had to question if it wasn't infatuation.

She figured this was exactly how groupies were made.

No, thank you. Not that she could make it through the barricade of women who were right up-front vying for his attention, anyway, even if she wanted to, which she most definitely did not.

Whatever the riot going down in her belly stood for could easily be ignored.

Right?

Still, she itched. Drawn. Her eyes locked on a man she'd never seen before.

Right before the band's set was coming to an end, she forced herself over to the bar to get refills on their drinks.

Needing a distraction

A diversion from drooling all over a stranger like some kind of wannabe fangirl, just like her sister had said.

Because seriously, what was wrong with her?

The band shouted goodnight to a thunder of applause.

Turning her back to it, she rested her forearms on the bar and waited for her turn. Canned music started to blare over the speakers again, the DJ striking up the dance floor.

"What can I get for you?" the bartender pretty much mouthed since it was so loud, and Violet popped onto her toes so she could shout her order over the volume.

"A pitcher of margaritas, please."

That was when she felt the stir beside her, the shift in the air, the awareness that whisked like a flashfire across her skin.

Heart stalling out, she glanced to her left at the man standing beside her.

His tattooed forearms were on the bar, and he grinned soft, eyes the color of a tranquil meadow tracing her face like he'd felt it, too.

"Hi," he said.

And she whispered, "No way."

Richard

A fist rapped at the bathroom door.

"Occupied," I grumbled low while I ran the towel over my face and down my chest, steam coating my skin and filling the air with mist and heat.

One thing about staying at my parents' was there was pretty much zero privacy. Everyone living on top of each other. But it was a small price to pay.

Being near when everything felt so precarious.

Ground unsteady and the world unsettled.

My mind this jumbled mess, torn between the penalty I had to pay and wanting to go straight to Violet and drop to my knees. Beg her for forgiveness when I knew there wasn't any to be had.

That adorable face flashed through my mind. My guts clutched in shame. In regret and this loyalty that ran like fermented poison through my veins. A corruption that smoldered and ulcerated.

Another round of impatient knocking thundered at the wood, and Royce's voice seeped through, lowered in dire emphasis, "Listen, man, I got bad news. Just got off the phone with the prosecutor."

Dread turned my heated flesh to ice.

Nothing but a flash freeze.

My blood ran stagnant, and my chest stretched so tight it felt like my ribs were being ripped apart in some kind of wishing bone match.

I stared at the wall. Locked in a fear that coursed.

This time, he knocked a single knuckle, his voice so low I could barely hear it. "Come on, man, open the door."

Hands shaking, I wrapped the towel around my waist and cracked it open, my teeth grating when I saw him standing out in the hall.

Expression grave.

Horror in his dark eyes.

"What happened?"

Dropping his head, his hand came out to support himself on the wall as he seemed to try to gather himself. "The two women who'd agreed to testify before the detective went in with the evidence against Fitzgerald?"

That dread took on a whole new life.

The detective Royce had been feeding information to, setting Fitzgerald up, had gotten sworn statements from two of the women Karl Fitzgerald had been holding. Two women who had gotten free and were going to take the stand and testify.

They were the smoking gun for the prosecution. Those who could vouch firsthand for the twisted depravity.

"Yeah?" I could barely force the question out. Wholly unprepared for anything he was gettin' ready to say.

Silence stretched between us.

Weighted with apprehension.

Finally, Royce lifted his head. It exposed the grim expression carved on his face. "Both of them went missing, man."

"What?" Sickness punched from me with the question, shock

hitting me like a landslide, disgust and hatred and outright fear rushing in behind it to knock me from my feet.

They were supposed to be under police protection.

My own hand was shooting for the doorframe to keep myself from dropping to my knees, the other coming to my mouth when my head slumped forward like it could calm the roil of nausea that burst in my stomach.

Bile rising in my throat.

"Fuck," I muttered toward the ground. "Can't fuckin' believe this."

Except I could, couldn't I? This was exactly why we were taking the measures we were. We knew just how dangerous these people were. Knew the lengths they would go to keep their perverted world under lock and key.

"How long have they been gone?" I managed to ask.

Royce roughed an agitated hand over his face, the king tattooed on the back of it flexing and jerking like it was itching to make its next move. "Since yesterday at least, maybe longer. Her last contact with them was a few days ago."

"Thought they were each assigned an officer to watch over them?" It was an accusation, venom ripping from my tongue.

Royce looked over his shoulder behind him, and he kept his voice lowered when he returned his attention to me. "Yeah. Thought so, too."

The implication hung thick in the stagnant air.

I blinked a thousand times. "His reach is long, man."

"Know it."

"Those poor girls." Hatred burned hot in my chest. Already sure of their fate. Not like this was the first time someone had gone missing who'd dared expose this warped, evil empire.

Royce's hand curled into a fist. "They've all gotta pay. Every single one of them." He trailed off, not even able to voice it.

"I know."

He shifted his hard gaze to mine, though his voice was laden with the plea. "We have to see this through. It's the only chance." Knew well enough that plea was for both our sisters.

For so many others out there that we couldn't come close to

knowing their names.

It was so fucked up how the tentacles of that sordid world had slithered and crept and overcome. Winding through our lives without us knowing it until all of us were tied. And it just kept going deeper and deeper.

"I won't stop until those savages see justice." Promise rolled from me on a threat.

Royce nodded then swallowed, tat on his throat bobbing heavily. "Prosecutor said she'd like to talk with you. Wants to know if you saw anything in the years you've known Karl Fitzgerald that you could use against him."

His brow quirked at that.

That dread doubled.

"What the fuck am I supposed to say to her? She's the last person I want to talk to."

I'd prayed I could stay off her radar. In the sidelines. Just an innocuous figure on the fringes there to support his sister.

"You don't fuckin' panic," he hissed. "Answer the questions you can *answer*. Make sure it's clear you don't know all that much."

Right.

Didn't know all that much.

"Sounds simple," I said, sarcasm dripping out.

"You don't have much of a choice, do you? It's game time. And it's not like you're under oath." His brow lifted. "It's your job to keep it that way."

"Yeah, well a lie's a fuckin' lie." I'd been telling so many they were going to bury me.

"It's the only shot we've got, man. Pretty sure this just proved that, yeah?"

With that, he turned and walked away, leaving me standing there watching behind him.

Wondering which of those lies would finally be the end of me.

"Come on, come on, come on," I muttered under my breath,

my feet wearing a path in my darkened room, anxiety clawing through me like a bitch.

Nearly choked on the relief when the low voice finally came through the line. "Richard."

"Kade." I exhaled. "Why the fuck haven't you called?"

He blew out a sigh. "Quieter we stay, the safer we are."

I rammed the heel of my hand into my eye and tried to focus. To remember my purpose. "How are they?"

"Secure," he said.

"You're sure?"

"There has been no new activity."

Relief blistered through my body. But it didn't last long. Not when I could feel all of this comin' to a head. Faster than we could let it.

"You need to tighten security."

He roughed out a menacing sound. "Think I've got it covered."

Dude was a badass, but this wasn't the time to get cocky.

"The two witnesses went missing," I told him.

Silence shocked through the line before he uttered a hushed, "Shit."

"They're cleaning their tracks."

"Knew they would, didn't we?"

"Yeah," I answered.

"We just have to push through and get them there safely. See it through. Only goal I've got." He issued it like a promise.

"We will," I said, resolute.

Sure of where I stood.

After that?

I would burn.

I knew I would.

Violet might hate me now? But when all was revealed, she was going to curse my existence.

Didn't matter.

This was the due that I owed.

"We can't fail them," Kade murmured, his worry coming through.

"And we won't."

That face flashed through my mind.

A splash of *Violet* lighting up behind my eyes. Color and life. That little girl at her side. Regret flashed and flared. Blinding my sight in my darkened room.

"Stay safe," I grated, "and keep me updated if you see *anything* out of the ordinary."

My mind flashed to the shadow I'd hunted in the night.

That uneasiness taking hold. Rooting itself deep.

"I will, brother."

I ended the call and clutched my phone in my hand, feeling like I was being skinned alive.

Walls too tight. Closing in. Everything I'd been running from gaining speed. Beating and thrashing.

Could feel a tornado approaching and getting ready to touch down.

A force that would annihilate.

Jagged rocks slayed my throat, and I tried to swallow around them.

Unable to sit still for a second longer, I grabbed my favorite guitar propped on a stand near the wall, the one I took with me everywhere.

Music was my only solace in the middle of this. Funny how it'd been what'd started it in the first place.

The culprit.

My love of a song clouding sound judgment.

I sank onto the floor and leaned against the bed. I propped her on my lap, my fingers playing across the strings as my left hand curled around the worn neck.

My head dropped back, and I closed my eyes, and I searched through the disorder for a melody.

For peace.

Every shade of Violet came rushing back.

Her eyes and that mouth and her sweet, delicate hands.

Body I wanted to get lost in forever.

Bliss.

My eternity that I would never touch.

The words gusted, swept in like a soft breeze through a

meadow.

I closed my eyes
I fell into a dream
Watching through a looking glass
Nothin's what it seems
Shards of ice
Cold, bitter bliss
That's what I get
For stealing that first kiss

My eyes slowly opened, my gaze on my fingers that played along the frets. I reached out and touched it, the tiny violet tattooed on the inside of my left wrist. No matter where I went, whatever faraway place.

A distant land.

A darkened room.

Lost in a trance.

She was there.

Violet

*I*t turned out, I was just getting myself deeper and deeper.

"Wallflowers would be honored to host your wedding," I whispered into my cell, silently cursing myself for agreeing. But how could I deny her when Emily had just spent the last twenty minutes asking for something and apologizing for it at the same time?

Asking for something she shouldn't when her request made complete sense.

The logical choice.

The only choice, really.

Which was why telling her yes was the only answer I could give.

The problem was, I had no idea how I would get through this.

I'd already been faltering. Running into Richard far too often. The man remaining in the distance but watching me through the space.

Showing up in random places.

Watching from afar.

Those eyes intent. His spirit unrelenting.

We hadn't actually spoken since the run-in at the grocery store, but still, I felt as if he were picking me apart, piece by piece, sifting through the wreckage for something salvageable.

Which I was nothing but a fool for even thinkin' it. For even letting the speck of a thought infiltrate my mind—the thought that he might want reconciliation rather than seeking our complete destruction.

Emily exhaled in relief from the other end of the line, but in it, I could still hear her concern. "Are you sure? I know it can't be easy for you."

I released a blustery sigh of indifference. "We host weddings here all the time. How could I refuse my best friend?"

By being sane and reasonable, that was how. But I guessed I wasn't either of those things.

I was a glutton.

A masochist.

Begging for the heartache.

Emily started to ramble, "You don't know what this means to me, Vi. I wanted to get married in my hometown, and there isn't a more gorgeous setting than Wallflowers. I mean, I tried to find someplace else, but it was clear they couldn't pull it together on such short notice. Besides, nothing else compares to Wallflowers. Not even close. It's going to be perfection," she gushed. "The first time I saw it, I fell in love. I can't imagine a better place to confess my love and my forever than under that tree."

Cut. Cut. Cut.

I didn't think she had the first clue that she was slaying me.

"It'll be perfect. We'll make sure of it," I promised.

"Are you sure we can pull it together? I know three weeks is short notice, and I'm sorry for that. But under the circumstances…" she trailed off.

"We can make it work. I promise."

Even from the distance, I could feel the gratefulness in her demeanor. "You are truly the best. I…" She hesitated, then murmured again, "I know how hard this has to be for you. I'm asking so much, and I know I don't have the right."

"Don't say that. You do have the right. I love you like a sister."

I guessed the hardest part of it was that I'd lost both my *sisters* at the same time. Not that Emily hadn't tried to keep in touch. That she hadn't reached out. But there'd been too much strain at that time. Too much pain.

Everything was raw and aching. The wounds fresh and ripe.

With the way thinkin' about Richard felt right then, I wondered just how well those wounds had healed.

"I love you, too. Forever. Nothing can change that," she said.

Emotion warbled through the silence that hung in the air, and finally, I cleared my throat, pasted on a smile, and prayed she could sense it from across the miles. "Okay, so I think we'd better plan a meeting. Tomorrow or Thursday? If we're going to pull this off, we're going to have to work fast. Do you have a caterer in mind?"

She giggled. "Oh, I have all kinds of things in mind."

My smile turned genuine.

Because this was what I was born to do.

To watch beauty blossom.

To foster and cultivate it.

And a wedding was the ultimate harvest.

"All right then. Let's do this."

Two days later, I was out in my workshop pruning flowers for a bouquet.

Watching the clock, not sure if I wanted time to speed away or to stand still. If it was the anticipation that was wrecking me or the actual meeting that might kill me dead.

My office and workspace sat at the bottom of the hill from the house, the acres of flowers growing out from behind the old structure that I'd restored.

It had been a broken-down barn that had been turned into a

rustic haven where I let my fingers go to work. Where I pruned and pieced and fashioned someone's sentiment into an expression.

Love.

Sympathy.

Mourning.

Congratulations and well wishes.

The truth was every flower had a story to tell. A wish to impart.

I found so much joy in being a part of it that I almost got lost in my work until the sound of tires crunching on the driveway and the low hum of an engine dragged me from the peace.

Heart lurching, I pulled the gloves from my hands, set them on the workbench, and took a couple steeling breaths before I gathered up my unwieldy emotions, bottled them for later, and slipped out the double wooden doors.

A black Suburban came to a stop in front of the house.

Squinting against the rays of the late afternoon sun, I peered into the distance at the people who climbed out of the extra-long SUV, trying to ignore the raging beat of my heart.

Telling myself it didn't matter.

That I could handle this, no matter who showed.

I was a big girl and I'd long since moved on.

Right?

Right.

I almost gave myself a little pat on the back for bein' so mature.

From the front passenger seat, Emily hopped out first.

Goodness, the excitement that blazed from her, so much that it was tweaking a grin at the corner of my mouth.

Melanie climbed out from the rear-passenger behind her, and I felt a buzz of my own excitement after not seeing her for so long.

But it was who followed her out that sent my lurching heart leaping in a shout of joy.

Mabel.

Emily's mother.

Richard's mother.

My spirit panged and danced and thrilled.

A song of old affection that raced across the field.

Emily's fiancé rounded the front of the Suburban and took her hand, and Melanie lifted the seat so another girl who I didn't recognize could climb out of the very back.

Relief blustered through me when I realized I'd dodged a bullet for a moment more.

Richard wasn't with them.

They all started down the path, making their way in my direction.

Then that balloon of hope I'd been feeling busted, spitting and sputtering out when I saw the shape of a tall figure show at the rear of the Suburban from where he'd come around from the opposite side.

Hovering and hesitating.

His hands stuffed in his pockets.

Wearing a tight tee that showed off his arms covered in intricate ink. Jeans just as snug. Hair whipping like mad around his rugged face.

The man hard and rough and raw. Like the sweet country boy I'd known had been scraped away by the things that he'd seen. By the years that had passed. By the fame and the money and the glory now tacked to his name.

A dichotomy where his aura danced in between.

It didn't matter that he was two football fields away.

I could feel the intensity of his stare.

The weight of him crashed through the atmosphere and pressed down on my chest. Saturating my senses.

How on earth was I supposed to handle this? It felt cruel and unjust. Like the world was out to end me. Every fear and hope and wound I'd ever sustained whirred and whipped and rebounded in a bid to annihilate.

All at the same damn time.

One hand wrapped in her fiancé's, Emily lifted her other, her words carrying on the slight breeze as they made their way down the pathway, "Hey, Violet. Sorry we're a few minutes late."

I waved in welcome and tried to make my voice match the feeling. "No worries at all. I was just wrappin' up prepping for tomorrow."

"I hope we're not interrupting."

"Nope. This is what I do. Besides, you know I wanted to be a part of this."

It was only half a lie.

Her smile was soft as they made it to the bottom of the hill. The second she got to where I stood, she wrapped her arms around me. "Thank you. Thank you a million times. I am so excited. I can't even tell you what this means to me."

I hugged her back and breathed in her sweetness, clinging to the memories of why I'd grown so attached to her. "Oh, you don't even need to explain. I can feel it radiating from you."

A thrill traveled her spine, and she pulled away so she could gesture to the man who stood like a guardian at her side.

Oh, was the man intimidating. Different than Richard, though. Screaming of a fast life and big city. Covered in ink.

The man left no question he'd seen a thing or two.

None of that held a smidge of importance, though.

He might look her opposite, like she'd said, but there was no denying the devotion that poured from him. No denying their connection. The man her match. "Violet, I'm so happy for you to officially meet my fiancé. Royce Reed. Royce, this is Violet. One of my favorite people in the world."

She looked back at me when she said it.

My heart panged.

Did she have to be so sweet?

His onyx eyes raked over me like they were searching for a secret. Peeling back my layers to see what was hidden underneath.

What he didn't know was I didn't have them.

I was an open book.

My heart written on my sleeve just as clear as the ink on his flesh.

Out in the open and visible for anyone to see.

I guessed that was why I'd made it so easy for people to take advantage of me.

A flashfire of severity gobbled up my skin.

There was nothing I could do but glance at the dark figure that slowly made his way down the path hedged in lavender.

Face chiseled, every distinct, glorious line glinting in the shimmering light of the fading day.

A beautiful invader.

A harbinger of treachery.

I should have recognized it before.

Not ever again.

Royce offered me a tattooed hand, drawing me back from the shadow that was descending. "It's nice to meet you, Violet. I've heard a ton about you. My girl said there was no chance we could do this without you, so we can't do it without you."

I shook his hand. "I'm honored to be a part of it."

Melanie suddenly came pushing around Emily, her dark brown ponytail swishing around her shoulders. "Um, excuse me. Can we get the pleasantries over with because this girl needs hugs." She gestured frantically at herself. "I haven't seen my Violet in way too many years. I'm over these withdrawals. Gimme some Violet."

She came at me like the powerhouse she was, and she threw her arms around me and squeezed me with all her might. She squealed low and jumped a little before she pulled away. "I can't believe we get to plan a weddin' together. O.M.G. Is this not the best thing in the world?"

Was it necessary to interject that I thought it was a horrible, terrible, bad idea or should it be plain obvious?

It wouldn't have made a difference, anyway, because she was rambling on before I could get in a word. "I told this one right here she was done for the second she met Royce."

She swatted in the direction of Emily while she simultaneously swooned, pressing her other hand over her heart. "I mean, you should have seen her the mornin' after she met him. She was walking around like she'd gotten struck upside the head and had a halo of stars dancing around her. You can't instantly hate someone that bad without loving them. And let me tell you, she hated him."

"Hey now," Royce rumbled with a slight, guilty chuckle.

Melanie kept right on. "She told me I was out of my mind when I started hunting for bridesmaids dresses that very morning. She should have known better than to question me. I mean come on, we know who's the genius here." She gestured to herself. "I called it. I think I'm the one who deserves the credit. They wouldn't be together if it wasn't for me."

A giggle slipped free.

I'd almost forgotten how over-the-top Melanie was.

Fun.

A joy that lightened the dark.

Emily rolled her eyes. "Oh, yeah, it was all you, Mel. I would have forgotten all about him had you not kept up with your pesterin'."

Royce wrapped his arms around Emily from behind, murmured at her cheek, "Forget about me? No chance I would let you."

A blush pinked her chest, and you could see them falling into the other.

My spirit danced and shivered, shaking in a way it hadn't in so long. I pinned a smile on my face and tried to forget the man standing twenty feet in the distance who I could feel washing through the atmosphere. Wave after wave of that deep, stark severity.

A chill taking to the air.

Mabel cleared her throat.

I jerked my attention to her.

Our gazes tangled for a beat.

In that second was a thousand apologies. Endless understanding and boundless sympathies.

"Mabel." I managed it on a whisper. Throat quivering.

She edged my way. Carefully. Her arms wrapping me tight the second she got to me. "I missed you, Violet."

I fought the pricking of tears.

And I wondered if she could feel the loss that echoed from the middle of me because she just drew me in tighter. Held me for the longest time before she edged back and brushed back a piece of hair that was whipping around my face. "I never should have been gone so long."

My head shook. "That was on me." The words cracked.

I'd lost track of the number of times she'd tried to reach out. After everything went down with Richard. When my sister went missing. With Daisy, offering help. When my mama had fallen ill.

Falling into You

Every time.

Unfailing.

I'd ignored each one because I couldn't fathom the pain of having to be in her space again. A sharp, gutting reminder of what I'd lost. But I guessed it'd come to the point where it hurt even worse being fully without, the vacancy too much to ignore, and I'd ended up at Emily's engagement party like a lost soul searching for its home.

Mabel brushed the pad of her thumb along my jaw.

Soft affection.

I wanted to weep.

When Emily cleared her throat as if it might be enough to break up the tension, Mabel reluctantly released me.

Emily held her hand out for the girl hanging in the periphery. "Violet, I want you to meet Maggie, Royce's sister. Soon to be mine."

Affection rolled from her tongue as she gestured to the timid girl who couldn't be more than nineteen or twenty. Dark, long hair, her eyes the same color as Royce's though they shined with something soft and innocent.

Beautiful.

Sweet.

A calm emanated from her. Her gift an ushering of peace.

"Maggie, this is Violet."

"Hi, Violet. It's so nice to meet you." She stepped forward, her attention darting all over. "You grow flowers?" Awe flooded from her voice.

I smiled. "I do."

"Wow, that has to be the coolest job in the world."

My smile widened, and I turned my gaze out to the acres of fields that grew behind us. Rows and rows of the flowers that were raised with love.

Blood, sweat, and tears.

"It is. But it's not that easy. It's a ton of work. Sometimes I wonder what I've gotten myself into."

"I bet."

"I can't take all the credit, though. I have help."

"I should hope so," she said with a small giggle before she was coming forward and hugging me. Not as if we were the oldest of friends. But as if we were gonna be.

God.

How could one moment be so perfect and horrible?

But my mama had always told me that was life.

Filled with grace and beauty and light.

Worn down by evils and tragedies and afflictions.

Your joy dependent on which you allowed to hold most in your heart. Which were given most residence and respect.

Me?

I was going to cherish *this*.

This restoration.

This revival of love that I'd found in these people.

Hell, I was even going to be cordial to those who didn't deserve it.

When Maggie stepped back, I lifted my chin to the man who lurked like the off-putting memory of a bad dream halfway down the path.

A perfect storm. Chaos in the midst of the serenity I had found.

"Richard." I tried and failed to make it sound as if I didn't mind that he was there, and he'd come a few steps closer. And there went my stupid eyes, immediately searching through the rubble on his flesh, seeking that tiny reminder he had tattooed on the inside of his wrist.

A violet.

I'd wondered if he would have erased it.

But it was there.

Hidden within the designs that whispered of brokenness and horrors unseen.

He grumbled a rough sound. The rumble of it rippled across my flesh, those eyes the color of a spruce severe and acute. So sharp he might as well have been touching me.

I shook myself out of it. There was no chance I could go traipsing into those memories that wanted to climb into my consciousness. To remind me of what it'd felt like to be wrapped in those arms and loved by that body.

Falling into You

What I needed to remember was how it felt to go without. What it was like to live in his aftermath.

"Well, we should head out to look at the layout." I started down the trail that led to the spot where we hosted weddings, taking on the persona of the event planner I used for our clients as the group followed behind. I gestured to our lush surroundings. "Since the last time you were here, we've added a multitude of new features to make this one of the state's most sought-after wedding destinations. A private drive to the tree loops around the north of us with a parking lot. It also gives easier access for deliveries. We do have a large tent for the reception, tables, chairs, as well as a dance floor. You will have to contact someone for the linens as we don't supply those, as well as any food and beverages."

Melanie whipped out an iPad, totally on top of it. "Tables. Chairs. Tent. Dance floor. Check, check, check. Mabel and I will procure the linens. Royce, get us on the hook of an amazing band, yeah? Someone yummy and sexy at the front. Yes and please and thank you." She mumbled the last before her attention shifted back to me. "I'm assuming you can provide the floral arrangements?" she asked with a quirk of her brow.

I let go of a light laugh. "Yes, we can definitely provide the floral arrangements. In fact, we insist on it." I sent her a wink.

We wound down through the rows of flowers.

Roses.

Lilies.

Lilacs.

A whole acre of poppies.

Daffodils and tulips.

I tried not to fumble when I saw Saul out working in the distance with a couple of other men on our team, the way he glanced our way in longing, worry, and speculation.

Like he could just…feel it. The turmoil I was in.

Goodness.

I couldn't deal with it all.

We wound down one hill and up another before we finally broke into the meadow where our weddings were held.

A whimper clawed at my throat when the gorgeous site came

into view. It struck me every time. But somehow—somehow—this evening it was different.

A huge American Elm sat at the far end of it. Stoic and proud. Its branches were thick and stretching wide, the leaves full. The entire area was surrounded by lush vegetation.

It was like stepping into Eden.

Paradise.

One I'd been cast from.

Keep it together, Violet. You can do this.

I forced myself into a semblance of normalcy when there wasn't a thing about this that felt normal. Still, I smiled and said, "I recommend sunset for the ceremony. Right about now. The view is breathtaking."

"I already know what will be stealing my breath." Royce proclaimed it just loud enough for everyone to hear.

I glanced at my sweet friend, at the way she sighed.

Joy spilled out for her. At the happiness she had found. It got mixed up with the hurt that wouldn't go away. The hurt that felt all the more profound with him standing in the backdrop.

An unwilling participant. The strain blistering through the air and searing our flesh. I wouldn't be surprised if the two of us combusted right there. Nothing left of us but the ash getting carried away by the wind.

"It's perfect," Emily whispered, taking in the view.

"Over here to the right is the best place to put up a tent if that's what you're planning for the reception. Unless you decide to have that in town?"

I'd gone over the options with her on the phone two days ago, and she'd said she would give it thought and make a decision by this evening.

Emily glanced at Royce, the two of them sharing a private conversation before she turned back to me. "No. I think everything taking place here is perfect. More than perfect. A dream come true, honestly. I can't imagine a more beautiful setting in the entire world."

"I think it's perfect, too," Mabel agreed, her face tipped toward the waning sky as if she were taking in the last rays and picturing the most joyous day for her daughter.

"Um…is there even a question? It has to be here. I can feel it." This from Melanie.

I started to reply only to pause when I sensed the whip of energy in the air and a rustle in the branches above.

My attention darted up to the tree, and I peered through the leaves, praying I was imagining things. That the direction my worry went was unwarranted.

Getting riled up for nothing.

But no.

My instinct was spot on because dark eyes stared down at me, her smile bigger than her surroundings where she was high up in the towering tree.

My heart bottomed out, and a blaze of fear went streaking across my skin. "Daisy. What do you think you're doing up there?"

"Hi, Mommy! I'm just checking out the weddings plans for your friend. Hi, are you my mommy's friend? You gonna get married?" she shouted from where she had climbed about halfway up and then out onto a thick branch, the child leaning over it and peering down.

My little daredevil.

Emily giggled though it was in discomfort. "Why, hello there. Are you supposed to be all the way up in that tree?"

Emily shot me a worried look.

"Oh, my," Mabel wheezed.

"No, she is most definitely not supposed to be all the way up in that tree," I scolded, my words meant for Daisy.

She knew better.

On top of that, I'd told her to stay in the house with her papa while I worked. The last thing I needed was her getting in the middle of this.

Getting close.

Involved.

Mixed in with the people who I had lost.

I couldn't handle it.

"Get down, right now. And be careful when you're doing it," I all but hissed, trying not to point to the ground and stamp my foot, or worse yet, break down and cry.

I could feel the surge of concern.

The way the air shifted and shook.

A shimmer of protectiveness.

I gulped, squeezed my eyes, tried to pretend that the man wasn't there.

Encroaching.

Coming closer.

"Ahh, Mommy. You're no fun. None ats all. Dontcha know life is supposed to be fun and full of the adventures? 'Sides, Papa said you used to climb this tree all the time. Never listenin' to a word you were told." She said it like I was the troublemaker.

"Do you like adventures?" She was back to talking to Emily who was still staring up at her.

"Yes, I love adventures. But you must be careful when doing them," Emily encouraged her.

Daisy started to climb down, talking while she did, "Like a weddin' adventure?"

"Yup."

"You need a pretty flower girl? I got new pretty shoes. You wanna see? I put them on so I could shows you. And I'm the best dancer. You think you want me to be in your weddin' like my mommy?"

I pressed my hand to my forehead. Oh, god, what in the world was she doing? Wearing her dress shoes up there and inviting herself to be in a wedding?

You are so gonna be in time-out, I silently shouted.

"Oh, oh, well," Emily stammered, trying to hold back a laugh. "I'm sure you would make such a pretty flower girl, but guess what? Royce has a little girl who is just about your age, and we were hoping she might get to be the flower girl as long as everything works out just right. But maybe you could help with everyone getting signed in on the guest book? I bet you would be great at that and so pretty doin' it."

Daisy squealed, her excitement a torpedo through the air. "Yes! I would be so good at that, I'm bettin'. I got a dollar. I'm so excited. You wanna see my shoes? I can get different ones if you want me to, but I like these ones the best!"

She started to rush, coming down fast.

My pulse spiked.

"Daisy, be careful!"

And I wondered if I'd seen it coming all along because that was the same second the slick sole of her shoe slipped off the branch she stepped down onto.

The child losing footing.

Losing hold.

She screamed as she started to fall through the dense branches.

My spirit groaned in a plea of agony.

A moaning from deep within as I stood there helpless.

My breath hitched when she caught onto one and held it by a single hand, but she was dangling way up high, and my heart was on the ground as terror took hold of every cell.

"Daisy. Don't let go." The words barely broke free from the fear locking up my throat.

Mabel whimpered.

"Oh, god," Emily whispered as everyone rushed forward.

"Shit," Royce grunted. He darted for the tree and started to scale it. "Hang on, Daisy."

"Don't let go. Hold on," I shouted, finally freeing the sound locked in my throat.

I rushed for the trunk of the tree, following behind Royce and shouting, "Hold on, baby. Hold on. We're comin' for you."

But she was screaming. Screaming my name. "Mommy! I slippin'."

No.

No. No. No. Her hold broke.

A whorl of black hair streaked through my vision.

My turmoil filled the air. "Daisy!" I screamed, trying to get to her but knowing there was no chance.

Out of reach.

Too late. Too late.

The Earth spun, and the ground quaked.

Dread took hold.

Because I knew it.

Knew she was too high. She was too high and I knew this was going to end bad and there was absolutely nothin' I could do.

The air whipped and dust flew where she made impact.

The magnitude of it brought me to my knees. I went for her, feeling like I was crawlin' through the rubble, moving in slow motion toward where she had fallen.

This child who was the world.

My reason.

My joy.

My light.

I'd almost made it to her by the time the dust settled.

I realized it wasn't just Daisy.

He was there.

The child was in a ball against Richard's chest.

"Oh god," I whimpered, shocked and unsure and trying to process what it was that I was seeing.

Wondering if I was hallucinating to save myself from the grief.

Sobs ripping from my throat, I climbed to my feet and staggered the rest of the way over to where Richard was holding her in those arms that I had once been so sure had been created to love and protect, my ribs feeling as if they were being ripped in two.

Everything holding me together pulling me apart.

From within the well of his hold, Daisy wailed.

I dropped back to my knees, tearing at his arms to get to her. "Daisy, oh baby, Daisy, are you hurt? Are you hurt?"

Reluctantly, Richard let his arms drop away.

She sat up on his lap. "My wrist hurts real bad." Then she wailed when she looked at the dirty shoes on her feet. "Oh no, I ruined my best shoes," she cried out.

I completely crumbled.

Relief. Relief.

The only strength I had left was enough to gather her into my lap. Into my arms.

Tears streamed free. Hot and hard and blinding my sight.

I hugged her close, shushed her, and whispered, "It's okay, it's okay. We'll get you another pair."

Falling into You

I looked at the man from over her head where he'd pushed up to sitting two feet away, roughing agitated hands through his hair.

The man who looked like he'd been wrecked.

Utterly destroyed.

If only he knew what that really felt like.

eleven

Richard

*W*hat the fuck just happened?

My heart stampeded, like a thousand thoroughbreds raced around a track carved in the void in my chest while I stared at the woman who was looking at me like she couldn't believe what I'd done.

Those eyes on me while her soul trembled and shook.

Her fear so patent I could taste it. The terror of what could have been.

The air was held in the meadow.

Like even the wind was afraid to move.

Everyone frozen in this shock that ricocheted between Violet and me.

Fuck.

It'd been instinct. Running to catch the child. Being there. Like my spirit had known exactly where it was supposed to be all along.

Her tiny body ascribed to the surety of my arms.

But that was the motherfucking problem.

I was made to protect her.

Made to protect them.

Thing was, doing it was a crime itself. Breaking the promise I'd made.

But if I hadn't been there?

At the thought, my pulse stuttered in dread, this thick, sticky fear that slugged through my veins.

Every second I was here it became clearer where I belonged.

Except I would never be accepted.

Just a fool's game hoping for forgiveness.

For redemption.

Didn't mean I would give so easily.

Violet was on the ground. So close. Making me itch.

Terror struck in those thunderbolt eyes.

She stared across at me through the connection that whipped and snapped.

Like she wondered if I could understand.

I wanted to get lost there. In her gaze. In this feeling that urged me to crawl to them, wrap them up, and promise I would never leave.

Bullshit.

A motherfucking pipe dream that would only burn me in the end.

Crush and destroy.

My mom was the first to shoot into action.

She ran around me to get to Violet and the child, and I scrubbed both palms over my face like it could eradicate every thought that had just blazed through my mind.

Like it could stop what I could feel being set into motion.

The greed that pulsed.

Devotion a drum that grew in intensity.

My mom knelt in front of them. Affection and agony oozed from her pores, and fuck, that slayed me, too.

Still, she managed to keep it together. "Daisy, it's Ms. Mabel.

Are you okay, sweetheart? Whew, that was some fall you took there. Scared the dickens out of us all."

"I ruins my shoes," the child wailed again. "Now I won't be able to be in the weddin'."

My mom chuckled low. "Well, they are a mighty fine pair of shoes, aren't they? But I think we can figure something out for the weddin'. Don't you worry about that."

"Are you sure?" Daisy asked her, sniffling and rubbing her hands over her tear-stained face, smearing the dirt into mud.

Mel, Em, and Maggie hovered over them. Unsure of what to do.

"Is she okay?" Emily shook out her hands like she could shake off the tremors. "God. That was…" she trailed off.

Royce was behind her, two feet away. I cut him a glance. He sent one back.

It was close. Too damn close.

"How about you let me take a look at those shoes?" my mother prodded, shifting her on Violet's lap so she could get a look.

Gentle in the way that only she could be.

While Violet struggled to maintain composure. But I knew the girl well enough to know when she was getting ready to crumble.

"My, these are fancy," Ma said in her soothing way. "I bet you could dance all night long in these beauties, couldn't you?"

Daisy sniffled but smiled this earth-shattering smile.

My chest tightened.

"Yups! My mommy said I'm the bestest dancer she's ever seen. I got lessons, you know."

"Wow, that is somethin'. You are a special girl, aren't you? A very special girl." My mother's voice hitched.

Daisy's shoulders lifted to her ears, a smile splitting her face that was smeared with dirt and tracks of tears.

So fuckin' cute.

So fuckin' dangerous.

My mom felt around her legs. "Any pain when I touch your legs?"

"Nope."

"Okay. Good. How about I take a look at that arm now?"

Daisy had it tucked to her chest, protecting it. Reluctantly, she let it go so my mom could take a look.

Daisy winced when she touched her right wrist. "Ouch!"

"Is that tender, right there?"

Clearly, the kid was trying to play it brave because her chin trembled, and her eyes filled with more tears, but she was acting like it was nothing. "Nope. I'm all okay now. I bet I can even fly. Watch this!"

She hopped up before Violet could stop her and flapped her arms. Second she did, she crumbled back to the ground.

Knocked down by an intense bolt of pain.

"I lied. I told a lie! It hurts real bad," she cried.

"I...I think I need to take her to the emergency room," Violet rambled. "I'm sorry, I think we're going to have to cut this meeting short."

Her entire being was shaking.

Shock and worry of what might have been rippling across her flesh.

Patent.

Palpable.

So real it was marching toward me like tiny soldiers on the invade.

An attack I couldn't stop or fight.

Standing, she picked Daisy up. Awkwardly, considering the child was almost half her size.

I was on my feet before I could talk any sense into myself. Before I thought over the consequences. Before I knew what this would mean.

"Let me take her."

Pain lashed through her expression. She held the child closer, trying to hoist her up. "I thank you for what you just did. But that's not necessary. She's fine. I've got her."

"Just let me help you, Violet. Your truck is all the way up by the house. You can't safely carry her that far." I leaned in, my mouth at her ear. "Let me help you."

Grieved disbelief gusted from her, that sweet, sweet mouth trembling all over the place. "You think I need you now? Six years late?"

"No, Violet. You've always been better off without me. Think we both know that."

"Then leave us alone." It was a plea. Girl as weak as me.

"I can't. Won't." My voice turned to stone.

Torment blistered between us, and there was no missing the tension that radiated from my mom and Emily. The vile choices I'd made. Their disappointment I'd carried around on my shoulders every bit as heavy as the burden of my debt.

Violet tried to drop her gaze, but it kept flicking up to meet my stare.

"Be careful with her." Violet's voice twisted around me. An agonized prayer. Trusting me when she knew full well she shouldn't.

I gathered the child in my arms.

Carefully.

Cradling her to my chest, her legs were draped over one of my arms, the other secured around her back and shoulders.

My heart panged. Fucking bled. "I've got you, flower girl," I murmured like a goddamn fool.

She grinned up at me. Cheeks covered in dirt and those dark eyes full of hope. "I want to be a flower girl, but the welcomes girl sounds second best, right?"

"No. Not second best. Not even close," I murmured at her forehead. Breathing her in.

Fuck.

I was getting too close. Touching on things I couldn't. But I couldn't find the willpower to walk.

They needed me, and this was the little I could give. I just wished I could offer everything.

Violet's storm raged around me as I began to carry the child back up the trail to the main house, the woman flustered and perturbed and agitated, flitting around behind me like a little bird.

Caught somewhere in the crux of wanting the best thing for Daisy and wanting to rip her out of my arms.

Save her from the pain that I would bring.

My attention darted to a man who was probably a year or two

older than me coming over the hill, rushing faster when he felt the turmoil that bound us.

"Violet...what happened? Is Daisy hurt?"

Could feel his eyes on Violet. Like he wanted to go to her. Wrap her up.

I attempted to shun the jolt of jealousy.

The possession that lifted and burned in my veins.

I tightened my arms around Daisy like some kind of selfish prick who had a right to make a claim on these girls.

"Yes...no...she's fine...she's gonna be," Violet stammered.

"I flew out of the tree, Saul...just like a bird. I wasn't even scared," Daisy shouted as she tried to poke her head up to see him.

I cringed.

She needed to be scared.

God knew, I was fucking terrified.

"Climbing that tree was not a good choice, Daisy," Violet chastised, worry bleeding out, the woman overwhelmed with this kid I was fast realizing was a handful. "You know that's against the rules. I've told you before that you were gonna get hurt."

"But just a little hurt, right?" She peeked up at me when she asked it, like she trusted me to have her back.

God, this kid.

"Can I be of help?" Saul offered. He came toward me like he actually thought I was going to hand her over.

Not happening.

"I, uh—" Violet started to answer.

"No," I shot at him with a scathing look, a warning in the single word.

Fucking no.

Back the fuck away.

Animosity poured from him. Undeniable.

My stomach curled in resentment. What the fuck was wrong with me?

I wanted to lay the fucker out.

I couldn't stop it. The fierce swell of envy that rose from the darkest depths. Where vengeance lived and hatred grew.

Where I was a prisoner to what I had missed.

To what I had lost.

"I think we're fine, Saul, thank you," Violet answered.

Could tell he didn't want to give up when he continued along a few feet behind us. He finally fumbled to a stop where he stood between two rows of roses while we continued to cut a path back toward the house.

My family trailed us.

Royce on edge, Emily fretting. Was pretty sure the only thing my mom wanted to do was smack me upside the head.

Couldn't blame her.

I could hear Melanie whispering to Maggie far in the distance.

No doubt, she was dishing the dirty details to Maggie since Royce's little sister didn't have the first clue about them.

But it didn't matter.

None of it did.

Nothing but the little girl who I carried in my arms. I didn't stop as I stormed up the last hill to where Violet's truck was parked in front of her house. I went directly to the back, opened the door, and carefully situated Daisy into her car seat, being careful of her injured arm.

"Is that good?" I asked, warily, glancing at her cherub face and trying not to get my heart smashed all over again as I buckled her in.

She grinned.

Fat chance.

I was toast.

A motherfuckin' goner.

"You did it right! Do you got a little girl to take care of? You are really very smart. My papa can never get these darned contraptions locked up right." She rolled her eyes that still had tears, clearly parroting her grandfather's sentiment.

I would have laughed if what she'd said didn't feel like razors dragging through my flesh.

Four inches deep.

Flaying me open wide.

"No, Daisy, I don't." It sounded like an apology.

Before I lost it, I shut the door and climbed into the driver's seat. Violet was right behind me, her voice lowered to a stunned hiss. "What the hell do you think you're doing?"

"Driving you and Daisy to the hospital."

"Oh, no, you're not."

"Just get in the truck, Violet. You are in no shape to drive and you don't need to be taking her yourself. You're upset."

"Yeah, well I can think of a hundred other people I would prefer to be doing the honors," she hissed under her breath.

I could tell Emily was getting ready to offer with the way she surged forward. I pitched her a warning glare.

My sister stopped in her tracks, confusion knitting her brow considering just a few days ago I'd been spitting teeth that she'd had the audacity to ask Violet to be in her wedding.

My actions nothing but contradictions.

"Get in, Violet."

"Get in, Mommy," Daisy shouted from the back seat. "I need to get my arm all fixed up so I can be good for dancin'. Don't go ruinin' this weddin' for me."

Violet scowled at me, and not an adorable, cute way. She looked like maybe she would stab me right then if she could get away with it. Or maybe she'd be willing to give it a shot, anyway.

"I'm not letting you do this to me, Richard," she grated under her breath, the anger shifting to desperation.

"What's that?"

"Toy with my heart."

"I never wanted to." My voice was as low as hers.

She stared at me, and I was trapped. Lost in the haze of those enchanting eyes as she took me in like she was trying to see through the garbage that had littered our lives.

Find the man she'd thought I'd been.

My lungs squeezed, and I kneaded at the steering wheel and forced myself not to say anything else. Not to tell her I missed her. That I still couldn't fucking sleep at night, and when I did, she was there.

A hostage I only knew in my dreams.

I was already doing so much damage just being there, and there wasn't a chance in hell that I could stay.

Finally, she gave a tight nod. "I need to get my purse and tell my daddy what happened. I'll be right back."

"Fine." The word was grit.

Maybe I was hoping she would refuse. Or maybe that Royce would come and drag my pathetic ass out of this truck and knock some sense into me.

But everyone was held.

Watching this shitshow go down.

Me as the star.

Violet fumbled around the truck, glancing back once as she took the steps onto the porch and then disappeared into the house.

I watched her go.

Unable to look away.

My heart raged. A caged beast screaming for its match.

"What do you think you're doin', Rich?" Emily's voice hit me from the side. A torrent of worry gushed out with her words.

I tossed a glance her way. My sister stood there twisting her fingers together. Our ma was behind her, brow twisted in concern and looking like she was itching to smack me again.

My tongue darted out to wet my lips, keeping quiet enough that only she could hear. "You asked me to come here. What did you think was going to happen?"

"I thought you were gonna stand up in my wedding."

"Next to her. Don't act like you don't know what you're doing, Em."

Her chin quivered. "I...I want you to get back on track, Rich. Find your joy. What's right in this world. I'm just prayin' you don't hurt her along the way."

"I think I've already done plenty of that."

The door reopened, and Violet came rushing out. Wearing that floral dress she'd been wearing all day, the one that had just about done me in, long locks of black hair braided in a pretty twist, errant pieces falling in delicate wisps around her gorgeous face.

Want fisted my stomach.

"Only question now is why," Emily pressed, the words secreted by the wind.

"Why doesn't matter. The only thing that does is it's too late," I grunted, shifting in the seat when Violet opened the front passenger door. "I'll give Rhys a text to come pick me up when we get back," I said.

Emily gave a wary nod.

"I'm sorry again, Emily," Violet rushed through the open door. "We can regroup tomorrow…for now, just start getting the invites prepared. Those need to go out ASAP."

"Don't worry about it. Take care of your sweet girl. That's the only thing that matters."

Violet sent her a bumbling nod as she climbed in. I was slammed with a wave of her.

Violets and dreams and the girl.

Emily angled her head in behind me so she could talk to Daisy. "You get all fixed up. We need our pretty dancer better for this wedding."

"I will," she sang, though it came out weaker than the kid's normal exuberance.

A sad smile graced Emily's face. It passed from Daisy to me and over to Violet. "Good luck. Text me later and let me know what they say."

Violet hugged her purse on her lap. "I will. Thank you."

Violet turned to check on Daisy, cooing a bunch of words, promising it was going to be okay.

Emily stepped back, and I leaned out to shut the door. I caught the disturbance that hovered around Royce.

The warning he wore in the set of his jaw.

I lifted my chin at him because I wasn't walking away from this.

For once…for one fuckin' time…I was going to be there for Violet, whether she wanted me there or not.

He just shook his head and pushed off from where he was leaning against the Suburban.

He knew it as well as I did.

I was in deep.

And I wasn't sure I wanted to get out.

Violet

*H*ad you ever felt like you were being conned?

The wool pulled over your eyes before you realized what was happening?

Deceived into thinking you were making the right choices for you and your family?

Problem was, too often you were opening doors better left shut.

Before you knew it, you were swindled right out of your heart and, if you let yourself unravel any further, most likely out of your panties, too.

I could feel the threat of it trembling in the air.

This tension that bounded and ricocheted and lashed.

Suffocating.

Curling through the cab like a million silenced questions that were never going to have any answers.

I peeked to my left at the man who was barreling down the road toward town. Leaned back in the driver's seat like he'd belonged there all along, one arm stretched out to hold the steering wheel and the other with his elbow propped on the windowsill with his head rested on his hand.

He would have come across as casual if it weren't for the fury that lined every inch of his glorious body.

If it weren't for that fierce jaw he had clenched tight.

The sun sank low on the horizon behind him, rays scattering through the window and casting him in a golden glow.

A music god who'd stolen the songs right out of my soul.

Pieces of myself missin' because they would forever belong to him.

"I don't know why you're actin' so angry. I didn't ask you to do this," I mumbled, so quiet, trying to keep my voice in check.

Hell, I'd begged him not to.

He grunted, that jaw working like mad.

I had the urge to touch it. To brush my fingertips through the stubble. Press my nose to it, too.

There went that spiral.

Down, down, down.

I dug my fingers into the seat, refusing to let myself falter.

He cut me a glare. "And you think I was just gonna let you handle this yourself?" He glanced in the rearview mirror at Daisy who was being uncharacteristically quiet. I wondered if she wasn't immune to any of this, either. If she felt the potency.

The roiling waves that grew higher and higher.

Sucking me deeper.

"Yes," I told him, point-blank.

His head shook, and he scrubbed a palm over his face. "I never should have come back here." He rumbled it under his breath. Like I wasn't going to hear. Or maybe that was exactly what he'd intended.

I stared out the windshield. "No, you shouldn't have."

Not when he was never going to stay.

"Fuck," he muttered with a shake of his head.

"That is a very bad word," Daisy piped in. Awesome. My little heckler was listening from the back after all.

He flinched and glanced her way again. "Sorry, Daisy. I wasn't thinking straight."

"That's okay 'cause you've got no little girls to watch over and then you're talkin' all those bad big people wordses, right?"

He cringed harder, and he gripped the steering wheel with both hands. "Something like that."

Slowing, he made a left into the hospital that was built on the outskirts of town.

Thank God.

I couldn't take much more of being cooped up with him in this cab.

I was beginning to think the only options I had left were either to kiss him or claw his eyes out, and I was not in the market to get my heart mangled all over again.

The alternative didn't seem all that prudent, either.

I hefted out a sigh of relief when he pulled into a parking spot in front of the small emergency room. Dalton was nothing but a speck on the map, and I figured we were lucky to have emergency services available at all.

"Here we are, sunshine. We're going to get you all checked out," I told her, doing my best to ignore the pinging of horror at what could have been. This could have been so much worse had Richard not been there to catch her when she fell.

And god, that destroyed me, too.

Knowing what he'd done. What he'd given. What he'd saved her from.

"I think I'm all the way fine. It's only hurtin' barely a bit." She sent me the fakest grin.

"Let's just see what the doctor says, deal?"

"Okay. Fine. It's a deal. Let's get this show on the road. I got reals important things to do," she said, all kinds of matter-of-fact.

Richard sent me an exasperated look. Like he didn't know what to make of her mischief, either. Whether to laugh or drop to his knees and cry.

My little angel child who was nothing but a hellion.

The second Richard put the truck in park, I climbed out. I rushed around to get Daisy, and then I was huffin' out my displeasure when he was already there. He unbuckled her and pulled her into his arms, murmuring these words that cut through me like a dull, rusted blade.

Agonizing and slow.

"Here you go. I've got you. Don't worry, flower girl, I've got you."

Did he think that bein' there now was gonna change anything? That it could make up for what he'd done?

"I can get her. I have to carry her to her room all the time when she falls asleep on the couch."

"I have her." It was a grunt. No room for argument.

I didn't even fight him.

At this point, I just wanted to get this over with.

Make sure my Daisy was okay and then get as far away from this man as possible. Set boundaries. Make him promise there would be no more of *this*.

The way he was infiltrating our lives as if he had a right.

Like he wanted to, which was a smack to the face in itself.

I couldn't handle it, the betrayal that had cleaved a hole in the middle of us.

Couldn't take his presence that screamed to fill it.

Couldn't risk getting swamped in his dark, decadent aura.

The last thing I could do was allow him to hold my hopes and my fears for a second time.

Give him that trust.

Because when he left me again? I wouldn't know how to stand.

Darkness cloaked the sky, heavy and oppressive in the moonless night.

A cascade of stars spiraled across the heavens, so low where they dipped down to meet the horizon that it felt as if we were driving through a glittering veil as we traveled the deserted two-lane road.

Headlights cut a path through the disorder that had become my world.

Silence a roaring presence in the cab.

Different than it'd been on the way to the emergency room.

It'd shifted.

Turned into something somber and quiet.

I glanced back at where Daisy was asleep in her car seat. Out cold. Sleep had already been chasing her down while we'd been waiting for the doctor to come in and cast her wrist.

I reached back and caressed it, my chest stretched tight as I took in the child who was filled with so much life and laughter and mischief, and still, so vulnerable and innocent.

Her well-being cast into my hands.

A shiver curled down my spine.

An ice-cold dread.

Maybe it hit me right then. After the shock had worn off.

What truly could have been. How close she'd come. That it could have been any other day when she was off on one of her escapades and no one would have been there to save her.

Gratefulness rocked me. Slamming me from out of nowhere. So intense it brought moisture burning at the back of my eyes.

"Shit," Richard muttered.

Like he'd been struck by the intensity, too, but in an entirely different way.

I jerked, and my attention rocked back to the man who kept hitting me like an earthquake. Quivers that staked through my being every time he said a word. Driven deeper with each glance.

Pain lashed across his face when he looked at me. "I'm sorry."

My brow twisted, and my heart skittered. "What exactly are you sorry for?"

Loaded question, much?

But I couldn't stop the gate that busted wide. Freeing something. Opening me up for one vulnerable second.

Truth billowing between us.

That connection zapping and zinging through the dense air.

"For not getting there sooner. For doing it wrong. For fuckin' it up." He mumbled it toward the windshield as if the night could take hold of his confession. Like there was more to it than what had happened this afternoon.

I needed to refuse it. Give him no credit.

But I couldn't ignore what he had done. That cresting of gratitude pouring from me.

Wave after wave.

"You saved her, Richard. If you hadn't been there...in that spot..."

I shuddered at the thought, unable to process a tragedy that great.

"She has a broken wrist." His voice cracked with some kind of unspent grief when he said it.

My head shook, that truth gettin' free. "And I'm thankin' God it wasn't a broken neck. Thankin' God that you were there. Right when she needed you. Right when we needed you."

The statement hovered in the cab.

Words smothering just as much as they were giving life.

The weight of it pressed down on our chests.

Our hearts drumming so fierce they'd become a lifebeat in the cab.

The two of us trapped in it.

Going under.

Clearing my throat, I ripped my attention from his profile and glanced back at her again, my voice filled with adoration and fear. With the burden I carried. "Sometimes I worry that I'm not enough for all that she is."

Richard's teeth clenched, his hands firm on the wheel as he stared out at the road ahead of him. "I'm pretty sure you're everything she needs."

My mouth trembled. "You don't even know me anymore."

He tossed me a glance. "Don't I?"

I got caught there, lost in the depth of his gaze. Unrelenting. Hard and soft and everything in between. I searched for a missing breath, finally tearing myself from the trance cast by this man and forcing myself to drop my focus to my lap.

I doubted that more than a blip of a second had passed that

we'd both been there watching it through the distance. But in it had been the eternity we were supposed to share.

His eclipse right there to swallow it up.

A black hole where I'd forever gotten lost.

I instantly felt the loss of it like a kick to the gut. This hollowed-out vacancy that moaned and ached.

Coming alive from where it'd lain only half dormant in the time he'd been gone.

Agony rushed me all at once.

I stifled it and tried to hold it together, but my chest constricted, and moisture clouded my eyes as a sea of sorrow threatened to sweep me away. Through the tears, I looked out the window at the passing countryside.

I just needed to make it home. Get inside and lock the door and shut him out.

Permanently.

Because I wasn't sure I could remain this close to him for a second longer, for my heart to be *right there* but no longer mine to keep.

Pressure filled the space. His breaths hot and heavy and saturating the air.

The man the oxygen in my lungs.

Questions vied to get free. Like talons trying to claw their way out of me. Eviscerating. No care for the destruction their seeking this closure might impose.

I bit down on my tongue, praying for the seconds to pass, holding my breath, feeling like I was nearly gonna faint by the time Richard rounded the last curve that brought the house into view.

A beacon on the hill.

In silence, we rambled up the dirt drive, old truck bouncing like crazy, my hand already curled around the doorlatch.

Before he came to a full stop, I was out the door like a gun had gone off, and I was launching myself into a 300-yard dash.

I rounded the back of the truck so I could get to my child.

And yet again, he was there.

Invading my space.

Stealing that breath that he'd supplied.

Before I could argue with him, he shot me a look that told me his actions were not up for debate when he opened the back door.

Oh, I was pretty sure there was plenty to quarrel about.

But still, I remained quiet as he picked her up, his entire demeanor at odds with the gentle way he handled her.

The way he pulled her sleeping form into his arms.

The way his breaths were short and ragged.

As if he were suffering.

Physically.

Mentally.

Like maybe he'd had his heart broken as severely as mine.

My spirit screamed, *Why, why, why? Why would you do this to me? Was loving her too much of me to ask?*

I sucked them down and instead ran ahead of him, keeping my footsteps quieted as I moved up to the porch and to the door. I pushed my key into the lock, and I could feel him behind me, the man towering, a dark fortress that eclipsed.

My bright star that had gone dim.

I struggled for clarity as I let us into the darkness of the sleeping house.

"Shh," I whispered as if the baited silence echoing back needed to be acknowledged. But the last thing I needed was for my daddy to come face-to-face with Richard having the nerve to come stand under his roof.

As it was, I'd been worried the man was going to have an aneurism when I'd told him what had happened—that Daisy had hurt her arm and Richard was driving us to the emergency room—that vein at his temple thumping like mad and gettin' ready to burst.

I hadn't stuck around for the lecture that I'd known was coming. It wasn't like I didn't already know exactly what my daddy would say.

"This way," I muttered, heading for the stairs. They creaked as we ascended, but I was worried it was the thunder of my heart that was going to wake the entire house.

Richard didn't say anything.

He didn't need to.

His presence profound.

Loud.

Already proclaiming that he was there.

At the landing, I took a right and ushered Richard into the room across from mine that had been Liliana's.

He slowed for a second, glancing down at me, this hard, tortured turmoil in his eyes.

Did he get it?

The pain I'd endured?

His thick throat bobbing with his heavy swallow, he tore his gaze from mine and carried Daisy inside.

The room had been redone since the last time he'd been there. It was now a painted oasis of rainbows and flowers and unicorns.

Magic.

Just like the little girl.

Richard's gaze darted around, taking it in before he moved to her bed that we'd made to look like she was floating on a cloud in that blue, blue sky.

I pulled back the covers, and he set her onto the mattress.

"She needs a bath but I'm pretty sure she would lose it if I woke her up right now," I said quietly, rambling more than I should. "She never wants to go to sleep and then she'll fight you tooth and nail if she has to get up."

He nodded, voice rough, sage eyes caressing over me. "Rest is probably more important right now. It's been a hard day. I think she had to have been in a lot more pain than she was letting on."

I returned a nod. "I think so, too. She doesn't want a thing to slow her down."

A soft smile played across those full, lush lips that sent a tremor racing through me, the shadows in the room dancing along with it. "Not sure a thing could. She's a force to be reckoned with."

I fiddled with my fingers. "She sure is."

God, this was awkward and horrible. Because I needed him to leave and the only thing I wanted to do was beg him to stay.

A fool.

A fool.

"She's tough. A fighter," Richard grumbled in this low drawl.

Showing just a hint of that southern accent he'd all but lost. "Brave."

He touched her forehead.

Gently.

Looking down at her with affection.

With this adoration I didn't understand.

My heart tumbled in my chest.

He ran his fingertips down her chubby cheek, and it was sorrow that came spilling out of his mouth, "Beautiful. So damn beautiful, Vi."

I gulped for the nonexistent air, and shivers raked through the length of my body.

Hurt wept from my soul, colliding with the old love I'd buried deep, where I'd held it there knowing it would never die.

It'd been too big and beautiful to ever succumb into nothingness, yet not strong enough to keep him there.

Had he been immune to it?

Had it been fake?

My stomach toiled in rejection because it'd felt so real to me that him not feeling it too seemed impossible.

Richard straightened, his spine going rigid, every muscle in that gorgeous body flexing and bowing as if he'd just gotten pummeled by every thought I'd had.

As if he felt the turmoil.

Did he know? Did he know?

"I should go," he said, barely able to glance at me. "I sent Rhys a text to pick me up. He should be here in a bit."

I nodded frantically. "Okay. Thank you." The last two words gushed out.

True in their form.

Thank you. Thank you.

He edged my way. Each step sent a tremor rocking through my body. Sage eyes caressed me slow. Lust and greed and shame.

He came to a stop just to the side of where I stood, and he angled in low, rough words grazing my ear, "Don't thank me, Violet. We both know I'm to blame."

There was no questioning what he was referring to had nothing to do with what had happened today.

He ripped himself away and headed out the door.

I squeezed my eyes closed almost as hard as I squeezed my fists. Praying for sanity. I could almost hear my daddy calling, *Make good choices.*

But I wasn't feeling quite so rational right then.

I guessed that sometimes things just needed to be said. They could no longer be held or quieted or contained.

Pulse a thunder, I rushed out into the hall where Richard was getting ready to take the stairs. "I didn't think I was going to make it. When you left me, when you walked away, I didn't think I would make it."

He froze, his hand on the railing, his head tipping toward the ground.

Impaled by my confession. Bound by the pain that bled through the admission. While I remained in the darkness of the hall. Wishing I could hide.

From what he'd done.

From the way he still made me feel.

From the fact he was there, destroying me all over again.

Richard warred. His lithe body rippled, sinewy muscle flexing and bowing and twitching.

With restraint or repulsion, I couldn't tell which.

But I realized I had none of it.

Restraint.

"How could you just wake up one day and not love me anymore?" The words quivered and shook with hushed misery. "Because I'm still waitin' on the day when I wake up and I'm no longer in love with you."

I had no time to prepare myself.

No time to put back up the walls I'd let down.

Richard was there, a phantom that moved through the shadows.

A plunderer.

A thief.

My love. My life. My greatest downfall.

He pressed me to the wall and planted his hands above my

head, that tall, strong body a fortress where it hovered over mine.

Flames leapt, the air charged.

A thousand volts of electricity.

He breathed out a harsh sound, the force of it covering me in his raw, potent energy.

Trapping me in that haze of seduction that had always hypnotized me. From the first second we'd met.

Crackles of need. Sparks of lust.

His nose ran along the curve of my jaw.

Inhaling.

Savoring.

Remembering.

Tingles raced, and my belly flipped.

My heart was beating so out of control I could feel the storm of it bashing at my rib cage.

Richard's was, too, this erratic drum, drum, drum that called to me.

Violent and fierce.

A warrior's song.

This was wrong. So wrong. I needed to shove him off. Cling to the reality of what he'd done.

Feelings were fleeting.

But the impact of heinous acts were not.

Thing was, I couldn't react. I couldn't move a muscle when his words were coming at me like a drug. "How could one lie negate a thousand truths?"

Richard took my left hand, and he let his thumb gently trace over the musical note on the inside of my wrist that I'd forever written there.

An imprint of him.

A sharp breath left me.

He inhaled it.

Sucked me down like I was the granter of life.

Our noses brushed and our chests heaved.

And I swore, in the middle of us, I saw our spirits tangle. Saw them start to dance and spiral and spin.

"Liar." The whisper curled into the air. It was an accusation. A plea.

"I am," he grunted. "But loving you was never one of them."

"Or maybe it was the biggest one you ever told."

"No," he rasped, and a shocked gasp raked from my lungs when he swept his lips against mine.

The softest tease.

Barely there.

He pulled back a fraction, the mossy haze of those green eyes mesmerizing. Filled with something I'd be a fool to believe.

Still, we rocked in time with the quivering of the ground. With the walls that began to spin. With my heart that faltered and sped.

"Then prove it."

Oh god, that was a reckless thing to say. Just begging for a little more devastation.

Because I saw the second he snapped. When those eyes flared in a shock of need, and his mouth was colliding with mine, his hands cupping my cheeks before one was twisting up in my braid and tugging my head back to meet the ferocity of his kiss.

I needed to push him away. Fight this. But I was opening to him, giving myself over to the desperation.

A possessive, dangerous plea.

I was lost.

Lost to the plucks and pulls of his plush, soft lips.

To the play of his tongue that stroked me into desire.

His hot, heated body pressed and urged, every inch of him hard and demanding.

We spun and shifted, both of us vying for the upper hand. I edged him out into the hall, two of us twisting and twirling, going round and round in a tug-of-war that neither of us would win.

Flames seared, and he had me banging back against the wall, the world nothing but grunts and whimpers and needy pants.

He moaned. "Violet."

A tiny cry pulled up my throat. "Why? Why would you leave me when I needed you most?"

He kissed me deeper, his hands rushing, searching across my body. Like he could chase the questions away. Like the trembling in his palms could give me an answer.

"Hurting you was the last thing I ever wanted to do."

My spirit wailed, and he hoisted me from my feet and plastered me to the wall.

I hit it with a thud, and my fingers drove into his hair and down to trace over his scruff. "Please. Take it away. Just take it away."

The pain and sufferin'.

Maybe this time when he went it wouldn't hurt so bad.

I was a fool to think it, but right then, I'd give anything for him to quell the agony.

To sate this need.

To satisfy what had been missin'.

I groaned into his kiss, rubbing myself against his body while he took handfuls of my hips. His erection pressed at my belly.

Fire lit, and god, I needed him. I needed him.

"Need you," I rambled into his kiss.

"Violeta." The choked, shocked voice hit us from the side.

It speared through the bubble that held us. The floor ripped right out of heaven.

I froze in dismay, and Richard jerked his head back, still pinning me to the wall while my father watched us through the shadows in pure horror.

The reality of what I'd done came crashing down.

I'd let Richard Ramsey touch me.

Had begged him for it.

Asking for the pain.

For the misery.

"You little bastard," my father sneered. "El tema de la alegria."

The thief of joy.

Richard stepped back and set me onto my wobbling feet.

His attention swung between us. Regret and guilt lashed through his expression.

I felt like I'd been doused by a vat of ice-cold water.

Woken from a blissful, perfect dream to the nightmare of what I'd done.

How could I have ever put myself in the position where he could steal it all over again?

Because there he stood with another piece of my heart in his hands.

I guessed the horrible truth of it was that he'd held it all along.

Richard

I staggered back while Violet's father glared at me like I was the antichrist.

The deliverer of wickedness and injustice.

The thief of joy.

He wouldn't be wrong.

My head shook as I looked between the two of them, guilt clotting off the air that was trying to scrape up my throat.

Lust ravaged my body. Clawing and wailing. Seeking a way out.

Dick hard and heart hemorrhaging.

Just a fan-fucking-tastic way for her father to find me.

Thing was, I respected the man with all that I had even while he looked at me like the vile, piece of shit that I was.

Didn't blame him a bit.

Dude deserved to hate me with every fiber of his being.

More than he already did.

I would do well to bolt.

Get the fuck out of there before I made it any worse than I already had which was damn close to being an impossibility.

Because this was pure selfishness.

Problem was, in the middle of it, I could feel what was coming off Violet. Desire coating every inch of her soft, seductive flesh. Her pulse drumming like mad, still caught up in the moment that had just been *us*.

Like we'd been taken back to the way it'd once been.

The way it should have still been.

Worst were the questions that throbbed and spun.

The reckless confession I had made.

I wanted it. To drop to my goddamn knees and confess it.

The lies I had told.

I bit them back because saying a word wouldn't help a thing.

I'd only destroy the one thing I had left to give.

There was no chance of redemption.

This woman would despise me with every fiber that knitted her beautiful being when she finally found out what I'd done.

The wickedness of my actions.

I was in deep. Nothing but a captive to what I had to do. To the choices I'd made.

Didn't mean I didn't want it.

To fall at this goddesses' feet.

Worship her.

Give into the hunger that lashed. A violent shout that demanded to be fed.

Getting a taste of this girl tonight had been like taking the first bite after a five-year famine and now I was ravenous.

Mouth watering and desperate to consume.

"I should go," I forced out.

Rejection slashed through Violet's expression.

"You never should have come," her father hissed.

He was right.

One-hundred-percent.

"No. I shouldn't have."

That rejection turned into a full-on tumult, torment crashing through Violet's demeanor.

I wanted to rush her.

Tell her it was a lie. That I would change it if I could.

But I was tied.

Obligated to this debt.

Still, I couldn't leave her there that way.

Not again.

The consequences could go fuck themselves.

I edged forward while her father seethed, and I traced my fingertip along the music note tattooed on her wrist, my admission low where I murmured it at her ear, "That is the one lie I never told."

A tiny cry slipped up her throat, and I forced myself to walk.

I needed to get out from under her roof.

Out from under her spell before I fucked this up more than I already had.

I headed back for the stairs. Mr. Marin stood on the other side of them where he'd come out of his room. I paused for a moment, looked him dead in the eye. "I'm sorry."

For his wife.

For his daughters.

For every-fucking-thing.

His lips flattened in misery. He gave me no response other than moving closer to his daughter. Shielding her from my depravity.

I turned and bounded downstairs, refusing to look back to meet her stare that I could feel following me.

Energy thinning. Stretching and pulling. Calling me back.

Gritting my teeth, I refused it and sped up. I flew out the door, and I thought for the first time in my life I was actually thanking God that Rhys drove like a lunatic.

I had to get out of there before I rushed back inside and told her everything.

Stumbling out onto the porch, I sucked for clear air like it might stand the chance of eradicating her from my lungs.

Like it might erase the feel of her hands that lingered on my flesh.

Rid the taste of her from my tongue that only made me want her more.

What I needed most was to obliterate the need of her from my soul.

I bent in two, trying to right myself. To get it together.

I had a purpose. A fucking purpose. I couldn't forget it.

I straightened, and then my spine went rigid when I saw a darkened shadow lurking at the side of Violet's truck.

A wave of protectiveness welled so fast I felt like I was going to come apart.

Rip someone to shreds before they had a chance to get close to these girls.

I would gladly die before I let that happen.

It was the one thing I could give.

I almost relaxed when the figure stepped forward, and I realized it was the worker from earlier who'd wanted to come to Violet's rescue.

Saul.

That relief lasted for the blip of a second before I saw the hatred that marred his face. His lip curled. "Who do you think you are, coming here?"

That was all it took to send anger burning through my blood, disbelief tightening my hands into fists. "I'm not sure how you think that's any of your concern."

He pointed toward the house. "Think you're wrong. Anything to do with them is my concern."

I saw it there.

Possession in his stance.

The way the asshole was staking a claim.

I inched forward, coming down the stairs, aggression curling through my veins as I moved toward him.

Couldn't stop it.

The jealousy that spun.

The riot that refused the idea of this prick touching my girl.

My girl.

My girl.

My chest clenched with the truth of it.

"I know who you are." He said it like a curse.

"Yeah, and who's that?"

"Her ex. One the town talks about like you're some kind of superstar. The one who let fame go to his head and dropped her like a rock. Trash to be cast aside."

Rage blinded me.

Asshole didn't know a fuckin' thing.

His head shook. "In the last year I've been working here, she's been happy. Moving on. You think I didn't notice her falling apart the second you showed your pathetic face back here? You're not welcome here, so why don't you pack your things and go back to wherever you came from."

"And you actually think it's you who gets to decide that?" Venom filled my mouth as I said it, and I edged deeper into the night.

Encroaching on him. Trying to rein it in and knowing the only thing I wanted to do was tear this asshole apart.

Rip him in two.

The dregs of the light from the porch cast a dim glow on his face.

I didn't need it to see the hostility there. The animosity that crawled over him.

If he were smart, he'd recognize mine. The way violence skated my flesh. Aggression coiling in my stomach, seeping through my veins and vying for a way out.

"Yup," he issued like a challenge as he crossed his arms over his chest.

My nod was slow and fueled by menace. Jaw cracking under the pressure. "You'd do well to rethink your position."

He barked a laugh. "You think I'm scared of you? You're nothin' but a fuckboy. Know your type. Think you're better than everyone else just because you wrote a song or two. Think you can come in and take whatever you want, whoever you want, just because you have a little fame tacked to your name. And I won't let an asshole like you mess with a girl like her."

"You don't know a thing about me. I'd suggest you don't act like you do." The warning hung heavy in the air.

He scoffed and took a step forward. "Yeah...and what is a pussy like you gonna do about it?"

Dude had the balls to spit on the ground when he said it.

I had him by the throat and shoved against the side of her truck before he knew what hit him.

Adrenaline coiled and rose.

This poison that surged.

The same bated violence that I'd lived by the last six years. So close to being unleashed.

I leaned down close to his face and seethed the words, "Keep your ass out of my business and you won't have to find out."

He laughed a sound of disgust while he thrashed against the hold I had on him. "Fuck you."

Anger blistered across my flesh, and I pressed him harder to the metal of the truck, trying not to lose it. "Stay the fuck away from me and stay the fuck away from her. You got me?"

I heard the roar of Rhys' car barreling up the road, and I jerked him by the collar of his tee and slammed him back down. "You're not gonna like it if I have to remind you."

I shoved him off, dude stumbling and trying to right himself.

I straightened myself as I turned to walk away.

If I stayed a second longer, things were going to get ugly.

Last thing Violet and Daisy needed was to see me coming unglued.

To witness the man I'd become.

The one who would fight to the death if it was required.

Saul's voice pierced me from behind. "It's time she moved on, and I'm going to see to it that it's with me. Nothin' you can do about it."

Possession slammed me like a punch to the face.

Devotion screaming.

Charring my insides with the betrayal that I had cast.

Spinning around, I walked backward, pointing at the bastard who thought he had everything figured out when he didn't have a fuckin' clue.

"Stay the fuck away from my wife. This will be the only time that I warn you."

Then I turned around and stormed down the drive toward the road, knowing my claim was nothing but selfish.

This distorted greed that warped all logic.

But I knew right then it didn't matter how much time or space or treachery I put between us. There was no lie I could tell that would cut her from my soul I'd given her years ago.

Richard
Eight Years Ago

"No way," she mouthed. Her eyes went wide in shock where he'd sidled up at her side at the bar after they'd finished their set.

He felt frozen, staring at her.

Girl casting some kind of spell. What he'd felt in an instant.

He'd been right. He hadn't been imagining it while he was onstage watching her through the raving crowd where she'd sat tucked back at a table like there was a chance she could hide from him.

This girl's eyes were dark, almost black. But what had held him rapt was the intense violet surrounding her pupils that fractured out in little veins through her irises.

Every time the light would strobe across her just right, they'd struck him like thunderbolts.

At first, he'd thought it was those crazy-ass eyes that had captured him. Nearly had him stumbling over the frets of his guitar when she'd come into view. Stomach lurching. Not knowing whether to climb off that stage right then to get a closer look or to wait and take the chance that she might be gone before the end of their show.

The girl was like looking at a glittering flare. A thousand sparkling colors in a sea of drab that gathered at the foot of the stage, same way as they did night after night.

But this girl? She was nothing but a jumpstart to his senses.

A kick of a million volts that had slammed him from across the space.

Which was damned ridiculous, so he'd spent the next hour trying to convince himself he was making it up. Envisioning himself a prize that didn't exist. This porcelain girl with soft, soft cheeks and softer lips. All pink and plush and plump and begging for his kiss.

"Hey there." His voice rumbled low, just loud enough for her to hear it over the clamor of the busy bar.

"Hi," she returned. Her voice was this cross between a bell and sensuality. Earnest and real and ripe with seduction.

A remedy.

Truth was, the stage was his life. The focus of each day. What got him out of bed in the morning.

The music that lived within him was the single purpose he'd been given. To breathe something magical into existence. Create something good in the middle of the atrocities and the strife.

Give a little hope and distraction.

Which was why he'd felt shocked when he'd had the compulsion to climb down from the stage and end a show early for the first time since he and his band had started touring years before.

All for this girl, right in his hometown.

"I'm Richard. You've gotta be new around here."

Redness pinked her cheeks. He wanted to press his nose to it to find out if she was as hot as he felt. "Violet. And no. Not new."

He kicked up a wry smirk, leaning in closer. "You're lying. No chance I could have seen you before and then forgotten you. Not when you are, without a doubt, unforgettable."

She turned to look at him. Those eyes flashed. "You know, you'd think with that whole stage thing and you playin' and lookin' the way you do, the cheesy pick-up lines wouldn't be necessary."

He barked out a laugh.

Shit.

This girl.

So different. And he fuckin' liked it.

He shifted around so he was facing her, one arm rested on the bar. His smirk deepened. "You're right. Not normally necessary. But normally I don't stumble into girls like you."

That blush deepened and she seemed thankful to have someplace to turn her attention when the bartender set a pitcher of margaritas and four glasses in front of her.

"Let me get that. Can you add a Michelob on tap to it?" he asked, going for his wallet.

"Sure," the bartender responded while Violet's hand shot out to stop him from tossing cash onto the bar. "No. I don't need you to buy me drinks."

His brows shot to the sky. "I can't buy you a drink?"

"Nope."

"And why's that?" Amusement danced around his mouth, his eyes drinking her in.

Fuck the beer.

He was pretty sure this girl was the only thing that could quench this thirst.

That violet stare raked over his arms, up his chest, until she was looking at his face, gaze sparking with something playful and real. "Because you're going to buy me a drink and then you're gonna think you can take me home. Then I'd have to go and disappoint you because that's not going to happen."

He edged in closer so he could whisper in her ear. He was slammed with a lungful of the girl.

Violets and color and dreams.

Infiltrating.

Invading.

In an instant, he was overcome with that intoxicating energy he'd sworn had zapped through the air the second she'd come into view.

What the fuck?

He tried to shake it off, the way she impacted him like she meant something.

"And what if I just wanna dance with the prettiest girl in the place?"

Music poured from the speakers, the dance floor packed, and lights strobed over them in time with the beat of the fast-paced country song.

Sensations flew, but the girl in his arms was the only thing he felt.

So soft. So right. Her spirit this palpable thing he swore danced around them. A vapor. Mist. Something faithful and right that he wanted to inhale.

It didn't matter a ton of people were two-stepping around them.

He held her tight, her sleek body tucked close, the thunder of her heart pounding against his as he led her in the slowest dance.

He had one hand splayed over the small of her back and the other twisted in her sleek, shiny hair.

She sighed.

And this time, he did, he inhaled her, brushed his lips across hers, and he fell into the bliss of her kiss.

"God, you're makin' a liar out of me." She whimpered the words as he pressed her against the door of his truck, kissing her with the madness she evoked.

Disorienting.

Dissolving him into something he'd never before been.

He nuzzled down the side of her face, breathing her in as he went, and kissed along the delicate column of her throat.

Her head rocked back, and her fingers fisted in his hair.

"And what kind of lies are you telling me? Because I don't think I've ever felt anything so real in all my life."

Darkness rained down from the heavens where they were behind his parents' house where he was staying the next two nights while Carolina George was passing through town. He'd pulled his truck around the back and parked in front of the stables and his father's workshop.

Where it was secluded.

Private.

Quiet.

Where it was just the pants of their breaths and the thunder of their hearts.

They'd talked for hours outside the bar and then had ended up there, neither of them ready to let go.

Gripped by the connection that stretched tight between them. Strangers who'd known each other all along.

A slash of moonlight filtered through the deep, dense sky, and bugs trilled in the trees that whooshed in the slight breeze.

It did nothing to quell the flames that consumed.

Her fingers dragged down the back of his neck, girl eliciting tremors of lust that rocked through his body. "This. You and me. Here, together. I told you I wasn't goin' home with you. My sister is never gonna let me live this down."

"Uh…didn't she go home with our drummer?" he murmured, his face buried in the flesh of her chest that he devoured.

"Well, she's usually a whole lot more adventurous than me."

A smirk pulled to his mouth as he kissed back up her throat and made a path in the direction of that delirium-inducing mouth.

"I disagree," he rumbled.

"You'd be wrong," she whispered back.

He was sure he'd never felt so drunk.

Entranced.

Mesmerized.

"You want me to take you home?" he grumbled.

Violet moaned as he nipped at her lip. "I should, but I don't. Not even a little bit."

"Good. Might die if you did." It was a chuckle of amusement when he said it, and she was giggling as he pulled her from his truck, swung her around, and hoisted her into his arms.

On a tiny squeal, she wrapped her legs around his waist and her arms around his neck. "Where are you takin' me?"

"Where I can show you how fuckin' beautiful you are."

He stared up at her as he carried her toward the stables.

Awed.

Sure he'd never felt quite like this.

A soft smile graced her mouth, her lips plump and moistened from his kiss, those eyes doing those crazy things that hit him like a punch to the chest.

Like every time this girl looked at him it cracked something open in the middle of him. Making room for something he'd never anticipated.

Moonlight poured around her head and cast her in a milky glow.

Girl a light in the middle of the night.

Colors and hope blossoming to life.

A moonflower.

"You are the most stunning thing I've ever seen."

Even in the dark, he could see the bloom of color flush her chest and climb to her cheeks, and she chewed at her bottom lip. "You don't need to feed me lines, Richard."

He angled around so he could slide open the door to the stable, still holding her, refusing to set her down. A light was on in the far back, barely illuminating the space. He slipped through the opening he'd made and carried her to the tack room off to the right.

"I do, Violet. I think you might be every line I've ever written. Interwoven in every song. There before I even knew you existed."

Hope.

Fear.

Grief.

Lust.

Passion.

Love.

Questioning life and where it was going to take you. Hoping on a forever no one knew for certain they'd be given.

The unforgettable moment you realized you'd stumbled on to what you'd been looking for.

"You can't go around sayin' things like that to me." Her voice was a rasp, and he let her slip down his body but didn't let her get far. He hooked an arm around her waist and tucked her close, letting his thumb trace along the striking angle of her jaw.

She gazed up at him.

The girl looked like a fairy.

Blown of delicate, intricate glass.

Fiction.

The magic he'd been missing.

"I can if it's true."

She shivered, and her expression flashed, and she set her fingers across his lips. "Stop talking right now unless this actually means somethin' to you."

He cupped her face, their movements getting lost in a slow sway. "It wouldn't matter if I stopped talking, Violet. My body would show you what I'm feeling, anyway."

He swept his lips across hers.

Tenderly.

The wind blew.

The earth rumbled.

He stepped back long enough to grab one of the clean blankets he knew his father kept there and spread it out on the ground.

He got onto his knees and stretched out his hand to the girl who stood fidgeting at the edge of the blanket.

Black hair framing her gorgeous face. Her spirit running manic in the space.

She tugged off her boots. They thunked against the ground as she dropped them, and then she climbed down to her knees in front of him.

He reached out and slipped the spaghetti strap off one delicate shoulder.

He pressed his mouth to where it had been.

She shivered beneath his caress, and her fingers trembled when she reached out and grabbed the hem of his shirt so she could pull it over his head.

Her eyes raced to take him in, same way as his lingered and searched, wanting to memorize every inch of this girl.

And they undressed each other that way.

Reverently.

Relishing every second. Every beat.

A soft, seductive exploration.

He laid her back on the blanket, the girl spread out, her hair a black halo that billowed around her head. Her pretty tits jutted with each heave of her breaths.

Lust consumed him.

But it was more than that. Bigger than anything he'd experienced before.

Kneeling, he edged forward and set his hands on her knees as he stared down at her.

Lost.

Taken.

Found.

"It means something, Violet. It fuckin' means something. Pretty sure it means everything."

He climbed over her and pressed into her tight, sweet body.

Bliss. Bliss. Bliss.

He groaned, and she whimpered as she dug her fingers into his shoulders. "Yes."

He gathered her up.

And they both let go.

Gave themselves over to the song of their souls.

Richard

Rhys' car roared down the desolate road. Flying through the night, hugging the corners tight.

While I shook. My damned knee bounced at warp speed. Agitation boiling my blood and setting fire to my veins.

Motherfucker's words banged through my mind.

"It's time she moved on, and I'm going to see to it that it's with me. Nothin' you can do about it." Knew it made me a prick that I couldn't let her go. That I hadn't in all this time. That in my fucked up, twisted mind, that girl had still been mine.

No matter what I'd said.

No matter the lies that had been told.

No matter the mistakes that had been made.

Had she really fallen for that bullshit?

Believed that I left her to chase down a dream? That I wanted that life more than I wanted her?

Fuck that.

But what was she supposed to believe?

Curiosity rippled through Rhys as he slanted me a glance. "You're lucky I love your mopey ass so much. You're about the only person in the world I'd crawl out of bed for in the middle of the night. Well, that and a text for a little Rhys-style lovin'." Dude waggled his brows.

"So, me and half the female population? I feel super special. Do I even want to know how many numbers are on your phone?" I tossed out.

"Not unless you feel like fallin' into jealousy. I mean, I know it's hard to be friends with a god like me, so I should probably keep that information on the down low. Out of the goodness of my heart, of course." He cracked a grin.

I shook my head. Dude almost managed to pull a laugh out of me.

But it was stunted.

Gloom came off me in plumes of thick, black smoke.

Rhys' inquisition turned speculative when he caught my mood.

"Care to tell me what you were doing over at Violet's in the middle of the night? Pretty obvious you weren't there to get a little of your own lovin' with that forlorn destitution on your face. Hell, you look so pathetic, you'd think you'd been sentenced to blue balls for life."

Sounded about right.

"You get your ass tossed off the property? Cockblocked? Or did she look at your ugly mug and come to her senses?" he razzed.

I rubbed my sweaty palms down my jeans. "Was only over there in the first place because Emily convinced me to go with them to check out the wedding venue."

Didn't take a fuckin' psychology degree to know my little sister was angling for something. What, I couldn't tell. Like Vi and I were just gonna somehow be friends?

Our pasts nothin' but water under the bridge?

Not possible considering I'd already burned that bitch to ash.

"And it lasted until two in the mornin'?" The question was

nothing but sly supposition.

Agitation taking me whole, I looked out the passenger-side window to the blur of landscape flashing by. "Daisy fell out of a tree and broke her wrist. Drove them to the ER. Couldn't ignore that."

Worry filled the cab.

"Well, fuck me," he wheezed.

Nah. I was the one who was fucked.

"She okay?"

I blew out a slow sigh. "Toughest little thing ever. Think she would have pretended it didn't hurt a bit until it healed wrong if Violet would have let her get away with it."

"Spitfire."

"Yup."

"Cute as fuck."

"Yup."

"You're toast, man. You know that, right? Are you about ready to stop lyin' to yourself and the rest of us? You could start with me. Not gonna bite. Well, I might. Should've kicked your ass from here to Kentucky when you walked away from her in the first place."

Reluctantly, I shifted my attention to him, for the first time broaching a subject I'd refused.

Unable to keep it in.

Pressure building until I had to let off a little of the steam.

"Didn't have a choice."

A scowl knitted his brow. "Didn't have a choice? Sorry to break it to you, brother, but life is nothin' but a fucking string of choices. Seems to me you made the wrong one."

"And making the choice to stay would have only hurt her more than I already did."

Shattered her.

What I'd done had been a showing of mercy. For her and myself. Euthanizing who we'd been to keep from subjecting us to a long, excruciating death.

Didn't matter.

This bullshit turned out to be excruciating, anyway. Living

without her a cold, bitter hell.

He scoffed. "Is this that whole 'being on the road is too much' bullshit? Letting her off the hook to give her a better life? Making that *choice* for her? Because believe me, y'all don't look better off to me."

A heavy breath pilfered free of my aching lungs. "No."

"You just didn't love her, anymore? You gonna keep claiming that? Because believe me, we have plenty of horseshit back at our parents' places. Could do without it being fed from you."

Frustrated, I stabbed my fingers through my hair. "Think the answer to that is plenty apparent, yeah?"

He roughed a hand over his face, and his eyes grew wide in disbelief. "So, what…it was the kid?"

Disgust poured through his words. "That's what it came down to? You were too much of a pussy to handle it?"

I flinched at the accusation that was so off base it would be hysterical if it wasn't so devastating.

A face I barely knew but would recognize anywhere flashed through my mind.

Dark, trusting eyes.

Carefree grin.

The memory of her sweet smile was demolished by the rush of realization. Every mistake that had been made. Every war. Everything I'd been fighting for and everything that had been lost.

Would be wise for me to accept there was nothing left to reclaim. Nothing to give but penance. Atonement for what had been inflicted.

That and to watch over them until it came to fruition.

Until the last nail was driven in my heart and Violet realized the vile secret I kept.

"Loving that kid wouldn't have been the issue. Deserving to do it was."

A frown took over Rhys' face as he whipped around a corner, ramming on the brakes and downshifting as we fast approached our turn. "The fuck are you talking about, man?"

I rubbed a palm over my mouth, trying to break up the torment that was rising fast. A flashflood. All the pain and grief and regret

I'd kept chained breaking free of the dam and swelling fast.

"I fucked up, Rhys. Fucked up bad."

He took the left, tires skidding on the pavement before he hit the dirt drive. Dust billowed behind like a ghost hunting us through the night, and he cut me a look through the slivers of moonlight that poured down through the darkness. Could feel the instant aggression that curled through his muscles.

"And what kind of trouble is that? You need someone to take up your back? Just say the word. Where and when. You know that, man."

Without a doubt, Rhys would go down for me in a blaze of burning glory.

"It was a long time ago. Doesn't matter anymore."

More lies.

But this was not something I was willing for him to get into. It'd already squandered enough of the people I cared about. Destroyed and decayed and trampled.

A fucking field of casualties.

It'd left a bloodied trail of destruction in its wake, and here I was, getting ready to go another round.

But this was the finale, and someone was getting knocked the fuck out.

He slowed as we got closer to our houses at the top of the hill. Agitation lined his thick, brawny muscles, dude ready for a fight. He jerked his attention toward me. Hurt slashed through his expression. "You been keepin' me in the dark, dude? What is this fresh shit? I'm your best friend. And here I thought this whole time that whirlwind you got swept into with Violet had just fizzled out, and all these years later, I'm hearin' you got your stupid ass mixed up in some kind of mess?"

A hard gush of air left me. "I make the mistakes. I'm the one who has to suffer for them."

"Alone?" he challenged.

"When getting you involved could only make it worse, yes."

He came to a stop at the fork in the road. Car idling. Dude was clenching his fists on the steering wheel like he was going to go Hulk on me. Uncontrolled chaos. He always kept it bridled, but I knew him well enough to know it was there.

"Bullshit. Your trouble is mine. Consequences don't matter, bro. We've been in this together from the beginning. Not sure when you decided to shut me out."

When it could have destroyed your life.

"You couldn't have fixed it, man. There was nothing you could do. And getting you involved would only make it worse. Kept you out of it because I care about you too much."

Too bad I'd done such a fucking terrible job of keeping it from the rest of the people I loved.

My sister's face flashed behind my eyes.

Guilt constricted.

So tight I thought I might pass out.

He turned to look at me. "So, what then, if it's in the past, tell me what it was. Tell me what was so goddamn awful you had to let your girl go."

I saw it for what it was. Knowledge running wild in his blue eyes. He'd already come to the conclusion before I could cut him off at the pass.

Dude might look like a jacked-up dolt. No brain cells left because his head was too full of arrogance and conceit.

Rhys Manning was nothing but obnoxious ego and secreted wisdom and fucking warm-hearted care.

Thing was, only people who got to witness those last two were the ones closest to him. Guy too terrified to let anyone else behind that brash demeanor that was just as real as the rest of them, but one he still used as a façade.

Walls too fortified to be toppled.

Guessed it was true that he and I had always had a ton in common.

And I knew right then he knew. That he could see right through me.

To the fear. To the ferocity. To the determination that singed and scorched and etched retribution on my soul.

There'd be nothing left of it when I was done.

"What are you in, man?" he finally asked, the dread in his tone warbling through the silence that bottled the cab.

I unlatched the door. "Nothing has changed, Rhys. Just…forget it. Thanks for the ride," I said to shut him down as I hurried to climb out, needing to get my head clear of this.

Clicking the door shut, I started toward the sleeping house. Didn't get three steps away before the window rolled down and he shouted after me, "One question."

I paused, shifted to look at him from over my shoulder, and lifted my chin to give him the go.

No doubt, I was going to regret it.

Rhys' expression was hard, as hard as the indictment lined in the demand. "Royce know?"

Disquiet curled down my spine, stomach coiling with a vile sickness that clawed and claimed.

Knew I shouldn't, but I gave him a tight nod, the bit of honesty that I could offer. "Yeah."

"Fuck," he hissed. Fear blanched his face. Ghost white. Dread painted him a ghastly gray.

Guessed that was all I had to say.

He turned away, looked out the windshield, and blew out from his nose before he was speaking toward the window, refusing to grace me with a glance, his jaw working like mad. "Tell me this isn't about those girls. Tell me you weren't fuckin' under Karl Fitzgerald's thumb. Know you were pushin' for us to sign with them. Before everything about Emily came out. Before Royce revealed the truth about Karl Fitzgerald. Tell me you didn't stoop that low."

Their faces flickered through my mind.

The agony.

What they'd gone through.

The ones that had gone missing.

In a flash, I was back at his car, my hands planted on the windowsill. I leaned down so I could jut my head inside.

Voice grit. "That bastard stole everything from me. Stole from the ones I love. Hurt and cheated and lied. Ruined innumerable lives. You really think I'd stoop that low, man? Force a girl? Only stoopin' I'm doing is getting on my knees to pray the motherfucker ends up dead."

Him and the rest of them.

Nodding, Rhys slanted his attention back at me. "Wouldn't have believed it…but fuck, man, what happened to Em…'"

He scrubbed a meaty palm over his face.

Shaken by what had come out.

Fitzgerald had had the intention of cutting the rest of us from the band once we'd signed so Emily would be the only one under his control.

All of us knew the very real reality of what could have become of her.

And I'd let it happen, fighting one battle and not realizing a whole different war was brewing right under my nose.

Royce had ripped his tarnished throne out from under him.

Stolen his crown and crumbled his empire.

It was a start, but I intended on setting that entire world on fire.

"Saw some things…in LA. Years ago." I let the confession bleed out. Let it ring with implication.

Worry streaked through his expression. "Royce using you? To testify?"

"No, man," I said solemnly. "I'm using Royce."

Rhys flinched.

Getting it.

That this went so much deeper than he knew.

The very reason I had to keep him out of it.

I angled in closer, vehemence curling through my muscles. "You're just a dude who got scammed by a greedy businessman, Rhys. You know nothing more. And you maintain that until we get to trial. Keep your nose out of it. You got me?"

He shook his head. "You're in trouble? Means I fuckin' am, too."

He didn't say anything else, just peeled out in the gravel as he lurched forward. I watched as he took the short distance to come to a stop in front of his mother's house.

Blowing out the strain, I turned and trudged back toward ours.

Night pressed down, as heavy as the exhaustion that weighed my bones. Every window in the house was blackened, only the light next to the door scattering a dim glow across the porch.

The air was cool, a light breeze ushering in the fall that consumed the last days of summer. Bugs hummed a low buzz from their perch in the swishing branches of the trees.

The stillness profound.

The hole inside me gaped wider than it ever had.

So close. So fucking close and she was still out of reach.

Girl on my tongue and dancing in my soul.

I tipped my head toward the sky to the spiral of stars that wrote the heavens in song.

Endless, ethereal beauty.

My fingers itched with the need to play.

With the need to create magic.

To sing this girl in a sonnet.

Weave her in poetry.

A horse whinnied from the stables, drawing my attention that direction. Far to the back of the property, a single light blazed from the smaller house my younger brother Lincoln had built a handful of years ago.

But the stables and workshop were still there.

Standing like a tribute.

A memorial.

Unable to resist the lure, I moved that way and crept through the shadows to a place that to me would forever be scripted in the delicate curve of her name. I eased open the sliding door, enough to slip inside, only to freeze when I heard the snapping of a stick coming from the other side of the stables.

A horse whinnied again, and I could hear Linc's dog, Cal, start barking from within his house.

Every hair on my body stood on end.

A shiver of awareness.

A slick of dread.

I eased back a step and peered into the lapping darkness. Through the shift of shadows that played and danced through the wispy tendrils of the night.

Another crunch.

Quieter this time.

Controlled.

Measured.

My heart rate spiked, and my breaths turned shallow as I slipped back out, keeping my footsteps as light as possible as I edged that way.

Caught somewhere between alarm and the bare determination to protect my family.

Another crunch echoed to my left, and my attention jerked that way to see a shadow suddenly bolt toward a grove of trees behind the stables.

Didn't think it through. Didn't consider.

I shot after him.

Pants of aggression puffed from my lungs, violence stretching every muscle thin.

Consuming.

Overwhelming.

I could feel the panic ripple from the bastard who tried to outrun me. The darkened silhouette dove into a thicket of trees, winding into their massive trunks and beneath the camouflage of their leaves that cast the ground in a murky obscurity.

I sprinted after him, feet thudding on the damp ground as I darted around the stables. Cal barked like mad, enough that it caused a light to flick on somewhere in Lincoln's house.

Fuck.

Last thing I wanted was my younger brother coming out here.

Couldn't allow him to get involved.

Couldn't put him in danger.

Problem was, I had no idea what I was up against. Didn't know who would dare come here. Who was wishing for death so badly that they would risk stepping foot in Dalton, though I'd lay down bets it was whatever prick had been snooping around Royce and Emily's engagement party.

Royce a clear target.

But my gut told me this went deeper.

I was determined to find out.

I made it around the stables and plunged into the disorienting haze of shadows. My eyes scanned, searching for movement.

For a sign of the fucker who was going down.

My hands desperate for retribution and knowing it wasn't time.

That I was supposed to be biding the days and the only thing I wanted was to end this now.

Violet's touch echoed from my flesh. Her words and her pain. Wanted it for her, even when she would fuckin' hate me in the end.

A creak rode on the air from somewhere in the distance, and I angled through the trees, ducking below branches and dodging undergrowth as I searched through the brush.

I thought I saw something off to my right, and I turned, running faster.

Asshole was gonna die.

I had no care—no focus—nothing but putting a hand on this asshole and bringing him to his end.

I jumped over a fallen log and darted around another tree.

I didn't even have the chance to process the rock coming for my head before it made impact.

No time to prepare myself for the gutting pain that fractured through my brain like a million tiny cracks.

It left me nothing but a pile of rubble.

Dropped me to the ground.

Facedown.

Barely coherent.

I came in and out of lucidity, no sound in the air but the piercing scream in my ears. Ricocheting agony through my head.

I gasped and writhed, trying to remain conscious. To fight.

I attempted to climb onto my hands and knees, but a rush of dizziness had me slumping back down into a pile of decaying, rotting leaves.

Darkness surged.

A morbid abyss threatening to suck me under.

Footsteps crunched as they neared, and I could feel the vileness in the air. Something wicked, the voice sounding distant though I knew he was whispering near my ear. "Where the fuck are they, you fuckin' thief?"

A riot of barking suddenly took hold of the atmosphere, and

another set of footsteps echoed through the night.

"Richard?" Linc shouted. "That you?"

The scumbag leaned in closer, oozing his depravity all over me. "Gonna end you, bitch. Gonna end you and all your friends."

Then he was gone.

A harsh gust of air jutted from my lungs, and I fully collapsed and faded into the darkness.

Richard

I glanced back at the restaurant where the girls were still huddled in a group,

at the way my wife bit her lip and sent me one of those sweet, seductive looks
that would forever have me on my knees.

I was half inclined to go back for her, take her back to our hotel and love
her right, but the hand landing on my shoulder and giving it a squeeze drew
me back.

"Car is here, man, let's roll." Shawn angled his head. Our drummer urged
me to follow. Rhys had bailed on this trip since his mother was sick. Dude
was nothing but a mama's boy. But it was cool. He'd already said he was
game. Ready to sign. He didn't need to be wined and dined and shown the life
that was getting ready to befall them. He'd known they were headed for it the
whole time.

"Later, baby," I mouthed the promise to my girl who gave me a wave as
she and the rest of the girls gathered to head out to go dancing to celebrate

Falling into You

Lily's birthday.

Hollywood style since the band had had to be here for the weekend, anyway.

Funny how some things just worked out.

Nerves rattled through me, this unchained excitement that burned through my senses. Anxious and eager when I slipped into the back of the black sedan and Shawn climbed down beside me. This was it. All the blood, sweat, and tears coming to fruition. Culminating in what we'd been working toward all along.

The car eased into the thick traffic. Neon lights glowed from the restaurants and clubs and hotels we passed, the sidewalks packed, laughter and voices seeping into the car and pumping a fever across our flesh.

The vibe in the air was like none other.

Ripe with potential. With riches and fame. Music and stars. Art and creativity.

The Mylton Records exec shifted around where he sat in the front seat next to the driver. Dude wearing a suit and his blond hair perfectly slicked back.

Reeking of money and power.

He smiled. "Are you two ready for what awaits you?"

"Hell, yeah," Shawn said.

Blue eyes shifted to me.

"Absolutely," I answered.

Though I itched, wiping my sweaty palms on my jeans as we twisted and turned through the city until we came to the sprawling fortress of a house just outside Beverly Hills.

The massive gate swung open at our approach.

Those nerves rattled.

Different this time.

Something uneasy shivering across my skin.

The Mylton Records exec waved his hand toward the pretentious house as the car eased into the sweeping curved drive. "This…all of it is yours. At your fingertips. Yours to keep. You just need to prove how much you want it."

I swallowed down the disquiet, and I hung onto the promise.

All of this was mine, and every dream of mine was a dream of hers, and I was going to do whatever it took to give it to her.

Heart hammering, I was jarred out of the memory when my

mother pressed the damp rag to my forehead, wincing as she cleaned my wound.

Gash right between my eyes.

Bullseye.

"I'm fine."

She tsked through the harsh lights of the small upstairs bathroom where I sat on the toilet and she doctored me up like she used to do when I was a kid. "Don't look so fine to me."

I scowled, and that shit hurt, too.

I was a mess. Disoriented. Head aching like I'd been pierced straight through.

More than any of that, I was raging mad. Fury roiling through my being, muscles knots of aggression, cells overflowing with the need to protect.

There was nothing more I wanted than to pick up the scent of that prick and hunt him down.

Prey becoming the predator.

Because there was no doubt in my mind that coward had been sent to sniff us out. That they'd picked up a trail and they were desperate to find out where it would lead.

"Try to hold still," she urged.

"I'm not twelve, Ma."

"Well, you might as well be with the way you're jitterin' all over the place."

"Someone was on our property. In the middle of the night. Asshole didn't think twice to take me down, either. Think I have a reason to be on edge."

She blew out the alarm she was trying to pretend didn't exist on a heavy sigh as she continued to dab at the wound. "You didn't get a good look at him?"

"No."

And I sure as hell wasn't about to tell her what I assumed. Was bad enough giving the vague statement to the sheriff who had shown up at our doorstep after Lincoln had called 9-1-1. I'd come to quickly and was able to refuse the need for an ambulance, but a cruiser had already been in route before I'd had time to talk Linc out of making that call.

My baby brother had no clue what he had stepped in on.

Disquiet shivered through my mother's demeanor, and her worried gaze searched my face like she was looking to make sure her oldest son was still intact. Her voice trembled when she admitted, "I was terrified, Lincoln calling the house and shoutin' that you'd been injured. Had no idea what we were gonna find when we went racing out the door."

Her hand shook as she continued to clean the wound. Sorrow winding through her being.

I reached out, took her by the wrist, and stared up at her warm eyes. "Ma, I'm okay."

My mother was the definition of care. So good and right. Tough as nails and as giving as grace.

Her graying hair was tied in a haphazard bun, and her green eyes the same color as mine were bloodshot from the tears she'd shed.

Knew she'd spilled too many of late.

Overwrought with the trauma of finding out what had happened to Emily.

"I can't stand for another one of my babies to be hurt. I think we've had enough of that around here, haven't we?"

In emphasis, I squeezed her wrist. "I'm fine. You don't need to worry. I had it under control. Was probably just some kids out on the property who got spooked and panicked."

Only wished.

Ma chewed at her bottom lip. "What if it wasn't, Richard? What if someone came prowlin' around here?" She cast a petrified glance at the closed door that led out to the rest of the bedrooms on the second floor. Finally, her gaze drifted back to me, sheer desperation written on her face. "What if someone is tryin' to strike fear in Emily? Keep her from testifyin' against that wicked man? I can't...I can't let anything else happen to her. With the baby..."

She trailed off.

Unable to say it.

Terror seeped from her pores. It manifested in the quivering of her bones. Like she was looking to me to see to it that she was safe. That I would protect her. That no more harm would come to her.

Not to her or anyone else.

Royce and I were going to see to it that remained a fact.

"I'm sorry. I'm sorry I wasn't there. That I let him get to her. If I could go back…"

Rage burned hot.

If I could go back, Cory Douglas would be dead.

But I'd been too blinded by my own hatred and agenda to even realize what was going down right under my nose.

She touched my cheek. "It's not your fault."

My teeth ground. "It is."

It was the first time I'd confessed it to her, but she had no idea what it really meant. The depth of what I'd done.

Her brows twisted in knowing concern. "You hold so much sadness, my sweet boy."

Regret clutching me in a fist, I forced a grin. "I'm just fine."

Her smile was small. "Don't even try to work your charm on me, young man. You might own a stage, all those women who go nuts at your feet, but your mama knows the real boy hidden under all that glitz and glam."

No.

She didn't know me at all.

Sorrow spiked through the consciousness.

She saw it, and she tightened her hold on my face. "And he's a good man. A good, good man who got lost somewhere along the way."

Not somewhere.

I knew the exact moment.

The one mistake.

The one misstep that had toppled me into a spiral of corruption.

"You still love her?" She searched my face, no need to even say her name.

I flinched.

"Thought so," she murmured.

Agony clawed across my chest. "No good for her, Ma."

She tipped up my chin. "What if you're exactly what she needs?"

"Doubt that."

"And that little girl." Ma said it like a statement.

My spirit panged. Guilt and grief and this glimmer of something that I refused to recognize.

"She's a handful," she continued softly. "Couldn't believe she got herself all the way up in that tree. That's a wild one for sure. Ain't it funny how instincts kicked right in when she fell? You were right there in a flash."

My head shook.

She was back to cupping my chin, forcing me to look at her. "Bet that sweet little thing has got a big ol' hole cut out in the middle of her and she's just searchin' for a way to fill it. Not quite sure what is missin' yet. Thing is, when a child grows up with a vacancy that big, they start lookin' in places they shouldn't."

Guilt lashed.

Constricting.

Suffocating.

I couldn't breathe.

I squeezed my eyes closed like it could block it out.

"Ma." I was about to start begging her to stop. "Violet is enough for her."

She had to be.

"And what if Violet's got a hole just as big? She lost two of the people who meant the most to her and she's about to lose another."

Lash. Lash. Lash.

I felt her words like the strike of a thin leather strap to my back. A scourge. Splitting skin and bleeding out.

"Please." The word cracked.

Because I knew every fucking thing she said was true.

She sighed and moved to fumble around in the medicine cabinet. She dabbed some ointment on the wound and butterflied it. Nothing was said between us, but the air was so thick it said plenty.

Disappointment radiated from her, ricocheting from the walls.

While I choked on my treachery.

"There," she said, searching my eyes for more than just a concussion. "You should put some ice on it. You're goin' to be hurting good come morning."

I nodded.

She started for the door then paused to look back. "I'm not putting undue pressure on you, Richard. Not asking you to step up and be a man. I'm asking you to find your heart because you and I both know where you left it."

Then she stepped out and left me sitting there stewing in the disaster I had made.

Finally, I forced myself onto my feet, and I was struck with another rush of dizziness. Dickhead had gotten me good. I looked at myself in the mirror. At the gash that was held by the makeshift stitch. Let it feed the fire.

The reality that this was not a game.

Violet's face flashed through my mind. Protectiveness gathered like a darkened storm.

Menace sinking all the way to the marrow.

The thought of someone being in the same town as her made me insane.

I moved out of the bathroom and down the hall to my bedroom. I let myself into the darkness and went for my phone I'd left on the nightstand.

Dialed the number.

It took four rings for Kade to finally answer, which considering it was in the middle of the night, it shouldn't have been a surprise, but still, I was on edge, eating up the floor as I paced.

"Richard."

"They know."

Disquiet dragged through the line on a clot of silence.

"What do you mean, they know?" he demanded low.

"Someone was here. On my property. Barely caught sight of him. I took off after him, and the asshole smashed my head with a rock before I could get him. Dropped me straight to my knees. He threatened me, right before I passed the fuck out—called me a thief. Implied I had something that belonged to him. Said he was comin' after me and my friends."

"What'd you say?"

"Didn't say a fuckin' thing," I hissed, voice held but filled with the rage that ripped me to shreds. "Fucker took off when my brother's dog went nuts and he came out to check what was happening. Don't know what would've happened if he hadn't gotten there when he did."

"Did he see him?"

"No. Scum was a ghost."

"Shit."

"Need to find him," I gritted.

"No," Kade shot out. "What you need to do is stay course. Act like you don't know a fuckin' thing. They're speculating. Manipulating the way they do. They had you once. Don't let them get you again."

"Someone threatens my family? Gonna end them, man. Sorry, but that's just the way it is."

I'd played off the dreamer.

Dude who only cared about his band and their success for so many years.

Couldn't sit around and do it anymore.

He heaved a breath of pure anxiety. "We're so close. String them along. Play it safe. You need to lay low? Lay low. You need to get lost? Get lost. But don't fuck this up. They are counting on us. We're all they have."

"Know that."

"Good."

"Okay." Wasn't even sure what that meant any longer. "I'll talk to you soon."

Ending the call, I tossed my phone to the mattress, grabbed my guitar, and sat down on the edge of the bed.

The sensations that had hit me earlier were overwhelming.

The girl was right there.

On my tongue and on my fingers and writhing in my memories.

But that feeling had turned frenzied.

Frantic with the need to make this right. No longer knowing

what that looked like or what it meant.

I strummed the quietest chord that resounded deep. The vibrations of the strings reverberated through my body.

Eyes shut, I swayed, got lost in that mystery.

Violet and dreams and the girl.

Almost silently, I began to sing.

> *I closed my eyes*
> *I fell into a dream*
> *Watching through a looking glass*
> *Nothin's what it seems*
> *Shards of ice*
> *Cold, bitter bliss*
> *That's what I get*
> *For stealing that first kiss*

I strummed through the verse as the chorus took hold. Framed in my mind and written from my soul.

> *Now I'm lost*
> *Lost in your mystery*
> *I lost sight. I lost my right*
> *Staring at eternity*
> *What's come, what's gone*
> *Never gonna be reclaimed*
> *Because clinging to this moonflower*
> *Is where I'll forever be chained*

Because I knew—knew it in her kiss.

She hadn't gotten over me any more than I'd gotten over her.

My hope.

My reason.

My *wife*.

I just didn't know what part of this life I had left to give her.

If there would be anything left at all.

If any forgiveness could be found in the mistakes that had been made. The heap of them had only grown higher as the years had passed.

I turned my gaze out to the sheer drapes at the window. The blink of the stars were barely visible.

But they were still clear.

Still inevitable.

And I knew right then I couldn't go on without taking back what was always supposed to be mine.

Violet

"*W*akes it up, Mommy!"

I was facedown, tossing in a tormented sleep when the tiny tornado made landing on my bed. Jolting through a gasp, I flung around to find Daisy actually jumping at my feet, waving her casted arm in sync with the other over her head.

I squinted at her through the harsh light breaking through the drapes. "What on earth do you think you're doin'?"

She didn't even seem to register that she'd been injured. That she might make it worse.

Goodness, I was gonna have to tie her up if I wanted to tame her, but I was pretty sure my spitfire would find a way to get herself free.

My own little Houdini.

"Wakeskin' you up, what do you think?" she said, matter-of-fact. "It's almost passed the whole day and Papa said I had to let you sleep because you had a reals rough night last night. You have a rough night? Lords knows I did." She tried to form a low whistle, but it was more a raspberry.

A laugh that was a cross between exasperation and adoration slipped up my throat, and I forced myself up to sitting. I scrubbed my palms over my face to break up the sleep.

The dreams that lingered.

The aura of him still holding me. Touching me. Luring me in the way he'd always done, willpower dust with a brush of his hand.

The man my destiny and my destruction.

How was it possible I could have succumbed so easily?

Put myself in the position to be wrecked all over again?

Hell, I was the one who'd begged for a little breakin' when I'd followed him out the door and into the hall.

But that's the way that boy had always made me.

Liquid.

Melted butter in his hands.

I blew out a heavy sigh and pushed back the matted, tangled bedhead that no doubt was givin' the scarecrow out in the field a run for its money.

I had to get myself together. Remember the pain of what he'd done before he had the chance to ration another deadly dose.

Just him being in this town meant I was traversing dangerous ground.

Heartache curled through my chest at the thought of it, that speck of me trying to hold on to what wasn't there, my wrist burnin' from the agonizing temptation of his touch, his mesmerizing voice a song that still whispered in my ear.

"That is the one lie I never told."

How could I even consider believing that B.S.?

Believe that charmer?

I knew better.

He was nothin' but a swindler and a fraud.

A snake lookin' for a snack.

I shook Richard Ramsey out of my thoughts because he didn't belong there, and I turned my attention to my little girl who continued to jump on my bed.

"You are somethin', you know that? You fell out of a tree last night and now you're trying to break your head by falling off my bed."

"But Imma bird! See how high I fly."

"And don't you know birds can't fly with a broken wing?" I teased, reaching out to grab her and haul her onto my lap because words didn't seem to do a whole lot of good.

Apparently, emergency room visits and broken bones didn't, either.

"How are you feeling?" I asked with her back tucked to my chest, my chin hooked over her little shoulder as I lifted her arm that was casted.

In pink, of course.

"It only hurts just a little tiny teensy bit." She tipped her head back to look up at me, her mess of hair bunched at my face and her sweet grin and scrunched-up nose splitting me open wide.

Joy pressed full.

Overflowing.

Overwhelming.

I kissed her forehead, and I tightened my arms around her and hugged her close.

Misery bound my consciousness.

Because I couldn't lose her. Not from an accident. Not from someone stealing her away. She was mine, and I would cling to her forever.

My voice dropped to a low plea, "You scared me yesterday. Don't ever do that again. You need to listen to Mommy even when you don't like what I have to say."

She huffed out a little sound, and she sagged her shoulders as she withered deeper into my hold. Her adorable voice shifted into an apology riddled with sass. "I know you are very right. I'm reals sorry. Papa said I'm nothin's but mischief and tomfooleries. I don't want to be a Tom, and Papa looked even extra sad when he was making my eggs this mornin'. I'll be good for now on. That is my promise."

She gave a resolute nod and lifted her hand in a solemn oath.

Yeah, and that would last for all of five seconds.

Still, I hugged her tight and whispered, "That's my girl. We just want you to be safe."

"It's real hard when rules are made to be broken." She said it with utmost sincerity.

A soft laugh rumbled out. "You are somethin' else, Daisy."

"Nope. I'm nothin' else. Just regular o' Daisy."

She shrugged.

A giggle floated out, and I ruffled her hair as I shifted her around so I could climb out of bed. She was hot on my tail as I went into the bathroom. I brushed my teeth while she made funny faces in the mirror.

With her right there, my life was complete.

Full.

Nothing missin' except for the place inside me that called out for him. The piece of me that needed to remain silent because I didn't need any bad ideas shouting in my ear.

When I finished, I tipped up her chin to look down at my sweet girl. "What should we do today?"

She didn't get time to answer before the doorbell chimed from downstairs.

Daisy's dark eyes went wide with excitement, while a bolt of terror zipped down my spine.

Would he dare show his ridiculously gorgeous face here after what my daddy had walked in on last night?

He was lucky he hadn't been chased off the property with a shotgun.

But this was Richard Ramsey we were talking about.

Of course, he was cocky enough to do that.

Daisy jumped up and down. "We gots company. Let's go. Let's go. You gotsta come because you know opening doors is another one of those rules I'm not supposed to be breakin'."

Ugh. Did I have to? Hiding under my bed seemed like a better solution.

"Come on!" She tugged at my hand.

"Fine." I followed her out, wearing only a tank and sleep pants and a heavy coat of anxiety, praying that it was a visitor for my mama. I edged out of my bedroom only to hear my daddy opening the front door.

And all that dread doubled.

Turbulence striking the air the second the door swung open and the shafts of bright light streaked into the room.

A silhouette stood in the blaze of them.

A god that had descended.

Graced the paupers with his immaculate presence.

The man so tall and powerful and stealing my breath.

Safe to say, Daddy was not impressed. "How dare you return to this home."

But Daisy was already clamoring downstairs and shrieking with delight. "Mr. Richard! Mr. Richard! Did you come to see me?"

She beelined for the door.

When she got to my daddy's side, he snatched her hand to keep her from going any farther. She popped up on her toes, leaning that way, like she was intent to do it, anyway.

Sheer, unmitigated enthusiasm.

Like she was immune to the violent tumult that raged and stroked through the air.

"I already missed you so much," she sang, grinning her grin and the man was returning one, too.

"Well, that must have been because I was thinking about you...missing you, too." That grumbly voice floated up to my ears.

A whisper.

A promise.

Agony pierced me. The stake of an arrow. Stalling my footsteps and expelling the breath from my lungs.

I'd warned him.

Warned him that she loved fast and loved hard.

She'd fall for him as hard as I had. Get swept up in the radiance of his presence. Consumed by what it felt like to stand in his flame.

Then he'd be gone. Attention hijacked by something more interesting. Something flashier and shinier and brand new.

Before we knew it, he'd be on to the next bigger, better thing.

I had the sudden, sharp urge to intervene. Stop it from happening. I hurried the rest of the way down the steps, only to falter when his face fully came into view.

When those intense sage eyes landed on me. A meadow in the middle of a raging storm.

An eclipse fighting against the light.

That gaze took me in like I was the piece he'd been missing.

What he was on the hunt for.

What he would fight for until the bitter end.

His presence a heavy, swelling sea.

A tidal wave that rushed.

But it was the gash and butterfly bandage on his forehead and the massive bruise surrounding it that hadn't been there yesterday that had me gasping and rushing the rest of the way toward him.

Nothing but a fool.

"Richard. Oh my god. What happened to you? Are you okay?"

Grimacing, he shook his head. "Guess karma came to pay a visit."

He glanced at my father when he said that.

My daddy scoffed. "Not soon enough."

"Daddy," I chastised.

He shot me a look over his shoulder that hiked to his ear. "What? I speak no lies. Unlike someone else around here." He shifted his attention back to Richard when he said that.

Discomfort bounded.

"Don't you know lyin' is one of the rules you aren't supposed to go breaking?" Daisy's sweet voice cut through the disquiet. "Hey, what you got there?"

She hopped from one subject to the next without taking a breath, and she freed her hand from my father's clutch when she noticed Richard was holding a wrapped box tucked to his hip.

She moved closer to him to get a better look.

But the only thing I could do was stare at his face.

That stunning, handsome face that was marred and deformed. Injured.

He knelt in front of my daughter.

My spirit thrashed.

Richard's expression flashed through a thousand emotions.

Regret and hope.

Hurt and love.

Worry and devotion.

Things he had no right to be feelin'.

It didn't matter a bit that I knew that fact. I was still frozen in them.

Ensnared.

The man nothin' but quicksand.

Eyes swimming with affection, he handed my daughter the present like he was offering a piece of himself. "Wanted to check on you. Give you this." His voice was raw, the man taking her in like he would be the one to single-handedly ensure her safety. "My ma, my sister, and I were super upset about what happened yesterday. We were worried about you, and we wanted you to know how much we were thinking about you. Thought you might like what's inside."

"Is that a present for me?" Daisy's voice lifted five octaves and her eyebrows shot to the sky with excitement when she realized he'd brought her a gift.

Shit.

This was spiraling out of control and fast.

"Yeah. It's for you."

"Oh yay! Oh, Mommy, looks it, I got a present." She took it without saying anything else and dropped to the floor so she could unwrap it.

Paper flew as she tore it free.

Then she was squealing more when she popped the lid from the box to reveal the pair of cute black patent leather dress shoes tucked inside.

She squeezed her hands together and held them to her chest, her shoulders hitching to her ears. "Oh, I got new dancin' shoes."

"Figured they'd be perfect for the wedding since the other ones got messed up," Richard told her. "What do you think? You think these will work out?"

"I love them," she drawled in the cutest awe, hugging the shoes to her chest. "Thank you, thank you, thank you! They are my favoritist ever. Do you want to be my best friend?" she asked, way too eager when she looked up at him with all her childlike hope shining through.

My chest panged. Dread shimmered.

I ignored the tiny spark of joy that this was the way it was supposed to be.

Daisy hopped to her feet. "Wait right there. I'll be back in a flash. Don't go anywhere." She tossed him a finger in the air before she darted into the kitchen.

Tension spun, winding and surging into the atmosphere. Stark hatred from my father who was the furthest thing from a hater. His care and concern rippling from his aging body as he stood glowering at the man who had hurt his baby girl.

A protector without weapons.

While Richard straightened to his towering height. Lookin' like a warrior. Something fierce and brutal coursed through his veins, though he dipped his head at my daddy in some kind of surrendered respect.

I eased forward and touched my father's arm. "Daddy."

He jumped like he'd been shocked by a bolt of electricity.

"It's fine," I told him, soft encouragement in my voice.

It was probably a lie.

A fallacy.

Shifting, he softly brushed my jaw with the pad of his thumb. "No, mi amor. It is not."

I gulped.

Shivered.

Because I knew he was right. Knew he was just as terrified as me after what he'd stumbled in on last night.

Richard was worming his way in. And for what reason? What could he offer other than more pain?

Daisy came blazing back out, waving a Sharpie in the air. "Got it! I need you to sign this, Mr. Richard. You get to first since you're the one who made sure I got all better."

Discomfort flamed and lapped, driving against the energy that curled and wafted from the man. The tether that stretched and stretched. Pulling at me.

Heartstrings that long ago should have been snipped.

Richard took the Sharpie and shifted on his feet at the door.

Unsure. His gaze both ruthless and wary when it traveled my way.

"Come in, silly," she told him, taking his hand with her uninjured one. She gave him a tug. "You got to come inside."

My daddy shot him a death glare. Daggers and ice and the most dastardly of curses.

It was a wonder he didn't drop dead right there.

I sighed. "Just…come in and sign the cast."

Richard nodded, those eyes on me as he angled by my father.

Goodness. This was a straight-up disaster.

Daisy moved over to the antique table that sat under the window overlooking the porch. She climbed onto a chair and pointed at the one next to it. "There. You sit right there, Mr. Richard."

She grinned with all her might, her black hair swishing around her cherub face, dimples denting in.

He pulled out the chair, shifted it around to face her, and eased down to sitting, gazing at her as he did. As if she were a strobe of light. A beacon in the middle of a raging storm.

Because that's what this felt like.

A hurricane that gusted and blew.

Hitting us at gale force.

I suppressed a cry when he reached out and touched her chin, when he murmured the words, "Was worried about you. How are you feeling?"

"Not so bad that I can't be in the weddin'. Let's be clear about that." She quirked a brow to let him know that was absolutely out of the question.

He chuckled a rough sound that reverberated through the space, though it was still filled with concern.

Chills lifted. The man touching me when he wasn't even looking my way.

Why? Why? Why? Why did he have to affect me this way? Why did it have to hurt so bad?

"We wouldn't dream of letting that happen now, would we?" he said, smiling soft and somehow sad. "My sister is going to need your help. Not a chance someone could do it better than you."

"Yep. I'm gonna do the best job ever! She'll want me to be in all her weddin's."

Through the emotion, I choked out an amused laugh. "I think Emily is hoping it's her only wedding, sunshine."

Yeah, I guessed I'd been hoping for that myself.

"Oh, right, yes," she said, nodding her head. "Together forever," she sang.

Richard suppressed one of those rough chuckles, his eyes cutting through the room to land on me.

Connection blinding.

I swallowed around the thickness, hardly able to stand under the force of it.

I had no idea how long we remained like that before Richard finally cleared his throat and turned back to look at Daisy. "Let me see that arm of yours."

Climbing onto her knees, she angled his way and leaned her arm on the table. "There you go. Do you like pink?"

He bit down on that plush bottom lip like he was trying to keep something on lockdown. Like he was struggling. This undercurrent of rage and desperation that I didn't understand mixed up with his care. "Do you?"

"Um, yes! I gotsta like pink. You know how many flowers are pink?" she said in her exuberant way.

Another grumbly laugh. "No. Do you?"

"Um...a gazillion million at least."

"Well, if you like pink, how could I not, considerin' how much I like you?"

I wanted to scream. Rip her away from him and keep her protected because I could feel the seams of our fabric getting snipped apart. The bindings that held me together getting clipped.

I couldn't let him do this.

Weasel his way into our lives. I'd wanted him there once.

The only thing he'd done was trample all over me.

Worse was the way I had that flicker of a feeling.

The dire need to believe it might be true. That maybe there was a bit of the man I'd thought he'd been, after all.

He scrawled something on the cast, something I couldn't make out from where I was standing. "There."

She beamed one of those smiles that could bring an entire town to its knees.

"It's pretty now." She waved it around.

He smiled this afflicted smile that stabbed and slayed.

My stomach tipped and my heart did that unforgiveable thing. The thing that went haywire whenever I got into his space. That thing that made me vulnerable and weak.

"Daisy…what do you say for the shoes?" I reminded her.

She threw herself at him.

Okay, that was so not what I meant. A simple thank you would suffice.

He caught her. Awkwardly at first. Then he hugged her back about as hard as she was hugging him.

Those strong arms wrapped around that little girl like he didn't want to let her go. His eyes closed and that spirit I'd always felt weeping something mad.

God. Was that all deceit, too? The way I'd felt like I'd known him to the very core? Tapped into his darkest, most private places?

Reluctantly, he released her, his voice rough with emotion, "You're welcome. But those are from my mother and my sister, too. Don't forget about them. My ma will have my hide if I take all the credit."

Her brow quirked in question. "Your hide? You been hidin' out? I want to hide. I love hides and seeks."

Richard barked out a laugh, and those eyes were searching for me from across the room, that warm sage spilling out with disbelieved affection at this child.

In it was an apology.

Something so stark and rippling with the secrets that I felt them knock me at the knees. I reached out to the back of the couch for support. To force myself to stay standin' right there before I went and did something stupid like dropping to them right at his feet.

But this was my *husband* we were talkin' about.

The man who was etched on my body, etched on my skin, etched on my soul.

The man who was supposed to share my life. Be the other half of it. There through every success and strife. Through all the joys and the sorrows.

The one who'd left me but never quite set me free.

That jaw clenching, he ripped his attention away and shifted it to Daisy. "Would love to play hide and seek with you sometime. Just be careful. I'm wicked good at it. I bet we could even talk Rhys into playing with us."

"Oh, I would love that to the moon."

She grinned up a plea.

He brushed back her hair.

Slay. Slay. Slay.

I was so not gonna make it through this.

Affection made a wistful dance through his expression.

I fidgeted. Shifted my feet. Hugged my arms over my chest. All of it a vain attempt at shielding myself from the potency of this man.

"Daisy, why don't you go have Nana sign your cast? You know she's gonna feel left out if she doesn't get to," I coaxed her. Desperate to put an end to this.

"Oh, yes! Good idea."

Daisy clamored off his lap and darted passed me up the stairs. "Bye, Mr. Richard. See ya tomorrow unless you want to have a sleepover tonight so we can play."

Uh.

Yeah.

No.

Richard seemed hesitant to stand, that gaze immediately latching onto me as he pushed to standing.

A snare.

Hooks.

I gulped.

"Need to have a word with you, Violet," he said, his voice nothing but smooth, cutting seduction.

My father grunted, reminding us that he was still there. I'd almost forgotten he was.

"That is, if it's okay with your father." Richard didn't seem all that much to be asking, though, the force behind his voice when he pitched my father a steady glance.

"My daughter is a grown woman and can make her own decisions," he said, though he looked at me like he was begging me to deny the request.

I should.

God, I should.

"It's fine, Daddy." Saying it again was nothing but heresy.

Because that storm whipped and blew and howled. Frigid cold against the flames that leapt.

Richard took the few steps back for the door. Hostility blazed from my father as he passed.

He paused, wavered, like he was going to say something before he seemed to think better of it and stepped out onto the porch.

I inhaled a couple shaky breaths, gathering myself, fortifying myself for whatever he had to say. Then I lifted my chin and started after him.

My father stopped me by grabbing onto my elbow. "Mija."

I looked to the worry carved on his face.

"Be careful. That man holds secrets. Ugly, dark secrets. I can *feel* them."

I swallowed down the fear that slicked across my skin.

The awareness of that truth.

The only thing I could do was tell him the same lie. "Don't worry. It's fine."

I slipped out into the brilliance of the day, to Richard who had paced away on the porch, the disturbance amplifying with each step he took.

Pieces of his long hair at the top whipping with the gust of wind.

His shoulders wide and the muscles in his back rippling with strength. The colors painted on his arms twitching and curling with the vibrations that rocked from his bones.

Reticent, my daddy clicked the door shut, and I took a couple shaky steps farther out onto the porch.

Richard turned around.

Energy snapped.

Electricity sizzled.

"What did you want to talk about?" I asked, the words cracking when I took in the ferocity that hardened his eyes.

Something feral and ruthless taking him over.

"This." He erased the space in two steps and swept me off my feet. One arm banded around my waist and the other bunching in the disaster that was my hair.

That was the very same second his mouth descended in a plundering, mind-bending kiss.

Richard

I curled my arm around her waist as I gave myself over to what

I'd been dying to do since the second I'd stepped through her door. Gave myself over to the fierce, unrelenting need to consume this girl.

Taste her and take her and touch her.

"Violet," I rumbled as I held onto the curves of her gorgeous body.

Lust blistered through my bloodstream. Careening through every cell. Thumping madness into my veins.

Violet gasped a throaty, needy sound, and instantly, our mouths went to war. Our lips vying to overtake the other. Our tongues battling for the control that neither of us possessed.

Insanity usurped logic.

All rationale shot.

Gone. Every fucking reservation I'd ever had slayed at the contact.

Could tell the girl was half in shock from the sudden shift, the air panting from her mouth, the other half wild as she sank her nails into my shoulders and hiked herself higher to get closer.

No chance we could get close enough.

Because this…this was the way we were supposed to be.

She was supposed to be mine and I was supposed to be hers.

Violet and I were written in the stars.

Fate.

Destiny.

My outcome before we'd even started.

Her mouth met mine in a frantic bid, her soul shivering all around like it was looking for a crack, for a way to get back to who we had been, to where I'd gone, when my heart had been with her all along.

This girl was nothing but a volatile ball of grief and need that I held in my hands.

A bomb that was getting ready to go off.

Heat coiled and lapped.

Flames that started at our feet. Leapt and curled and ravaged.

It wound around our bodies to set us afire.

Shouldn't have been surprised considering the choices I'd made had left us burning at the stake.

In the middle of the storm, I couldn't stop kissing her. Couldn't stop from asking her for more when I knew I would never deserve it. That I'd never be worthy. But knowing I was going to fight for her with every fiber of who I was, anyway.

Even if those fibers were frayed.

Even if they were ragged and worn.

Tarnished and defamed.

My dick was hard as stone. Pressing and begging at her soft belly, the physical embodiment of how fuckin' bad I'd missed this girl, while my spirit wept with every promise I'd made but had not kept.

I angled my head in a demand to deepen the kiss, like it might make up for the disloyalty.

For the deceit and deceptions that I still had to keep stashed in the deepest recesses where only the monsters could see.

My wife. My wife.

I found myself murmuring it at her soft, lush lips, my hands moving to frame her precious face. "My wife."

Violet whimpered. Fingernails scraped at my back. Need tore through her body. "Richard. Why did you leave me? Why would you hurt me so bad?"

Frantic, her tongue stroked against mine. In the middle of it, I could taste the bitter salt from the tears that fell down her face.

The fingers at my back turned to fists.

Curling into my shirt before she pounded into my back, her kiss becoming more desperate as the offense flooded out.

"How could you? How could you just leave me?"

My hands gripped and pled, riding down her shoulders and locking around her back, holding her tight like I could keep her from floating away. From disappearing into the expanse of nothingness that had been born between us.

The void we were trying to fill in a single moment too vast and extraordinary.

"I know I hurt you, Violet. I know I hurt you. I didn't want to. It killed me. Fucking destroyed me."

A sob hitched in her throat.

Guilt throbbed, violent in its lash, and I forced myself to pull away.

But I couldn't go far.

My forehead dropped to hers as I fought the compulsion to show her the scars the years without her had left.

Marred and stained and disfigured.

Because without her, I'd never looked the same.

My hands were on her hips when I set her on unsteady feet.

She dropped her attention to the ground as a cry wrenched free, and she started to back away. My hands shot out to take her by the face. To stop her from running. From hiding. "Violet."

"No." It cracked like a bullet from a gun. Her head shook and she wound out of my hold, putting her hands up between us. "No. Richard. You can't do this to me. I can't let you do this to me all over again. I won't make it. I already warned you…warned you that our hearts can't take it, and you keep comin' back here with the intention of wreckin' me all over again. And this time it's not just gonna be me who you're going to ruin."

"Last thing in the world I want to do is hurt either of you. I won't." It was the stab of a confession. Probably the vilest lie I'd ever told. I didn't want to hurt her. But there was no stopping this train that was barreling out of control.

Asshole out on our property last night had proved that.

"But you already did, Richard. You hurt me worse than anyone has ever hurt me before. You left me."

The last words cracked, and she touched her chest.

Like the girl wanted to give me access to see what I'd done.

She didn't need to show me. I'd known it all along.

"I'd take it back if I could. If I could go back and erase what was done, I would. I don't want to hurt you anymore, Violet. I want to be here. Right here, with you. I need you to trust that."

A motherfuckin' fool. But I couldn't turn back. Couldn't turn away. Couldn't *leave*.

She blinked up at me with those mesmerizing eyes.

Violets and the sky and eternity.

The girl delicate and raw.

Fragile and fierce.

Every fucking day since I'd met her, I'd been in awe.

She scoffed out a disbelieving sound. "And that's the problem. I can't trust you. Can't trust that you'll stay."

She stared up at me, wading through the turmoil, wearing this skintight white tank with no bra and sleep pants that hugged her in all the right ways.

Distracting to say the least.

"What do you even want, Richard? I'm over here telling you I can't trust you, and I don't even know what you're asking me to give."

I took a step forward, cocking my head to the side, my words grit. "Not asking for a thing, Violet, because you and I both know you're already mine."

Misery sliced through her being. A physical rendering. I felt it like a blow. "You're right. I have always belonged to you. And look what's left."

Stepping back, she held her arms out to the sides, tears streaming down her stunning face and glinting in the reflection of the sun.

Wisps of black hair fluttering around her.

My fairy girl.

I was in front of her in a flash, one arm looping around her waist and the other cupping one cheek.

Emotion crested through her features.

Girl overcome.

Disgust.

Love.

Goodness.

Grief.

Everything I wanted to gather up and hold forever.

"You think you're in pieces, Violet? Look at me. Look at us without each other."

That crystalized gaze blinked and fluttered, her lips parting and making me want to devour her all over again.

"That's your fault."

"I know it's my fault. I know it. And I can't change what I've done, no matter how badly I might want to. Question is, can you forgive me?" The last scraped up my throat.

Violet stared at me, wavering and confused and unsure. Her attention moved to the injury between my eyes, and her hand trembled when she lifted it and feathered it over the butterfly stitch. "How could you ask me to forgive you when I know you're hiding something from me, Richard? I see it. I feel it. What have you gotten yourself into? What happened last night?"

I flinched. "My past is catching up to me, Violet. Every mistake I've made is right here, and I'm doing everything in my power to fix it. To make it right the only way that I can."

"I don't understand."

Anger blistered across my flesh. "There are things at play that I can't show you, Violet. That I can't let you see. But you need to know I'm going to destroy it. I'm going to end it. Burn it to the ground. And when it's done? I'm going to pray you can find a way to forgive the unforgivable."

I was so close, our mouths grazed.

Tiny wildfires erupted.

"Just remember when you find out? Remember I did it for you."

That energy whipped. Agitated and wild. The girl's heart started to pang in a disturbed, unsettled way.

"You're scarin' me, Richard."

I exhaled a heavy breath. "Believe me, baby, I'm scared, too." Not for myself. But I couldn't shake the terror that I might not be able to pull this off.

And if I didn't?

None of us could afford the cost.

"One thing I need you to know is I'm not going anywhere," I told her. "I'm going to be right here, taking care of you and Daisy, protecting you, until it's over."

Confusion bound her, her defenses trying to make a rise. "When did you start caring about me and Daisy?"

My fingertips played across her knitted brow. "When did I start caring about you and Daisy? Told you last night, I never stopped. Never stopped loving you. Never stopped wanting you. Not for one fuckin' second."

"You didn't sign the papers," she whispered, still staring at me like she was going to stumble upon the answers hidden in my eyes.

I recoiled at the memory.

Way I'd nearly lost my mind when the divorce papers had been delivered to one of the hotels we were staying at on the road. The words had read like my own goddamn tragedy that I'd personally penned.

In a fit of rage, I'd ripped them up and tossed them over the balcony.

"Couldn't."

"Why?"

I snatched her wrist and brought it to my nose, inhaled across the tiny piece of art that represented us.

A music note.

Swore, the violet on my wrist throbbed, desperate for its match.

"Because that would mean completely letting you go."

She exhaled a shaky breath, and I kissed across the lifebeat that thundered at her wrist and murmured the words like they were proof, "Funny how I never heard another word about it from you after that. Funny how you didn't push. Funny how you felt the exact same way as me."

I let the implication hang in the air.

Fact that we belonged.

That it didn't matter the space I tried to put between us.

Our hearts were still touching from across the miles.

"It was easier just to let you go," she whispered.

"Let me go? Don't lie to me, Violet. Your heart wouldn't be doing this if you had."

I set my palm flat against her chest. Against the thunder that raged and banged and fought for what was right.

"Taking you to dinner tonight." I was back to kissing across the tattoo on her wrist. "Want to take you out. You and me," I rumbled at the tender flesh.

Needed her alone.

She raked out a surprised sound while goosebumps pebbled her skin. Her blood sloshed and her chest heaved. "Are you crazy?"

Obviously.

"Always have been for you."

"You're insane."

"Exactly."

I edged back, gazing down at my fairy girl. "Things were never quite logical for us, were they?"

They were instant.

Rash and reckless.

Rejection shook her head, those cheeks so pink and her eyes so dark. "I'm not gettin' back together with you, Richard. I might be a fool, but I'm smarter than that."

"I never said you were."

"You're acting like I am."

"Just making it clear what I want."

She crossed her arms over her chest. "I agree we need to talk, and we can do that over dinner. But no more kissin' or touchin'."

I grinned in victory.

She scowled the cutest scowl I wanted to trace with the tip of my finger. "I mean it, Richard. We are just talkin'."

I backed toward the steps, never taking my eyes off the girl who tried to keep her cool. To pretend like this wasn't more than what she'd just agreed to.

"I'll pick you up at six."

Air huffed from her nose.

"Don't text me later giving me some line about you not feeling well." It was almost a tease.

"Fine," she shot out.

I turned and ambled down the porch steps, heading for my truck. I opened the door and glanced back at her through the intensity that shivered through the air.

Like I was physically tied to the one thing I'd been missing.

"Oh...and wear one of those sundresses I love so much."

I sent her a wink and hopped into my truck.

I was fairly sure she stomped her foot.

And I realized I was grinning when I turned around, took the long dirt drive, and pulled out onto the road.

Like the dormant violet inside of me decided it was time to come to life.

nineteen

Violet

What had I done? What had I done?

I was barely breathing when I stumbled back into the house. My daddy was there, concern disguised as disappointment etched on his face. Like that man was written on me. His touch leaving the glow of neon imprints all over my skin.

I figured my swollen, reddened lips were proof enough.

What was I doing?

Despair swept through me, and my shoulders sagged as I leaned back against the door the second I closed it. My head banged against the wood.

Several times.

Where the hell was my resolve?

"So?" my father asked from across the room.

"So, we're going to go to dinner to talk through the past. Figure out how we can get on until the wedding is through. Gonna have to be around him until then. He and I have some things we need to hash out."

At least that's what I was telling myself.

He sighed and ran a hand over his face. "I have a bad feeling, Violet."

"We have unfinished business. We need to finish it. That's it."

Sniffling, I rubbed the back of my hand under my chin that felt crusty with the tears that had dripped down my face. I had been tugged through so many emotions out on that porch that I didn't know what I felt.

Need.

Hurt.

Sorrow.

Fear.

Unrest curled in my belly.

What the hell was he talking about? Protecting us? Not going anywhere?

I wanted to reject it. Chalk it up to another flimsy, lame excuse. But I knew him well enough to know there was something there.

I could feel his agitation.

The burden on his shoulders.

"I…I'm going to go check on Daisy."

I headed up the stairs, but I had another destination in mind. Needing to go to the one who always understood.

My lifeline.

My buoy.

My advocate.

I climbed to the top of the stairs, slowing when I got to the landing, my steps suddenly dragging with the weight of the reality I wasn't ready to face. The thought of losing her, too, ripped that hole inside me wider. Demons clawing and grasping and tearing away more of what was most important to me.

Leaving me gaping and bleeding out.

I eased up to her door. The floor creaked under my footsteps, and I peeked in to find her already looking at the doorway. Expecting me. Anticipating me.

"Come sit with me, my angel." She patted the bed with a frail hand.

A torrent of sorrow swelled in my chest. An eternal spring that would gush forever.

Under it, it felt impossible to breathe.

Her grayed hair was matted and stringy, her hazel eyes deep set in the shallow pools that sunk in her pallid face.

It didn't matter. It would still be the loveliest face that I'd ever seen.

Choking back the tears I could feel burning in my throat, I eased inside and moved over to her. "Hi, Mama."

I leaned in and pressed a kiss to her forehead. Lingering. Wanting to stay in the warmth of who she was forever.

Finally, I peeled myself back to look down at the woman who'd always had every answer.

She smiled up at me, her eyes twinkling with mischief. "I heard you had a visitor."

I sighed and sat down on her bed, facing her, bringing my knees to my chest like it could hold the brittle pieces together. Every crack running through the middle of me aching like mad. "He brought Daisy a present from him, Mabel, and Emily."

She hummed. She didn't believe for a second that was the full story.

A sigh pilfered free, and I hugged my knees tighter. "He kissed me. Last night and today," I admitted in a rush, cheeks blazing with embarrassment.

"That's that boy's way, isn't it? Sweeping in like a storm that hits in the middle of the night without warning, and you can never tell what kind of damage has been done until the sun comes up in the mornin'." She said it with a soft smile. Disappointment and affection.

We'd all loved Richard Ramsey which was probably why my daddy had come to hate him so much. Because he'd put his trust in him even when he'd swept me up in the whirlwind that was his life.

"I'm afraid if I let him, he'll demolish me again. All of us." My gaze shifted out the door into the hall where we could hear Daisy playing in her room. Her imagination running wild as she prattled on to herself. "And I don't want to walk blindly in the night."

Understanding moved through her expression.

"And what's he saying, Violet?"

My lips pursed. "He's actin' like he wants me back."

"And what do you want?"

I choked out a laugh. "Not to be a fool. Not to stumble out and get lost in his darkness."

The man a total eclipse.

Awestriking.

Earthmoving.

Heart-altering.

A curtain pulled over your eyes so quickly you were caught unaware.

"He left me with nothing."

A lame excuse and a faulty explanation.

That and a shattered heart.

She reached out and curled her hand around my ankle, her voice rough and low and filled with emphasis. "You are no fool. Not even close. But you are not driven by the sensible. You are driven by the *sensation*. By the feeling you get buzzing through your veins. Are you *listening* with your heart? What are you feelin' right now?" she asked, those dark eyes searching me with their unending warmth. With her belief and hope.

"Terrified."

It was the bare, basic truth.

Sympathy pulsed through her expression. "That should probably tell you something."

My head shook, knowing how crazy it was. "I think he's in trouble, Mama."

A frown pinched her brow. "What kind of trouble?"

I hugged my knees tighter, mind spinning as I tried to add up the pieces he'd given. The secrets he held. "That, I don't know. But whatever it is? I think it just might have been bad enough to rip us apart."

Anguish flayed through my heart. Every wrong he could have committed. The ideas of what he had done. When I'd gotten that pathetic letter six years ago, I'd come to the quick, undeniable conclusion—he'd fallen for someone else.

It'd hurt. Hurt so badly, but I'd done my best over the years to come to terms. But then why would he say the things he had? Imply he'd had no choice?

My tongue darted out to wet my lips, and I forced out the admission, "I agreed to go to dinner with him tonight. To *talk*."

Mama laughed out a wry sound. "Oh, I doubt very much that man has talkin' on his mind. Look at you, already loved up and he's barely touched you."

Redness streaked. "Well, there won't be any more of that *touchin'*. I already told him that was it. That I wasn't taking him back and if he wanted to have dinner, we would talk, lay out the past, and get over it. Move on. It's time."

She looked at me like I was the one telling the lies. "That's just it, huh?"

"Yep."

Her mouth slipped into a disbelieving grin. "Don't be so sure there's not more."

"Why do you defend him?"

Her features morphed in understanding, her goodness pouring out. "I'm not defending him, Violeta. Not at all. But I saw what was between you two. Something real and instant. An instinct you both possessed that recognized the other. There was no mistaking it."

"Then maybe I should have known he would leave me."

Her face pinched.

"What?" I asked.

"I just never believed the reason he gave."

All those questions spiraled and blazed. I shoved them down. "The reason doesn't matter. He left me, Mama. He walked away. *For six years*."

"And now he's here."

I exhaled a heavy sound. "And now he's here."

"And in trouble."

I huffed out a heavy sigh through my nose. "I think he's always been trouble."

"Yes, he has. The best kind of trouble." Her eyes danced.

"Mama," I chastised, not sure if I wanted to laugh or cry.

She reached out and took my hand, squeezed it tight. "I just want my baby to be happy. To know her heart is free. With Richard or without him."

She didn't need to say it, the rest of what she'd thought.

Before I go.

I squeezed her hand fiercely, sorrow a thousand bricks piled on my chest. "I will be fine, Mama. I promise you."

"I know you will be fine, my angel. But I want you to fly. To soar. For your joy to blossom with more color and beauty than every flower in the field."

My voice hitched in desperation. "I love you. Love you with all of that."

"And I love you," she whispered. "I've had it, Violet. That true joy. My family."

Heartbreak blanketed her ashen face, hopeful desperation in her quieted voice. "Have you had any news on Liliana?"

My heart clanged against my ribs, but I forced a wary smile that I hoped came across as positive when just thinking about it made me want to spiral. "The private investigator said it would take time, but he felt confident he would find her."

But would she be dead or alive?

Would she come?

Would she steal away that joy my mama was talking about?

Staggering fear slammed me, my lungs squeezing in a fist.

"I'll bring her here, Mama. If there is any way possible, I will bring her here."

She nodded through the streaks of moisture that dripped out of the corners of her eyes and rushed into her hair. I crawled over to her, laid down on my side, and wrapped my arms around her.

A silent promise.

And a wish that I didn't have to let her go.

Richard

*A*wareness panged in my chest, heart giving an extra beat at the sight of her.

Eyes eating up the girl who stepped out the front door and clicked it shut behind her.

She was wearing a sundress.

The sexiest sundress I'd ever seen.

Red.

Thin straps and a ruffle that ran across the straight neckline, exposing the gorgeous skin of her chest and shoulders, arms thin but built from working out in the fields. A mess of black hair was tied up high on her head in a ponytail and wrapped in a ribbon.

A few tendrils got free and kissed along her collarbones that I could barely glimpse over the top of the billowy fabric.

The dress landed just above her knees.

Black cowgirl boots on her feet.

My insides tightened.

She looked like a picture of home.

Wanting to get to her faster, I stepped out of my truck, rushed anew with the sense of standing on even ground when I'd been clawing through desolation for the last six years. That I was there, right in the place where I'd been purposed. Where I would have belonged if I hadn't been condemned.

I shoved those thoughts down. Wanted to savor this moment. To give myself over to the fantasy of what this could have been if I hadn't made that one mistake that had sent me toppling into a black hole.

One that just got darker and uglier and vaster the farther I fell.

If I hadn't thirsted for success so desperately.

She edged across the porch while I took a couple steps her direction. A cool breeze blew through, whipping those strands around her gorgeous face, that mouth covered in a shiny gloss, her eyes luminous and mysterious and overflowing with every question that I'd left her with.

That stunning body written in nerves.

Toiling and shivering.

I was wracked with a bout of longing, so intense and fierce, it almost dropped me to my knees.

"Hey, gorgeous," I said, leaning against the front of my truck and waiting for her to come my direction.

"Hi," she whispered. Wariness bled from her demeanor. But beneath it was something more.

Something that had been *us*.

That relentless energy that had staked its claim on who we were.

A connection unending even when it should have been ripped up at the root.

It banged and lashed and heaved through the dense air.

Girl's eyes flashed and those lips parted.

Affected.

I pushed off the truck and strolled her way. Hands stuffed in my pockets to keep from doing something stupid like reaching out and *touching*.

Because I was achin' like mad to do the very thing she'd asked me not to do.

To taste and to kiss and to fuck.

Reclaim.

I stopped at the base of the steps. Holding onto the railing, she took the first step down. It sent tremors rocking the earth. When she climbed down to the next, it might as well have been an earthquake with the way she hit me.

A landslide.

A complete collapse.

She stopped on the last, leaving us face-to-face.

Our breaths mingled in the air.

Whirring around us with the whisper of possibility.

Could I be such a fool to think that I might have this again? So selfish to go after the girl who deserved so much better than what I had done?

Stomach contorting in conflict, I reached out and grabbed a single piece of her hair.

She jerked in a sharp inhale.

I tucked it behind her ear, keeping clear of her skin, my breath close to her ear. "You are stunning. You have any idea what you do to me? Finding you like this? Fucking most beautiful thing I've ever seen."

Old wounds opened up and rushed from her pores. "You can't go around sayin' stuff like that to me. We already talked about this."

"You said no touching or kissing. Not doing either of those. And I came here planning on telling you the truth."

At least what I could give her which wasn't gonna be a whole lot.

She huffed out a painfully cute sound. "You just touched my hair."

I quirked her a grin. "Hair doesn't count."

She rolled her eyes. "Lord help me if you're the one making the rules."

"I thought it was plenty established that I'm the rule breaker, not the rule maker?" It came off playful.

Her laugh was droll. "Rule breaker. Heart breaker. Same thing, isn't it?"

"Violet." Her name tumbled off my tongue in an apology.

She shook her head, lifted her chin. "Come on...let's get this over with."

I pushed out a sigh and stepped to the side so she could make her way to my truck. I followed close behind, my hand hovering at the small of her back but not quite touching. Probably didn't matter a whole ton considering the heat of us created a fiery ball of energy in that bare space, burning us alive, anticipation a razor-sharp edge in the atmosphere.

Her breaths were coming short and swift as I reached around and opened the door for her. She climbed in. "Thank you."

"My pleasure."

She'd always been.

My sheer and utter pleasure.

I shut her in, rounded the front, and hopped into the driver's seat. "You ready?"

She huffed a little sound, though there was something light playing around her mouth. "I don't think I've ever been ready for you, Richard Ramsey."

"Funny because I think you were the only thing in my life I've ever been ready for."

Pain creased the corner of her eyes, and I started the truck and backed out without saying anything else.

My intentions clear.

She was just going to have to catch up to them.

We started the trip into town in basic silence.

Violet's apprehension was heavy and dragging in the cab, the minutes slugging by and racing too fast.

I glanced across at her, girl shifting in the seat more than she had been the day I'd gone with her to take Daisy to the emergency room.

Because then her focus had been the child.

The sweet, adorable child who lodged a rock at the base of my throat.

Guilt came at me like a sledgehammer sent to crush my tainted soul to dust and debris.

I reached out and broke another of those rules. Caressed the pad of my thumb along the edge of her hand she held on her lap.

Tingles ravaged her flesh.

Palpable.

The beat of her heart a hammer, a clanging riot, so loud I could feel it like a shout at my spirit. Mine raced to catch time. I glanced her way for a second, still touching that spot and wishing I could sink all the way inside and make her understand.

"Want to make one thing clear before we start this night, Violet. Need you to know I never meant to hurt you," I said, shifting to stare out the windshield. The countryside blinked by, passing in a blur, same way as our love.

Gorgeous and wilting. Bright and fading.

Blooming before it'd been sentenced to decay.

"You were the one thing I cherished beyond any other in this world. *The one thing.*" The words scraped from my raw throat.

Sadness rippled from her being, filling up the space and stealing the air. My lungs wanted to cave. "You keep sayin' that, Richard, but you chose to do it anyway. You think you comin' back here can just erase that?"

"No. I don't." I huffed out an uncomfortable laugh. "Do I wish it could? Fuck yeah. Would do anything to take away the pain. But I can't escape this."

My attention drifted to her, like she might be able to see to the bare truth of what I was tellin' her.

The hidden confession.

I was a prisoner.

Bound to what I'd done. To what I had to do.

Her expression was tortured. "What have you been runnin' from? What you said back at the house..."

She trailed off. The implication clear.

My teeth mashed together. "Won't let anyone get near you, Violet. Won't let anyone touch you."

This whole mission was about saving the innocent. The pure who had been defiled.

"Who is it I need protected from?"

My jaw clenched tight, voice only half a tease. "Apparently only me. Anyone else won't get close."

She choked out a wry sound. "Now that is something I can believe."

I slowed as we got into town, and I took a left into the restaurant parking lot. I pulled into a spot, turned off the truck, and released a heavy sigh as I roughed a disturbed hand through my hair, staring ahead before I finally forced myself to look at her. "It's a bad world, Violet. That's the truth."

"What's a bad world?"

I looked out the windshield. "Fame. Striving to be something, to stand in the limelight, not having the first clue you're gonna get burned by it."

Sorrow swam in the depths of those fathomless eyes.

Mystery and mourning and fidelity.

Girl so fuckin' genuine and sweet and real that she made it difficult to sit in the purity of who she was.

"Every life has its hardships, Richard. Its trials. We could have gone through them together." Her mouth trembled when she said it, with the loss of the years and the what-could-have-beens.

Hand shaking like a bitch, with the truth of the corruption this girl didn't understand or see, I shifted so I could set my hand on her cheek.

"You're not getting what I'm saying."

Didn't want her to.

It was what I was protecting her from in the first place.

"It's bad, Violet. And when I say bad, I mean *bad*. Cruel and wicked and perverse. You don't know what I've seen."

What I'd been involved in.

How it would wreck her if she even caught a glimpse.

Moisture filled her eyes, and she attempted to blink away the tears, but one got free, her voice quivering with dread and sympathy. "You mean...like what happened to Emily? I saw, Richard, on the news. That somethin' bad happened to her. It's horrible. I can't..."

She trailed off, her breath hitching in pain.

Grieved.

Gutted.

Blame lashed like a whip. Gashes that would forever bleed. "Like that. Even worse."

And fuck, I hated to even compare what my sister had gone through because that was bad enough. But I'd seen to the full depths of depravity.

"You would have protected me."

"What if I couldn't? What if it was the only way to keep you safe?"

"Then you never should have been there in the first place."

There she was.

Honest.

Real.

Right.

I never should have been there in the first place, and that had been the first mistake I had made.

"And sometimes you're standin' in the middle of something, and you have no idea how you got there," I told her, words an abrasion that scraped and ground. "You'd do anything to get out, but you're already a prisoner and there's no hope for escape."

Dread dampened her expression. "If you were in trouble, why couldn't you have trusted me?"

My teeth gnawed at my bottom lip, and I stared at the woman who meant everything. I warred with what to say, finally settling, not sure if it was the whole truth or an excuse. "Because I didn't trust myself."

Didn't know if the reality was that every faulty choice I'd made had been ushered in by shame.

Our gazes tangled. A fusion in the dusky light that poured from the lamppost that lit the parking lot. A labyrinth between us that I had no idea how to cross.

Finally, I pulled away and expelled the tension on a heavy exhale. Then I sent her a smile. "Come on, let's put this all away for a while. Enjoy tonight. Each other. Have fun."

Apparently, I'd grown another head because she looked at me like I was insane.

It could be argued.

"You want me to *have fun* with you?" It was all a disbelieving accusation, but beneath it was a lightness that hadn't been there before. "And don't think I didn't notice you changin' the subject. You want to talk? Then you need to actually talk."

"We will, Vi. Soon enough. Just...want to spend a minute with you. Breathe. Besides, you and I used to have a ton of fun." So what if the innuendo made its way in.

"Don't you dare, Richard Ramsey."

I hitched up an innocent grin that wasn't innocent at all. "What?"

"Don't try to sweet talk me." A smile played around her lips.

"Don't you know sweet talking you is my favorite pastime?"

"You are impossible, you know that?" She bit her lip, trying not to laugh.

A chuckle rumbled in my chest, lost to the sudden buoyancy that fluttered in the air. I reached out, touched her face, this time in straight-up adoration. Heart pressing full. My thumb traced the angle of her cheek. "God, I missed you."

Agony and affection vied for dominance on that sweet, stunning face, girl just staring at me, our connection a steady thrum in the atmosphere.

A tether.

A bond.

Didn't know how long we stared before she shook herself out of it. "Are you going to feed me or what, Superstar?" It was a tease. A taunt.

"Superstar? Not even close," I told her.

"Pssh...I've heard the rumors about you and your band. Know you made it big. Just like I knew you would."

She started to climb out.

"Stay right there. Don't move."

I hopped out and rushed around the front, opened her door, and extended my hand for her to take it.

She glared at it like it was a viper. "Richard."

"I'm just bein' a gentleman like my ma taught me to be."

Those captivating eyes rolled. "You really do love to sweet talk me, don't you?" She took my hand, those long legs exposed as she shifted around to slip out, skin glimmering in the light, that fabric sweeping up those thighs I was dying to get lost in.

To lose myself in that delirium-inducing body.

Need pulsed.

I swallowed it down, but it didn't want to go anywhere when she climbed out and it left her standing an inch away.

Lust. Greed. Want.

They pummeled me at gale force.

I somehow got it together and took a step back.

I should have been awarded a gold medal.

"Let's feed you, gorgeous girl."

So I was pretty sure the no touching thing might be off the table because I couldn't let go of her hand, and she didn't seem like she could let go of mine as I led her into the upscale restaurant, the best in Dalton.

Inside, it was dim and swanky. Place decorated in an antique, lush vibe.

Heavy tapestries and oversized carved wooden furniture, small alcoves lit by candlelight to create an intimate setting.

At the hostess stand, I gave my name. I thought the girl who couldn't have been more than nineteen working it might have pissed her pants because her eyes went round when she saw me. She started to stammer, "O-oh...oh yes. Richard Ramsey. Right this way."

The girl kept stealing peeks at me as she led us through the main floor to one of the private tables. She was way younger than me. Someone I didn't recognize or know. Which was kind of unsettling considering this was my hometown.

But I guessed things did change.

We ducked into the secluded nook, and I held out Violet's chair. She slipped into it, and I moved to sit on the opposite side. The girl passed us our menus.

"I...um...so...have a good dinner." She ducked out without saying anything else.

Violet suppressed a giggle.

"Don't even," I mumbled, pretending to turn my attention to

the menu.

Her giggle got louder. "Told you."

"What did you tell me?"

A blush was lighting her face. But it wasn't shyness eliciting that alluring color. It was pride. "Superstar," she mouthed.

"Not even," I said again.

She laughed, and she kept her voice subdued considering the entire restaurant was held in a low drone of voices and clanking dishes. "Did you see that girl back there? She tripped all over herself with the mention of your name."

I waved it off. "She did not."

"Yes, she did. I bet you could go up to her right now, ask her to go home with you, and she would."

Somehow, she was all playful grins when she said it.

But I wasn't laughing. "Wouldn't happen."

"Bet you a hundred bucks." Violet's grin was even wider.

Faster than she could process it, I had tossed my menu onto the table and had shifted so I was right in her face, leaning off to the side and over the small circular table.

I was assaulted anew.

Violets and dreams and life.

Wanted to glut myself on it.

"It wouldn't happen." The words were hard.

Emphasized.

Confusion filled those violet eyes, that perplexed gaze searching my face.

My teeth ground with the ferocity of the confession. "It wouldn't happen because I would never ask her to go home with me. Not her or anyone else."

That confusion grew in strength, girl's mind racing toward disbelief.

The energy shifted.

A fierce severity that blustered from my flesh.

The determination.

Her entire being rattled. "Don't you dare start tellin' me lies, Richard. I've come to terms."

It was such a lie, I could taste her defense on my tongue.

I squeezed her wrist, my nose at her cheek, brushing across the silky flesh before I was moving for her ear. "You. Are. My. Wife."

It was hard.

Vicious.

Possession bounded through my blood.

"And that fuckin' means something to me."

Shock froze her, like she didn't dare breathe. Didn't dare move.

I couldn't bear to ask if the same had applied to her.

I couldn't blame her if it hadn't even if the thought made me want to go on a crime spree.

It'd been six fucking years, and believe me, that truly could drive a man to insanity.

"Six fuckin' years." The declaration came on a roll of pain.

Physical.

Mental.

Tension ricocheted.

Dancing through the flames that leapt and lapped in the secluded space.

I edged back enough to meet those eyes.

To stare into eternity.

Didn't matter if I had her or not.

She was the forever that had been written on my heart.

Violet

$\mathcal{S}$age eyes stared me down with the sort of severity that could blast through a concrete wall that was ten-feet thick. Sear through every resistance. Blow through every reserve until there wasn't a single thing left but vulnerabilities.

Oh God, did it ever put my rationale at a stark, glaring disadvantage.

My daddy was right.

I was not just *fine*.

Every fractured piece that I was trying to hold together was quaking and quiverin', my shredded insides I'd sewn up in flimsy threads threatening to bust apart.

He hovered an inch from my face, our noses close to brushing, that dark aura shifting into something far more dangerous. The carved, sharp angles of his gorgeous, chiseled face were tense with the truth there was no denying.

That energy spiked.

Like tiny daggers impaled in my spirit.

I couldn't allow myself to get lost in those eyes and those hands and that body. To get lost in those words that wanted to soothe away some of the hurt.

To heal a small portion of the hole that gaped from within, knowing that maybe there was a chance that this man had been as lonely as I had been.

I cleared my throat and sat back in my chair, breaking the connection that strained and swelled, doing its best to cast its hypnotizing spell.

One that could so easily leave me swept away.

Adrift.

Forever lost in his eclipse.

"Violet." It was a soft breath. Frustration and helplessness.

"I don't know what to say to that, Richard."

The waiter appeared at our table, bursting the bubble.

Richard sat back with a sigh of disappointment.

"Welcome to Delonge's. Can I bring you something to drink to get you started with tonight?"

Richard looked at me, watching me like every word I said was precious in his sight.

I cleared the agony from my throat.

This was not easy.

Not easy at all.

Sitting in his space was making it monumentally more difficult to keep my wits about me.

To remember.

"I'll have a glass of moscato," I managed.

"Sir?" the man asked, swiveling his attention to Richard.

"I'll have whatever local beer you have on tap. You pick." Richard said it like he couldn't be bothered.

"Perfect. I'll be right back with the specials."

He left, allowing the tension to come sweeping back in.

Shifting, I forced a smile, swearing to myself I could get through this.

I just needed to deflect.

Stay on safer topics and not the ones that would crush me.

"Tell me about the band. About Rhys and Emily. What it's been like the last six years. I bet you all got up to some shenanigans."

A true smile twitched along Richard's plush lips. He sat farther back in the chair, that lean body built of sinew and strength slung back in the seat, wearing jeans and a button-down, the sleeves rolled up his forearms that my gaze kept drifting to. He had one tattooed arm stretched out to the table so he could fiddle with the corner of the fabric napkin folded by his bread plate.

I couldn't help but watch the muscles tick and jump. The way his easiness was fueled by an undercurrent of hostility.

"We've written some damn good songs, that's for sure."

"I bet."

He quirked a brow. "Have you listened?"

I huffed out a reticent sound. "I did my best not to, but seein' as how every time I turn on the radio of late, your band is suddenly playin', it's been a whole ton harder."

I sent him a wry smile.

Superstar.

I shouldn't care to be proud, but I was.

A light chuckle rumbled off Richard's tongue, and he rubbed his hand on the back of his neck. "After playing that awards show, things happened fast."

My brow pinched, realizing I'd missed so much. Six years gone, and I had no idea what had happened in between.

"But I thought that big record company had been trying to get y'all to sign a long time ago? All the way back to when…" I trailed off at that because I couldn't bring myself to say it.

Back when we'd come to our end.

Anger flashed across Richard's face. So sudden and shocking it jarred me back.

"It wasn't a good deal for us."

I could feel the frown pinching my brow. "If you didn't sign, how did Emily end up back there? In that position?"

That lump in my throat throbbed. The same horrible, sick

feeling I'd gotten when I'd seen Emily on the news. What I'd felt when Richard had mentioned it back in his truck.

The vein in his thick neck pulsed, and the hand on the table that had been relaxed tightened into a fist. "We were back in talks with them when everything went down."

Uncomfortable laughter filtered out because I didn't have the first clue how to navigate this. Actually *talking* with Richard. Not when every time I mentioned something serious, I could see the barricades go up. Walls fifteen miles high. The man giving me nothing but vague answers and indistinguishable reasoning.

Every word laced with ambiguity. With an undercurrent of a warning.

The problem was, when he looked at me with those eyes, I felt like a floodgate had been opened somewhere in those colossal walls. An access point.

It was becoming harder and harder to disregard what my daddy had said. About him having secrets. Ugly secrets.

Him telling me he was in trouble.

God. Maybe I should just cut and run. Save myself the agony. I glanced toward the door as if making the escape might eradicate it all.

The hurt and the questions and the need that wouldn't let me go.

His hand shot out, pinning mine to the table. "Don't be afraid. Not of me."

I laughed a harrowed sound. "You might be an asshole, Richard. Selfish to the extreme. But I know you're not a monster."

Richard stared me down, looking at me through the lapping flame of the candle in the middle of the table, the man revealing more than he'd ever shown.

This stark, cutting grief.

"Want to make it right, Vi. I'm asking you for that chance."

I flushed when the waiter suddenly returned with our drinks, and I jerked my hand back, thankful for the reprieve.

The weight too heavy.

The questions more than I could bear.

The man rattled off five or six specials that I barely processed.

Because it didn't matter how desperately I was trying to protect myself, I was too enraptured by the man sitting across from me.

I fought for normalcy. To act like this was no big deal. That we were just two old friends catching up and I couldn't feel myself splintering apart.

I ordered a filet, then I took a shaky sip of my drink, and I was back to searching for lighter subjects before I fell.

Stumbled.

Completely tripped.

I forced a bright smile. "But now you have a new label. That's so great. Just like I knew y'all would. When are you going to be recording? Is anything going to change for y'all? When do you leave? Is there a big tour coming up? Goodness, I bet you get to fly on a private jet now."

I was slinging out the words like they could fill up the space and blot out the tension. Like I could erase the things we were really wanting to say.

A smirk quirked his sexy mouth, and he set his elbow on the arm of his chair, his index finger propped against his temple to keep his head supported.

The locks of his brown hair flopped that way.

Gorgeous.

Sexy.

A punch to my senses.

I shifted in my seat.

"What, are you trying to get rid of me?" The words teased from that wicked tongue.

"I think I'd be wise to," I told him honestly.

"And what if I asked you to keep me?"

"Then I would ask you to stop breaking my heart."

Nope.

There were officially no safe subjects with us because in an instant, we were already right back in the toil of it.

The waters holding us under starting to boil.

Richard leaned forward, the movement stealing my breath, his features flashing grief. "I'm sorry, Violet, so fuckin' sorry that I wasn't there for Daisy. That I wasn't there for you."

Hurt slashed with the mention of her name.

So intense and fast that a shudder raked through my body. My hands shot to the edge of the table to cling to it for support.

I guessed he really did want to talk.

Cutting out the fluff and going right for the gullet.

"Are you?" It wheezed from my aching throat. "Are you really sorry, Richard, for taking the easy way out when I reached out to you? When I swallowed my pride and begged you to come back to me? To be there for us?"

"Yes."

He said it so simply.

Frank.

Sure.

And still with enough regret to blow me to bits.

"I don't believe you."

The scariest part was the words I'd tossed back were nothing but a lie. Because I did. I knew he was telling the truth, even though I was terrified to accept it.

A song came on over the speakers, playing softly like they'd been doing all night. But this time, I took notice because that captivating voice was filling my ears.

Overtaking my senses.

Richard.

Singing soft and smooth and low.

Raw, unbridled emotion.

Carolina George was playing on the radio. The lead on this one belonged to Richard, Emily's sultry voice lamenting in the background.

My stomach twisted in a roil of knots.

God, I couldn't outrun him anywhere I went. Considering he was sitting there right across from me, I figured I was pretty much screwed.

Those eyes flared.

Lust and love.

The man taking in my reaction and knowing exactly what he did to me.

His voice alone could be my demise.

He slowly stood, rising to his towering, powerful height, covering me in a shadow that I knew could obliterate.

The hand he extended completely decimate.

"Come here."

It didn't come close to feeling like a request.

"Why?" The word was a tremor.

"I want to dance with the prettiest girl in the place."

Oh god.

He remembered.

Every cell in my body ignited with the need I still felt, with this love that wouldn't let go, with the terror that bound and raced and wailed of the danger he posed.

But I was a fool.

A fool who took his hand and let him pull me into his arms. I let him start to lead me in a slow, sensuous sway. Just moving from side-to-side, one strong arm looped around my waist and the other curled around the back of my bare neck.

Tingles streaked.

Emotion surged.

Tears burned in the back of my throat as he held me close.

He leaned down and began to quietly sing along to the mournful love song.

I've been livin' a lie
Without you by my side
When did I surrender
When did I let go
When did life become a gamble
Your heart on the cutting line
Didn't mean to stumble
Wish I had the strength to stand
Still lovin' you and I'm not able
To forget the touch of your hand

Richard heaved out a breath and curled his arms tighter around me, words a grunt of desperation, "Every song, Violet. Every fuckin' song is about you."

His confession covered me like the warmest caress.

Cascaded over me like seduction.

Like the lulling waves of a faraway dream that I'd had for so long.

I wanted to slip into it.

Into his warmth and his safety and the comfort of his touch.

Just let go.

Fall.

Soar in this surrender.

With that single thought, panic hit.

Realization of where I was letting myself go.

My entire body shivered.

Terror and dread.

I couldn't do this. I couldn't do this.

He tried to hold me tighter. I fought him off, slapping at him as alarm took me over. I wrangled out of his arms, my heart hammering so hard I could feel it in my ears.

It hurts too much.

It hurts too much.

Even though we were secluded, I could feel the weight of the eyes of the nearest tables shifting to stare at the drama going down.

That's all we needed.

To start a flashfire in the Dalton gossip gang. The news would be back to my daddy before we even made it home.

I stared at the floor, barely able to find my shuddering voice, "I think you should take me home."

"Violet." He reached for me again.

I stepped out of his reach.

"Please. Just take me home. I can't handle this, Richard. It's too much."

He sighed. Frustration and devastation.

Sage eyes churned with sadness and calamity, and he roughed a hand through the locks of his hair that my fingers itched to feel. But I knew goin' there would only bring me more sorrow.

That I was slipping.

Falling into him.

Falling into his abyss.

Into an endless, starry night.

And if I let go, I'd be the one to blame if there was no one there to catch me before I hit the jagged rocks waiting at the bottom.

Finally, he gave a clipped nod of resignation.

He dug into his wallet and pulled out a few hundred-dollar bills and tossed them onto the table to cover the meals that hadn't yet arrived.

"Let's go."

Shame covered us as we walked out, people watchin' in prying, morbid interest.

Too bad it wasn't a ridiculous datin' show and there weren't actual hearts at stake.

All of it draped us in a heavy, oppressive silence that felt as if it would suffocate. So dense and sluggish that I was having a hard time getting my feet to cooperate as I treaded across the dimly-lit parking lot.

But I had to do this.

I had to protect myself.

Had to protect Daisy.

Had to remember.

He opened the door for me, and I was struck with another shockwave of need when he gripped my elbow to help me into his fancy new truck.

Leather seats were there to welcome me while I felt like anything touching me would burn right through my flesh.

Consume me.

Leave me nothing but bones and regret.

Richard shut the door, hurried around to his side, and climbed in.

He drove us home through the bated unease that lapped with the questions that begged to be answered. The problem was that I wasn't sure I could handle the answers.

The one truth I had was that I was terrified of forgiving him.

Of accepting that vulnerability.

Above anything else? I knew my father was right.

Richard Ramsey held ugly, horrible secrets.

We made the twenty-minute trip in abject silence. The wreckage of our hearts clanking so loud that nothing else could be heard above it. Headlights speared through the darkness and spread out on the deserted country road as he sped through the night.

I didn't look at him.

Didn't dare glance at the rigid, hard beauty of his profile. At those hands that I could feel clutching the steering wheel in a grief I'd grown to believe he wasn't capable of.

Finally, he took the last sweeping curve that would bring the simple home into view. A haven where it rested on the grassy hilltop with the expanse of darkened, sleeping flowers making up the backdrop.

He slowed and eased onto the long drive, winding up it and coming to a stop in front of my house.

I was out the door before he had the chance to be a *gentleman*. Couldn't take him touching me without completely falling apart.

I started for the house. He flew out of the truck and was standing in front of me before I could prepare myself. Cutting off my path. Eyes wild. As unchained as my insides felt.

"Violet." My name grated through the air.

Shards of broken glass.

Panic setting in, I shifted gears, and I darted away from him and down the path that led to my sanctuary. To where the flowers grew and blossomed and became something so tangibly beautiful.

A labor of my love.

Footsteps pounded behind me, that energy jolting through the cool air with each step that he took.

"Violet," Richard shouted again, and I just drove deeper, flying through the low rows of flowers.

Hydrangeas and carnations and lavender. Until the rows grew higher.

Until I was surrounded by every color of roses.

Thorns snagged my dress and pricked my arms.

I didn't care.

I just ran.

Not even sure where I thought I was going. How I thought I

would escape.

I angled through a narrow row of holly, leaves smacking across my bare shoulders on both sides.

I swore under the starlit sky every fear I had came to a head. Climbing out of those cracks and getting free. Gathering as a united force to take me hostage.

I almost gasped out in relief when I no longer heard his footsteps pounding behind me.

I should have known better.

Should have known better.

Because his voice coming at me trampled me with the same force as if he'd tackled me to the ground. "What are you afraid of, Violet?"

I tried to keep running.

"What in this world are you most afraid of? Because what I'm most afraid of is losing you."

A haggard breath raked up my lungs. Harsh and hard and disbelieving.

I whirled on him.

Anger flashed through my bloodstream.

"You're afraid of losing me, Richard? You left me. You. Left. Me." I slammed a fist against my chest. "And you don't get to stand there and act like any of this was my fault. No matter the circumstances, no matter what happened, it was still on you."

Richard stood beneath the pour of moonlight. So ruggedly beautiful it hurt. Hair striking like bronzed silk, the sculpted, immaculate lines of his face glinting in the milky rays, the span of him tall and oppressive and making me lose my mind.

"You're right. It was my fault. *My fault.*" His voice slashed and scraped, and he curled his hands into fists at his sides.

"Your fault," I wheezed into the breezy air, fighting tears that stung and burned. Leaves rustled all around us, the hedges tall enough that it left us hidden in the maze of vegetation. "It's your fault that I'm broken like this. It's your fault that I don't trust. It's your fault that I've been livin' alone for the last six years to raise a little girl by myself."

The words grew with intensity as I spewed each one.

I didn't know if admitting this was assuaging something or making it worse, but I couldn't stop. "A little girl who became my entire world. *My entire life.*"

I took a surging step toward him, holding my chest like it would keep that bleeding organ in the middle from tumbling out to land at his feet.

"And you want to know what I'm afraid of most in this world, Richard?" My tone was laced with ridicule and accusation. With a violent despair that came on a torrent from within.

"What I'm afraid of is losing her. I'm afraid that one day my sister is going to show up at my door and take her away. I'm afraid of not getting to be her mama, anymore."

I guessed I hadn't allowed myself to realize the true weight of that fear.

The sheer terror of what dredging up the past was going to do.

The fact my sister had abandoned that baby at our doorstep when she was three days old. Said she couldn't keep her. I'd chased her down, begged her to stay before she'd jumped into a car I didn't recognize and disappeared into the night.

Now I was petrified of her changing her mind.

In that second, the full impact of that burden pressed down on my shoulders.

Daisy.

Richard.

My mama.

The private investigator who was currently searching for the one person who I loved with every piece of me and selfishly prayed I would never see again.

Guilt and shame and grief.

They hit me all at once.

Too heavy.

Too much.

And I crumpled to the ground.

Richard

*G*rief tore through me like a raze of gunfire. Penetrating through flesh and bone. Blowing me back and toppling me forward.

My knees hit the soft dirt and trampled grasses in front of her, and in two seconds flat, I had her pulled onto my lap and my arms wrapped around her sweet, trembling body. I started rocking this girl who was shaking and weeping so uncontrollably I didn't think I could hold her pain.

Knew I couldn't.

But I was going to try.

It made me a bastard. I knew it did. But I was fuckin' gonna try.

I pressed my lips to the top of her head while sobs ripped from her heaving chest.

"I've got you, Violet. I've got you," I murmured into that wild mane of black.

Fingers curled into the fabric of my shirt, and she pressed her face into the well of my neck. "Why does it have to hurt so bad, Richard? Why does it feel like every good thing in my life gets ripped away?" she cried through gasping, quaking words.

"I'm sorry. I would take it away if I could."

"Why did you have to do it in the first place? I needed you. I needed you." The words continued to spill in a deluge. The barriers she'd tried to keep fortified between us broken down to nothing. Rubble in this mess that was our lives.

I held her closer. "I didn't want to. It killed me, baby. Killed me."

"I don't understand." It was a whimper. A plea. Questions billowed, trying to take hold.

The confession burned on my tongue.

She was going to hate me. Soon enough, she was going to hate me.

"Wished I could make you understand, but I can't. Can't give you that, baby. I would if I could. Please believe that. Please trust that. Please believe I am trying to make it right."

A tremor ruptured through her entire being. She burrowed deeper into the security of my arms. The cries she was emitting didn't lessen but they were changing shape.

Becoming guttural. Whimpers of something that bellowed through the night. The sky hung low, the stars so bright and close where they dangled from the heavens that I was sure I could pluck one out and offer it to her.

A dream that we'd shared but had burned out far too fast.

The canopy held us.

Covered us.

A bubble of protection that refused to allow in anything else.

That energy thrashed in the confines of it. Whipping and wrapping us in the same twine that had bound us at first glance.

Our connection fierce.

Unrelenting.

Endless.

Eternal.

A little fist pummeled on my chest. Then another.

No. They weren't to injure.

Just got the sense she wanted to bash her way in and get to the truth of what had become of the love we were supposed to share for all our days.

"I'm so mad at you. I'm so mad at you. I want to hate you. I *need* to hate you." She rambled the words against the rampage battering my chest.

"I know. I know," I whispered back, and she was kissing across the spot where she'd just been releasing her torment over my heart.

"Let me hate you," she said there. "Don't let me trust you again."

It was a broken plea, and she kept kissing higher, over the fabric of my shirt. Tremors shivered and need rushed.

"Violet." It hit somewhere between a petition and a warning.

The exploration of her hands became frantic as she searched me in the night below the murky, opalescent glow of the moon that sagged low.

Under it, something hysterical came over her being, girl's spirit screaming out in this madness I didn't know how to sate.

How to tame.

How to fix.

"I'm sorry. I'm so fuckin' sorry," I kept murmuring into her hair. At her temple. At her cheek.

Like I could offer the comfort that she needed.

Take it away.

Do something to make her life better.

"I hate you," she said again, trying to convince herself of the lie.

It'd be so much better if I wanted her to.

If I could let her go.

I'd tried. Fuck I'd tried.

Impossible.

My hands splayed across her back and rode up toward her shoulders. A covering of affection.

Need blistered.

I tried to force it down. To beat it into submission. This wasn't the time nor the place.

But Violet was kissing higher, those lips making a frenetic path up the column of my throat, tiny caresses of her mouth sending me into madness.

"Richard, Richard," she chanted.

Her hands gripped.

Her spirit grasped.

"Violet. Baby. You need to stop."

She just nipped at the scruff of my jaw, her tongue coming out to taste the flesh.

Lust bounded.

I hissed.

Didn't she remember the admission I'd made to her back at the restaurant? Because this was brutal. Torture. She kept up like this, and I was gonna blow.

Guessed the sentence was fitting. The temptation she was meting. This girl kissing on me and not being able to have her.

She shifted her position to sit on my lap and wrapped her legs around my waist.

Fuck. Fuck. Fuck.

She started rocking, and my hands shot to her waist to attempt to stop her, but I was moaning out a greedy sound when she rubbed herself on my rock-hard cock. She did the same, the sexy mewl rolling from her throat.

"Why do you make me feel this way? Richard. Please."

She nipped the corner of my mouth with her teeth and her fingers drove into my hair. "Please."

"What do you need, baby? What do you need?" My voice was a growl. Desperation and the knowledge that I shouldn't do this. That this girl had reached a breaking point and I wasn't fit to hold her together.

The secrets I was keeping from her were more than enough to make me a criminal just for touching her.

Still, I was edging back to look into the expanse of those eyes, unable to push her away when she was clinging to me like I was the one thing that was going to keep her grounded.

Like maybe I wouldn't be the one to destroy her in the end.

"I need to go back. I need to remember. I need to remember the way it used to be when you loved me. I need you to remind me what it feels like."

"There is no *used to* in this equation," I rumbled beneath her assault.

She leaned in and whispered at my ear, "Touch me."

I nearly came undone.

"You don't want this, Violet."

At least the girl who'd run out of the restaurant because of the declarations I'd been making didn't. Wasn't so sure about the girl who was currently grinding her sweet heat all over the bulge in my jeans.

Friction flying.

Zinging through the air and making it hard to cling to reason.

"You owe me. Remember the way you used to touch me? The way you used to make me fly? Remember when you told me you'd do it forever? I'm achin'."

Well, fuck me.

How was I supposed to argue with that?

She kissed across my mouth. Lips brushing lips in a tender caress.

Flames leapt in the space.

Enticing, excruciating heat.

She exhaled at my mouth, and I swallowed it down, muttered, "I do. I owe you. I owe you everything." Then I followed the words with my tongue, delving into the treasure that was this girl's mouth. "Want to give you the world. Anything. Everything."

Hot flesh stroked the other. Tangling in this desire that caught fire.

A blaze that burned right through the middle of us.

Sparking and spreading.

This girl was straight-up arson.

Torching all reason and discretion.

No longer gave a shit about anything other than making this girl feel good. Satisfying this one request.

Stupid?

Hell yeah.

So fuckin' stupid because Violet was still trembling and shaking and expelling tears while she clamored to get to me, moisture glinting and striking as it rolled down that breathtaking face, and my guts got jumbled in a warning that she was going to regret this.

That I was only making this coming end worse.

But those thoughts were drowned by the desperation that rose and lifted between us.

Stirring the disorder.

Each movement more delirious than the last.

Hands and tongues and teeth.

Wild kisses.

Needy pants.

My palms glided up the smooth, bare skin at the outside of her thighs, riding underneath the fabric of her dress.

Tremors raced across her flesh.

"Richard. You…your touch has always burned me alive. Left me ash."

She pressed her knees onto the ground on either side of my lap, rising higher so she was hovering over me.

My head tilted back, and I devoured that mouth as the girl consumed mine, her hands riding over my shoulders.

Cupping my face.

Yanking my hair.

Delirium.

Ecstasy.

A travesty because I knew it couldn't last.

I let my hands wander higher. High enough that I held two handfuls of perfect, round ass.

My dick jumped as I gripped her bottom.

"God. I missed you. Missed you, baby. So bad."

She whimpered, and she edged back, staring down at me when I brought a hand around to the front and pushed the silky scrap of material covering her aside.

"Want me to touch you? This what you're asking for?"

She nodded. Frantic. Quick. Tongue darting out to wet her lips.

I gazed up at her when I slowly pressed two fingers into her tight, wet heat.

Hot, slick flesh.

Shivers wracked her.

I nearly came.

Fucking beauty.

Awe-inspiring beauty.

I dragged my fingers in and out. Pumping into her pussy. Watching her as I wound her up. As her thighs quivered and her stomach shook and her fingers dug deeper into my shoulders.

Her mouth dropped open and her eyes drifted closed.

Girl giving herself over to me.

Trust. Trust. Trust.

She yelped when I suddenly swept her up and shifted so I could lay her out on the ground. Patches of grass had been trampled beneath her, creating a soft bed.

Wild hair strewn around to frame her gorgeous face.

That dress twisted and bunched up her thighs.

Moonlight poured down from above and cast her face in an ethereal glow.

A fairy made of blown glass.

Gorgeous and fragile.

The prettiest thing just waitin' to bloom.

Moonflower.

Love gusted through my veins.

Real. Intense. Inescapable.

Heaving out a strained breath, I sat up on my knees at her feet, staring at her through the wisps of light. "You are the most stunning creature I've ever seen. Magic, baby. You are the magic inside me. The best thing that ever happened to me. The *light* that went dim when I lost you."

She shuddered, and I set my hands on her knees and pressed them apart. I glided up the insides of her quivering thighs, following the trail of chills that lifted on her skin, taking the skirt of her dress with me. I didn't stop until it was all the way around her waist.

Her hips bucked from the ground. "Please. Don't tease me."

Gripping both edges of her underwear, I ripped them free.

She gasped.

A smirk crawled across my face. "You forget, sweet girl, what you do to me? How I love you? How I make you shake? How I make you scream?"

"I tried," she whimpered, "Lord knows, I tried. But I can't, Richard. I can't forget you, no matter how many years have gone by."

And there was a nagging thought at the back of my mind that told me to end this, but I was nudging her legs farther apart and getting a good look at the pink, swollen flesh tucked at the juncture of her thighs.

Wet and glistening.

My mouth watered.

I dove in.

Forgetting reservations.

Forgetting regret.

Just needing a taste.

Violet cried out with the exploit. Her delicious body convulsed with the shock of intensity.

With the zap of energy that struck.

I licked deep into her slit.

Diving deep before I edged off, kissing across her lips, nuzzling into the cleft of her thighs.

I drove her into another frenzy.

A ball of desire.

Girl a live wire I held in the palms of my hands.

Hers were catching in my hair. Urgent and dire. "Please. Richard. It's been too long. Too long. Don't tease me."

"You want this fast?"

"Yes. No. I just…need. I just need you."

I gave, turning my attention to her clit that was engorged and as needy as me. I licked it, stroked it with my flattened tongue, lapped and suckled while I drove two fingers deep. Dragging at that sensitive spot on the way out.

My free hand spread over the lower part of her flat belly and pressed down above her pelvic bone.

She moaned.

So deep.

Desperate fingers yanked on my hair. "Oh god. I almost forgot. Almost forgot."

I drove faster. Rushed her toward the precipice while my body screamed to get lost in this fantasy. Cock so hard I couldn't see.

Intoxicated.

Half mad.

Wanting to climb to heaven.

Ride out this bliss.

Violet came on my tongue, walls clenching around my fingers. Girl writhing as she rode out the ecstasy. As the stars fell around us. Like a thousand glittering wishes I'd do anything to keep.

I needed her.

Fuck, I needed her.

And I was kissing up her stomach, over the fabric of that dress. I pressed up on one hand, my mouth going higher and higher, licking over the swell of her breasts and the turbulence of her heart.

With the other, I frantically unbuttoned my jeans and pushed them down far enough to get my cock free.

Lust stampeded.

Clouded my vision.

Made me dizzy with greed.

My lips were at her chin, her jaw, kissing across the plush line of her mouth, murmuring, "Can I have this?" as I wedged a spot for myself between her thighs. "Want you more than I want life."

I felt it. The slight shift of her chin away from me.

They slammed me all at once.

Her reservations.

Her fears.

And I groaned out in pain.

At my recklessness.

Fuck.

Fuck.

I fucked this up. Such a botch job there was no chance for recovery.

Jeans halfway down my thighs, I hustled back.

Scrambled away.

Shame battering my senses.

I have no right. I have no right.

But this girl had me in her hand before I could make sense of it.

The thrill screamed through my veins, and a groan ripped up my throat, and Violet was on her knees where I was on mine, girl stroking me with greed.

With desperation.

"I want to hate you. I want to hate you, but there's never been any hatin' you, Richard Ramsey," she rumbled right before she plunged downward and took me into her mouth.

Sucking on my aching head. Long and hard.

Those words were probably the last thing a man wanted to hear before a girl had his dick in her mouth.

But I didn't mind.

I'd take any pain she gave if it meant experiencing a second of this.

Her sweet mouth and her wicked tongue.

Swirling and lapping while both those little hands curled around the base of my cock.

Then she was taking me deeper.

Deeper and deeper.

Tongue driving me into madness.

Hands stroking in time.

Sucks and licks.

Faster and faster.

So good.

So good.

My hands were in her hair. Tight. Tugging. Not sure if I should push her away or beg her for more.

"Shit. Violet. Baby. That mouth. That mouth. You. I need you. I need you."

Doubted truer words had been spoken.

"Motherfuckin' magic," I rasped.

Pleasure built with the friction.

Gathering fast.

She took me all the way down to the back of her throat.

Bliss gathered to a pinpoint before I split apart.

Combustion.

Devastation.

I came and came in her mouth. Orgasm going on for days. Every cell in my body taking part.

I wanted to cling to that feeling forever, but I could feel the girl pulling away.

She tried to keep her attention averted as she wiped her mouth with the back of her hand and readjusted her dress.

I didn't even take the time to tuck myself back into my pants. I took her by the face, hands on both cheeks, urging her to meet my gaze.

First thing I saw was the horror in her eyes.

Shame and guilt.

"Don't," I grated. "Don't regret this."

She exhaled a tiny sound, those eyes overwhelmed. "Don't regret this? How could I not?"

I brushed back the hair matted to her face, caressed the pad of my thumb over the angle of her jaw, stared down at the one who meant everything. "Because you and I both know where we belong. That you and me? We're right, baby. We belong. No denying that."

Pain lanced through her expression. "I can't even control myself when I'm around you. You make me weak. You make me so weak, Richard. I don't even recognize myself when you're around."

"You're wrong. When we're together? Both of us are exactly who we are supposed to be." My voice ground with sincerity.

Sorrow sifted through her demeanor, and she tried to wipe away the dried tears on her cheeks. I pulled my jeans up before I stood, and I reached a hand for her where she was still on her knees. "Come here, sweet girl."

Instead of taking it, she looked up at me with that false determination written on her in dark, chaotic colors. "This can't happen again."

I didn't say anything. I just nudged my hand out closer to her.

Sighing, she took it, and I helped her onto her feet.

I snatched her underwear from the ground and tucked them into my pocket.

She rolled her eyes, mumbled in that adorable drawl, "God, you are such a man."

I got back in her space, towering over this seductive thing who looked like she didn't know if she wanted to climb me again or bolt. I fluttered my fingertips across her trembling bottom lip. "A man who's gone without for far too long."

Her teeth ground, and she forced out the words, "Maybe it's time you found someone else."

My thumb grazed her jaw, voice rough, "That what you want?"

"I wish that it was."

"And I wish I could be the man good enough to give you everything you deserve."

I didn't say anything else. I just followed her back through the rows of flowers and hedges that this girl watched over.

Made them flourish.

The kindler of beauty.

Silence moved around us in wisps and vapors. That energy lulled yet unsatisfied.

She climbed the main hill back toward her house. She started for the porch, and I reached out for her hand and stopped her at the first step.

Warily, she turned.

Rays of milky light shined down on her precious face.

Her spirit a hammer in the atmosphere.

"Not gonna give up, Violet. Until my last day, I will be loving you. I will be protecting you. Whatever the cost. Hate me or not."

Then I dropped her hand, turned, and left her there as I headed back to my truck. I climbed in and watched her staring at me in the distance.

She stood like a statue.

A fortress.

Black hair billowing around her vulnerable strength as the breeze blew through.

A goddess to be revered.

Had no clue how long we just sat that way. Like our pasts raced to see if there was a way to carve out a future from the barricades and trenches the years and betrayals had formed.

Finally, she turned, slowly climbed the steps, and crossed to the door. She glanced back. Her soul on display.

Sheer, unmitigated love.

Hope.

Belief.

And the glaring hole left by distrust and doubt.

She opened the door a crack and slipped inside.

And I wondered how big of a fool it made me that the one thing I was clinging to was that hope.

The tiny, threadbare dangling string of hope that I could pull this off and she wouldn't completely hate me in the end.

Violet
Seven Years Ago

*N*erves rolled through her being. Body and soul. Heart and mind.

She inhaled an anxious breath as she straightened out her dress. She was at the base of the rolling hill, hidden from everyone else. Her bridesmaids marched a path ahead of her as the strains of the violin drifted through the cool evening breeze. The heat of the day waned as the sun began to sink toward the horizon, making a descent toward the tops of the lush copse of trees that surrounded the area.

Her daddy stepped up to her side, his face spilling over with the amount of love that shone. "Oh, mi amor, you are a sight to behold," he told her, his smile so soft and filled with abundant warmth.

"Thank you, Daddy."

"I am nothing but the speaker of the truth." He touched his chest. Sincere.

She fiddled with her dress that was made of white embroidered leaves and flowers. A plunging neckline and fitted waist, giving way to a full skirt that was covered in the same delicate pattern.

A modern take on a traditional.

A dress her mama and sister and Emily had basically demanded was the one when she'd been concerned it was too much even when her heart was screaming yes.

She'd thought to go for practical when in reality none of this was practical at all.

Marrying a man she'd known for all of six months.

A man who'd shown her what that old adage of being swept off your feet really meant.

Head over heels, only she'd been tumbling heart over feet since the second they'd met.

A man who was destined to be great.

To be famous.

A superstar.

A man who'd spent half their relationship on the road.

And she was getting ready to walk down the aisle to meet him.

No.

She wasn't scared.

She was itching to run down it to get there faster.

Her daddy lifted her chin. "Are you sure you're ready for this? I can't believe my baby girl is taking the hand of a man."

Soft affection played through her spirit. "Yes, Daddy. I'm ready. I've never been so ready for anything in my life. The question is, are you?"

He chuckled a gentle sound. "Never," he teased, then sobered, "but I am happy. So happy to see the way my daughter glows. The love shines in your eyes."

Violet nodded at him, and the music shifted, and Violet knew it was her time.

That her life was getting ready to change forever.

Her daddy extended his elbow, and she looped her arm through his, and he began to lead her up the path covered in a dozen different petals of flowers.

Each from their farm.

A token of wishes in each.

They came to the hilltop where the massive tree came into view. Branches stretched out wide with the sun just dipping down enough to touch the top. Lanterns hung from the lowest limbs, and long pieces of chiffon were draped from them as well, billowing down to touch the earth.

A few rows of chairs sat in front of that awe-inspiring tree.

Her bridesmaids and the groomsmen stood there to welcome them.

But it was the man waiting at the end of the aisle that stole her breath.

Bronze hair whipping in the wind, that face hewn in sharp angles and lines, sage eyes intense and spearing her from across the space.

Energy billowed. Curling around her like a warm embrace.

Home.

Her daddy leaned in and whispered in her ear, "And it shines in his, too."

Night had descended. Lanterns glowed and strings of light twinkled in the trees and in the shrubs that surrounded the lush, gorgeous setting.

Round tables and a makeshift dance floor had been set up under that gorgeous tree, and another band Carolina George was friends with was playing for the reception.

Richard wrapped his arms around her and exhaled his potent aura into her hair. "I can't believe you're my wife. My Violet. My inspiration. My world."

She could feel the contentment and excitement burning through his blood. The outright awe in his touch.

Her heart ran manic, flooded with an amount of joy she didn't know existed. She grinned up at him. "Believe it. You're mine now.

Husband."

Richard grumbled a needy groan. "I like the sound of that."

"Good…because you're going to hear it for all my life."

He brushed back a piece of her hair, gazing down at her with adoration. "And then forever after it."

Joy burst, and he tightened the arm he had around her waist and tucked her closer to his side where they stood beneath their tree with both sets of their parents flanking them on each side.

Where he'd proposed two months before. When he'd taken a red eye from Los Angeles on a one-day break and confessed that he couldn't live without her permanently in his life.

Their guests were scattered throughout the tables, having just finished their meals, while the rest of the wedding party had risen from their table and moved over to the tiered cake covered in bright edible flowers.

Emily, Melanie, and Violet's sister, Liliana, had stood up as bridesmaids. Richard's groomsmen were his brother Lincoln, Rhys, and Shawn, the band's drummer.

They'd kept it simple. Only the few people closest to them.

Violet thought it looked like a perfect picture plucked out of a magazine.

A picture that would forever be emblazoned in her mind.

Rhys clicked a knife on the side of his champagne flute to get everyone's attention. "Now, now, now, I've got somethin' to say. A toast is in order before we get to the dancin'."

"Oh, this is bound to be good." With a light chuckle, Richard tossed out the razz and curled his arm a little tighter around Violet's waist.

Melanie groaned from where she was standing to the right of Rhys. "Make it snappy, cowboy! You are not the star of this rodeo."

"Cowboy? Bite your tongue woman. I'm a stallion. The. Best. Man. Pretty sure everyone knows who's the star around here."

When Rhys claimed it, Lincoln gave him a playful shove on the shoulder. "Uh, excuse me, dude. Check yourself. I'm pretty sure I am the best man."

Violet giggled.

Only Rhys would try to usurp the position.

"Semantics," Rhys said with a grin. "We all know who Richey-Poo here really loves best."

He lifted his glass higher in the direction where Violet and Richard stood, a smug, affable grin playing all over his face.

A ripple of laughter blew through. The mood light. Joy in the air.

"Just hurry it up, man, we know the way you do," Shawn goaded, taking a drink of his beer.

Shawn was the one Violet knew least. The one member the rest of them hadn't grown up with, but he'd become close friends with them once he'd joined the band. He was the one her sister had a mad crush on. Had gone home with the same night as Violet had gone home with Richard, though Violet was worried that was where their connection ended.

Shawn was not into her the same way.

Treating her with an air of indifference except for the times when he was in town and texted her for *company*.

Just a good old-fashioned booty call.

Violet hoped her Lily would cut the ties.

Shawn pointed at Rhys with the index finger of the hand he had wrapped around a beer bottle. "We leave it up to you and our poor man Richard here is gonna be missin' out on the good stuff on his wedding night."

It was pure suggestion.

"Fine. Fine. We definitely wouldn't want our boy here to go without. And I mean, have you seen his wife?" Rhys said with a glint in his eye. "I'm not sure how he's still hanging out here."

He lifted his glass. "To one beautiful bride and one lucky asshole who gets to forever have her by his side."

A chorus of hoots and hollers went up through the wedding party and the small number of guests, and this time Violet really was blushing when her sister was quick to add, "Have you seen her husband? I'm thinkin' it's my sister who is antsy to get the heck out of here."

"Liliana," Violet hissed under her breath with a laugh.

They were all gonna get it.

Her sister waved her off, lifting her glass, looking so gorgeous in her slinky, dusty blue chiffon dress that Violet was certain she was the one who was stealing the show. "I second what Rhys said—to one beautiful bride—the most beautiful bride to ever live—and to her husband who gets to live his days with someone as amazing as her."

She met her sister's eye.

Adoration pulsed.

The sincerity of what she'd said.

"I love you, Violet. I couldn't ask for a better sister. For a better friend. There is no bigger joy than getting to witness you find the kind of joy you have found because you deserve it more than anyone else. You are the meaning of family. I respect you with all I have and can't wait to see the love and happiness you find in this life."

Liliana's voice turned wry, "And to Richard because he is a great guy even though I was pretty sure I was goin' to have to chop off his hands and another important piece of his body that first night with how handsy he got. One look, and the boy was a goner."

She quirked a brow.

Their daddy rumbled a low grumble.

Embarrassed, Violet pressed her face into her husband's chest, unable to believe these were the kind of toasts their friends and family were gettin' up to, even though she shouldn't have been surprised at all.

Richard only held her by the back of the head and laughed, his low, seductive voice reverberating through her, "All right, is someone gonna give a real toast so we can eat that cake? Because truth be told, I *am* anxious to get my gorgeous wife out of here."

Violet curled her hand in his shirt and grinned up at him. "You're in so much trouble."

He smirked down at her. "I hope so."

"Yes, someone is going to make a real toast," her daddy interjected. He walked up to where Rhys had been holding the microphone, took it, and ribbed Rhys with his elbow. "My turn, cowboy," he teased with a smile.

Chuckling, Rhys stepped aside, while Violet's mama sidled in closer and took her free hand.

Her mama turned her gaze on her.

Her dark eyes filled with pure, absolute affection. Black hair the same color as Violet's billowed in the wind.

Love filled Violet to overflowing.

So intense.

So much.

So beautiful.

She squeezed her mama's hand and mouthed, *I love you.*

I love you more, she returned.

Her daddy lifted his glass. "To two beautiful people with the proof of love shining in their eyes. To passion. To joy. To family. To fidelity. To everything that will make your relationship continue to flourish and grow like the blooms that flourish around us. May you have a love like the love I've shared with your mother. The kind of love that never ends but only grows so deep in your soul it has no chance of wilting."

Her chest squeezed.

"Violet and Richard...live your life. Run it together. Never stray. I know you have what it takes. Never let that light go dim."

Everyone lifted their glasses. Richard turned Violet to face him, and she took a sip of the bubbly champagne while everyone cheered, and Richard did the same, their eyes never leaving the others'.

He set both their flutes aside and took her by the hand so he could lead her onto the middle of the dance floor.

On cue, the band struck up.

Richard gathered her in his strong, protective arms, and he began to sway her to the slow song that she hadn't anticipated would play for their first dance.

But oh, was it familiar.

It hitched her breath in a lump at the base of her trembling throat.

Overwhelming.

Completing.

It was a song that Richard had written one long, beautiful night when they'd stayed up until the day was breaking with the dawn. When they'd dreamed and loved and made vows that would forever go on.

He sang it in her ear while he held her in the strength of his arms.

Life spent running
Chasing down a dream
Never saw you coming
Tripping up my feet
You had my heart stalling
Learning how to beat
Never expected love
Beauty breaking the mold
Ripping up the seams
Getting lost in violet
Colors and dreams
Your love a landslide
I'll follow you to the end
And then I'll find you all over again

They were giggling like mad when they burst into the tattoo parlor at just before midnight. Violet was still wearing her dress and Richard was in his fitted suit.

Standing out. They could hardly care about that.

Richard had arranged the appointment, so two artists were already waiting, the work done in a flash, but still, Violet felt every vibration of what they seared on their skin.

A tiny violet on the inside of Richard's left wrist, and a miniature music note on the inside of Violet's.

Music and inspiration.

Trust and fidelity.

Hope and commitment.

Her husband watched her as they marked her, those sage eyes

staring right into her soul, that tether that bound them thrumming with devotion.

With the moment.

With the magnitude of what it meant.

They were giggling again as they rushed back out.

Richard pressed her to the wall the second they were outside. He kissed her hard.

"My wife," he mumbled into her mouth and then he was sweeping her off her feet and into his arms.

She squealed.

Joy rushed.

Intense.

Profound.

She curled her arms around his thick neck, and he carried her up the sidewalk. The night was all around them, the bugs trilling from their shelter in the trees.

Refusing to set her down, he carried her all the way to the nicest hotel in Dalton where they were staying, right through the posh lobby and up the lavish stairway to the second floor.

He opened the door to their suite, still holding on, whispering, "My wife, my wife," as he carried her over the threshold.

My wife.

His confession wound through her being.

The proclamation.

He set her onto her feet at the end of the massive, luxurious bed. He tickled his fingertips along her collarbone exposed by the dress.

Chills raced.

Those eyes traced her, took her in, memorized the moment.

"Beauty. Life. Light. Now I know what it all really means."

"I love you," she exhaled. "Forever."

He slowly undressed her while she undressed him.

Reverent hands. Whispered promises. Their forever bounding out in front of them.

He laid her out on the bed, and he climbed over her, hovering an inch away.

Their bodies hummed.

Heat flooded the space.

Liquid.

Molten.

"My wife. My moonflower in the darkest night. You will always be the song of my heart."

"My husband. My sun that ushers in the day. You will always be the beat of my heart."

And their spirits sang together. Their bodies one. Their love abounding.

He held her wrapped tight as he moved over her.

Slow.

Treasured.

A revelry.

Sweat drenched their skin, their passion in sync.

He kissed her deep before he curled an arm around the top of her head, held her face with the other.

Nose to nose.

Breath to breath.

Soul to soul.

"I will never let you go."

Twenty-four

Violet

"**H**ey, Violet, over here!"

I jerked around from where I stood waiting on the sidewalk in front of the single wedding dress shop in Dalton when I heard the voice calling my name from across the parking lot. Emily waved furiously from where she, Melanie, and Royce's younger sister, Maggie, were climbing out of her car, a huge smile of excitement on her face.

While my insides twisted. Caught in a clamp of dread and this messed up hope that I knew I shouldn't feel. A smidge of guilt for giving in the way that I had, letting that man touch me last night, all mixed up with the residual of that *touch* that was still coursing through my veins and heating my flesh.

I was a proper mess.

Bags under my eyes. No sleep to be found. Tossing and turning all night. Eyes still red from crying and body still flying from gettin' sent to the stars when I'd least expected it.

A goner before I'd even known I'd been struck.

I should have known that's what would happen when I let Richard Ramsey invade my space.

I wondered if she could see it as she approached, Richard's sister coming up the sidewalk, wearing shorts and a pretty, flowy tank and wedge heels, blonde hair falling around her shoulders. If she'd notice the way I shifted and tried to hide the evidence of the flush I could feel climbing to my cheeks. If his touch might be glowing on my skin like it felt like it was.

Hell, he might as well have been dipping those wicked hands in paint and leaving the proof all over my skin.

"You beat us," Emily said, the woman exuding happiness.

I smoothed out the skirt of my sundress. "Just by a minute."

She had her arms out, reaching for me by the time she was two feet away. She squeezed me in a fierce hug. "I missed you."

Light laughter rumbled out, affection so thick, my mind so muddled that I had no idea what to do. I pulled back so I could grip her by the hands, voice thick with emotion. "I saw you just two days ago."

"And that's far too long." She squeezed my hands tighter. "How is Daisy?"

"As rambunctious as ever. Apparently, there isn't a thing that will slow that child down."

Laughing, Mel edged in for a quick hug. "For real, Vi. I am in straight awe of you. That child is a whip. Nothing but a firecracker. I swear, I didn't know whether to laugh or cry when she was trying to convince you she was *just fine*. You have your hands full with that adorable thing."

I tugged at a piece of my hair. "There's a solid chance I'm going gray."

She giggled and stepped back, her tawny hair held in a sleek ponytail that swished around her shoulders. A coy grin split her pretty face. "Oh, don't even talk to me about goin' gray. At least you don't have to deal with the nonsense of the boys in that band day after day. Good god, I'm lucky I haven't stroked out. Between

Rhys and his constant carousin', brute nothing but a publicity nightmare, and Richard's grumbly, brooding ass, it's a wonder I manage to get any of them out on a stage."

I ignored the panging in my heart at the mention of his name. "I think she's askin' for a raise," I teased, glancing at Emily.

Emily giggled. "Oh, don't worry, with the new deal, I'd say she's sittin' pretty."

Mel quirked a brow. "Barely enough to deal with the two of them. I deserve trauma pay."

"Well, I guess if it's so horrible, we can find a replacement," Emily said, words droll. "I wouldn't want to put you in the position of having to do something you don't want to do."

"You wouldn't dare," Mel shot out, hand over her heart.

"I just don't want my best friend to be miserable or anything. I know how much you *hate* Rhys." Her brows lifted in suggestion.

I suppressed a giggle. I had no idea how those two hadn't spit out ten babies by now. Rhys and Mel had always gone round and round like kids on a playground. Rhys might as well have pulled her hair and told her she was ugly with the way that boy chased her around.

Of course, Rhys had a reputation. Women for days, and on most of those days, he was takin' two or three. But as much as he flirted with Mel, she'd never given in. I'd always figured she didn't want to be another number. A sideshow. Looking at her now, I doubted very much any of that had changed.

"Rhys is still the same? Actin' a fool?"

"A blubberin' idiot is what that boy is," she grumbled.

"And you get to walk down the aisle with him." Emily giggled, biting her bottom lip when she said it.

"Shoot me now," Mel said.

"No can do. I need you for the wedding."

"I see what's important." Mel was laughing when she said it. "I demand a new partner."

"Fine. Rhys can walk with poor Maggie here. Welcome to the family." Emily shot Maggie a playful wink.

Maggie blushed. "I think I can handle him."

"Oh no, poor girl won't know what hit her," Melanie said,

words wry.

Maggie had been hanging back, watching us, taking us in, so quiet and shy and cute. I raised my hand in a small wave. "It's nice to see you again, Maggie."

"Same." She hugged me in another one of those warm embraces. "I've been thinking about you."

I edged back, catching the expression on her face.

Worry.

Understanding.

This young girl's spirit was obviously much older than her given years.

"You have?"

Her tongue swept across her lips in discomfort. "It was really hard watching your fear that evening. When she fell. I saw your face."

She winced.

Her compassion was stark.

Boundless.

Real.

I fought the glimmer of that fear I'd felt that night, and instead chose to be thankful that Richard had been there.

That he'd saved her.

Circumstances didn't matter.

There were just some things that trumped all else.

"Thank you. It was definitely scary. Luckily, we only came home with an arm casted and nothing worse."

She nodded, and Emily gestured to the store. "We'd better get inside. Our appointment is at one. They'll be waiting for us."

I tried not to cringe. That was the thing about living in a small town. Memories were going to haunt you wherever you went.

We filtered inside.

"Oh good, Emily and party. Welcome. I'm Letty, and I'll be assisting you today." The woman running the store turned her attention to Melanie and gestured to a large rack. "I've set aside the dresses you requested."

By the time I could even orient myself, Melanie had gone all business and was placing a pile of dresses in my arms. "You try on these." She handed some off to Maggie. "And you'll model these."

She took about seventeen of them for herself and hung them in a dressing room.

That was right before she whipped out an iPad from her bag, mumbling at Emily as she scrolled through the screen, "Emily, you still want to do same colors but different styles?"

Emily shifted on her feet. Unsure. "I…I think so. I wanted to see a few options on y'all before we decide. Mia won't be here until two days before the wedding, so we'll have to pick one for her and the final alterations will be done then."

I looked at her in question.

Emily's smile was almost sympathetic. My sister-in-law who I hardly knew any longer. The details of her life or the people who had become most important to her.

"Mia is Leif's wife," she explained.

"Ah."

Leif was the new drummer. He had taken Shawn's place after he'd left the band, which I didn't know the details about that, either. Whatever falling out they'd gone through had happened after I'd been cut from the loop.

Emily reached out and squeezed my hand. "She's amazin'. You'll love her. Super sweet. Do you know the band, Sunder?"

I gave a nod. Of course, I knew Sunder. You'd have to live under a rock not to, and considering I kinda did, anyway, meant they were really famous. "Sure."

"She's Lyrik West's younger sister. They met when Leif was playing with Sunder as a fill-in for one of their albums. You'll love both of them. All of Sunder will actually be here for the wedding. I've become really good friends with their wives, and with Carolina George now being under the Stone Industries label, it's brought us all close together."

My head shook. Pride rising high. "Wow…y'all really did make it big."

Mel waved an indulgent hand in the air. "Um…so big…you don't even know. I mean, they played live at the ACB Awards. You can't get any bigger than that."

Emily blushed. "It's not that big a deal."

"Huge deal," Melanie said with her back to us as she arranged the dresses.

"I think it's a pretty big deal," Maggie added in her shy way.

"I do, too," I agreed, smiling at my friend.

Wistfully.

Nostalgia hitting me full-on.

The dreams they'd had. They were going to do whatever it took to chase them down. Reaching for the stars. The only difference was I'd somehow been fool enough to believe I was going to be there with them while they did it.

Not that I was a starfucker.

Wanting a claim to their fame.

I'd just loved them all so much I couldn't wait to see them achieve every single dream.

"We're truly blessed," Emily said as she stared at me for a beat. "Grateful for how far we've come."

"I can't wait to see how far you go."

Finally, I cleared my throat when the tension felt too thick. "Well, we'd better try these dresses on. We've got a weddin' to plan."

"Good idea. In you go, sexy pants." Melanie waved an emphatic hand to my dressing room. "God...these pictures are gonna be amazing. Like, your bridesmaids are legit the most gorgeous women in the world," Melanie said, her attention shifting to Emily.

Emily quirked a brow. "You are one of my bridesmaids."

"And?" she drew out.

I laughed.

Only Mel.

We tried on the dresses, coming out each time we put on a new one to show it off.

Mel gathered up the ones we liked and put the rest in a discard pile for Letty who was running around trying to meet her demands.

After spending two hours with her steering this party, there was no question she was worth every cent of whatever they were paying her to manage the band.

She had it in her blood.

Quick wit and organization and no fear to tell it like it was.

On my second to last dress I'd been given to model, I stepped out of the dressing room. It was a light-rose, clingy dress. It had a ridiculously deep neckline, the material expanding from the cinched straps and widening to cover your breasts, a fitted band that went all the way from beneath the bustline to the waist. The A-line skirt draped to the ground and had a high slit riding up the left leg to expose the thigh.

Sexy and sleek.

Cleavage for days.

Mel's eyes went wide the second she saw me. "Oh my god, that's the one." She pointed at me in glee.

I turned to look in the mirror.

God, it really was stunning.

"Turn a circle." Mel whirled a finger in the air.

I obeyed. It wasn't like I was about to argue with her.

"That's it." She looked at Emily. "What do you think?"

"It is so perfect. Beyond perfect. I think you all should wear this one. Forget the mismatched look."

Emily turned to Maggie. "What do you think?" she asked, hopefully, but with some kind of concern that I didn't understand.

"I think I would be honored to wear that dress in yours and my brother's wedding."

Melanie squealed. Threw herself at Emily. Hugged her tight. "I can't believe you're actually gettin' married. For real this time. And not to that fucknugget, Nile."

Emily scowled but let go of a barking laugh. "Wow. Thanks for bringing up my ex."

"Hey, just a friendly reminder that sometimes when you think your life is falling apart, it's actually shaking you up and setting you on the right path to get you where you're really supposed to go. I.E. Royce's bed."

Emily smacked her arm. "God, Mel."

Mel laughed. "What? We all know that's where you want to live. Pretty sure that baby in your belly is proof of that."

Maggie smiled a shy grin. "I can't wait to be an aunt. I hope a ton of times. You just go on living there."

"Um, okay you two. I think Maggie is going to have to stop hanging around Mel."

Melanie swatted at her. "Not a chance. I love her. She's mine," she breezed as she carried the dress over to Letty. "We're actually going to go with this dress for everyone. I've sent everyone's sizes over to you via email. Except for Violet. She needs to be fitted. You're sure you can get these expedited in time?"

"Absolutely."

"Great. Now...on to *the* dress."

Letty smiled wide. "The dress."

She pulled the garment bag from the hook where it waited. The name of one of those uber famous wedding dress designers embroidered down the side.

"The dress," Emily wheezed, biting down on her lip.

Emily was ushered into one of the larger rooms with Letty to help her, and a few minutes later, she came out wearing the most gorgeous dress I'd ever seen.

Mel was right—these pictures were going to be incredible.

Emily stepped onto the round riser with mirrors angled all around it. The satiny white single-shoulder dress clung to every curve of her body. Fitted from top to bottom with a slit running up one side.

Her baby bump was just beginning to show.

She set her hand on the tiny swell, and I could see the tear slip from her eye.

A joyous, awe-filled tear.

I met her gaze through the mirror, mouthed, "You are so beautiful. I'm so happy for you."

She shifted just a fraction to look back at me. "Do you remember when we were doing this for you? How beautiful you were standing up here?"

Her words struck me like an arrow. A stake that pierced all the way through. I'd been trying to forget. Not to make these memories about me, just like I'd been trying to do at the tree and failing miserably.

I was pretty sure my face showed it.

"Oh, Vi...I'm sorry. I didn't mean—"

I waved her off to stop her from continuing. "It's fine."

She frowned.

Just like my daddy, she didn't believe me a bit.

An hour later, we were all under an umbrella in front of a cafe drinking iced lattes.

"Why is shopping so exhausting?" Emily groaned as she slumped back in the chair and took a sip from her straw.

"Uh...because you never have to do it. You have a personal shopper. Hello, remember me?" Mel gestured to herself.

"Thank God."

"Um, yes, thank God. Could you imagine if I let you get on a stage left to your own devices? The band would've had to kick you a long time ago."

"Hey," Emily whined with a smile.

"What? You'd probably try to get up there without a lick of makeup and the pajamas you were wearing the night before."

"Call me a trendsetter."

"I would think slob would be more fittin'." Melanie grinned.

Emily laughed, then sighed, her mood shifting to serious as she glanced between each of us. "Thank you for doing this, for bein' a part of my wedding. This is the most important day of my life, and I couldn't imagine a single one of you not being there to share it with me."

That disquiet rumbled. The feeling I'd been fighting all day. The unease of standing up there in that same spot with Richard so near.

I'd grown accustomed to it with the other weddings we hosted. Was able to block it out. Make it a part of the job on our land and nothing more. It wasn't like the tree wasn't sitting in that very spot day after day, anyway.

But this...this was different.

This was intimate.

Important.

My family that was no longer really my family, and I no longer knew how to fit.

Maggie touched my knee where she sat next to me. "Are you okay?"

Empath.

I was sure of it.

I sent her a soft, shaky smile. "Of course."

She frowned, not biting the lie. "I know I don't know you that well, and it isn't my place, but...but what I said earlier about seeing your face when Daisy fell?"

Unsure of what she was getting at, I managed a tight nod.

"I saw your face the whole time we were at your farm. From the second we drove up until you were leaving to the E.R. The way you looked at him."

Undoubtedly, Emily had told her about mine and Richard's history.

I swallowed down the tears I could feel burning at the back of my throat. "Sometimes it's hard looking into the past."

"It looked to me like you were looking at what should have been your future."

"That's the same thing, isn't it?" I asked her, confused and uneasy.

Maggie shook her head. "No. Looking into your past, you might miss it, but you know it's over. That's not what your expression was saying, and it sure wasn't what Richard's was saying, either."

Wow.

Okay.

I was getting read by a nineteen-year-old. I guessed I really was transparent.

Melanie laughed a quiet, wry sound. "You should have seen him on the way over there. Man looked like he was going to come out of his skin and the only thing that was gonna be left was his big bleeding heart and his poor, miserable, lonely dick."

"Melanie," Emily scolded below her breath.

"What? You know it's the truth. That guy is always on edge,

wound up like a kite, high and then low."

I frowned. "That doesn't sound like him at all."

He was ferocity. Intensity. The beauty in his soul pouring from his heart and through his fingers.

A shining light wherever he went.

Mel leaned forward and rested her elbows on the table, sipping her drink and staring over at me. "A man changes when he gets his heart broken."

I scoffed. I couldn't help it. "I think it was the other way around."

"Maybe he broke his own," Mel hedged.

Emily was nervously chewing her bottom lip, looking between us. Whatever she'd been trying to hold back came spewing out, "You two went on a date last night?"

"Oh my god," Melanie gushed and smacked her hand on the table. "I knew it. I knew it, I knew it, I knew it."

"It was not a date," I hissed low, holding it back like it was a secret and like the whole town wouldn't know by then about the debacle that had unfolded in the middle of the restaurant.

"He took you to dinner," Emily argued, pushing, searching my face when she did.

"He just wanted to talk."

"And that's it? You just talked?" Emily's brow pitched high in speculation.

Redness raced. Blood sloshing at the reminder. At the thoughts that slammed me in prickly, lustful bits.

I dropped my head a fraction to hide it.

"Oh my god," Emily whispered and edged forward. "Did you—"

"God, no."

Except it was close.

Oh god, had it been close. Me nearly fully giving in, wanting him so desperately that I felt like I might physically succumb.

Death by celibacy.

Mel angled down, trying to see my face. "Look at her, Emily. She is lyin' through her teeth. What did you two get up to last night?"

"Something I am sure to regret," I admitted, wondering why I was trying to deny it in the first place.

The evidence was written all over me.

The testimony of my bleeding, mangled heart.

Melanie slammed her hand down again. "I knew it. Finally, Richard got himself a little lovin'. Maybe he'll stop being such a Mr. Crabby Pants. All that pent-up energy and a giant dick and no one to sink it into—now that is one volatile combination."

Her assertion was all kinds of solemn with a dash of amusement.

My eyes widened, and Emily smacked her on the shoulder. "What in the world is wrong with you?"

Mel shrugged. "I'm not going to apologize for telling the truth to my friend. Besides, stumbling in on Richard and Rhys in various states of undress while on tour is a hazard of my job."

Maggie giggled in embarrassment. Maybe a little interest, too.

Cheeks pinking when she dropped her head to hide it.

"That's it, all your hotel key cards are gettin' revoked," Emily told Mel.

But I was staring across at Mel, taken aback again by what she'd said. Trying not to believe it. For it not to matter.

"Is it true?" It came rasping out without my full consent, words scraping my raw throat, cutting me open wide to reveal the pain that wouldn't abate.

And I didn't mean the size of his dick. I was already well-acquainted with that.

"That he's been alone since you?" Melanie clarified.

My nod was brittle.

Mel's lips pressed together, grim and sure. "I'm not with him every second of every day, Violet. But never in the last six years have I known him to even acknowledge another woman other than a polite hello, let alone sleep with one. It would shock the hell out of me to learn that he had. That's the truth."

Maggie touched my knee again. "See. The future."

But I didn't know how to have a dream of a future with a man when he had been the downfall of the past.

Violet

*T*wilight hung across the skyline in swaths of pinks and lavenders and blues as I eased up the drive to our house sitting on the hill.

I was still reeling. Reeling from last night and today and all the things that felt like they were catching up to me. The threat of destruction all around. Too many uncertainties to feel stable.

Whole or sound.

The world trembling underfoot.

I parked my truck in front of the porch and killed the loud engine.

Daisy came barreling out, her arms in the air and her goodness bursting from her tiny, innocent spirit, black hair flying around her precious face.

My chest squeezed. My heart in a fist.

This was the good.

The right.

The purpose of *everything.*

I climbed out of the truck and caught her in my arms.

"Mommy! I missed you. Did you have the best day tryin' on all the dresses? Did you get one? I bet you are gonna be the prettiest, prettiest ever. Except for your *prettiest* picture. Now that is the real prettiest."

She'd always been a smidge obsessed with the mystery of my wedding picture. The unknown man who had stood by my side. The one who was supposed to remain there but had left me high and dry.

I hadn't had the heart to get rid of it.

She'd only become more interested in it now that she had a name to the face.

"It was a great day. And yep, we found the perfect dress to go along with Emily's."

She grinned as she looked at me, her cheeks pink and her dark eyes dancing with unending joy.

My heart.

My heart.

It panged.

Shivered in the distress of uncertainty and clutched in those sparks of hope that were growing brighter with every second.

"I am so, so excited to wear mine. Did you know it came in the mail today from the package man? Papa let me try it on. It's sooo pretty with my new, new shoes, and my cast doesn't even look a little bit bad in it."

She lifted her broken wing.

I touched her chin. Devotion rode free on the waves of affection that pressed from my being. "You will be the prettiest little hostess in the whole world."

Daisy beamed. A ray of light. "Come on, you've gotsta see it. I bet Mr. Richard will think I'm so pretty."

Yeah.

Obsessed.

I understood the affliction.

She dragged me inside and upstairs to her room where she'd

ripped apart the box, packaging strewn, her dress a crumpled mess on her bed. "Papa said I haves to be so careful not to get it dirty so I can't play with it until the special day."

"That's a great idea," I told her as she was whipping off her shirt and fumbling into the fluffy pink dress that I had ordered online, my little whirlwind shrugging into the garment and struggling to get it on over her cast.

"Let me help you," I told her, situating it over the bulkiness of her arm and helping her to get it over her body.

She slid her feet into those shoes that I worried were going to be worn out before the wedding day two weeks from now. She brushed the wild mane out of her face with two hands, grinning in the floor-length mirror hanging on the back of her door. She swayed from side-to-side. "See, Mommy! It's so pretty. I loves it." She squeezed her hands together in a grateful prayer.

I edged up behind her, planted a kiss to the top of her head, fought the tumble of fear I felt.

This unending worry that I was stumbling toward something I wouldn't recover from.

But I would fight for her.

For the best thing for her.

Whatever that was.

"You are so beautiful. Inside and out. My sunshine," I whispered.

She grinned wider. "Take a picture and send it to Mr. Richard."

I cringed.

She frowned. "You don't like him?"

She touched the handwriting on her cast, and my eyes were drawn to the inscription he'd left.

Daisy, a precious, perfect flower. Never be afraid to explore, learn, and bloom. Grow with all the love because love is what you are.

"No, sweetheart, I don't *dislike* him. Things are just very complicated between us."

"But you love him?" she asked almost carefully. Hopefully.

"I used to. A lot. But that was a long time ago." My words were soft. Cautious. I wouldn't lie to my child, but she sure didn't need to hear the sordid details.

"I think he loves you a lot a lot."

My spirit thrashed, and I met her gaze through the mirror, fiddling with an errant lock of her hair. "Why would you say that?"

"Because he looks at you that special way. Like when Papa looks at Nana."

Old sadness pulsed. "I don't think so, sweetheart."

Except sayin' it felt like a lie. The confessions he had left me with. The way he'd touched me. The way he'd looked at me in the very way that Daisy was talking about.

Like I was the stars in his sky.

Endless.

The light at the end of his forever that he had promised to me.

"I know so." It wasn't even an argument.

I shifted her around and knelt in front of her, pushing back the disaster of hair from her face, trying to frame it into words that she might understand. "I think he used to love me that way. Maybe it just makes him sad when he looks at me and remembers what that was like."

"No, Mommy. I see it. Amor, amor, amor." She sang it like a love song the way my daddy would.

My heart clutched. "You are the amor." I barely managed to get it out around the emotion that warbled in my throat.

"We all got amor," she told me, resolute. Her voice dropped to a secretive whisper when she said, "Mr. Richard, too."

I pressed a kiss to her forehead because I couldn't answer it or respond to it. There were too many questions that swirled and toiled and dug up the dirt on the grave that had been our marriage.

Ripping me to shreds.

Eddies of distrust and surges of the need to believe. The hope I'd always sworn I would cling to but was terrified I'd only be a fool to trust in now.

Terrified of letting myself go. Of giving in. Because if I lost him again...

My chest nearly caved at the thought.

I tipped up her chin, my sweet child looking up at me with all the faith in the world. Trusting me to give her the right answers when I couldn't seem to come up with a proper answer for a single one.

"Every person deserves to be loved, Daisy. Every single one."

But no one deserved to be destroyed the way he'd destroyed me.

"And sometimes people are so, so sad, and they need to be loved an extra little bit."

God.

This child.

I touched her nose with mine. A soft caress. "Sometimes I think your heart is too big."

She stared at me, our eyes connected, our souls one when we were together.

This child that hadn't grown of my body but was one-hundred-percent mine.

"I just need it to grow big enough to be as big as yours, Mommy...then I'll be perfect."

I choked over the emotion lodged in my throat. "You are perfect."

Before I fell apart right there, I gathered myself and pushed to standing. "Okay, let's get that dress off so we can keep it clean for the ceremony."

"Picture first." There she was, right back to that.

She actually propped her hands on her hips.

How she went from the sweetest little thing in the world to cheeky in a second flat, I'd never know.

Exasperation blew between my lips. "Fine, sassy pants."

I pulled my phone from my pocket and snapped a picture of her grinning like mad. Nothing but dimples and adorableness.

"Send it."

I widened my eyes at her in feigned annoyance.

She giggled.

I tapped into my text thread with Emily and attached the picture with my message.

Me: Daisy wanted to say thank you for the shoes and let you know she's ready to help with the wedding. If you could forward to your mom and Richard to say thank you,

that would be great. Don't worry, we'll actually make sure her hair is brushed for the ceremony.

I capped it with a winky face.

There. That was painless. The right thing to do. Richard would get his thanks, but it wouldn't come directly from me, not that I had his number, anyway.

"Now scoot and get that dress off."

"Okay, Mommy."

She changed back into her regular clothes and then at the first intonation of my daddy singing in the kitchen, she went racing downstairs to help him with dinner.

Soft sorrow filled my smile when she disappeared, this overwhelming mix of love and grief and dread.

I fought it.

But I could feel myself coming up to a ledge.

A steep cliff that was eroding.

This trembling sense that everything was gonna shift and change.

I followed her out of her room only to pop my head into my mama's. She was asleep, dragging in deep, uneven breaths. I eased in as silent as I could, pressed a lingering kiss to her cheek, and brushed back the sticky, damp hair clinging to her forehead.

That grief tried to become a stronghold. To fully take me over.

I forced it down and left as quietly as I'd come, heading downstairs. My phone buzzed in my pocket.

Emily: Oh my god, she is sooooooo adorbs! Tell her I can't wait for her to help. Give her kisses from Auntie Emily. <3 <3

My guts twisted. God, I'd gotten too close too fast. Danger lurking all around. My heart at risk. It'd already been battered so desperately I didn't know if I could handle it all again. Getting wound up in their lives. I was already achin' thinking about them leaving again after the wedding.

I was letting pieces of myself go when I knew full well I

shouldn't. Richard was already chiseling out more of the broken pieces that were barely being held together as it was. The problem was, they'd always belonged to him, anyway.

From the second I'd seen him.

The man my downfall.

My dark night sky.

A million glittering stars that I could never reach far enough to touch.

The hell I'd never imagined I'd be sentenced to.

I walked into the kitchen to Daisy standing on her stool next to my daddy, washing the potatoes for dinner.

"You got a message, Daisy."

Her eyes lit in excitement. "From Mr. Richard?"

Daddy grumbled his disapproval.

"Nope. From Emily. She said the dress is perfect, and she can't wait for you to help with the wedding."

"Yay!" she sang.

I kissed her cheek. "I need to head out to the workshop and get a few things in order for deliveries in the mornin'. Shoot me a text when dinner is ready?"

This I addressed to my daddy who was watching me with concern and all his fatherly love. "You work too hard."

A soft giggle rippled out. "What are you talkin' about? I took the whole day off. If I keep it up, you're going to have to find someone more worthy to fill your shoes."

He tipped up my chin in a show of affection. "You've overfilled my shoes. Look at the land."

He gestured out the kitchen window that overlooked the abundantly colored fields.

Pride pressed at my ribs. "I had a good teacher."

His smile was adoring. "And I had the best student."

"The best!" Daisy shouted her agreement.

On light laughter, I kissed them both again before I headed out the back door and down the porch steps to where the world was darkening, the solar lights lining the path flickering to life, illuminating the trail in a glittering haze.

My phone buzzed again, and I clicked into the message.

It was from a number that wasn't in my contacts. It didn't take a whole lot to decipher who it was from.

Richard: Beautiful. Like her mother.

I knew he wasn't referring to my sister, and somehow that hurt, too. That he would assert it. That he was doing this to me.

Me: She is beautiful. Innocent. Vulnerable.

I sent my warning.
My phone buzzed back a second later, more texts following right behind.

Richard: I'd never hurt her. Just like I never wanted to hurt you. Last night was…

Richard: It was magic, Violet. Fucking magic. I almost forgot how perfect we are together, and the only reason I tried to put it out of my mind was for my own sanity, dyin' from missing you.

Richard: But like you said—I'm insane. Insane with my love for you. My need for you.

My stomach climbed to my chest, that energy flapping with the butterflies that spread their wings in my belly. I tapped out a response while I begged my foolish heart to build up a resistance.

Me: Last night was a mistake.

Richard: No. It might have scared you, but you and I both know it wasn't a mistake. We never were. It was all the other decisions surrounding it that were wrong.

Tears blurred my eyes.

Me: I need to go.

I couldn't handle it, the man feeding me lines so sweet they were going to decimate my logic and leave me massacred in the end.

I wasn't expecting another message, but my phone buzzed again.

Richard: And I need you to stay. Need to keep close. Please, just be safe.

What the hell was he trying to say?

Unable to handle it, I shoved my phone into my pocket and continued to wind down the long path. When I made it to the workshop, I entered the code to open the door, propped it open, flicked on the lights, and powered up the old MacBook I kept in there on my desk so I could verify the orders that needed to go out tomorrow.

The sounds of the night surrounded me, the peace of this place, and I got lost in my work. I focused on the minute details to ensure each order was perfect. Nothing forgotten. It might not seem like a whole lot to some people, but this job was so important to me.

The fact that flowers brought joy.

They expressed grief.

They showed love.

A message given in each one.

So engrossed in it, I jumped when my phone started to ring on the desk beside me.

Those nerves doubled when I saw the caller ID.

The private investigator.

Heart jolting in fear, I rushed to grab it with trembling hands, answering, "Hello, this is Violet Marin."

It was the worst feeling being desperate for news and, at the same time, praying there wouldn't be any.

Guilt flooded my being.

Wave after wave.

How selfish did that make me? What kind of person would make a wish so wicked?

"Hello, Violet. This is David Jacobs."

"Mr. Jacobs. Have you found something?"

"Possibly. We tracked her to California. Do you recognize the name Martin Jennings?"

My pulse chugged like I was trying to wake from a bad dream, my mind sifting through the memories and faces.

It landed on one night in Hollywood.

My sister's birthday years before. She and I had flown out there for the weekend because Carolina George had been in talks with a record label.

Mylton Records.

A disturbance curled through my belly.

A face flashed through my mind.

Slicked back blond hair and a smarmy smile on his arrogant face.

Martin Jennings had been the Mylton Records exec that had taken us out to a fancy dinner. The one who'd been sent to schmooze and flatter and fawn over the band. Show them a good time. Convince them signing on that dotted line was going to catapult them to stardom.

After the few things I'd heard about that company, it was clear falling for it would have been a bad call.

"Yes. I met him once…years ago," I forced out.

"I found her in a picture with him dating back to close to six years ago. She was pregnant in the image."

My stomach twisted in confusion. She'd only met him that one time.

"Are you sure?"

"I'm going to forward it to you for verification."

"Okay. Could she be with him?" My words hitched in my throat. The plea right there. The walls beginning to spin.

Closing me in.

"Unfortunately, or fortunately, however you want to look at it, no. Five years ago, he was sentenced to life in prison in connection with the death of a man named Mark Kennedy. Mark was the original drummer of the band, Sunder."

What?

Fear slugged through my veins, and my stomach completely bottomed out.

Terror whipping up a storm.

Trying to connect the dots.

We'd only been in Los Angeles for two days. My mind raced back to that time. How it had gone down. Parts of it were still a gutting blur in my mind.

Lily had only come home for a couple days after, and then she'd been gone.

I'd thought she was spreading her wings.

Finding herself.

Nine months later, she'd been abandoning that precious baby girl at my doorstep.

I'd been so overwrought with despair and the new life I'd been given, adjusting, trying to make sense, that I'd never put the dates together.

"And you haven't found anything since? No pictures? No word?" The words left me on sheer desperation. "Someone has to know something. Someone has to have seen her."

He blew out a sigh. "I don't have anything solid at the moment, but I think we're getting close."

There was something he wasn't telling me. I could feel it.

Unsettled waves lapped high.

"Do you think she's alive?" It rasped from the depths of me. Hope and apprehension and all the things I didn't know how to process.

"I can't tell you that, Ms. Marin. I don't want to speculate. The only thing I know is I believe I've picked up on a trail that I might be able to follow. Be patient. This is probably going to take a little time."

Time.

Always time.

My heart reached for the house where my mama rested. Where the cancer ate away at her body while her soul continued to glimmer with hope.

And I knew…I knew we were running out of time.

"Okay. But please…do your best to find her. We need to find her soon."

"I will."

Hands trembling like mad, I ended the call, set my phone on the desk, and dropped my face into my hands.

The urge to cry was overwhelming.

Guts twisted.

So much hope.

So much horror.

The thought of reclaiming one of the most important people to me and losing another was so hard to bear.

The truth that sometimes to gain a piece of your heart, you had to let another go.

I had no idea how much time passed like that. Lost to the worry. Minutes or an hour.

When I froze.

Dread lifted the fine hairs at the nape of my neck.

Prickles a flashfire.

Awareness that pushed nausea up my throat and sent my pulse slugging in fear.

The crunch of a footstep.

But it was the evil that I could feel invading the space that made me want to throw up.

I started to whirl around but couldn't before those footsteps stampeded and something was pulled over my head.

Darkness took me hostage.

Disorienting.

Suffocating.

It was a bag that was cinched down tight.

A scream ripped up my throat, and panic flooded my system. Rushing and gripping and beating my heart into mayhem.

What was happening? Oh god. What was happening?

I flailed, trying to rip the bag from my face.

Two arms locked around me from behind and dragged me from the stool, my legs knocking it over as I was yanked into the air.

The sound of the metal clattering against the concrete floor was deafening.

Reverberating through the chaos.

"What do you want? Don't touch me. Who are you?" I shrieked as I kicked and clawed and thrashed, but my arms were pinned to my sides.

Overpowered.

Unable to break free.

In the flash of a second, I was flying, thrown to the ground. I crashed against the hard floor.

Pain splintered up my shoulder, and a wail tore from my throat.

Terror rushed, surged, and clouded my thoughts.

"Help," I moaned and choked, dazed, completely caught off guard and turned around and clueless to what was happening.

Darkness blinding.

Unable to see my attacker.

Unable to anticipate what was coming next.

I made it to my hands and knees, and I started to crawl across the floor, hands feeling around to try to make an escape.

There was no bracing myself for the blow.

No preparing myself for the searing agony when I was kicked in the stomach from out of nowhere.

A haggard cry screamed from my throat, and I curled into a ball on my side in the staggering agony.

I gasped, writhed, tried to get back onto my hands and knees.

To find a way out.

But there was no escape.

No fighting someone who wasn't fightin' fair.

A vicious voice growled at my ear, "You shouldn't go diggin' up graves. You never know when you might fall in."

That was the only thing I heard before a fist landed on my cheek.

So hard it shot me straight into a dark, bottomless abyss.

Richard

I sped through the night with the accelerator pushed all the way
to the floorboards. Vision a haze of red.

Fury and fear.

Sickness clawing at my insides. Eatin' me alive.

I skidded into the parking lot of the hospital where I'd been
with Violet and Daisy only a few nights before. But tonight, it was
completely different.

Ominous and dark. A foreboding that sagged and shivered in
the night.

I flew into a parking spot, and I was out of my truck in a blip
of time that hardly existed and still seemed to go on forever,
sprinting into the emergency room entrance. First thing I saw was
her father pacing in the waiting room.

His attention snapped up when he felt me coming like an

earthquake.

That's what I felt like. Pummeling the earth with my fists until I shook down whoever was stupid enough to hurt her. Hunt down the motherfucker. Skin him alive. Stand for this girl who I should have been standing for all along.

"Where is she? Is she okay? What happened?" I blurted the second I got to him.

He glowered with the force of a nuclear power plant. "How dare you show your face in this place."

The outrage of it should have blown me back, but I stood ground.

"She's my wife."

"You no longer get to claim that."

I angled toward him. No matter how much I respected him, I wasn't about to stand down. "You have every right to hate me, Mr. Marin. I get it. Accept it. But she is *my* wife, and I'm not going anywhere."

His protective demeanor shifted, his shoulders sagging to the floor, horror in his expression.

"She was beaten." The words fumbled from his mouth in a roll of confusion. "I...I called the ambulance when I found her. Who would do this?"

Rage singed through my body. A flashfire. Nothing left but the need to hunt down whoever had done this.

Had promised her that I wouldn't let anything happen to her. And this?

Guilt clutched me by the aching throat, and I swallowed it down, focused on the only thing I could change.

The one thing I could do.

Protect her.

"Where is she? Is she okay?"

When Emily had woken me, she didn't have any information other than Violet's father had called her from his car in hysterics, asking her if she could come pick up Daisy at the hospital since he couldn't leave her with Mrs. Marin.

They didn't have anyone else they could trust.

I was flying out the door ahead of Emily before she could stop me.

Wasn't like my sister didn't know what reaction she was going to get out of me, anyway.

His head shook.

"I do not know. I cannot bear to take Daisy back there."

Helplessly, he gestured to the little girl who was curled up on two plastic chairs, her head propped on a rolled-up blanket that had been ripped off her bed, child fast asleep.

My spirit throbbed.

Affection rushed to occupy my chest.

A straight-up invasion.

It got whipped up with the intense need to decimate.

To destroy.

"Give me one second."

Panic seizing my breaths, I moved to the reception desk, voice a desperate growl, "You have a patient...my wife...Violet Ramsey. Need to know where she is."

Knew she went by Marin. But legally? She was mine.

Mine.

My wife.

My reason.

My life.

My light.

The woman clicked into her computer before she looked up at me. "She's in room 3B. You can go back."

That was right when Emily and Royce came rushing in. Worry was written all over my sister's face, her attention darting everywhere, looking for an answer. "Oh god...Rich...what's goin' on? Have you heard anything? Is Violet okay?"

"We don't know yet. We need to get back there. Watch Daisy so I can take her father back, yeah?"

Her brow pinched. "Of course."

We moved back to Mr. Marin who had sunk down onto the chair next to Daisy.

Helplessness slumped his shoulders. The man weary and worn. Weathered and worn to the brittle bone.

I curled my hand around his shoulder. "Come with me. Emily

and Royce will see to it that Daisy is safe."

I sent Royce a look at that. My eyes cutting with the message.

Guard that little girl with your life.

Evil's afoot.

He gave me a clipped nod, tat on his throat bobbing with aggression, hands already in fists.

Mr. Marin pushed to his feet, and I kept a hand on his upper arm to guide him toward the double doors. The receptionist buzzed us through.

Anxiety battered me with each step.

Heart on the thrashing floor.

Because I would never fuckin' forgive myself if something happened to this girl.

If I failed again.

My eyes jumped over the numbers outside the draped-off enclosures.

Second I saw hers, we moved that way, my heart beating a storm of chaos.

I pushed the drape aside, holding my breath, and I peered in to find Violet propped up on the bed.

Eyes open.

Heart beating.

Brutalized but whole.

Relief rocked me. Body and soul and mind. It butted with the rage that curled and twisted and glowed like a hot iron searing a brand on my spirit.

A crush of protectiveness rose so fast that I couldn't see.

Couldn't feel anything but the need to hold this girl.

Care for her.

Love her the way she'd always deserved to be.

My eyes swept her. From her head to her feet and back to that gorgeous face again.

That fury flashed. Hatred boiling my blood when I saw the way her jaw was swollen, clearly taking the brunt impact of a fist.

But it was the fear and shock in those violet eyes that was going to destroy me.

"Oh, mi amor," her father wheezed in pain from my side when

he caught sight of his daughter.

"Daddy," she whispered.

He rushed to her side while I hung back at the far side of the enclosure.

He flitted around her, uncertain, desperate to make it better but having no idea how to make it right.

I did.

Hunting the fucker down and ending him sounded about right.

Thunderbolt eyes found mine from across the space.

Energy lashed. Surges of intensity. Of possession. Of greed.

I eased that way, going around to the opposite side of the bed from where her father was.

I was struck with her aura.

Violets and dreams and the girl.

The one real thing in my life.

Light. Light. Light.

Compelled, I leaned in, unable to stop myself. I brushed back the hair matted to her cheek, my gaze adoring as I stared down at this girl who'd been battered. And for the sake of what?

"Are you okay?" It raked from my throat. Barbs and thorns. "Tell me who did this to you."

"Why are you here?" she asked instead of answering.

I kept brushing my fingers tenderly through her hair. "Because I don't know how to be where you are not."

"Richard—"

My head shook to cut off the defense I knew she was going to give. "Not going anywhere, Violet. This? This just fortifies that. I never should have left you. Never."

Those eyes softened, but in them swam the turmoil. Confusion and pain and fear.

"Tell me you're okay." Didn't mean for it to come out a demand, but that was honestly the only answer I could handle.

She heaved out a mirthless laugh. "Physically? Yes. Or at least I'm gonna be. The rest of me, I'm not so sure."

I attempted to rein in the fury, but it was getting loose. Seeping from its confines and igniting in my bloodstream. "Did you see the attacker?"

Violet winced when she barely moved. That made me want to end someone, too. "No. I didn't see anyone. Didn't get a chance to before a bag was pulled over my head to keep me from seeing." She blinked rapidly. "I don't understand...why would anyone attack me that way?"

Anger grabbed me, claws sinking into my flesh.

Terrified that I'd brought this to her doorstep.

My mind immediately moved to that prick who'd shown on our property, prying for something.

I forced the words around the tight clamp in my throat, "Did he say anything? Say what he wanted?"

Fear blanched her face, and Violet's throat trembled when she swallowed. "Can we talk about this later? I'm tired."

Her eyes told me there was more. That she couldn't burden her father with more than he was already shouldering.

She turned to him, trying to force a smile, but there was no hiding her worry. "Where's Daisy?"

"Emily came," he assured her. "She is going to watch over her so I can be with you."

Relief flashed across her face before she flinched. "Did she witness anything? Did she see me like this?"

"No," he said. "She was in the house when I went down to check on you when you didn't answer my texts or calls. I made sure she stayed inside while the paramedics attended to you."

His words were a balm, the girl slumping down lower, her shoulders sinking into the bed. "Thank God. I can't...if something would have happened to her—"

I was back to holding her face.

Not with force.

With care.

With the love that was never going to stop. "It won't. Won't let anyone get near her. Just like I won't let anyone get near you again."

The promise echoed through the tiny space, and her dried lips parted, those eyes watching me like they were desperate for a way to believe.

Mr. Marin edged forward and captured her attention. "I'm so

sorry, mija. I am so sorry."

A frown dented between her eyes. "It's not your fault."

"How could I not have known someone was on my land? How was I not there to protect you?"

Grief churned through his eyes.

I touched his shoulder. "It's not your fault. You couldn't have known. I won't let anything happen to her again."

I was going to end this.

Ensure she was safe.

My attention drifted back to her. She was fighting tears. Wisps of that black hair was spread out on the pillow, girl so pretty it hurt.

My dream.

My fantasy.

Battered and bruised.

"You need to rest," I murmured, "I'm sure the doctor will be in soon enough to poke and prod you."

She almost smiled at that, and I wound her hand in mine, brought her knuckles to my lips, whispered, "Why don't you sleep a bit until then? We'll be right here. Watching over you. You don't have to be afraid."

She nodded again, and her eyes dropped closed.

I sat down on the hard-plastic chair next to her while she slept. Her father was on the other side. Both of us refusing to budge.

Two of us just…watching over her.

An hour must have passed before he spoke. "Please, don't hurt her again. You already wrecked her spirit. I can't stand to watch you return to ruin her life again."

A knife of shame sliced through me.

"Ruining her is the last thing I want to do," I told him, voice barely loud enough for him to hear.

He looked up at me in a challenge. "Do you know anything else?"

"I'm trying to figure that out. How to be everything she needs me to be."

His gaze drifted back to her sleeping form. "This beautiful girl should never be a test."

Guilt constricted my chest. When he found out what I had done, what would he think? How far would the hatred go? Could there ever be forgiveness?

Didn't expect forgiveness.

Didn't deserve it.

But I'd fight for it anyway.

Give this man back a little of what I'd taken.

The confession left me. No reservations. "I love her. I always have, and I'm not ever going to stop."

He blanched when I claimed it, and his lips pursed in confusion. "Then why would you leave?"

"Need you to know, I never wanted to. I wasn't left with another choice. That choice was taken from me the day I was forced into a battle I'd never signed up to fight. I left because it was the only way to keep her out of it. The last thing I wanted was for her to be a casualty."

His chin lifted, his mouth warbling at the side. "I see secrets in your eyes."

I gave him a tight nod of affirmation.

No sense in denying it. It would only make it worse in the end.

He looked at his daughter before he looked back at me. "Are you responsible for this?"

Knew he wasn't asking if I'd physically hurt her.

Think he already knew the answer to that.

Never.

I gulped down the agony, the fire that burned my throat and blazed through every cell in my body. "Not gonna lie. I've got enemies. And if one of them came to her through me? They will wish they never knew my name."

His throat bobbed. Got the sense he felt the ferocity of what I was saying.

He'd have every right to kick me to the curb.

That's where I belonged.

"There is so much pain in our lives right now. We cannot shoulder another burden. Please…take care of her. Protect her. Protect them."

"I will. I promise you that."

Violet and that little girl? They were mine.

My duty.

I slumped down farther in the chair, watching her sleep. Could do it forever.

Didn't know if I'd started to drift, but I jumped when my phone buzzed in my pocket. I dug it out and swiped into the screen.

Royce: What the fuck, man?

I glanced over at Mr. Marin who had nodded off, his head rocked back against the wall, the rage I'd felt earlier still right there. Bated. Waiting on direction.

Me: Know, man. I know. No chance this isn't related.

Royce: She get a look?

Me: Don't think so. But she got something. Could tell from her expression. I will find out.

I sent another text right behind it.

Me: Daisy?

Royce and Emily had taken Daisy back to our parents' house to sleep. Where we knew she would be safe.

Royce: Currently snuggled up next to Emily in her bed, asleep. Fucking cute.

I almost smiled. Could feel Royce's affection through the miles. Guy wearing this shield of menace that hid the biggest, bleeding heart.

Me: And you got relegated to the chair. Poor bastard.

Royce: Not like I'm sleeping anyway.

I blew out a sigh of relief. Knowing Royce had this. That he would have our backs just as much as I'd always have his.

Me: Thanks, man. I owe you.

Royce: Nah. Family. It's what we do. But you know this is messy? Don't pretend like this complication isn't going to come back to bite you in the ass.

I looked at Violet's sleeping form.
My chest tightened.
Need.
Hope.
Desperation.
Light.
She was no complication. She was the incentive. The purpose. My heart's single goal.

It was close to morning by the time they discharged Violet after she'd given her statement to the police.

My tongue burned with the urge to give mine. To lay it out. But it wasn't time. Couldn't do it until I saw this through to its completion.

With my arm curled around Violet's waist to support her, the three of us stepped out of the sliding doors and into the witching hour. Night so still and deep you could imagine you were slipping into another realm. A time and a place where ghosts and spirits roamed.

Violet didn't even fight me on it. She just leaned into my hold, limping out into the parking lot, making my heart roll and boom and thunder.

Emily had driven Mr. Marin's car home since he had a car seat, so I clicked the locks to my truck, and I helped Violet climb into the front passenger seat.

Her spirit was all around.

Subdued.

Dampened in its uncertainty.

Wary and waiting for what was to come.

We both knew it.

Felt it.

The storm that gathered on the horizon like the sun gathering for the day. Building in energy. In intensity.

Eyes on the girl, hers on me, I reclined her seat a bit and leaned over her so I could buckle her in.

"I've got you," I murmured as I adjusted the belt and then clicked it into the lock, my face an inch from hers when I angled back, voice gruff, "I've got you."

"Richard," she whispered. Needy and low.

I cupped one side of her precious face, my thumb tracing the angle, my soul shouting for its reclaim. "Rest."

Her teeth clamped down on her bottom lip, and she gave a tiny nod. I stepped back and shut the door.

Mr. Marin got into the back seat.

Almost immediately, Violet fell back asleep as I headed in the direction of their house.

Her sweet spirit filled the cab.

Intoxicating.

Fascinating.

Entrancing me in a dream that this girl could be mine.

Really mine.

That I wouldn't have to let her go.

That there was a chance she might not hate me when it was revealed.

Stupid, blind hope.

But that's what it was.

This blinding, obliterating hope burning in me that one day— one day she would look at me and actually see the man I'd wanted to be for her. The husband I'd wanted to be. This girl the treasure.

The goddess.

And I'd be the one worshipping at her feet.

I kept glancing over at her, making sure she was fine, and I kept catching her father staring at me through the rearview mirror. The man unsure. As confused as me. Horrified by what had happened and willing to do anything to keep her safe. Not sure if that was with me or without me.

By the time we were making the final curve along the two-lane road approaching their house, a tinge of gray was striking at the edge of the sky.

It felt like wishing on a new day.

Like maybe there could be a chance that something better could come this way.

My truck bounced as I took the dirt lane and came to a stop in front of their house. I turned off the ignition, looked at the girl, my whole being overtaken.

Every cell compressed.

Filled with this devotion that made it impossible to breathe.

I climbed out and moved around to the passenger door. Mr. Marin warred, torn between stepping in to shield her from me and fully giving me that trust.

"I have her," I said, the words barely breaking the atmosphere.

Still, they sounded of a proclamation.

Truth.

Swallowing hard, he gave a tight nod before he slowly ambled up the porch steps to unlock the door. Knew he wanted to get to his wife, to check on her, even though he'd texted with her a few times through the night to update her, and each time, she had assured him that she was okay.

Not to worry.

To take care of their daughter.

He turned the key in the lock and opened the door.

I angled in so I could release her seat belt, violets filling my nose, overtaking my senses.

Sweet.

Sweet.

Sweet.

I slipped my arms under her and pulled her into my arms.

The weight of her perfect and precious in my hold.

She sighed, muttered my name in her sleep, and burrowed her nose into my shirt. I held her close. Pressed a kiss to her forehead, whispered at her skin, "I've got you."

I climbed to the porch and angled through the door, and her father shut it behind us.

Carefully, I carried her upstairs, ascending to the second floor and through the door to her room.

Without looking back or giving an explanation, I nudged the door shut behind us with my foot and carried her to her bed that was still made. I pulled back the white, lush comforter and lay the girl on the white and gray striped sheets.

A vision of beauty.

The epitome of grace.

She whimpered, and her eyes barely blinked open as I pulled her shoes from her feet.

"Need you," she rambled incoherently.

"You've got me, baby," I promised her. "You've got me. I'm right here. Not going anywhere."

On my knees, I leaned up enough so I could unbutton her jeans, and I pulled them down her slim legs, did my best not to give into the fantasies that wanted to come flying at me at the delectable sight.

Girl an angel.

A lyric.

A song.

I tucked her under the covers, kissed her forehead. Breathed her in and silently promised I would never let anything happen to her again. Then I pushed to standing and headed back downstairs, slipping out into the day that was breaking at the horizon, the darkness being eaten away by the rays of light that climbed over the hill to the east.

My eyes roved over the rolling fields.

To the flowers and down to where I could make out the roof of her workshop at the bottom of the path. My feet carried me that way, heart rate ratcheting with each step that I took, and my spirit clanged against the chains wrapped around my being when I came to where the door still stood partially open.

The local investigators had already done their thing, but I was bettin' they'd come up empty-handed. Because this wouldn't be close to being a hack job.

A professional sent to do someone's dirty business.

I peeked inside, chest squeezing tight. I looked around, searching for a footprint or a sign or a motherfucking presence to still be lurking in the depths.

Silence echoed back.

Glancing out the door, I took in the surroundings, making sure I was in the clear before I pulled out my phone and dialed the number. It rang twice before Kade's voice was on the line.

"Yo, brother. All good?"

Probably not if I was calling at five-thirty in the goddamn morning.

"Violet…my wife…she was attacked." Menace oozed with the words.

"Fuck," he muttered in his gruff voice. "Who?"

"Not sure, but I'm not gonna buy into the idea it was coincidence."

I gulped, tried to see through the blaze of shame. "You need to ask them to reconsider. Think about going to the police."

Kade hissed, words spitting from his mouth, "Not a fucking chance, man. You know what happened the last time someone opened their mouth. Won't risk it."

I roughed an agitated hand over my face, trying to keep cool. I looked at my feet. "Shit. I know. I fucking know. I just…I can't bring this back to Dalton."

It pressed through gritted teeth.

Emphasized.

Fact.

"It's already in Dalton, Richard. Think you know it's always been."

Dread spiraled through my body, and I scraped restless fingers through my hair, my nod reticent. Calculating. Desperate for a different solution.

"You have to see it through," Kade added.

My gaze moved to Violet's workbench, where her computer had been smashed, scrapes on the ground where the stool had been ripped out from under her.

A vile, vicious attack.

"And what if we're running out of time?"

"Then you find a fucking way to stall them. Throw them off. Give them a different path to follow. You change lanes and pretend like you know where you're headed."

Knew exactly where I was headed.

To Violet.

To the child.

"I'll do my best."

He sighed like he heard exactly where my brain had gone. "Don't fuck this up, Richard."

"I won't."

I was going to fix this. All of it.

Ending the call, I clutched the phone in my hand, trying to rein it in, before I started out so I could get back to Violet.

I stumbled in my tracks when the figure stepped out in front of me, cutting off my path.

Saul.

His face twisted in a sneer. "I told you. I told you that you would wreck everything coming here. Everything was fine. Completely fine until you came. She was good."

My attention darted back to the workshop, wondering just how much he'd overheard while a surge of possession slammed me so hard I felt like I ran face-first into a brick wall.

I sucked it down.

"Not in the mood for bullshit this morning."

His head cocked. "No? You in the mood for putting a sweet, innocent girl in danger? Is that what you're in the mood for?"

His taunts filled the crisp morning air.

I sucked it down in an attempt to cool the fire.

Last thing I needed was to expend any energy on this.

"Not doing this with you." I angled around him.

The time of day did not belong to him. It belonged to her.

I started up the path toward the house.

Felt the commotion of his footsteps coming up behind me, the roar of his outcry filling my ears. "You don't deserve her!"

Every muscle in my body tensed. Flexing for the fight. Knew it was coming. The way he plowed into my back. His momentum tossed us both to the ground. Bodies a tumble of ire.

The hate, the jealousy, the possession I'd tried to keep bound wrenched against their chains.

Face in the dirt, I pushed up, scrambling around in a bid to toss him off. He clocked me in the jaw.

Motherfucker.

All that hate broke free, and I had him pinned to his back in a second flat.

Crack. Crack. I landed two quick punches to his face.

A moan of agony ripped from his throat, and his eyes grew round in fear. I gripped two fistfuls of his shirt, lifting him up and slamming him back to the ground.

My teeth gnashed, the threat boiling out from the darkest place in me. "You want to fuck with me, asshole? You're going to learn what that means."

"She's better than you," he wheezed.

No fuckin' shit.

I picked him up and slammed him down again, and then I leaned in and ground the words close to his face, "You don't listen very well, do you? Warned you to stay the fuck away from my wife."

I pushed him deeper into the ground, fighting the urge to bury him there. Before I lost control, I shoved off him and climbed to my feet. I swiped the bitterness from my mouth, dabbing at the dot of blood dripping from the corner of my lip.

Fucker.

Dude laid there glaring up at me, not daring to move. I pointed at him. "Already warned you, asshole. This will be the last time before I personally throw your ass from this farm."

I turned and started to storm up the path, a riot of rage pummeling my insides. Wanting to take it out on the poor bastard who was fighting for what he thought was right. Problem was, he had no fucking clue.

But that was the way—people only saw the surface. Made their judgments. Cast their stones without knowing the full story.

Just a twisted, fucked-up factor of human nature.

Which was the only reason I left the prick breathing.

I was halfway up the hill when he shouted behind me, "You're going to pay for this. I won't sit idle and let you do this."

I slowly turned to look at him from over my shoulder. "Stay out of my way. You don't? You're going to find out what it really means to pay."

Then I turned and left him standing there.

The commitment flaring.

Filling up my chest.

Overwhelming.

Because nothing—nothing in the world was going to stop me from finishing this. From protecting them. From setting one thing right.

Violet

Facedown in my bed, I blinked my eyes open to the rays of
sunlight that slanted through the cracks in the drapes covering the
window. It cut through the shadows that lurked within the
bedroom, but it was the subdued chatter of voices echoing from
downstairs that pulled me from sleep.

Yawning and fighting the exhaustion that threatened to pull me
back under, I stretched and rolled over.

Every inch of my body moaned in protest.

All it took was the riot of pain to send a flashfire of memories
assaulting me.

The fear.

The confusion.

The outright horror.

The attack in the workshop.

Waking up in the emergency room.

Richard showing up with my father.

Him driving me home and seeing to it that I was safe.

What screamed the loudest was the lashing memory of the cruel voice in my ear making that threat. I was sure that I would never forget it.

I scrubbed both hands over my face to break up the images, wishing it were nothing but a bad dream, but I knew full well I had to wake up and face this nightmare.

Forcing myself to climb out of bed, I went straight into my bathroom, cleaned myself up a bit, and pulled on a pair of sleep pants to cover my bare legs.

A shiver rolled over me as I was touched with another memory. This one soft. A loving caress. The man gently undressing me while he promised he would always be there. That he wasn't going anywhere.

Sucking in a stuttered breath, I eased out my door and followed the sound of voices that grew louder the second I stepped out.

The scent of bacon and biscuits hit my senses. A warmth emanating that wrapped me in solace.

Home.

Home.

Home.

I moved down the hall to the narrow set of stairs that led into the kitchen, my back pressed to the wall as I inched down and listened to the muted chaos that was happening at the bottom.

I stopped at the base of the staircase so I could take it in, confusion twisting up my brow and somehow my heart knowing this was the way it should have been all along.

My daddy and Daisy were in their favorite spot, Daisy on her stool standing next to her papa at the counter, two of them singing one of their favorite songs.

My heart swelled, then it nearly tumbled over when my eyes drifted over the rest of the room.

Emily and Maggie were beside Daisy at the counter. Daisy was trying to teach them the words while they chopped up fruit for a salad. Emily's voice so pretty that it danced through the atmosphere on ripples of peace.

Royce, Melanie, and Rhys were at the kitchen table, drinking from mugs of coffee and chatting away like they did it most every mornin'.

Like it was normal.

Like it was right.

My chest pressed full. So tight it was close to overwhelming.

Because sitting at the head of the table was my mama. My mama who was propped up in her wheelchair and drinking from a cup, too.

But it was my knees that were wobbling and my stomach that was tipping when my gaze traveled to the far side of the room. To where the man was standing, leaned against the wall next to the back door with his arms folded over his chest.

Fierce.

Unrelenting.

A warrior who stood guard.

Sage eyes found mine like he'd felt me coming from a mile away.

Our gazes tangled.

Fire crackled in the middle of the room. It was so severe that I guessed the rest of the room must have felt it because every voice fell silent.

Richard pushed off the wall and came toward me. His lithe body vibrated with fury and strength.

Sinewy muscle packed—flexing and twitching.

Little earthquakes trembled underfoot with every step that he took. My breaths came shorter and shallower as he slowly, purposefully closed the distance between us.

And then he was there, standing in front of me.

One massive hand cupped the uninjured side of my face, and the other brushed back the hair that was tousled in disaccord.

This feeling of security infiltrated. Wrapping me like a dream. That dark aura covering me in a shroud of protection.

Hard and savage.

Somehow soft.

Hungry eyes took me in like he was watching the sunrise

breaking the day after living through a total eclipse.

And that's what it felt like—standing in the sun.

"You're awake." Richard's gruff voice scraped through the air and wrapped me like an embrace that I wanted to sink into forever.

Was I terrified? Of him repeating our bad history? Of him leaving me with a crater in the shape of him that I would never recover from?

Yes.

Wholly yes.

I would be a fool not to have reservations.

But there was a bigger part of me that was crying out to be heard. Screaming at me to listen to what was in his cryptic words and see what was hidden in his caring eyes.

"How are you feeling?" Richard's head pitched to the side, his nose so close to mine that he might as well have been kissin' me.

I thought maybe he was actually thinkin' about doing it.

Right there.

Right out in the open.

My attention darted over his shoulder to the mass of faces that were watching us. We might as well have been on the big screen. Our love story playing out in vivid technicolor.

Witnesses to if we would ride off into the sunset or if we were written in tragedy.

I swallowed around the pressure, my tongue darting out to wet my dried, cracked lips. "Sore," I managed to force out.

Richard growled. I didn't know if it was from him watching the action, his needy stare on my lips, or if it was from the anger that blistered across his flesh.

Truth was, the side of my face pounded in a dull, throbbing ache, and my stomach was still agonizing with the blow.

But it was more the fear than anything.

The warning that vile, disgusting voice had hissed in my ear.

"You shouldn't go diggin' up graves. You never know when you might fall in."

A shiver streaked down my spine.

Richard reached out and tipped up my chin, and I knew he was reading me. That he felt the terror wedge itself deep into my psyche. "Won't let anyone touch you."

It was a rumble.

Thunder that boomed through the space.

I nodded at him.

Surrendering to that truth. Believed that whatever was going on, he would do his best to take care of us.

The scraping of chair legs jolted us from the bubble. "Hell no, no one's touchin' you, sweet thing. We've got you."

Rhys had pushed to standing. The brawny, hulking man with dimples in his cheeks actually cracked his knuckles in a show of support.

From where Royce remained sitting like some kind of tatted king in his chair, violence came on a rush, his own show of loyalty, even though he didn't need to say a thing.

My father pushed back from the stove and stood staunch.

I understood it immediately. The fact that everyone was there for me. That they were surrounding me in a hedge of protection.

Steadfast.

Unfailing.

Daisy lifted her unbroken arm and curled it into a fist, her voice a shout of solidarity. "Hell, no. No one's touchin' my mommy!"

I choked out a shocked laugh, and Emily slapped her hand over her mouth to hold hers in, while Melanie fell into a fit of cackled giggles where she sat at the table. "Oh my god...I think Daisy is my soul mate."

Rhys stampeded like a bull across the kitchen and swept my daughter into his arms. He tossed her in the air. "No way, Daisy Mae! We've got her, don't we?"

"Heck, yes!"

"We will prevail!"

"We will prevail!" she parroted.

"We won't back down!"

"No's backin' down!"

"And we won't say bad words!" Rhys slid that right in there like he was still chanting his war song.

Her mouth popped open. "Oopsie."

"You probably shouldn't talk like that, little miss, yeah?" He ruffled her hair. "You know what my mama used to do when she'd catch me saying things I shouldn't say?"

Her eyes went wide. "What?"

"She'd wash my mouth out with soap."

Horror struck her little features. "Soap? But my mouth isn't dirty. I already brushed all my teeth."

"But you're spouting dirty words. You don't be careful, they're gonna grow in there just like the weeds out in the field."

Daisy stuck out her tongue and frantically wiped her tongue with her hand. "Eww...I don't want nothin' growing in there. Yuck."

Rhys chuckled.

She grinned in all her adorableness, and she reached out and tried to pry his mouth open. "I bet you got somethin' real gross growin' in there with all the dirty bad things I bet you say."

Richard released a snort through his nose, trying to contain it, my poor baby girl having no idea the undertone of what she was saying.

Melanie cracked up, her hand smacking the table. "Watch out for that cowboy, Daisy. There are definitely all kinds of dirty, filthy things going on in there."

"Cowboy? How many times do I have to remind you? It's stallion, baby. You know this," he tossed out to Mel.

He turned back to Daisy, dimples denting his cheeks, and he opened his mouth wide. "Anything? Tell me I'm clear. I can't take it. Help. Save me," he sang on a playful plea.

She inspected his tongue before she gripped him by both cheeks, her little fingernails scratching into the scruffy beard he was sporting. "Nope. You're all in the good and safe. Just like we're savin' my mommy."

"Yes, we are."

He glanced at me, the ferocity in his eyes belying the lightness in his tone.

Gratefulness tugged at my mouth.

My daddy clapped his hands together. "Okay, my beautiful people. Let's eat."

Rhys bounced Daisy in his arms. "Woohoo! I'm starving."

"Woohoo!" Daisy sang, too.

Richard wound an arm around my waist like that was the way it was supposed to be.

Casual.

Natural.

Again, like it was done every day.

"Dude's always hungry. You all better make your plates before there's nothing left," he said.

Rhys smacked a hand over his heart. "As if I would be so selfish. I'm nothin' but a giver."

He winked at Maggie when he said it.

Redness climbed her neck and blossomed on her cheeks.

I glanced at my mama who was watching Richard at my side. His hand curled into my opposite hip.

Sinking in.

Standing firm.

And I knew we had so much to talk about.

But right then?

Right then, I needed to rest in this.

In peace.

In family.

In the spark of hope that I could feel illuminating at the edges of the darkness.

Richard pressed a kiss to my temple. "Why don't you go sit down and rest? We'll talk soon."

I felt the undercurrent. There were hard times coming, hard discussions and hard decisions, but they'd gathered here to give me a moment of reprieve.

I nodded and untangled myself from him, kinda wishing that I didn't have to.

I ambled over to the table.

Melanie beamed a smile at me and patted the seat between her and my mama. "Come sit your sexy butt down next to me."

"Sexy butt. Sexy butt." There went Daisy, her little ears way too keen, the child jumping up and down and chanting it where Rhys had set her back onto her stool. "My mommy is a sexy butt."

Melanie covered her eyes. "Crap. Where's my filter for five-year-olds?"

"Pretty sure you left it on the schoolyard in kindergarten," Emily teased, mischief dancing around her while she finished scooping the diced fruit into a big bowl.

I sank down into the chair, my eyes wide and my heart pounding this frantic, beautiful rhythm, hardly able to process the activity happening in my kitchen. More than had been there in years.

The life. The joy. The faith and the hope and the love.

It didn't matter if it felt like things were falling apart.

That I was sitting on a razor-sharp edge.

I could feel the fullness of the peace that climbed the walls and hovered in the air.

Richard moved over to Daisy, and he ran a hand down the back of her head before he leaned down to press a kiss to her crown. "You better watch out or Uncle Rhys is gonna get that soap after you."

Daisy clapped her hand over her mouth. "Oops! There I go, breaking the rules. I guess I really am a Tomfoolery, right, Papa?"

My daddy laughed with soft affection. "Yup. You are nothin' but mischief and tomfooleries."

Affection lifted and soared. My spirit dancing out around me.

I felt the movement to my left, and I glanced that way to my mama spreading her hand out on the table toward me. I twined my fingers with hers. Squeezed tight.

Amor. Amor. Amor.

It banged and shivered and bound.

My daddy filled two plates, and Richard took them from him, crossed the kitchen, and set them in front of me and my mama. "There we go. Before Rhys can get his grubby hands on it." He sent a grin to Mama and then shifted to give me a wink.

Love poured out, gushing from the dam where it was supposed to be contained.

And I thought it might have been the most wonderfully terrifying thing I'd ever felt.

Most of the day gone, we were outside in the backyard. Richard had helped my mama out into the sun where she sat under a blanket in her wheelchair, and Maggie, Emily, Mel, and I had gathered around her.

The guys were playing with Daisy where she climbed the ladder to her slide what had to have been a thousand times, and the three of them took turns catching her at the bottom.

My daddy was napping, exhausted from the trauma from the night before.

Daisy whooped as she hopped onto the platform, rushed across it, and sat back down at the top of the slide. "Here I come! Imma bird, watch me fly!"

She threw her arms into the air and propelled herself into action.

This time it was Royce's turn to catch her, that dark, intimidating man covered in tats with this stoic, fervent spirit. When she got to the bottom, he lifted her and tossed her into the sky, catching her, the little girl squealing and laughing, her joy palpable in the fall air.

Emily inhaled a sharp breath, and she rubbed her hand over the tiny bump on her belly.

Melanie swatted her arm. "Stop drooling over your man. It's unbecoming."

"Um...you're gonna start blaming me now?" Emily tossed her a grin.

Mel laughed. "Okay, okay, fine. Maybe the rest of us are just jealous you snagged yourself one of the good ones. I mean, seriously, look at that fine ass man. Hot as Hades, he sings and plays, and then he goes around looking at you like that. How is that fair? And I know just because you walk around with that ridiculous grin on your face that the man has to be blowing your mind in bed. And I'm over here scrounging through the dregs."

I laughed. "Well, Rhys doesn't look so bad."

"Nope. He sure doesn't," my mama said in her wry, playful

way.

Okay.

I thought we could all agree the man was gorgeous in his over-the-top way.

Big and outrageous and full of life.

Melanie grinned, brows disappearing behind her bangs. "Tell me you don't think Rhys and I are actually a thing?"

"Haven't you always been? I mean…the tension between you two—"

"Is not close to bein' sexual," she cut me off. "He teases the crap out of me, and I give it right back. Honest, kissing that brute would be like kissin' my brother. My role in his life is trying to keep that bad boy in line. Besides, I've seen him in action. Hard pass. Believe me, I was not exaggerating when I told Daisy that boy is nothing but dirt and filth." Mel laughed when she said it.

"I bet there's a whole lot more to him than that filthy exterior," Maggie said, a shot of defensiveness breaking right through the timidity.

Melanie's brown eyes grew wide with mock horror. "Oh, lord, don't let that charm and that body and those dimples get to you. That 'stallion…'"—Mel air-quoted it—"…has starred in far too many rodeos. You do not want to sign up for a ride."

Emily laughed a light sound. "I'm with Maggie…he's not that bad."

Maggie shook her head. "It's… it's not like that…no…never mind."

"Just watch yourself, unless what you're looking for is a little fun. I'm sure he'd be all too happy to oblige. Just don't let your brother know. We don't want to set any fires we can't put out." Mel smirked.

Maggie's eyes flashed up to take in Rhys who had climbed to the top of the playset with Daisy, setting the child on his lap and sliding down with her.

They both had their arms in the air like they were riding a rollercoaster.

At the bottom, they toppled to the ground, both cracking up.

My mama's voice wrapped through the mood. "Oh, good men

come in all shapes and forms and fashions. Not one looks alike. Just the same as bad men. The one thing I've learned in my life is to listen with my heart."

Memories swamped me.

Her hand on my chest when I was a child. When I'd be afraid or nervous or excited to try something new.

Listen with your heart.

My attention moved to Richard who'd snatched Daisy into the security of his arms and was currently darting around the lawn, Rhys trying to catch them, Richard outmaneuvering him with each pass.

Everything ached.

My heart listening too hard, screaming against the rational part of me that was terrified to accept what it heard.

"Talk about finding a man who's all the things." Maggie touched my knee, her head tilting, her moment of fluster shifting to understanding. "Don't see any scraps there."

I tried not to physically react, but it was useless, the way my gaze locked on Richard who kept stealing glimpses of me.

Emily took my hand and squeezed it tight. "No. There are no scraps there. Just a good man who's scarred in so many ways, looking for a way to repair the damage he has done."

She looked over at me in worried inspection. "I thought he was gonna lose his mind when I woke him up last night. I mean, not that we all weren't freaking out, but Richard...I swear I could actually see a piece of him chipped away when I said you were hurt. Or maybe it was a piece being righted. Snapping back into place."

My spirit shivered and thrashed.

Sorrow pulsed through Emily's expression. "I can't believe that happened. Right here on your property."

Fear slithered in a slow slide across my skin. "Neither can I."

"Do you...do you have any idea of who it could have been?"

I swallowed around the knot in my throat, glancing around the property as if it might offer insight. Knowing somehow...somehow it had to do with my sister, which was more terrifying than anything else. "I don't know who it was, but they clearly couldn't say the same thing about me."

This attack was not by chance.

It was targeted.

I knew it all the way down to the depths of my soul.

Emily continued to hold my hand. Mel took the other and then reached for my mama's. Maggie touched my knee.

"You aren't alone," Emily urged, her sweet voice tilted in emphasis. "Not even close. We are all right here with you until we find out who is responsible."

Richard's watch snapped our way, as if he'd felt the potency of the moment. As if he were a part of it. At the center of that promise.

I ignored the sting of tears, gulped down the terror, and pinned on a smile that faltered when I glanced over and noticed that my mama had slumped down farther. Her frail body sagging with exhaustion.

"Mama...you look tired. Why don't we get you inside so you can rest?"

Mama smiled. So much joy that it shattered through me. A balm and destruction. "I am feeling a little tired."

I pushed to standing and moved to lean over her, my hand twining back with hers. I hugged our threaded hands to my chest. "I love seeing your face shine under the sun."

I didn't want to acknowledge the fact that the day had begun to set.

The heavens changing shape. Strewn in hues of pinks and blues and oranges as the day drifted away.

Soon, darkness would come.

She reached up and touched my cheek. "As horrible as last night was, today has been one of my greatest joys. Being out here with you. With your friends. With this beautiful family who has come to surround my baby girl in their love." She lowered her voice, her hand going to the thunder of my chest. "Listen to what it says."

Emotion clutched and squeezed.

Warmth covered me in a bough of shivers when I felt the presence cover me from behind.

Profound severity.

That darkness I wanted to get lost in forever.

I could feel his footsteps as they thudded up the porch steps.

Measured.

Purposed.

Mama touched my chin. "Listen."

I could barely nod around the crash of sensation, and I swiped at the single tear that got free and straightened when Richard came to stand at my side.

As if he'd heard the call from across the yard and come.

He didn't even hesitate. Didn't question.

He edged around me so he could angle down and scoop my mama into his arms.

Care and love and life.

They struck down like thunderbolts of lightning.

Rumbled through the air. A storm hidden to the eye but clear in the mind.

"Are you good?" he rumbled just as deep, curling those arms around my mama tenderly.

Protectively.

"Oh, I am now."

Mischief glinted in her eye.

I choked around a laugh, around the fullness, around the realization that I could feel gathering to a breaking point.

I moved for the back door and held it open so he could carry her inside. His aura covered me when he shifted slightly to carry her through the threshold, and I found myself holding my breath to keep from completely losing myself.

To keep from floating away.

He carried her through the kitchen and living room and started up the stairs, murmuring words I couldn't hear as I trailed along behind at a distance, my pulse stampeding and my spirit rioting as he carried her all the way into her room.

And when I watched him settle her onto her bed, when I saw him adjust her pillows and her blanket, when I recognized he'd given her *this day*, a day to live to its fullest, I knew that was where I wanted to be.

Lost.

And when he knelt at her bedside, when they shared whispered words, when he took her weathered hand in both of his and began to sing in the way that only the man could, I realized I was already there.

Tripping.

Nothing below but the darkness of his abyss.

I was in a free fall.

And there was no chance of stopping *this*.

twenty-eight

Richard

*H*ad you ever experienced a turning point in your life? A single, defining moment that changed everything? I'd venture to say we all had. Probably multiple times.

I could pinpoint a few of mine.

The first time I'd picked up a guitar and felt the freedom of holding it in my hands.

The first time I'd stood on a stage in front of an audience and felt the rush of adrenaline surge with the first beat of the song. The way it felt like flying.

The night I'd met Violet Marin. Yeah, that'd felt like flyin', too.

The night I'd lost her.

And right fucking then.

Violet's mother in my arms as I carried her upstairs, her dark eyes rimmed in violet that were so much like Violet's, the woman watching me in this way that made me certain she could see right through me.

To the guilt.

To the shame.

To the secrets buried underneath.

And still, like there was a bridge of trust that we were crossing together.

Thought my ribs were being cracked open wide, the woman so light it felt like I was carrying papier-mâché. All except for the weight of her spirit.

The fullness of it.

The realness of it.

"I've got you," I found myself saying, repeating what I'd told her daughter.

I've got you.

It was a promise that meant so much more than simply carrying her to her bedroom, same way as I carried her downstairs this morning so she could be in the kitchen with the rest of us when Violet woke up.

It was a promise that I would hold her.

Fight for her.

Fight for her family.

Fight for what was right.

I carried her into her room and situated her onto her bed, adjusted her pillows, and pulled the blanket over her feeble body. "There we go," I murmured softly. "How's that?"

"Perfect." Knew from the way she watched me that it had nothing to do with her getting comfortable in bed.

My smile was meek, riddled with remorse, and I started to back away, but she reached out and gripped me by the hand. "Thank you," she rushed to say.

I sank to my knees at the side of her bed, and I cupped her bony hand in between both of mine. "Don't thank me. I'm the one who's done all the damage."

Her head shook against her pillow. "I never believed that."

Emotion clogged my throat, and I struggled to breathe around it. To pretend like I wasn't affected. Like sitting here at her bedside wasn't killing me. "I wish it weren't true."

Her mouth trembled at the side. "Will you be there for her?" she implored, tendrils of her spirit reaching for me.

Her attention shifted toward the doorway where I could feel Violet hanging back. Observing from the distance.

Mrs. Marin kept her voice low. "My Violet is strong. Fierce and brave. A fighter. She is a quiet warrior. She may have been knocked down, but she will stand. I *know* this. She doesn't need anyone to take care of her. Overshadow her. But she deserves to have someone come alongside her. To support her. To stand for her. Tell me, Richard Ramsey, will you be the one?"

"I will be by her side for as long as she will allow me to be."

Her eyes deepened like she'd seen all the way to a new layer. Dark depths swimming in awareness. "And you need her to come alongside you. To heal the brokenness inside you. To show you the power of forgiveness. To remind you that you deserve it, too. I see it, dear boy."

My forehead dropped to our intertwined hands, and I exhaled a shaky breath. One of apology. "I don't deserve it. But I pray that someday…someday I might."

I squeezed her hands tighter, began to sing, and prayed one day she might forgive me, too.

Rhys had manned the BBQ, dude playing it up, having a good time, when in reality, we were there as guards.

All of us on high alert.

Watching.

Waiting.

The mood had shifted with the faint rays of moonlight that crept into the sky, had shifted with the streaks of clouds that hazed out its light.

Royce kept shooting me glances through dinner. Dude knowing just as well as I did what this meant. What had gone down.

Still hadn't had the chance to talk with Violet in private considering Daisy wouldn't budge on a nap, kid so full of life and loving every second of us being there that I'd had the hardest time pushing it.

Honestly, I'd been thankful for the reprieve.

Thankful to spend the day pretending like I couldn't feel the earth trembling at its seams. Axis tilting. Worlds colliding that weren't ever supposed to meet.

Never should have come back here. Never should have dragged my mess into this town, leaving trouble at the doorstep of the ones I loved most.

But I couldn't change that now.

The goal might remain the same, but I had to split the focus.

From where we were out on the front porch, darkness swimming around us, the hum of bugs trilling in the trees and the sweet floral scent saturating the night, I hugged Daisy tight. "Goodnight, silly bird."

I tickled her side.

She howled with laughter, squeezing my neck tighter. "Goodnight, Mr. Richard. I'll see you so early in the morning. Right when the sun comes up."

Couldn't help my grin when I edged back and ran my hand over the top of her head. "Yeah. I'll see you in the morning."

I wasn't going anywhere.

I was posting myself outside their door. Would sleep on the goddamn lawn if that was what it took.

Reluctantly, I set her onto her feet, catching Violet's wary stare.

The two of us had hovered around each other the entire day.

Magnets that didn't quite touch.

She stretched her hand out for the child. "Come on, Daisy. Let's get you into bed."

"Are you really that sure that I've got to go to sleep? I'm not even tired a little bit."

Of course, she followed it up with a massive yawn.

"I think there's a little bit of tired in there."

"Just this much." Daisy held her fingers in a pinch.

"I think that's enough."

Daisy blew out a flabbergasted sigh. "Fine. Make me miss out on all the fun."

"I think the fun is over for the night, Daisy Mae. Uncle Rhys here is leaving. Don't think there's any more fun to be had." Rhys grinned at her as he gestured to himself.

"Will you come back and play with me tomorrow?"

"I just might."

"Shake it, don't break it." Daisy stuck out her hand for him to shake on it.

Rhys cracked up. "A future ballbuster in the making."

Her nose scrunched in confusion. "Ballbuster? I don't think I kick hard enough to go bustin' any balls."

Between Mel and this clown, the poor kid was going to be scarred.

I smacked Rhys on the back of the head. "Watch it, dude. Little ears."

His hands flew up in surrender and he started to back away. "My bad. My bad."

Asshole shot me a look, mouthed with a grin so only I could see, *You're so fucked. It's all over, man.*

Was over a long time ago. Now it was time to restart.

"Goodnight, everyone. Thank you again for being here today. It means more than you could know," Violet said, her voice cracking.

"We wouldn't have been anywhere else," Emily promised.

Emotion crested from Violet. Could see weariness creeping in, chasing away the solace of the day.

Reality setting in.

Crowds were a good distraction.

Comfort in numbers.

But I think we could see that false security being stripped away.

"Goodnight," everyone else told her before she retreated into the house to get Daisy ready for bed.

Once they disappeared inside, I turned, hands shoved in my pockets. "Thanks for being here."

Rhys clapped me on the shoulder. "Uh, no brainer, man. Who else were you gonna call? Look at me. If I were in trouble, I'd want me on my side, too."

I shoved him off with a laugh. "Dead weight, man, dead weight."

He smacked his hand over his heart. "Blasphemy. You know who's got your back."

I fist bumped him. "Know it. Thank you."

"Always, brother," he told me.

I hugged Mel, Emily, and Maggie, saying goodnight, and the three of them headed for Royce's rental car, Rhys right behind them, each piling in.

Royce hung back, eyes darting over the fields, looking for anything out of place. "It's not right, man."

"Nope," I agreed, rocking back on my heels.

"You gonna be good here with her, or do you want me to stay?"

"I'm good…just watch my parents. Emily. Maggie. Who the fuck knows who they'll be coming for next. No one goes anywhere alone."

No doubt, their goal was sending a message.

A message of fear.

It was the message they'd been perpetrating all along.

My teeth grated.

No more.

Rage pulsed through his expression, our thoughts mirroring the other. "This has to end. All of it."

"It will," I promised him. "We just have to get to the trial."

When we did, this would end.

On a slight nod, he backed away and lifted his chin. "Anything goes amiss? Call. I'll be here."

"I know."

Turning on his heel, he jogged around the front of the car and slipped into the driver's seat. Rhys rolled down the back-passenger window, poked his head out, and slapped his hand on the roof. "Be safe, brother. You need the cavalry, holler, this boy right here is in the mood to do a little ass-kickin'."

"No fightin' for you, cowboy," Mel tossed out, yanking him back inside.

Royce backed out, shooting me a glance of warning while Rhys' razzing voice still carried to my ears. "No fightin'. No lovin'. No drinkin'. What good are you? That's it. You're fired."

"You wish, cowboy. This band would fall apart without me," Mel punted back.

"Cowboy? How many times do I have to tell you, darlin'? It's stallion, baby. Stallion."

"That's it, you're walkin' home. Royce, toss his ass out right here. I can't take another minute."

It was still a tumble of teasing controversy as the car shifted into drive, and I stood there watching until they made it to the end of the long drive and turned left onto the two-lane road.

Second the silence hit, my attention scanned, searching the shadows.

Watching.

Waiting.

Hands itching with the thirst for revenge. To expose it all. Right then and there.

When nothing moved but the leaves on the rustling trees, I blew out a sigh and headed back inside the quiet house.

Most of the lights had been cut. Mr. Marin had turned in about an hour before, curling up at his wife's side.

I sent up a silent promise that I wouldn't fail them this time.

After I locked every lock on the door and rechecked to make sure they were secure, I moved through the living room and into the kitchen, dipping out onto the back porch, doing the same inspection as out front.

Silence echoed back.

Nerves on edge, I scanned one more time before I retreated back into the house and deadbolted the lock behind me.

Under the strain of it, I sank down onto a chair at the kitchen table and dropped my head into my hands, rubbing at my hair like it would conjure a solution.

A true way to fix this without breaking more in the end.

My chest tightened when I heard the delicate footsteps coming down the second set of stairs that led into the kitchen.

Could feel her presence rush me.

Violets and grace and the girl.

She stopped at the bottom of the steps, her face barely visible in the lapping, jumping shadows.

Energy surged.

Chills lifted.

A shaft of electricity struck in the air.

Slowly, I pushed to standing.

The atmosphere sizzled.

My breaths hardened while my heart careened out of control.

I moved her way.

A storm hovered over me.

Thunder and greed.

I felt her harsh inhalation, the girl sucking me down into the well of her lungs.

She stood at the foot of the staircase, wisps of black hair falling over her shoulders, those eyes strikes of lightning in the night.

Those plush lips parted, and her chin quivered.

Hand shaking, I reached up and traced the tremor. Like it might be possible to hold it in my hand.

"I'm scared, Richard. So scared." Violet whispered the admission. Breaching the subject we'd been skirting all day.

Giving me her truth.

I cupped one side of her gorgeous face, thumb brushing across the defined angle of her trembling jaw. "I'm scared, too. Scared of what I'm willing to do to protect you."

Her throat bobbed when she swallowed, and she lifted her hand, fingertips grazing the healing wound between my eyes.

A silent confession zinged between us.

Acknowledgement that none of this had been random.

She blinked up at me, and her tongue darted out to wet those full, pink lips. "I didn't see anything, Richard. But I heard. My mama always taught me to listen with my heart…and I heard it, Richard. I heard the wickedness. I heard the evil. He said…"

I inched forward. Possession gripping me in its storm. I tipped up her chin, staring down at her through the dim, bleary light.

"What did he say?"

She choked, barely able to press out the words, "He said not to go diggin' up graves. That I'd never know when I might fall in."

What the fuck?

I'd expected some veiled warning for me.

Panic seized me. My chest constricted in a bluster of rage. Tongue the lash of a blade. "What graves? What the fuck was he saying? Who?"

Her head shook, her own panic vibrating through her being, and she was clutching me by the shirt.

Her little fists curled so tight they might as well have been embedded in my soul. "I just need to know one thing right now. Tell me it's true. Tell me you still love me because I'm done pretending like I don't need you."

Violet

Sage eyes flared, and a play of shadows danced across the carved lines that made up his formidable shape. He took my face in both of those big hands.

A tender bid of possession. "You want to know if I love you, Violet? Fuck. The only thing I feel is love for you. Loving you is the composition of who I am."

He looped an arm around my waist and tucked me close.

The air thinned and my lungs squeezed, the beat of our hearts racing, racing, racing. A thunder that boomed.

Encroaching.

Rumbling

A storm that gathered strength.

And I knew—I knew it was getting ready to hit land.

"Told you," he murmured in his rough way. "You are every

song I have ever written." He brushed back the hair from my face and tucked it behind my ear. "You are every lyric. Every riff. Every strum. Every echo. You are the song of my heart. I love you, Violet Ramsey. I love you with everything I've got and with everything I've got left to give."

And I was swept away.

My feet no longer touching solid ground as he lifted me, my toes barely brushing the floor as he tucked me close against the warmth of his body.

Joy slammed me.

Overwhelming.

Beautiful and terrifying because I knew I was giving myself over to this. There was no more fighting these feelings.

They were free.

Running rampant.

His nose brushed mine, and he kissed the corner of my mouth. "I love what comes out of this beautiful mouth."

He ran his nose up my cheek, and then he pressed a tender kiss to my eye, then moved to the other, his voice a low roll of emphasis, "I love the way these eyes see the world."

He ran his lips to my temple, murmured there, "I love the way this mind thinks. The way it processes."

Then his hand was shifting, running down to palm flat over the erratic thud of my heart that expanded, swelling to overflowing, breaking free of its chains. "And most of all, I love this. I love the heart of you. The trueness of you. I love *who you are* in the deepest places that only I can see."

He grabbed my hand and pressed it over the battering in his chest. "Do you feel it, Violet? Do you feel it beating for you? It always has. And it's never gonna stop."

"I feel it," I rushed the whisper. "I feel it, Richard. I feel it to my soul. I feel it in every one of those places that you love. I can feel you lovin' them. Do you feel mine?"

My nails clawed at the fabric of his shirt. Digging in.

His fingers curled into my hair, scraping into my scalp, Richard's voice raw, "I've felt you all along."

That was it.

The walls crashed down.

Every reservation dismantled.

The rubble in flames at our feet.

We stood in them, in the fire that we'd walked through to get to this place, and I knew it didn't matter that I didn't have every answer—I trusted in this.

Richard watched me with those eyes for a baited beat.

In a moment of reverent silence.

"I don't want to hurt you." He brushed a thumb over the swelling on my jaw.

"You won't. Just…kiss me, and don't you dare stop."

Then he curled his fingers tighter in my hair and dragged my mouth to his in a fiery, unapologetic kiss.

That storm hit land.

Mayhem.

A beautiful, unrelenting disaster.

A sudden deluge of desire.

A tidal wave of greed.

Bodies a needy collision of lust and everything we'd missed.

Our mouths hungry for what we'd been starving for over the last six years, nothing but nips of teeth and tugs of lips. Tongues delving into a tangle of devotion.

Richard hiked me higher, angling toward the wall to keep us balanced as I wrapped my legs around his waist.

The second I made contact, I moaned, rubbing myself at the hot, delicious friction of his hard cock that pressed at his jeans.

"Fuck. Baby." He pressed a single hand to the wall and kept the other banded around my waist, angling me in the exact way he knew would light me up. "You are gonna kill me. Ruin me. Ruined me a long time ago," he mumbled at my mouth.

I kept kissing him, biting and licking and stroking my tongue into his beautiful mouth, like I could taste the meaning of his song.

Knowing he would sing me.

That he would write me with those fingers and love me with that soul.

And I wanted it. Surrendered to it.

My nails sank into his shoulders. "Richard. I need you. I need you more than I've ever needed anything. I'm so tired of goin' this alone."

"You're not alone. I'm right here, baby. Fall into me. Let me hold you. Let me support you. Everything I've ever done, I've done for you."

His words spun around as frantic as our bodies reached and begged and hummed.

Those secrets there, vibrating, fracturing the stones, so close to being set free.

He hiked me higher and started to carry me up the stairs, both hands on the outside of my hips, holding me tight, the man never breaking our kiss. "I've got you. I've got you."

He kept repeating it as we ascended the stairs and he rushed down the hall. He stopped outside my bedroom door to kiss me deeper. "I go inside your room…you're mine, Violet. This isn't a quick fuck. It's not a distraction. This is you and me going back to the way we were meant to be."

"I think you know full well that I've always been yours."

"Mine," Richard grumbled in something that sounded akin to pain, and he jerked me from the wall and carried me the rest of the way into my room. He set me onto unsteady feet, shut the door, and flicked the lock. "Mine," he said.

The man was a dark tower in the room, his shape an eclipse that covered me in warmth, sage eyes flashing in that magnetic way.

For a beat, we stared, our hearts a mangle of the years we'd lost, writhing in the space between us.

It was Richard who breached it, broke through the disorder, and my breath hitched when he dove in for a possessive, mind-altering kiss. No room left for questions. No space for reservations.

We were bare.

Vulnerable.

We turned a circle, orbiting the other, our mouths fused while we fought to free the other of their clothes. He grabbed the hem of my shirt and eased it over my head, remembering my injuries, while I ripped and fumbled to get his shirt over his head.

He helped me, stepping back to peel it up his gorgeous body and tossing it to the floor.

A gasp ripped up my throat, and I gaped at him.

Walls spinning around us while my eyes ate him up.

Devouring the hard, carved lines of his abdomen.

The man a sculpture.

A god.

But it was the tattoo that covered the entirety of his left side and chest that had me shaken. A haunting full moon hung over his ribs, and it was surrounded by a cluster of violets where it sat in the sky. Stars fell from that sky, falling and falling, disintegrating into nothing.

It was suspended over what was unmistakably the rolling hills of Dalton.

It gave me the impression that the tiny promise on the inside of his wrist hadn't been enough.

Like he'd gotten lost and this had been his map, only somewhere along the way, his compass had gone missing.

"Richard," I whispered, overcome, taken.

I could feel myself falling right through the sorrowful abyss of that sky.

Stepping forward, I kissed across the image, my hands gliding up his sides. "Richard. My husband. My sun that ushers in the day. You will always be the beat of my heart."

I murmured my confession against the raging of his heart.

He set a hand on my cheek and gently urged me to look at him.

"My wife. My moonflower in my darkest night. You will always be the song of my heart."

He repeated the same words he'd given me on our wedding day.

Our devotion.

Our loyalty.

My palm pressed over the thunder that rioted at his chest. "Then listen to what it says."

I repeated what my mama had taught me.

My own compass beating strong inside of me.

And it was pointed directly to him.

In an instant, we crashed together.

I felt desperate with the need to touch him everywhere. To sink in. To erase any distance. Blot out the past and fill it with the future.

"Richard. Oh god. I missed you. I missed you." The ramble of words poured out of my mouth while I left a frenzy of kisses over his twitching stomach and up his chest.

Kissing me and kissing me, he flicked the hook of my bra and dragged the straps down my trembling arms. My breasts felt heavy, aching for his touch, my nipples tightened into hard, needy peaks.

Richard obliged, diving down and taking one into his mouth.

A moan tremored through me, chills streaking across my skin and pumping need through every vein in my body.

Dumping it into every cell.

That deluge just grew higher.

I was drowning in a sea of fire.

Richard's palms spread down my sides and around to grip me by the bottom while he kissed a line down between my breasts. He kept going, moving lower and lower until he was lightly kissing over the bruise marring my abdomen.

A second later, he was on his knees.

He stared up at me with those mesmerizing eyes as he hooked his fingers in the elastic band of the sleep pants I'd been wearing the entire day, and I was shaking and shaking as he slowly dragged them down, taking my underwear with them.

He left me standing there, wholly bared to him.

He hissed, and I could see the wave of lust crash through his body. "Shit, baby. Vi. How do you do this to me? Have to be dreamin'. Have to be. Moonflower. Never thought I'd get to see you like this again. Any idea how fuckin' stunning you are? How you make me ache?"

My gaze wandered over his wide shoulders and the packed strength of his chest, to the muscles taut across his abdomen.

God, he was miraculous.

The man art.

A mold of heaven. But it was his face that had always done me in.

Falling into You

"Funny how every night when I closed my eyes, the only thing I could see was you. You were emblazoned in my mind," I admitted.

A growl ripped through the air, and he pushed to standing.

Without hesitating, I reached out and flicked the button of his jeans. "Get these off. It's hardly fair I'm standing here completely naked while you're still hiding some of that from me."

A smirk pulled to one side of his mouth. "Got nothin' to hide."

Okay.

That was clearly a lie. But right then, there were no barriers between us.

He shoved down his jeans and kicked off his shoes at the same time, shucking the heavy material from his ankles before he was standing bold and powerful in front of me.

I rained a million kisses across his chest, across the art representing me that he'd adorned himself with.

"Every song," he grumbled.

And I was singing back softly as my lips traipsed over the inked flesh, "Amor, amor, amor."

Richard moaned and fisted his hand in my hair, dragging me flush to his body. His cock thick and hard where it was trapped between us. "Can't wait to get inside of you. Can't wait to feel this body again. Fucking perfection."

I whimpered, rushed with need, with a desire so overwhelming it knocked through my senses.

Amplifying each one.

"Beauty."

Every touch.

Every word.

Every action.

"La historia de mi vida," Richard murmured low.

The story of my life.

My knees wobbled.

It wasn't sarcasm.

It wasn't mockery.

It was *meaning*.

"You are the start and the ending. The days in between. Even when you weren't there."

Richard scooped me up when I said it, his nostrils flaring, devotion so thick and severe I could almost see it hovering in the air.

He laid me on the bed, trailing a finger from my trembling throat straight down my body. He circled my belly button. "If you could see what I see when I look at you. You are inspiration. Awe. The first wonder of my world."

My body arched. Desperate for his touch.

I whimpered as I watched him where he stood at the side of my bed looking down on me. The man massive where he hung hard and heavy. His cock swollen. Long since past ready.

My insides quaked.

"You want this, sweet girl?" It came off sounding like a warning when he stroked himself once.

Throat dry, I couldn't speak, could barely manage an erratic nod.

"Need you to be sure. Don't want to hurt you. After last night…"

"You won't. I need this."

He parted my knees and continued that line over my pubic bone, the faintest touch across my clit, even lighter as he barely brushed through my lips. "First time I saw you, it was over. I was done for, baby. Don't want anyone else. Never."

Richard crawled onto the bed, stealing the breath from my lungs when he came to hover over me.

Gazing down.

My soul sang. I reached out to flutter my fingertips across his lips. He kissed the tips, sucking them gently, his eyes watching me with all his shadowy darkness.

Grief and guilt there, held in his devotion.

"Never, not once. You are the piece that is missing inside me. My match," I whispered.

My heart carved in the shape of him.

"Won't let anything happen to you. Not to you or Daisy. Will die first before I let anyone get near you."

"I trust you," I murmured back.

Simmering flames lapped across our flesh.

Heat rising.

"I love you, Violet. Never stopped. Whatever you do, whatever you think, I need you to remember that."

"I believe you."

Then he drove into me with a single thrust that I had no time to anticipate.

It was nothing but vicious, exquisite bliss.

A shout of pleasure ripped up my throat, and I clamored to get a better hold around his neck, to adjust to the size of him filling me up.

Taking me whole.

A deep growl rumbled in his throat while he kept himself still. "So fuckin' good. Being in you. There is nothing better than this. Do you remember, baby, what we're like together?"

He pulled back a fraction and nudged back in to the hilt.

Pinpricks of pleasure lit up all over.

My fingers sank into his shoulders, and his nose was at my cheek, his pants expelled at the overheated skin. "I remember," I whispered.

How could I forget when there wasn't a thing in the world that felt better than this?

"It's been too long. Too fuckin' long. You know what it feels like to be inside you after all this time?"

"I hope as good as you feel to me."

He edged back, tucking his fingers in my hair, the man staring down at me as if I were light.

Incandescent.

A smile played across his plush, sexy mouth. "Don't doubt that. Fucking heaven, baby. Magic."

I tipped my chin up toward him, meeting his eyes. "Then let's make it."

A rough, needy chuckle left him, and he dipped down to take my mouth as he pressed up on both hands and began to move over me.

Deep, deep thrusts.

Hard and measured.

Our bodies in time.

Our rhythm in sync.

His mouth devotion.

His fucks possession.

I met him with each one.

It didn't take long for our movements to become frantic.

Heat lighting up, flames growing higher, drowning in that sea of fire.

He pushed back onto his knees, gripping me by the outside of the hips, those eyes moving to take in where he drove us straight into delirium.

The drive of his hips and the pant of his mouth and the surrender of his soul.

"Never…never experienced anything like this. Nothing compares to being in you. Living in you. Not gonna stop, Violet. Wanna be right here."

He lifted his right hand and licked his thumb.

My insides tumbled.

My heart shattered.

I was nothing but pieces for him to hold.

He reached down and started to stroke me into madness. Winding me straight into ecstasy. "Touchin' you, Violet. It's like touching the stars."

My body writhed and my hips lifted and my spirit soared.

He fucked me harder, penetrating to the innermost places I'd kept secret, shattering the last of the reservations I'd had.

Emotion surged.

Crested with the sensation.

Whipping into a storm that would leave me changed.

Marked in a brand-new way.

Because it was easy to hate. To hold on to the betrayal. But it wasn't so easy to let it go.

Forgiveness was both terrifying and freeing.

"Richard. Richard. I don't want to go another day. Not another day without you. I need you. I need you. I need you."

I chanted it as pleasure gathered fast.

Like it swept in from the ends of the earth and raced to meet in one singular place.

In a place that was only me and him.

That connection shivered and shook and stretched taut.

So intense that it pulled Richard back to me, his body angling over mine, the man wrapping me up, his eyes on me as he thrust and drove and promised me with those eyes that he would never let me go.

"Always," he grunted.

And there was nothing left.

Only the two of us.

Bound by something sacred.

Captives of the divine.

In that singular moment, I felt something coming back together.

Brokenness hewn.

Fractures fused.

Molten.

Liquid.

Solid.

Ash.

One.

One.

One.

Where I was his beginning and he was my end and we were all the days written in between.

Flying through his darkest night.

The man my eclipse.

My sun.

My every star in the sky.

And I was falling…falling into him.

Into his eyes and into his heart and into the safety of his hands.

He gathered up my hand and pressed it against the riot in his chest. Held me close. Like he could keep me from floating away as the orgasm rocked through me.

A thousand tiny explosions of perfection.

Wave after wave after wave.

Pleasure racing, reaching out for him, my body pulsing around him for eternity.

"Heaven, Violet. You are fuckin' heaven. Watching you glow. Nothin' better than this. Right here. With you."

"Come with me," I begged.

Hips snapping, and his muscles bowing, he took me deeper.

Harder.

Faster.

More.

Chains broken.

No heed.

No sense.

Just us.

He kissed me hard, his words a mumble at my lips as I felt the orgasm take him over. "You."

"You," I whispered back.

Richard tremored and shook, gripping me like he thought I might disappear.

Holding me tight.

His mouth at my ear. "My wife."

Richard

I couldn't get my breath on account that I was inhaling all of hers.

Wanting more. To swallow her down and feed on her beauty and drink from her soul.

This gorgeous, hypnotizing girl with thunderbolt eyes.

My fairy girl.

My moonflower.

God knew I was no match for the magic she cast.

I pressed a kiss to her delicious mouth, and she hummed, those arms still wrapped around my neck.

I twitched and jerked and wanted to take her all over again when I eased out of her body, kinda wishing I could just live right there.

Set up shop.

Hang up a sign that read *Home, Sweet Home.*

But that's what this was.

Coming home.

Violet whimpered when I pulled out, and I got the sense she was thinking the exact same thing.

"Tell me you missed it." I let a grin slide to my mouth, but I knew it had to appear adoring as I stared down at her on her bed, all that lush hair spread around her, the softest smile playing on her face and love swimming in her eyes.

"What? Mediocre sex with you?" The tease slipped from her mouth, and she was holding back laughter, and I was tickling her, the girl shrieking out a laugh, squealing and flailing and kicking her legs as she tried to block my playful attack.

Giggles rippled free that she tried to temper in favor of not waking up the entire house.

I thought there might be too much joy for that.

This moment sublime.

I flipped her around until the girl was straddling me, Violet's expression like looking at the first dawn.

I bucked my hips, and she let out a throaty sound. "Mediocre, huh?" I challenged.

Her face softened, and she played her fingertips along the tattoo I'd marked of her about three years ago. When I knew my love for her was never going to set.

"There isn't a single thing that is mediocre about you, Richard Ramsey."

My fingers threaded through the soft wisps of her black hair that hung like a veil around her face. "That's good...because you are spectacular."

"Oh, you enjoyed that, did you?"

My grin grew. "Think that's pretty clear. Six years without bein' in you? Without lovin' you? Without touchin' you? My poor dick was on a hunger strike. Nearly died."

I gave her a faked, mopey frown at that.

She barked out a laugh, and then slapped her hand over her mouth to mute it, her voice shifting into a sexy whisper. "Poor, baby. Now you know how I feel."

My hands cupped the outside of her bare thighs, and I was

trying to keep it together considering the girl was sitting on me naked. Still wet. My poor, destitute dick was very, very aware of the exciting change in our situation.

"I knew all along."

Could feel the shift, the lightness shifting into the darkness that surrounded us. No chance of eradicating it until all was exposed.

I just had to hang on for a few more weeks.

Pray she'd understand.

Forgive me.

Understand what I'd had to do.

"I hate that you left me," she said, blatantly honest.

I pulled her down and shifted us so we were lying on our sides facing each other. Her little heart beating manic and those thunderbolt eyes searching me for the truth. "I hate that I had to."

Her tongue darted out to wet her lips, and she glanced away before she looked back at me. "What that man said last night..."

My stomach clamped in a vice of rage. I managed to keep it in check. To just keep looking at her, waiting for her confession.

"I think I know why he came."

My chest tightened. "You recognize something about him?"

Her lips pressed together, and she slightly shook her head where it was rested in the crook of my arm. "No, Richard, but I *heard* it. Where the threat was comin' from. This is about my sister."

Her throat bobbed in a shock of pain when she said the last while I tried not to lose my shit.

Instinctively, my arms tightened around her. "Why do you say that?"

The girl hesitated, warring. "Because I hired a private investigator to find her, and I think someone doesn't want her to be found."

Horror froze every cell in my body.

She sat up, and the words started to fly from her mouth in a tumble of desperation. "Richard, it absolutely terrifies me what that might mean. If it's her that doesn't want to be found or if it's someone else. What...what if she's in danger?"

I pushed up to sitting, too, taking her by both sides of the face, searching her through the grainy haze of her room.

"Baby," I whispered, the word nothing but gravel. "When did you hire this person? What has he found?"

I mean...fuck.

Her chin quivered, and she spread her fingers over her chest like she could feel a part of herself bleeding out. "A few weeks ago. My mama...Richard...my mama needs to see her one last time. It's the last bit of peace that she needs to say goodbye. The resolution she needs. The last I love you she needs to say."

Gutting brokenness seeped from her pores, and I wrapped her up like I could hold those shattered pieces together and not be the one who was going to send it all crashing to bits in the end. My mouth moved to her ear. "Has he found anything?"

Her head shook in confusion, and she curled her arms around my neck. "A picture. A picture from back in LA. You remember that man, Martin Jennings? The one who took us out to eat all those years ago when they were trying to get Carolina George to sign?"

Fury went on a tangent in my rib cage.

A battering.

A storm.

It took everything I had not to fly from the bed.

"Yeah," I managed to say.

"She was with him. How was she with him?" Violet begged, clinging to me tighter. "I'm terrified, Richard, terrified that I got her into something that she couldn't get out of when I invited her there. That I'm somehow responsible for this. For whatever happened to her. And I'm so selfish...so selfish," she wheezed, "so selfishly scared to find out. Scared to learn what it might mean. Scared of what is going to happen with Daisy. How could I be so cruel? How, Richard? I...I..."

Despair rushed out with the words, and she choked over a sob.

Deep gashes of pain that pierced her.

"It makes me sick to be this person, but I don't know how to stop this feelin'. This feeling that makes me want to wrap that little girl up and run away. Hide her away forever."

Hitched, pleading cries ripped up her throat.

This girl breaking apart.

No walls left to hide behind.

Revealing it all.

I wrapped her tighter, wishing I could do the same, and I pulled her to straddle me where I was sitting up on her bed. I kept brushing back her hair that was matted and tangled, the fine wisps sticking to her cheeks.

"You aren't a horrible person, Violet. Not even close, baby. You are everything. Everything. You are a *good* mother who is just trying to protect her child. What you're feeling is instinct. There's not a thing wrong with that."

"What if she takes her, Richard? What if the investigator finds her and Lily comes back and she takes her away? What do I do then? How will I survive?"

Her heartbreak cracked through the room.

A violent explosion that banged against the walls.

She hiccupped and struggled to get closer. "How could I ever let her go?"

Problem was, I couldn't give her an answer.

Couldn't promise it wouldn't happen.

"No matter what happens, I'm here. With you. You aren't alone. You aren't alone," I murmured, desperate for a way to make it better. To take away her pain.

But that was the problem.

I was helpless.

Fuckin' helpless.

Especially considering I was the one responsible for it in the first place.

Richard
Six Years Ago

*T*he sedan came to a stop in the huge circular drive that was surrounded by a rambling, manicured lawn. Flowered hedges outlined the sidewalks and a waterfall shot toward the haze of city sky before it spilled back down to splash into the reservoir. The entire property was surrounded by an imposing brick wall, trees growing even higher above the towering walls to provide privacy where the residence sat in the middle of the bustling city.

A man dressed in uniform opened the back door, and Shawn and Richard slipped out to the muted thrum of music echoing through the thick walls of the grand estate.

The man dipped his head in a curt nod. "Enjoy, gentlemen."

Shawn howled and clapped him on the back. "Oh, I'm sure that we will."

Falling into You

Martin Jennings climbed out of the front seat and adjusted his suit jacket before he waved an indulgent hand toward the entrance of the extravagant home. "You are our guests of honor tonight. Anything behind those doors is yours. Feel free to indulge. Our parties are *invite only*, so you can be sure of full discretion by all attendees."

Disquiet rumbled in the periphery. Somewhere at the edges of Richard's brain. He hadn't ever been to a party where a disclaimer was a necessity.

But he was too excited to acknowledge it. This feeling coming over him as they climbed the ten massive steps that led to the double-doors that had to be twenty-feet high.

This was it.

They were being invited into this world.

The Mylton Records world.

Everything they'd been striving for was right there, within their reach.

Their music was good. Really good. But it was going to take a label like Mylton Records backing them to shoot them into the stratosphere.

One side of the double doors opened to the sprawling home, nothing but sky-high ceilings and modern furniture and wealth seeping from the walls. Music blared from the speakers that pulsed a frenetic beat through the entire house.

Place packed.

Wall-to-wall.

Bodies crushed in the space like it was some kind of trendy nightclub rather than a mansion in Beverly Hills which was a mindfuck in itself.

Lights strobed and music blared, and his heart rate ratcheted, trying to take it all in.

Sex, drugs, and rock 'n' roll.

Sure, he'd seen his fair share of shit out on the road, but he didn't think he'd ever seen the unmitigated evidence of it quite like then.

Girls half dressed. Sitting on laps. Dancing on tables.

Dudes totally buck and running through the house.

Some in collars. Grinning. Dancing.

Nothing but a freak show.

A tumbler full of glittering amber was shoved into his hand.

Martin Jennings lifted his above his head. "To Carolina George rising to their full, unobstructed potential."

"Fuck yeah, I will drink to that!" Shawn shouted, and they clinked glasses before they were clinking theirs with his, and Richard was tossing back the alcohol in a bid to settle his nerves that rattled and shook.

A disorder that blew.

The liquid burned a fiery path down his throat and pooled in his stomach. He was quickly given another, and he felt those nerves unfurl into a shaky confidence as he tossed the next one back and followed Martin through the throng. He led them into another room that was just as packed as the last.

Lights cut into a low, dizzying haze, a daze of strobing white and blue lights that thudded over the room. Semi-private sitting areas made up of plush couches were tucked along the edges of the walls and a full bar sat at the far end of the room.

There was a raging dance floor in the middle.

Martin gestured for them to follow, and he led them to one of the alcoves at the very back. Richard sank down into the comfort of a couch, watching the mayhem that hammered and thrashed.

A woman appeared in front of them carrying a tray, dressed in a thong and these little shiny dots covering her nipples. She dropped off a bottle and three shot glasses before she disappeared back into the crush.

Shawn laughed this seedy laugh, cut him a look, and said, "Holy fuck. Told you, man. We're about to be kings."

Martin poured three shots. "To tonight."

Richard tossed it back.

Welcomed the burn and the fire.

The night moved on, and that haze grew, his mind slipping and sliding and shifting the more drinks that he sucked down. The woman returned with another bottle, though this time she also set a little tray with a small pile of white powder onto the coffee table.

Martin sat forward and cut it.

"Tomorrow we make you superstars. Tomorrow you sign and you become part of the Mylton Records family. But tonight…tonight we celebrate. Tonight, you get to see who you're going to be." Martin sent Richard a glance. Something that almost looked like a warning.

And fuck.

Richard had the urge to get the fuck up and run out the door, all the way back to Dalton. But this—this was what they'd fought for. Years spent on the road. Half starved. Penniless.

It was one night.

One goddamn night.

What could it hurt to *indulge*?

Shawn didn't hesitate to do a line when the tray was passed his way.

Richard did. He felt this shiver of dread that curled down his spine like a slick of ice. And he was wondering just what the fame was gonna cost when he leaned forward and dragged the poison through his nose.

The burn was different this time. A sharp sting that didn't take all that long to shift into bliss.

A flush of power.

A rush of truth.

Fact that this was where they'd been heading all along.

Lyrics hummed through his mind and the beat of a bass drummed through his soul.

He grinned and sat back on the couch.

Tonight.

Tonight.

Shawn banged an agitated fist on his knee.

"You know who we should call?"

"Yeah?" he asked, lifting his chin.

"Lily. She's a ton of fun."

Richard guessed he was too far gone to catch what flashed in Martin Jennings' eyes when he said, "I agree."

Violet

I wasn't sure I'd ever felt so exhausted and alive at the same time.

My spirit soaring and my body aching.

Not that I was going to complain about that considering it was wholly due to the number of times Richard and I had reached for each other last night.

The man taking me again and again.

Loving me soft.

Fucking me hard.

Our reconnection taking us through every emotion.

The highs and the lows. The desperation and the savoring. The joy and the sorrow. The adoration and the lust. The laughter and the tears.

I should have slept like a rock.

Instead, I'd been unable to drift. Just wanting to cling to it. To the moment. To the truth. To the promises that we had made.

Finally, at the breaking of dawn, I'd pried myself from his gorgeous, sleeping form, climbed from my bed, and crept downstairs. Needing to clear my head. To figure out what I would tell Daisy. What I was gonna tell my daddy.

Truth was, I was still having a hard time wrapping my own head around it, so I sure as heck didn't know how my daddy would handle it.

Yesterday, there'd been camaraderie. A sense of coming together for a purpose.

I just wasn't quite sure what the reaction was going to be to the *purpose* that went down all through last night.

Blowing out a heavy sigh, I poured myself a cup of coffee while I stood in the warmth of the first rays of daylight streaming in through the window, not even trying to hide the giddy grin plastered to my face even when there wasn't a soul there to witness it.

But I figured if there was, they'd see what was written all over me. The loved-up happiness that had me awash.

Floatin'.

Flyin'.

That only amplified when I heard the shuffle of feet. The warmth of the rising sun didn't have a thing on the warmth of the strong arms that wrapped around me from behind. Nothing on the way I felt when Richard pressed his cheek to mine, when he nuzzled my jaw, the man tilting my head so he could press a lingering kiss to the side of my neck.

Chills raced and my heart expanded in the most magnificent way.

"Good mornin'," he rumbled, his voice this throaty, sleepy growl.

Oh yeah.

That got me going, too.

Apparently, I really had gone without for too long.

"Mornin'. What are you doing up so early?"

"I was gonna ask the same thing about you. You don't like sleeping next to me? Because believe me, baby, I'm done sleeping without lying next to you."

His mouth grazed the shell of my ear. "That a good enough answer?" he murmured.

Need curled down my spine, and one of those happy sighs was exhaling some of the weight from my chest.

Like I no longer had to bear the full burden on my own.

"I couldn't sleep because I was afraid if I closed my eyes, I might wake up and it'd be a dream," I confessed.

Those hands splayed wide across my belly, and he pulled my back to his front.

Gluing us together.

His mouth trailed up and down the side of my neck, eliciting a tiny moan, his grip just tugging me tighter. "No dreamin' this, baby. Believe me…I've spent the last six years dreaming of you. Wishing for you. My mind didn't stand a fuckin' chance at competing with the real thing. Nothin' better than you."

I whimpered, and then I froze when the kitchen door swung open. My attention whipped that way to find Daisy racing in, my daddy's hand wrapped up in hers as she hauled him inside.

Oh, crap.

Her eyes went wide with excitement. "Mr. Richard. You're here! You're here! Did you stay for a sleeps over?"

Clearly, my daddy wanted to know the answer to that, too. Or more importantly, where he'd slept.

Richard chuckled, not even considering releasing me. He just turned us a little so we were facing out, those arms locked around me.

A clear statement given.

Mine.

"Well, since you're here, where else was I supposed to go?"

"You love me?" She asked like she was floored by the idea, and her beaming smile filled the entire room.

Her sweet innocence so genuine.

So real.

The child just seeing things for what they were.

I guessed maybe it was the only thing that could unfasten those arms from me because Richard spread his hands over my stomach, dragged them to either of my hips, and left a kiss behind my ear before he stepped around me and knelt in front of her.

He tucked an unruly dark lock behind her ear. So tenderly that I nearly succumbed right there.

A goner.

"Yeah, precious flower girl, I do. I love you."

"Just like you love my mommy?"

He grinned, a light chuckle rippling free. "Different but the same."

Then she threw herself into his hold, and he picked her up and spun her around, and she lifted her arms in the air, that blundering cast waving all around. "Amor, amor, amor," she sang.

She grinned at me from over his shoulder. "Told you."

I choked out a laugh. "You did, didn't you?"

She turned her attention back to Richard. One hundred percent serious. "I am the smartest girl in the worlds. Just ask my papa."

She waved an over-eager hand his way.

Daddy smiled.

His love abounding, though there was no missing the remnants of uncertainty still lingering in his eyes. "Yes, you are, mi amor. The smartest girl in all the worlds."

"Well, then, I guess you must be," Richard said, all too keen to agree to the logic.

I didn't have the heart to make this a deeper life lesson. That all children were smart in their own special way.

I figured all of this was life-lesson enough.

The truth that sometimes…sometimes when your heart refused to give up, it ended up exactly where it was supposed to be.

"Still not sure this is a good idea." Richard had his hands shoved in his jeans' pockets. Man standing at the side of the long SUV that had shown fifteen minutes before, the whole crew piling out.

Richard's concern was that half of them needed to leave.

"Um…hello. We've got her." Melanie took a step in front of me. With the way she puffed out her chest and widened her stance, she might as well have been wearing camo like some kind of commando.

Richard shot her a glare. "Really?"

Emily giggled and took a step toward her brother. "It's fine, Richard. We're all here. None of us will let Violet out of our sight."

She gestured at Maggie and Mel who were flanking me.

Royce's brow lifted, the man leaned back against the front grill of the SUV. He sent Richard a glance before letting his attention drift toward the four of us. "Not so sure. What's Mag-Pie here gonna do? Kill 'em with kindness?"

He sent an overbearing look to his adorable little sister. She returned him an offended pout.

Rhys cracked up. "Oh, I bet that little thing can kick some butt. Besides, Mel's here. Biggest ballbuster there is. Not a man alive who'd get in the way of that."

"Damn straight, cowboy. Lord save us, turns out the man knows a thing or two after all."

Richard huffed. Not close to being amused.

I stepped toward him and set a placating hand on his forearm. "It's okay. I'm gonna be fine. All four of us are gonna be together the entire day, and my daddy has Saul and two of our other guys watching the land."

I swore fire puffed from the man's nostrils.

A bull about to charge as his gaze prowled across the rolling fields. "Saul? Is that supposed to make me feel better?"

Jealous.

No question.

I almost laughed.

Saul was harmless.

I squeezed his arm tighter. "The weddin' is in less than two weeks. Y'all have to pick up your suits and run the rest of the errands." I pointed at the bridesmaids. "We're going to be busy the entire day getting things ready. I mean, unless you want to stand around playing with ribbon and tulle all day?"

Rhys dropped to his knees and clamped his hands together in a prayer, crying out in mock horror. "Oh god. Don't make me. I'd rather be hog tied."

"You need to be hog tied," Mel tossed out.

"Ah…know you want me tied up, darlin'. All's you gotta do is ask."

Mel gagged. "Gross."

Royce jerked him up by the arm. "On your feet, asshole. Don't make me kick your ridiculousness out of my wedding." I was thinking it was only half a tease.

"The audacity," Rhys cracked, dusting off his boots, laughing as he rubbed at his beard that was growing thicker by the day.

"Yeah, we know who's the ass," Royce grumbled.

Rhys clapped him on the back. "You know you love me. I mean, shit, I'm lettin' you get hitched to my Emily. You should be on your knees thanking me."

Lincoln shoved him. "Dude. Step down from that overinflated pedestal. That's my sister you're talkin' about."

"Hey. Em's my girl."

God. The guy was a handful. I'd almost forgotten how crazy he was.

I gave a little nudge to my man.

My man.

Oh, did that ever feel good.

"Go on. This is important to your sister. To your future brother. I promise I'll be careful."

I mean, it wasn't like I would dare go traipsing this land alone. I wasn't about to be that reckless. But I felt sure in this—that everyone was watchin' over me.

That we would be just fine.

Richard grumbled.

Royce scanned the fields, checking the three farmhands who'd gathered in the periphery. He shifted to look at Richard, lifted his chin. "They should be covered, man. Not like I'm cool being away from my girl, either. We'll be quick. In and out, and we'll get back."

Richard wavered, not quite agreeing before he stepped toward me and grabbed me by both sides of the face.

He kissed me hard.

It was the kind of kiss I felt all the way to my toes. The kind that blazed through my bloodstream. Left me hot and needy and breathless.

Finally, he dropped his forehead to mine and exhaled a shaky breath. "Be careful. I won't survive if something happens to you."

I let him breathe me in. Suck me down. Let him feel my whispered words. "Nothing is going to happen to me. We've waited too long for this. We can't lose it now."

So yeah.

They were all gaping.

Mouths unhinged, watching Richard claim me right out in the open.

Different than yesterday.

Because today?

Today we were standing in our new beginning.

"Go," I coaxed him.

He ripped himself away and walked to the SUV. He slipped into the front seat, watching me with that raw potency through the windshield. Rhys and Lincoln climbed into the back on either side, and Royce hopped into the driver's seat.

I didn't say a word, didn't move a muscle while I remained planted, held in the grips of his unrelenting gaze.

Royce whipped the SUV around and rambled down the drive, the powerful engine accelerating as they hit the main road.

"Oh my god." Melanie's voice yanked me from the trance.

My attention whipped that way. "What?"

"Don't *what* me, young lady." Her eyes took me in from head to toe, and then her face was splitting into a wry grin. "Look at you. All freshly fucked. I should have known something was different."

A blush rushed to my face.

Not because I was embarrassed.

But because I was assaulted with the distinct images of Richard doing just that.

My hands gripping the bedframe while he'd owned me from

behind.

Sweat drenching our skin.

Our bodies freed.

No boundaries we wouldn't breach.

I bit down on my bottom lip and squeezed my thighs together.

"Ahh...I see someone is still reelin' from the effects of that giant dick."

"Melanie," Emily hissed, smacking Mel's upper arm with the back of her hand.

Mel shrugged. "I don't know how she's walkin', honestly."

I cleared my throat. "Not walkin'. Flyin'."

Mel cracked up.

Emily's smile was full of affection.

Of relief.

Maggie reached out and took my hand. "See. Your future. You're brave to step into it."

My brow curled. "I'm not sure I'd call myself brave."

Honestly, I was barely rising above the debilitating fear.

She shook her head. "No, Violet. It's brave. Because some of us are too fearful to step out of our pasts. We remain prisoners to them. Chained. No way to move forward."

Emily took her opposite hand since Maggie was still holding mine. My gaze flicked between them, and I squeezed her hand tight. "I don't know your story, Maggie. I don't know what you've been through. But I see a brave girl."

A tear slipped from her eye, and she choked it back. "I'm not feeling so brave right now."

I wished I understood.

Emily cleared the roughness from her throat. "Maggie and I are supposed to testify against the man who violated both of us, three weeks from now."

A tremor rolled through Maggie.

Violent in its path.

I clung to her tighter. Of course, I knew Emily was involved, but I hadn't realized Maggie had been, too.

Melanie moved forward so she could take my free hand as well as Emily's.

It brought the four of us into an unbroken circle.

Emily's throat quivered, and I saw the fear there, as well, saw how deep it went, normally covered by her natural joy.

But right then, she pulled the veil back.

"It was supposed to be in the bag. No question of these men seeing justice."

She met my eye. "Two of the women who were supposed to testify with us? Two women who'd been forced into a life of sex slavery? They disappeared last week."

Horror spiraled through my being. A blade cutting directly into my soul.

Because I knew what was in their eyes.

True terror.

The fate of those women unknown but unfortunately obvious.

"Oh my god," I whimpered, hardly able to stand when it finally became clear what the two of them had been through.

What Richard had implied.

"You mean...like what happened to Emily? I saw, Richard, on the news. That somethin' bad happened to her. It's horrible. I can't..."

"Like that. Even worse."

His words suddenly made full, complete, horrible sense.

Melanie squeezed our hands so tight that it sent a pulse of commitment running through the circuit. "Nothin's happening to any of you. You hear me? It ends now. Here."

I nodded frantically like my doing it would cause the threat to pass. "We're behind you."

And I didn't know why I got the sudden, sinking feeling that I was right there with them.

Twilight teased at the dwindling day, the bright, endless blue giving way to swashes of pink, cool air riding on the breeze and twisting through the quieted, peaceful mood.

The four of us were in the workshop, where we'd basically been for the last week, getting everything finalized for the wedding. Emily was singing low, perfectly in key without a lick of music to guide her, Maggie humming along.

I swayed to the beat of it, stuffing twinkle lights into mason jars and wrapping brown twine around their necks. They would be filled with fresh flowers on the day of the wedding and used as centerpieces for the tables.

We worked together.

Our hearts and our minds lulled.

Leaving our fears at the door in a hope that Emily and Royce could have a normal wedding. We'd made the conscious choice to focus on only this rather than the fear that lingered at the outskirts of our minds, choosing to shut out the stress and worry so we could focus on their special day.

On her beautiful day that I was determined to give her.

In a few days, the wedding guests would begin arriving.

A few distant relatives.

The last member of their band, Leif, his wife, Mia, and their children.

The members of Sunder and their families.

Plus, the members of Royce's band that he'd recently been reunited with, A Riot of Roses.

The invitation list wasn't huge. The number of guests was small enough so that everyone could truly feel a part of it, which was what Emily had wanted most.

Most were staying at the same hotel in Dalton where the engagement party had been held.

We had these last few days left to put together the finishing touches.

And truth be told, I was in my element.

Decorating.

Putting pieces together that would mark her special night.

Plotting out the flowers that would amplify the beauty and joy.

"Last one," she said as she started to wind the twine around the jar.

"It's gonna be beautiful," I told her.

"Perfect," she agreed.

It was.

I believed it.

Held onto the hope and the faith I could feel burning inside me.

It only intensified when I felt it.

That rush of energy that stirred through the air right before the sound of voices and footsteps reached out to touch my ears.

The guys were all suddenly there. Standing in the sliding doorway to the workshop we'd left wide open.

Royce moved directly for Emily. Wrapping her up, his tatted hands spread out to cover her tiny baby bump. "Hey, you."

"Hi," she whispered, leaning back into his touch. "Are you nervous?" she asked, tipping her head back on his shoulder so she could take in his expression.

His daughter, Anna, was flying in tonight. The child who I'd learned he'd been unjustifiably separated from since she was only a baby. The man sent to prison for attacking his sister's attacker, his rights stripped away while he'd been there. The atrocious actions so unfair.

Thank God, they'd been reunited.

He'd gotten to see her a handful of times before they'd come to South Carolina to plan the wedding, and tonight they would be picking her up and she would be staying with them for the next week.

Maggie would be there to help considering there was still so much to do for the wedding.

"Nervous. Excited. Just…ready to have my family together," he said.

"I can't wait to have this time with her," Emily said, love riding through her features. "I love her already, and I hardly know her."

She almost blushed at that, turning self-conscious as she peeked at her fiancé.

God.

She was amazing.

So good.

So kind.

So real.

"I imagine it's natural to immediately love a child you know you're going to be responsible for. That you're going to care for. A child who's going to look to you to teach her. To protect her. To *love* her. It doesn't matter if she was born of your body or not."

There was Maggie again.

The empath.

So insightful that it stole the words from everyone's tongues.

But Richard was looking at me.

Understanding the stark, instant impact of what Maggie had said.

The crash of devotion.

The truth that I would do whatever was required for Daisy.

Live and die and fight and pray.

She was the core of who I was.

The focus.

The reason.

Our gazes danced. Twirling and twirling as the silence hovered around us.

The truth that by stepping up, she'd become his, too.

He reached for my hand. "Almost finished?"

With shaky hands, I set down the last of the jars I'd been working on. "I think so. It's all coming together."

Emily came for me, hugged me tight. "Thank you."

Why I suddenly felt like crying, I didn't know. But I felt awash in it. In the emotion. In the love. In the true meaning of family.

I hugged Melanie something fierce, Maggie the same, Lincoln and Rhys.

Royce, too, his voice a murmured, "Thank you," at my ear.

I swiped the tear that got free. "It is my honor."

Violet

"**Y**ou look stunning." I smiled softly at my sister-in-law where she stood at the full-length mirror in my bedroom.

Wearing her wedding dress.

Twenty minutes from walking down the aisle.

Waves of blonde were twisted in a loose side braid, and tons of wisps fell out, fresh flowers from the field pinned into the plaits.

"Um. Stunning might be an understatement. Royce is gonna lose his shit." Mel grinned.

Emily released a shaky exhale, and she spread her hand over her belly, emotion cresting in her eyes that were the same color as her brother's.

Her mama stepped up to her and took her by the hand. "You are so incredibly beautiful, sweet girl. Look at you. Mel is right. Royce is gonna lose his shit."

I choked out a laugh, and Maggie took Emily's other hand. "I agree. You walk in the room, and my brother can't look anywhere else. Come in looking like this? You're going to be lucky if you make it all the way through dinner before he's hauling you to privacy to get you out of this dress."

Mabel tossed her a grin. "That's what weddin' dresses are—a gift for the groom. A present to be unwrapped."

"Torn to shreds, more like it," Mel said. "It might as well be five-thousand-dollar tissue paper."

"Um, if he destroys this dress, he's in trouble." Mia sent a playful smile to Emily.

Mia Godwin was dressed in the same bridesmaids dress I'd modeled just a couple weeks before. The clingy, gorgeous fabric hugged her shape flawlessly.

I'd met the wife of Carolina George's drummer two days ago. Emily had been right.

I loved her.

Instantly.

So honest and open. Direct but soft.

This striking beauty who undoubtedly stopped traffic when she walked on the street.

Melanie hadn't been exaggerating—there were gonna be some epic pictures from the event. The way the photographer was currently scurrying around and clicking a gazillion shots and groaning in pleasure as she did was proof of that.

"Mommy!" The door banged open to Daisy running in with Anna in tow.

The two little black-haired angels had been inseparable from the second they'd met.

"Me and my's bestest new cousin friend are all ready. We didn't even get no dirt on our dresses when we went down the slide."

Lord help me.

"Daisy. You were supposed to be reading books in your room. Not playing on the swing set."

"Well, I was telling her a story when we played. That counts, right?"

"This kid's gonna be an attorney." Mel sent me one of those

looks that prayed for my sanity. "Pretty sure she can talk herself out of any bit of trouble. Hell, all she needs to do is smile."

Daisy beamed the evidence.

Exhibit one.

Emily giggled at poor Anna standing looking like she'd been cornered.

"I think my daughter is a bad influence," I said, twisting my face up in a hapless apology.

"That's what cousins are for," Daisy informed me. "We gotta learn from each other. And have all the fun together. Right, Anna?"

Anna nodded in her shy way.

The child was quiet and timid and probably feeling a bit out of sorts, but we were doin' our absolute best to show her this was where she belonged.

That she fit right in.

Cousins.

I doubted either Daisy or Anna had expected that. Rhys had brought it up like a tease during the dress rehearsal last night. Afterward, the two hadn't been able to stop claiming it.

It was crazy how a few short weeks ago, I'd felt as if I were shouldering so much alone. Loving for so many. Trying to hold up my mama and daddy. To provide for my daughter. To be everything.

And now we were surrounded.

Lifted.

Elevated.

Loved.

Mabel sent me a tender smile as if she'd had a direct connection to my thoughts, her mouth moving in a silent whisper, *I am so thankful to have you back in our lives.*

Maybe I never should have rejected their support in the first place. Never should have let the choices Richard had made steal them away.

Truth was, most of the time it felt easier to close yourself off than to admit your need.

"Auntie Emily, you look smokins' hot. Just like my mommy."

A disbelieving laugh scraped from my throat.

This kid.

"True story," Melanie told her, giving Daisy a high-five.

"You do, too, Mells Bells," she added with a resolute nod of her head, child nothing but happy chaos.

Oh, she got that from Rhys. Apparently, my little troublemaker wasn't the only bad influence around here.

There was a knock at the door, and it swung open to the minister poking his head in. "Everyone ready? I'm about to head to the meadow."

Emily sucked in a flurried breath. "I'm ready."

We all filed out, carrying our heels in our hands and wearing flip-flops on our feet so we could make it down the pathway in one piece.

The day was beginning to set so perfectly. That gorgeous fusion of color gathering at the horizon and painting the sky in a portrait of beauty.

Picture perfect.

We made it all the way down to the bottom of the hill where I'd had a small stand built with storage and a cooler for the bouquets. Stopping there, we quickly changed into our heels, all of us giggling like crazy as we shoved our flip-flops into the slots and figured out which bouquet belonged to who.

Excitement billowing.

Nerves rippling.

Daisy went running along to check on the guest book that was set up on the other side of the meadow where the guests came in from the parking lot. Funny how the job she'd been so desperate for had all but been forgotten once she'd gained her new best friend.

Luckily, Shea Stone had been happy to stand in and assist.

We resituated Emily's dress, made sure her hair was just right, and adjusted her bouquet.

Emily heaved out a sigh of skittering nerves. "Goodness. I just might pass out. If I do, you better carry me to the altar. I don't wanna miss this no matter the circumstance. Let it be known I give permission for the weddin' to go on even if I'm not conscious for it." She forced out the flustered joke.

"You're doin' great," I promised her. "Everything is perfect. Just like I said. Don't worry. Just enjoy your day."

"I love you," she said, her chin tremoring. "This just feels right. You takin' up your spot in the family. Where you've always belonged."

My heart pushed against my ribs, and that emotion climbed higher. "I wouldn't want to be anywhere else."

I stepped back so her mama could press a kiss to her cheek, and then Mabel walked over to me and drew me in for a long hug that caught me by surprise, her mouth at my ear when she said, "It's the most beautiful thing to get to watch both of my daughters get married in this sacred spot."

Her words were packed with meaning.

With love.

With unending support.

Stepping back, she squeezed both my hands, and I did my best not to weep right there. The stunning highs and the gutting lows I'd been riding the last weeks.

But I knew…right then. This was where I wanted to be.

"I am so thankful for that, too."

She touched my cheek. "Precious girl."

Then she turned and walked over to Lincoln who held out his arm to escort her to her seat. The woman was wearing this pretty sequined gown with a swooping left shoulder.

A beauty aged through the years. Stoic and real and true.

When she disappeared up the hill, Lenny Ramsey came down it.

Looking sharp in his suit, the man grayed at the temples and his face worn rugged from his years spent out on their ranch.

His smile was out of this world when he saw his daughter standing there.

My heart leapt.

Not quite sure how to stand under the magnitude of this beauty.

Amor. Amor. Amor.

My daddy had always taught me that's what this place was. That it bled it. Rooted it. Grew it and heightened it.

I'd never been so sure of that truth than right then.

The music changed, and a furor rippled through the air.

Palpable.

Lifting chills on my flesh.

"Are you ready for this?" I whispered to Emily.

"I've never been so ready for anything in my life."

A wistful smile pulled to my mouth. I could remember so clearly feeling the exact same thing.

No reservations.

All the bridesmaids got into place. Mia started up the hill. Mel paced behind her, then Maggie trailed behind. I gulped down a steeling breath when I knew it was my time to follow. I walked up the incline where we were hidden at the base of the sweeping hill, inhaling a sharp breath when I crested the top and the meadow came into view.

Rows of chairs covered in white fabric sat on either side of the tree with an aisle running down the middle.

Abundant bouquets made up of roses, lilies, and peonies with an assortment of draping greenery sat at the end of each one. Bouquets I'd handpicked the last two days and painstakingly worked to piece together.

A blessing issued with each one.

At the center of it was the massive tree with its stately branches that stretched out to form a ceiling, rising high toward the twilight sky, casting the entire place in its protection and warmth.

Royce stood on the right waitin' on his bride.

The man rocked back on his heels with his hands linked behind his back.

Anxious.

Purposed.

But it was the man standing at his side that ripped the air from my lungs and sent my axis tipping.

That compass pointed directly at him.

I might as well have been gazing on him for the very first time.

Face chiseled, every distinct, glorious line glinting in the shimmering light of the fading day.

A beautiful protector.

A savage lover.

He watched me like he was having a hard time standing still and not making his way for me.

Sage eyes traveling from my face and slowly drifting down.

I swore, in the distance, I saw him gulp. Clearly, the man appreciated the dress.

Energy zapped through our atmosphere.

Shockwaves.

Wrapping me in chills and warmth.

Hope and need.

I bit down on my bottom lip and tried to focus on not tripping over my own feet, and decided it would be much safer to be glancing around to take in the faces that had shifted in their seats to watch the wedding party come up the aisle.

A ton of faces I recognized.

Some I'd only met.

A few I'd never seen before.

My heart swelled with an onslaught of adoration when I saw where my mama and daddy had been seated in the second row behind Emily's family, Daisy sitting on her knees backward and holding onto the back of the chair next to my mama so she could see.

Richard had undone me again.

An hour ago, he'd been there to carry my mama's frail body all the way from our house and out to the meadow. Her wheelchair was placed off to the side so she could be moved into it after the ceremony where she could enjoy the night before the exhaustion set in.

Mama smiled in her wistful, loving way.

Tender and knowing.

My spirit thrashed, and I smiled back, right before my gaze was being drawn back to the man.

To the man who was watching me as if he couldn't look anywhere else.

And I trusted.

Trusted the care.

Trusted the concern.

I trusted in the beautiful heart that lived underneath the ghosts that covered him like a howling shroud, concealing the secrets he told me he couldn't yet give.

But I chose to believe.

To believe in him.

To believe in us.

I wondered if he felt it.

The way my spirit cracked wide open and a torrent of devotion went flooding toward him.

The way that big body itched in that sexy suit that fit better than should be allowed.

The way my mouth watered, and my stomach somersaulted, and I was physically aching to take part.

He tugged at his bottom lip with his teeth, fightin' a smirk.

A shiver toppled and twisted down my spine.

Yeah.

He felt it.

I guessed I was far too excited by the prospect of him reminding me of it later.

I moved over to my spot and turned around to face the aisle.

As soon as I was in place, the violinist shifted her song. Everyone stood in anticipation.

A second later, Anna came dancing up between the chairs.

Grinning shy but tossing her petals into the air and letting them rain down around her.

Ooohs and *ahhs* rippled the space.

Daisy waved at her, and she waved back.

Adorable and sweet.

When she got halfway, she went racing for her father who'd knelt to catch her, the man sweeping the little girl into his arms and tucking her to his side.

The two of them stood waiting for Emily.

A moment later, she was slowly coming into view as she and her father made their way to the top of the hill.

A collective round of gasps went up. Their lungs held in a moment of reverence.

The bride striking awe in the guests.

Royce held the little girl tighter, eyes eating Emily up with such a divine adoration that it brought tears to mine.

The way her own expression flared and flamed and softened.

Their love so apparent and clear.

When she made it to the end of the aisle, her daddy leaned in and pressed a kiss to her cheek, whispered something that none of us could hear. She nodded, her smile so soft, and he stepped back, bringing the fingers of both hands to his lips and blowing her a kiss.

Oh goodness. So sweet.

Then he turned and shook Royce's hand, and then the man reached out for the little girl that he'd just met. Pulled her into his arms. Hugged her tight and carried her over to where Mabel was sitting.

A statement.

A proclamation.

Like they were offering their own vows.

Accepting her into their precious family.

My chest stretched so tight, and that burning at the back of my eyes was at full force.

The minister began, opening in the typical way, talking about marriage and what it really meant. Why it was sacred.

When he finished, Royce fumbled into his pocket to find the vows he and Emily had written. There was no missing the way his hands were shaking as he unfolded the piece of paper. He swallowed hard, shook his head, overcome with emotion.

His voice clogged with the immensity of it.

"Emily. My love. *My soulshine.* I give you my life. My days. My love. My devotion. My loyalty. Everything I do, I will do for us. For our marriage. For our family. I know you know I'm not perfect, but when I make mistakes, I promise to learn from them. I promise to hear you. To see you. To never forget you in the times when it matters most and in the moments that seem insignificant. Because every second with you is significant. You are my life. And I stand here, offering you mine."

Emily sniffled, laughed through her joy, and touched her nose with the back of her hand.

Trying to gather herself.

While my mind raced back to that evening seven years ago, to the man who currently stood like a fortress of fidelity behind Royce.

Staring at me.

My mind whirred with the memory of what he'd promised. The way his voice had tremored and shook as he'd read the words he'd written for me.

"It's funny when you meet someone, and you just know. Funny how your heart instantly recognizes someone who was meant for you. Violet Marin, you opened my eyes to so many things. Our love came on fast, this wedding faster. But I have zero hesitation standing here before you now. Know we talked about this—about what it takes to make a marriage work. We've discussed our parents who are still loving each other to this day, wondering how they did it when so many people never seem to get that far. We came to the conclusion that we have to want more joy for each other than we want for ourselves. That a love that lasts is an unselfish love. It's a giving love. And we know that ideal has to go both ways or it's just not gonna work. But standing here, Violet, under this tree, I promise every day of my life I will wake up wanting to give you more joy than you had the day before. I will wake up and sacrifice for you, whatever it takes. I will wake up with respect. I will wake up with devotion. Every single day, everything I do, I'll be doing it for you."

Emotion tightened my throat, and I swallowed, hoping my knees didn't start knocking right there.

Richard's jaw clenched, teeth grinding, and I wondered if he wasn't reiterating those words all over again.

Emily and Royce's hands swung between them, their bond unending, moving between them and covering those who had gathered to share this day. Emily attempted to clear the roughness from her voice, but her words were hitched, lumbering with the emphasis.

"Royce. My love. My joy. I give you my life. My days. My love. My devotion. My loyalty. Everything I do, I will do for us. For our marriage. For our family. I know you know I'm not perfect, but when I make mistakes, I promise to learn from them. I promise to hear you. To see you. To never forget you in the times when it matters most and in the moments that seem insignificant. Because every second with you is significant. You are my life. And I stand here, offering you mine."

The minister pronounced them married, and Royce was sweeping her off her feet and swinging her around and kissing her fierce and hard and soft.

A seal of every promise they had made.

Everyone cheered.

That little girl went running back to him. He hiked her up into his arms, and Emily reached out and took her hand. The three of them walked back down the aisle together. I followed to the spot where I was supposed to meet my escort.

My life.

My husband.

Richard was there, so tall and fierce, extending his elbow.

I grabbed it.

Held on for dear life.

Not understanding his sacrifice.

But knowing it was true.

Twinkle lights glittered from where they were wound in the branches above. The rows of chairs had been moved out and round tables set in their place, the centerpieces glowing and gorgeous in the middle of each.

A makeshift dance floor had been set up in the middle, and a two-foot stage was on the far right.

The delicious dinner had just been cleared away.

Emily was glowin' where she sat directly across the table, Royce glued to her side, his hands all over her every second, never breaking their connection.

I guessed I could say the same thing for the man beside me.

I glanced to my right. Richard shifted to look at me the second I did, no doubt sensing me peeking at him.

Since we were surrounded by the rest of the wedding party,

Richard squeezed the hand he had rested on my bare thigh under the table.

It hadn't taken him long to find that high slit, taking advantage of the situation, not that I was gonna complain. His fingertips kept making leisurely passes up and down my leg.

Flesh tingling.

Lifting with chills.

My stomach in constant knots of needy anticipation.

A smirk ticked up at the corner of those lush lips, and Richard dipped down to whisper in my ear, "You have any idea what this dress is doin' to me?"

I gave him an innocent look.

He chuckled low, and his mouth went traipsing along my jaw, teeth nipping at my earlobe. "If you aren't sure now, don't worry, I'll be showing you later."

Need sloshed and spun and throbbed between my thighs. A tangible, perceptible flush.

One that Richard felt.

He groaned, and his fingers twitched on my leg. He gripped me tighter.

I heaved out a shaky breath.

Rhys was suddenly there, draping his arms around both of our shoulders and poking his head between us. "And what are you two up to over here?"

He cracked a cheeky grin.

Redness flushed.

Richard elbowed him in the gut.

Rhys howled, ducking back, laughing and guarding the spot. "What's wrong with you, man? I'm just coming over to say hi. Be friendly and genial. And you go around gettin' violent."

"I'll show you violent."

He clapped Richard on the shoulder. "Oh, I think you were definitely gettin' ready to show us *something* until I intervened." Rhys shot me a wink.

Embarrassment went racing.

"Huh. Funny you were watching. You lookin' for lessons?" Richard tipped him a smirk.

These two.

Rhys howled with laughter and curled his arm tighter around my shoulders. "No, man. Just worried for our beautiful Vi, here. Need to make sure your sorry ass knows what he's doing. Poor girl."

My head shook with the flush I was choking down, and I couldn't stop the smile when I looked up at the goof grinning down at me. "Don't worry, Rhys. I'm just fine."

"Just fine?" Richard challenged.

I shrugged a tease.

His nostrils flared.

I laughed.

Feeling free.

Light.

So different.

So right.

"Well…" I said, the ribbing twitching all over my mouth.

Those fingers were sinking into my thigh again, and Richard dipped his face down close to mine.

"You're gonna pay for that later." His eyes danced and played.

My teeth clamped down on my bottom lip. "I sure hope so. I wouldn't want to walk around bein' *just fine* for all my life, would I?"

Melanie cracked up. "Oh, Vi. I love you. Thank God you took this sorry sucker back."

Yeah.

Thank God.

I smiled at him.

He shook his head, lips fighting their smile.

Amor. Amor. Amor.

I felt it shimmer and dance.

Rhys grabbed Richard's arm and tugged at him. "Was actually here for a reason other than pointing out that you're a wet noodle in bed. It's time."

Richard's brow lifted in warning.

Rhys grinned. No shame. "Come on, let's do this."

Richard gave me another little squeeze before he pushed to

standing. "I'll be right back."

I frowned in confusion.

"It's a surprise," he added low.

That was right about the same time a bunch of different people started popping up from the tables spread around the meadow.

Rhys and Richard started it.

Leif pushed back from the table where we sat and stood with them.

At the next table over, the rest of Royce's band, A Riot of Roses, stood, chugging their beers and setting the empties on their table before they joined the group that gathered.

The members of A Riot of Roses—Van, Arson, and Hunter—gave off this unruly vibe. This disordered crew who were ridiculously tight.

Best of friends that carried their secrets like mysteries on their skin.

Covered in mayhem. Rough and raw. Screaming of trouble and big city. But man, did they make something to look at in their fitted suits, tats twisting out from their sleeves and necks.

They all started to climb to the small stage.

Off to the left, almost the whole table stood.

Sunder.

I'd gotten to meet them earlier.

Austin Stone.

Lyrik West.

Ash Evans.

Zachary Kennedy.

Their original lead singer, Sebastian Stone, had joined them.

His wife Shea was at his side.

All of them were superstars who were so down to earth that it hardly made sense, and I realized that Richard would soon be like them.

Recognizable at every turn.

It was like we'd been hidden out here at my small farm, in our tiny town that could hardly be considered a city, the country so far from the stardom that Richard had reached that it didn't seem real.

Out of touch with the fame.

But it was impossible not to recognize it then.

Not when Richard climbed to the stage with everyone and the hired band stepped aside. Everyone picked up their instruments.

Excitement rippled through the air.

Every person attuned as the sound of feedback came through the speakers.

They quickly set up, and Richard moved to the mic as he slung the strap of his guitar over his head.

Oh god.

I was not gonna make it, seeing him onstage.

Not when it was all so new.

Not when I was still reeling.

Not when I was still trying to catch up to the sudden shift in my life.

But this wasn't about me, and he was pressing that gorgeous mouth to the mic, saying, "Emily and Royce, please report to the dance floor."

He winked at that.

Everyone laughed as Emily pressed her hand to her mouth and tears sprang to her eyes.

The woman totally surprised.

Royce stood and offered her his hand. She took it, his bride shaking all over as he led her out into the middle of the dance floor.

The guests gathered around the three sides to witness their first dance.

A thrill that drew us to the boundary.

Mesmerized, I watched as Richard wrapped his big hand around the neck of his acoustic guitar and strummed a single chord.

It resonated right through the middle of me.

"We figured since there were a whole ton of people here who could serenade you two on your wedding night, we'd better make good use of it. This is something we put together for y'all. A gift. Our blessing. Our prayer that your lives are filled with all the love the two of you deserve. That all your days are a love song."

That thrill sizzled as the artists on the stage took their spots, this mesh of country and rock.

I was pretty sure what was getting ready to transpire right then was gonna be straight-up musical history.

Something special. Something you couldn't experience anywhere else.

Some of the world's greatest talent standing on one stage and playing for the smallest crowd.

Talk about intimate.

Oh, but that was what it was. The way Royce looked at Emily in that moment. Their worlds colliding in a kaleidoscope of beauty.

He took her in his arms.

Love billowed in the breeze.

Richard and Van both had acoustic guitars, and Lyrik West had an electric. The three of them played through the intricate notes that began the song.

Soft and mesmerizing.

Instantly entrancing.

Their guitars harmonized, while Leif, Zee, and Hunter quietly drummed this rising beat that started off slow and gained in an escalating intensity.

Leif played a bongo with his bare hands, Zee and Hunter with smaller drums that were perched between their knees.

Rhys and Ash both had their basses, and A Riot of Roses' bassist, Hunter, had gotten ahold of a cello.

Shea Stone began to hum into the mic she held, while her husband gently played the acoustic guitar he'd strapped over his body.

It was like Royce and Emily had their own personal symphony.

Richard pressed his mouth to the mic and began to sing.

That voice rough and sensuous.

Wrapping around me like a dream.

Shadows playing across his gorgeous, chiseled face, his cheeks cut in that severe, distinct fashion.

Still the most beautiful man I'd ever seen.

That voice twisted and rose and lowered, so thick with emotion I could taste it, Shea's extraordinary voice wrapping with his as they sang this duet that curled and whispered and stunned.

Singing about love.

About cherishing.

About never lettin' go.

Those sage eyes found me from the stage. The way they always had. As if he felt me. Two of us tied in this tangible, impossible way.

Our connection thrummed.

My love rising, coiling in the air, his meeting mine in the middle.

My stomach tightened and my spirit shook.

His voice, his words, his entrancing, dark beauty the only thing I could breathe.

The cadence lifted and rose and heightened. The music becoming this driving force that shivered and shook and rumbled in the air. Their voices climbed and soared with it, and everyone on stage had begun to sing along with them.

The song reached this crescendo that I was pretty sure left every single person there shaken.

Changed.

Impacted by the magnificence.

My throat tightened, burning like crazy, my chest expanding in time. I pressed my hands against it, trying to keep my heart from bursting right out.

The last note was held. It reverberated the ground and echoed across the fields until it trailed off on the last, tinkling notes.

Everyone stood there gaping.

Royce and Emily were melded together on the dance floor, barely swaying where they'd become one.

"Royce and Emily would now like the rest of their wedding party to join them on the dance floor," Shea said.

Leif and Rhys hopped down from the stage. Leif went right for his wife and Rhys was grinning like mad when he took Maggie's hand where she stood off to the side of the dance floor.

Lincoln and Melanie joined them, and then those sage eyes were on me as the man climbed down from the stage and began to stalk my way.

I felt like prey in that moment.

His hunger wild.

His need fierce.

As fierce as the devotion that I could feel drumming from his every step.

Hot hands landed on my hips and his lips landed on my jaw. "You have any idea what it's like to be on that stage singing and look out and know the most beautiful girl in the world belongs to me?"

Shivers raced.

"Probably a whole lot of the same as looking up on that stage and knowing you belong to me," I whispered.

The rest of the band members remaining onstage began to play the megahit duet that Shea and Sebastian Stone had recorded together years before.

A song I'd heard what felt like a million times and would never get old.

This soft, seductive love song that filled my ears and struck a chord in my being.

Richard pulled me into the strength of his arms.

A bright burst of light flashed behind my eyes.

Every nerve ending in my body sparked.

He felt it.

Groaned as he tugged me closer, up tight against all that hard, packed muscle that twitched and jerked.

He led me deeper out onto the dance floor, whispered, "I just want to dance with the prettiest girl in the place."

And tonight—tonight, I was no longer afraid of being that girl.

I curled my fingers into the lapels of his suit jacket, desperate to erase the space. For a way to cling to this feeling. To make it last forever.

He pulled me tighter, wrapping me in strong arms. Where I knew I belonged.

Shea's voice lamented in our ears, her husband singing low.

Daisy and Anna had joined the couples, the two of them holding each other by the hands and spinning round and round.

Leif and Mia were lost in each other.

Mel and Linc goofing around.

Rhys had Maggie by the hand and was spinning her fast, catching her, dipping her, spinning her again.

Peals of carefree laughter rode through the air.

Joy. Joy. Joy.

Richard spun me, too, only he stopped me when I was facing away and pulled my back to his chest.

He held me there, rocking us slow, nuzzling at my neck. His lips brushed the shell of my ear.

Chills spread.

"Look at you, Violet Ramsey. So fuckin' sexy in this dress. Stealing my breath. Stealing my heart. It always belonged to you, and I'm begging you to never give it back."

His words spiraled around me, and I nodded my head and felt the thunder of his heart where it rampaged at his ribs.

Severity rushed around us.

Threading his fingers through mine, he curled my arms and pressed our hands against my chest, hugging me tight from behind. "Forever."

Then he extended our left hands out in front of us and brushed his thumb over the bare spot on my ring finger.

Then I was choking over the affection that filled every crevice in my being when I saw what he held in his right hand.

The ring.

The ring that had been his grandmother's. I hadn't felt right keeping it, so I'd sent it certified mail to his mama rather than facing any of them to return it.

I'd felt the loss of it ever since.

"This has always belonged to you, Violet. Just like my heart."

I exhaled a shaky sigh, almost as shaky as my hands, barely able to keep it together when he slipped the ring back onto my finger.

Then he spun me again and curled me into his arms. "You," he said. "It's always been you."

Richard

I laid Daisy's sleeping form on her bed, tugging the shoes she'd danced in all night from her precious little feet.

"She lived that wedding large, didn't she?" I murmured into the dusky light that barely infiltrated her room, gazing down at the child.

Warmth spread through my veins.

Nothing but an intoxicating drug.

Wanting more and more of it. So reliant on it that the thought of not having it made me think I just might die.

Except this drug?

It wasn't artificial.

It didn't numb the pain.

It just cut me wide open and let me feel everything.

All this love that I'd been terrified to feel. To recognize. To hold.

I glanced back at the woman who hovered over by the door, wearing that sexy-ass dress that'd had me hard the entire fuckin' day.

"I thought she was going to pass out right on the dance floor, she was so tired," she whispered. "Mama tried to convince her to head back to the house with her, but she wasn't having it."

"She wasn't about to miss out on a bit of the fun," I murmured quietly.

"No chance of that," Violet whispered, her sweet voice wrapping me in tendrils and ribbons.

Woman a straight shot of lust to my veins.

I glanced her way before I looked back at the child. "She's incredible, Violet. Incredible because she has the most incredible mother."

That fact lodged itself in my throat.

Heavy and dense.

Pushing out.

Knew I had to tell her.

Just fucking tell her.

The confession burned on my tongue, but I had no idea how the hell I would be able to let it out.

Her head shook, thunderbolt eyes striking in the darkness, her subdued laughter full of self-conscious adoration. "Half the time I don't know what to do with her."

"Pretty clear to me you know exactly what to do. She's courageous, Violet. Feisty and sweet. Speaks her mind but also wants the joy for everyone around her. She's a giver. She's a fighter."

"You mean she's a handful."

A light chuckle rumbled free. "That, too."

Nerves had her chewing at her bottom lip, and her gaze caressed over the sleeping child. "I'm trying. Trying to do right by her. The only thing I want is for her to grow strong. To feel love. To know she's secure."

Her confession trembled on the last.

I pushed to my feet.

Violet stood across the room.

Black hair twisted in these flowy knots and curls.

Her silky skin glowing beneath that plush, rose dress, the plunging neckline teasing me with the delicious swell of her tits. But it was that ridiculously high slit that had nearly undone me.

My fairy girl was nothin' but a miracle.

Magic.

My moonflower.

"So fuckin' pretty," I murmured.

The ring I'd put back in its rightful place glinted and shined in the spray of moonlight that slanted through the window.

Streaks of it lighting up her face.

"So fuckin' sexy."

I moved across the room with measured steps. Energy lit. A shockwave of electricity.

It was like the flick of a switch.

A shockwave that blinded.

Violets and grace and the girl.

Violet sucked in a staggered breath as I stalked her way, and I edged her out the door and into the hall.

Her back thudded against the opposite wall.

I took my fingertip and trailed it from her jaw, down her trembling throat, and let it trace down that lust-inducing line that dipped deep between her breasts.

"Do you get it yet, Violet? What you mean to me? That you're everything? That everything I've done is because of my love for you?"

Her chin lifted. Those eyes on me. Letting me in. All the way down into their vast, staggering depths. "I trust you."

A groan rumbled in my chest.

Wasn't sure if it was because she shouldn't, or because I was thankful that she did.

That confession burned on my tongue again.

Rancid, venomous fire.

I swallowed it down and let it fuel the flames.

Let it stoke the need.

I trailed the pad of my thumb across her sexpot mouth.

Girl a motherfucking fantasy.

Impossible where she stood with her back hooked to the wall.

A moan climbed her throat. I kept caressing my thumb along that lush bottom lip, gazing down at the girl who owned my world.

Possessed me with a glance.

Her heart beating this manic rhythm, mine picking up time.

I took her left hand and brought her ring finger to my mouth, pressed the glittering stone to my lips. "I love you, Violet Ramsey."

"I love you, Richard. I love you with all my soul."

I swooped her up. She squealed in surprise, and then she wrapped her arms around my neck and melted into me.

I carried her into her room. The whole time, I kissed her slow and desperate.

I wondered if she could feel the apology.

The truth that I'd take it all back if there was a chance that I could. The truth that it didn't matter what happened when I told her, I would fight for her.

She whimpered and sighed, that honeyed tongue playing and dancing and teasing against mine.

Strokes and licks.

Desire lapped and sizzled and flamed.

Growing in strength.

I only stopped long enough to shut her door and click the lock before I set her in the middle of her room. "Let me look at you."

"I think you've been lookin' at me all night," she teased.

A rough chuckle curled up my chest. "Not possible to pay attention to anything else when I've got heaven staring back at me."

Heat crept up her chest and splashed her cheeks.

Girl so fucking sexy and so fucking sweet.

"You wreck me, Violet. Absolutely destroy me."

"You ruined me the first time you touched me."

"Hope you're good with me touchin' you time and time again." It came out a warning.

She breezed out the wisp of a sigh. "I'm just fine with you ripping me apart while you're keeping me together."

There she was.

My wife who wasn't shy to ask for what she wanted.

To give it just as good as she took it.

Lust burst in my blood. A dam breaking way and sweeping away all control.

Need overwhelming.

Crushing.

Guts tied up and body aching to get lost in this girl.

"Gonna devour every inch of that delicious body," I muttered, voice scraping the heated air.

Energy banged against the walls.

Trembled underfoot.

"You better." I heard it for what it was. A demand.

My hands drove into her hair, and I jerked her mouth against mine in a punishing kiss.

She returned it, this girl giving me her all.

My hands found her neck, and I rode them all the way down to tease at her nipples through the clingy fabric. "This dress. This fucking dress, Violet. You are killing me, baby. Can't handle how bad I want you. Every second. Every day. Not ever gonna let you go."

"That's good because I won't let you leave me." She pushed her hands to my chest and ran them up under my jacket, shoving it from my shoulders. I twisted out of it and let it drop to the floor, my hands rushing back to grip her by the hips.

I tugged her against my throbbing cock. "Feel that? What you do to me?"

Violet whimpered, and she started jerking through the buttons on my shirt. "I want to feel it. Want to feel it all."

Yes-fucking-please.

My hands slipped down, all the way to that slit, getting greedy where I palmed her thigh. Hooking her leg around my hip, I slid my hand up higher until I was getting a good handful of her ass.

I rubbed against her.

"Richard. Please. Need you." She made it through the last button of my shirt, her palms flat as she raked the material back to expose my chest. She immediately dove in as I shrugged the shirt the rest of the way free, girl frantically kissing across the canvas of art.

Fire streaked.

This flood of devotion that careened and crashed.

Overcame every obstacle. Made me sure we could make it through what was coming and coming fast.

That possession rose with it. Purposed protectiveness. Truth that I was going to do whatever it took to take care of her. To be there for her no matter what happened.

My spirit clutched at that.

Daisy's face flashing through my mind.

I blocked it out.

Not tonight.

Not tonight.

I would tell her tomorrow.

Tonight—we needed this.

I slipped my hands up her back and found the zipper of her dress. I peeled it down. The sound of it sparked in the air.

Electrified.

Every molecule charged.

A second away from when we would completely combust.

I dragged the straps of the dress from her shoulders and pulled it down, letting the entire thing pool at her feet.

Holy fuck.

"You really are trying to kill me, aren't you?"

Violet stood there in this one-piece body suit. White lace and satin. The thinnest strip of material making up the straps and barely covering her nipples, the fullness of her breasts peeking out on both sides. Plunging down to go with the rest of her dress, so deep her belly button was exposed.

It rode high on her hips, her ass bare.

"You like?" she asked, standing there in only that and her high, high heels.

I choked through a needy laugh. "I am not okay. Turn around."

Violet obeyed, turning around in a slow, tempting tease.

The bodysuit was backless, the slips of fabric that had covered her tits getting thinner and thinner until they were nothing but spaghetti straps that went over her shoulders and down her back.

Those two straps T'd into one strip that disappeared between the lush cheeks of her ass.

I pressed my hand to her upper back and pushed her down. Her hands flew out to catch herself on the mattress of her bed.

With her bent over, I spread both palms over her bottom and squeezed tight. "You got any idea how perfect you are? What it's like to be standing like this looking at you?"

She wiggled in my hold.

I nearly died right there.

She shifted so she could look back at me, thunderbolt eyes filled with hunger. "I need you, Richard. Need you right now. Need you in a way I've never needed anything in my life."

"You already have me," I promised, letting my fingertips part her cheeks, following the line of the strip. "So pretty," I murmured.

She whimpered and pressed back when I barely grazed over her lips. Girl dripping wet. "See how much you need me, baby?"

"So much. More than you could ever know." She pressed her face into the bed, and I was spreading my hands up her back, easing her up as I let my fingers slip under the straps at her shoulders. I dragged them down, pulling the bodysuit away at the same time and sliding it down her body as I towered over her from behind.

I shifted her just a fraction so she could see herself in the full-length mirror standing in the corner of her room.

Her tits jutted and perfectly round. Nipples puckered and begging for my touch. "Look at you," I whispered at her ear.

I cupped her tits in my hands. She pressed into my hold as I rubbed my thumbs across the diamond tips.

A quiver rolled down her spine.

"Perfection."

I turned her around and urged her back onto the bed.

Girl naked.

Staring up at me as I flicked the button of the dress pants and shoved them down. My cock steel. Pointing toward the sky. Begging for her.

She whimpered when she saw me. Girl devouring me with

those eyes. Same way as I was devouring her. "It's you, Richard. You who makes me shake. Never before have I met a man who can command my breath."

"You own me," I murmured low.

The truth.

The girl was my sheer, utter undoing.

The one thing that could make me veer course. Should have known I'd been heading for her all along.

She leaned back on her elbows, her heels planted on the bed, stomach quivering in anticipation. She watched me with that molten, trusting gaze.

"You've shattered me."

And I was gone.

Lost in her eyes and that stare and her heart.

I climbed up over her and kissed her hard. Demanding it all. Her sweet heart thundering in the space and her shy wickedness coming out to play.

Girl this perfect combination of innocent and vixen.

Loved that about her.

Our tongues stroked. Taunted and teased while our bodies rose to this heightened level.

Heat lapping.

Flames steadily filling the space.

Our spirits humming.

Perfected in *this*.

And I needed her. Fucking needed her to know what she really meant.

"Love you, Violet. Love you," I muttered at her mouth while her fingers scraped and pled and tried to drag me closer.

I rocked back onto my knees and took hers in my hands, spreading her wide. I didn't stall before I dove down and took a long lick through her slick, hot pussy.

Girl nearly shot from the bed. "Richard. Oh. God. Please."

"Love the way you taste," I growled, edging back to get a good look before I went back in and parted her slit with my tongue.

Hands fisted in my hair.

Close to painful.

It sent a shock of lust rocking down my spine. My dick so hard I could barely see.

Lust sending waves of dizziness through my head.

Rational side of me knew this should be impossible. That I shouldn't be touching this girl. And the selfish part of me knew there was no chance I would ever let her go. "Could stay right here forever, Violet. Right here between these legs."

She moaned, writhed, begged for more.

I gave it to her. Teasing her with my tongue, licking and suckling at her swollen, engorged clit.

Cries jutted from her mouth, and she pushed closer. "Oh. God. Richard. Love you touchin' me. Missed it. Don't stop. Don't ever stop."

Didn't plan on it.

I pressed two fingers into the tight warmth of her sweet cunt. Her walls clamped around them. I fucked them deep, dragging them across that spot that kept making her buck and moan, licking and sucking her the whole time.

"Richard."

The air shivered.

Crackles of greed.

I pulled my fingers out so I could spread her on both sides, and I fucked her with my tongue.

Driving her mad.

Wild.

Girl bucking and pleading and demanding more.

More. More. More.

Wanted to give it all.

My love and my life and this devotion that wasn't ever gonna end.

I kissed all the way back along the crease of her ass, tongue rimming that hole, girl nearly coming undone right there.

I grinned.

Couldn't fucking help it.

Loved that she loved to play.

That she trusted.

That she craved it.

Gave it.

Took it.

I edged back so I could give it to her.

"On your hands and knees, baby."

Violet's eyes flashed in need, and she flipped around, no hesitation, pressing back toward me as she swung her gaze over her shoulder.

Girl holding me with that unrelenting stare.

I took two handfuls of that bottom, my dick rubbing along her crease.

"Please, Richard. I'm long past teasing."

"You need this?"

"I'm beggin' for it."

I grabbed myself by the base, running the tip of my dick down her cleft until just the head was dipping into the welcome of her delicious folds.

I nudged in an inch, a moan locking in my throat, girl whimpering and pushing back.

"Take it," I told her.

She did, wiggling and adjusting and taking me deeper.

I groaned, watching my cock disappear into her body.

So good.

So right.

This girl my all.

"Yes," I hissed.

She slammed back, taking me to the hilt.

Her thighs trembled, and I could tell she was struggling to adjust.

She was so tight. Her walls held me in a needy clutch.

No girl should feel this good.

My cock throbbed in a thousand tiny pinpricks of bliss.

"You feel that, Violet? Feel what you do to me? How good you feel? Nothing. Nothing in the world compares to this. Nothing like being in you."

"No one. Never. Richard."

I grabbed her by the hips and started to take her in rigid, deep, demanding strokes.

Her sweet body rocking back to meet me with each thrust.

Violet's head was rolling from side-to-side, her hair all over the place. I grabbed a fistful of it, tugging her back so I could get to that mouth.

Our tongues fucking in time.

This war of greed that both of us were gonna win. "Not gonna let you go, Violet. Never again."

"I wouldn't survive," she whispered, her truth banging against the walls.

"You're mine. Mine, sweet girl. You feel it…what I do to you? You were made for me."

Pleasure wracked my cells. Gathering fast. Gaining speed as I watched my cock driving into the sweet relief of her pussy.

Violet whimpered, "More," as her hands curled into her comforter to keep herself steady.

That pleasure whipped. Streaking my spine and lifting my balls.

I eased back so I could circle her ass with my thumb, and I pressed into that tight, puckered hole.

A desperate whine left her, her pants rising into the air.

Whipping around me.

The girl dropped her chest to the bed, her head turned to the side, watching me as she reached under us. Blunted fingernails scratched at my balls. Nails raking that sensitive flesh, swirling around my hole.

"Oh god. Fuck. Violet. You are destroying me."

I took her faster and harder. She met me thrust for thrust.

Girl demanding it.

I would give her my all.

Everything.

My heart. My truth. My life.

"Touch yourself, baby."

And she went to town on that clit.

That was all it took, and the two of us were going off like an atom bomb.

Leveling everything. Girl writhing and moaning and trying to cover her cries by burying her face in her mattress as this fire took us whole.

Boundaries incinerated.

Nothing left but ashes.

Words falling from her mouth that she tried to bury in the sheets. "Don't ever leave me, Richard. Don't. My heart can't take it. I can't. I can't."

All those vulnerabilities slipped back in.

Two of us completely bare.

Nothing left to hide.

I had to tell her.

Had to.

Couldn't go another day keeping this deceit because I no longer knew who it was that I was betraying.

Knees giving out under the weight of what I had to do, I eased us down to our sides and I curled my body around my girl.

Her spirit thrashed and her heart hammered out of control.

Like that moment we'd just shared had crushed every wall. Stripped every barrier. Tore away the veil.

Got the sense she was lying there, staring right at my secrets.

I pressed a kiss to the base of her skull. "Baby...I need you to listen...need you to hear the truth."

It cracked on the fear.

Every cell in her body seized, and she gripped me by the hand, twining our fingers together, her ring glinting in the hazy rays of infiltrating moonlight. "Not tonight, Richard. Give us tonight."

I nodded against the back of her head, my nose in her hair, inhaling the girl.

Violets and grace and the good.

I tugged her sweat-drenched body closer.

Refusing to let her go.

Refusing the wedge of terror that tried to slice its way into my soul.

"When we wake up in the morning, I need you to hear me out. Listen. Let me explain."

Her nod was wary. "Okay."

I breathed out in something that wasn't quite relief. "Okay."

I held her as we drifted. As we floated. As we soared.

Girl content to lie in my darkness.

Falling into You

I opened my mouth and began to quietly sing.

I closed my eyes
I fell into a dream
Watching through a looking glass
Nothin's what it seems
Shards of ice
Cold, bitter bliss
That's what I get
For stealing that first kiss

She sighed and sank deeper into my hold as I moved into the chorus.

Now I'm lost
Lost in your mystery
I lost sight. I lost my right
Staring at eternity
What's come. What's gone
Never gonna be reclaimed
Because clinging to this moonflower
Is where I'll forever be chained
Clinging to this moonflower is where I'll forever be chained

I eased up and whispered in her ear, "And I'm never going to let you go."

Violet

$\mathcal{M}$y phone vibrating on the wood of my nightstand nudged me from the most blissful sleep I'd ever had. Powerful arms were wrapped around me from behind, and he held me in the haven of his body, his heart this steady thrum, thrum, thrum that lulled me into a transcendent peace.

The barest light glowed against the window, and I carefully untangled myself from Richard's hold when my phone vibrated again. I pushed up to sitting on the side of my bed. Squinting against the sleepiness still trying to drag me under, I thumbed into the screen so I could find out what was so important this early in the morning, and I saw that I'd missed three calls and a bunch of texts.

David Jacobs: I need to speak with you.

Falling into You

David Jacobs: I've been calling. Please return my call.

David Jacobs: It's vital I speak with you immediately. I'm coming to your house.

A shudder ripped through me.

Head to toe.

This sticky chill that slicked my spine.

Ice cold.

It sent alarm freezing my heart to a stalling point.

Sitting there staring at my phone, I knew I was about to get news that I wasn't sure I was ready for.

Wasn't sure I could handle.

I blinked through the waves of grief that threatened to take me under.

A dark, dark sea I could feel coaxing me into its depths.

Fear slogged through my veins, slowing my movements when I pushed from the bed, unplugged my phone, and quickly fumbled to get into a pair of jeans and a tee, my hair a wild disorder from the twist it'd been in for the wedding and then Richard destroying it last night.

My gaze moved to where he'd shifted when I'd slipped out. He now lay facedown with the sheet dipping low around his waist, just the faintest hint of his ass peeking out.

Gulping around the jagged rocks that had gathered at the base of my throat, I tried to cling to the sight of him there. To use it as encouragement. As the reminder that I would do whatever was best for Daisy.

No matter what.

I did my best to claim the knowledge that I wasn't alone. Richard would be there to support us. To help us. But I was having a hard time feeling any sort of security.

Not when this feeling of dread rose to wash out anything else.

This sense that doom was encroaching.

I blinked back the tears burning at the back of my eyes, turned, and crept out of my room. Quietly, I clicked my bedroom door shut behind me and tiptoed downstairs and toward the front door.

With each step, I felt that swell growing higher.

A tidal wave that gathered strength.

It rushed and surged and, by the time I was unlocking the front door and stepping out into the breaking day, I could barely stand.

Stranded in a riptide.

Because I could feel it.

The devastation that approached.

My mind banged with the reality of what was coming.

I was gettin' ready to be told my sister was no longer alive.

I wasn't ready. I wasn't ready.

"I love you, Violet," her voice twisted through the air, choked and emphasized. "I couldn't ask for a better sister. For a better friend. There is no bigger joy than getting to witness you find the kind of joy you have found because you deserve it more than anyone else. You are the meaning of family. I respect you with all I have and can't wait to see the love and happiness you find in this life."

And I missed her. I missed her and I missed her, and oh god, it ached.

It ached like mad as I watched a sedan blaze a trail up the drive, dust a dark cloud billowing behind it.

He came to a stop, and David Jacobs climbed from the front seat of his car. His expression grim.

He was in his mid-40s maybe, his hair receding at the front, the rest parted and tamed with product. Wearing slacks and a button-down.

He held a thick folder in his hand that I knew revealed my sister's fate.

I tried to stand firm. To keep the trembling of my jaw and the shivering in my soul at bay.

He edged forward. "I apologize for waking you so early in the morning, but I stumbled into some evidence a couple days ago. I followed the trail, and yesterday evening I received some pictures I'd been waiting on from a colleague in California. I was up through the night putting everything together. I was able to verify it this morning."

A tear slipped free. I swatted at it and tried to put on a brave front, when really, I was crumbling. "What did you find?"

His grimace confirmed it was bad.

"You might want to sit down."

"Just tell me." It was a wheeze.

He climbed the steps and moved over to the small table tucked at the far end of the porch. He set the stuffed folder on top of it, but he pinned it closed with his fingers. "What's inside here is going to be hard to look at."

I braced myself, nodded, and those tears kept falling. "She's gone."

It wasn't even a question.

"No, Violet. She's not. At least, I don't think so."

Relief slammed me.

Staggering.

My knees went weak, and I had to plant my hands on the table for support. "Where is she?" I begged.

His head shook. "I've contacted the police in Los Angeles, Violet. I believe she's been held against her will."

A horrified frown of disbelief pulled to my brow. "I...how could that be? She left here. I watched her leave."

I'd chased her down.

Begged her not to go.

"I'm not sure of the circumstances yet. The only thing I know is I've traced her to a house in an upscale neighborhood in Los Angeles. It's empty now. We have confirmation that up until three months ago, there were both men and women being held there. Forced into sex slavery. Kept there against their will. Most strung out. Fed drugs and coerced into submission. The house was owned by the same record label Martin Jennings had worked for, Mylton Records."

He inhaled. "There was a raid several months ago. Two women had managed to get to the police and make statements. They were going to testify against Karl Fitzgerald. But by the time the police showed for the raid after Karl Fitzgerald was in custody, the house was empty."

Oh god. Oh god. Oh god.

Nausea swirled and the earth spun. Whipping and whirling so fast I thought I was going to black out. I struggled to remain upright. To process what he was tellin' me.

My sister. What had she been through?

And the two women—I instantly knew—felt it in the sinking of my spirit. They were the two women Emily and Maggie were talking about. The two who were supposed to testify against the men who had hurt them, the ones who were the smoking gun, the ones all of us were sure had seen their demise when they'd gone missing.

Dizziness spun my head.

So fast I barely could remain standing.

"I have photographic evidence that your sister had been kept in that house."

My knees rocked again.

He hesitated, his fingers still nailed to the folder, looking at me like he wasn't sure I could handle what was inside.

I wasn't sure I could, either.

My shaking hand went to my stomach like I could keep the nausea from crawling out.

"Open it," I told him, words scraping the brisk morning air while I felt like I was burning up from the inside.

"These pictures are—"

"Open it," I shouted, cutting him off, unable to take it a second longer.

He gave a wary nod before he flipped it open.

Horrified grief gripped me by the throat, bile racing it, making me choke.

She was there.

Picture after picture.

My beautiful Liliana.

Far too thin.

Bruises littering her body.

The once brilliant life that had shined in her eyes sucked dry.

Each image of her was with vile, disgusting men. Draped across them for show.

Naked.

Paraded.

Used.

I wanted to retch when I realized some of the faces were familiar.

Famous.

Abhorrent.

Depraved.

Like they could just reach out and take whatever they wanted.

I shuffled through them while sickness roiled in my body.

This boiling, seething fury that made me want to go on a rampage for the first time in my life.

Want to slam the folder shut and deny the evidence but unable to stop looking at her.

Made me want to reach into them and lift her up and protect her for all my days.

My big sister who'd always done it for me.

"Lily," I whimpered, running my fingertips over the evidence of her face.

How?

Why?

I frantically flipped through like it might bring me to the end of where she was.

Then I stumbled.

Blown back.

Stuck on one of the images buried in the middle.

Lily was kneeling. A collar around her neck and wearing nothing else. On her knees in front of a man.

A man.

Richard.

Richard.

Richard.

There was another.

My sister on his lap.

Another of two other women with them.

Revulsion sped through my veins.

That bile erupted, and I barely made it to the railing before I vomited over the side.

"No. No, no, no." Tears blurred my eyes, and I clutched my stomach as my body bent in half, unable to see through the streams of anguish that flooded free.

I stumbled.

Reeling.

The pieces of my barely mending broken heart shattered permanently.

Pieces scattered from here to eternity.

A hand touched my arm. "I'm very sorry. I wish we had found her under better circumstances, but we are incredibly close, Ms. Marin. A family member of one of the women in some of the other pictures received a call. We have reason to believe there are other women with her."

"Where?" I demanded.

"We still aren't sure."

"Where?" I screeched.

He blinked before he dug into his pocket and pulled out a small slip of paper. "This is the name and number of the man who had his daughter contact him some weeks ago. He was wary to provide me more information. You might be able to get through to him."

I snatched it and shoved it into my pocket, not sure how my feet were holding me up when I was no longer solid.

Nothing but fragments and decay.

"Thank you."

"I'll be in touch with more news. Just...please lay low. Stay safe. I heard what happened to you."

The implication hung in the air.

He didn't even need to give it.

I knew. I knew.

My mouth trembled with the grief I could no longer contain. "Just find her and bring her home to us."

"I will. I promise you that. If you get through to Mr. Baronson, please, let me know. I'm inclined to believe that is our one missing link."

Nodding, I hugged my arms over my chest to keep my bleeding heart from tumbling out.

He jogged back for his car. I watched him until he disappeared, my eyes on the billowing dust of his tires as he bounced down the long drive, until he took a left at the main road.

While I tried to ignore the overpowering presence that swallowed me from behind.

For the first time, I realized all that darkness was sinister.

A true, malicious threat.

The man nothing but ugly secrets and dark lies.

Just like my daddy had warned.

His aura rushed and howled, and I slowly turned around to face him.

The man stood in the doorway.

And I didn't want to believe it. Wanted to refuse the evidence. Wanted to plead with him that it wasn't true.

But this was the man who'd left me.

Just...left me.

At the very same time as Lily had.

Oh god.

A rush of fear tumbled through me, head to toe. Saturating my spirit. Soiling my stomach.

Belief smashed.

He took a step toward me, and I took a fumbling one back. "Violet."

"Don't." It was a jagged, gutted cry.

His attention darted to the pictures scattered on the table.

Guilt streaked across his face.

Bile rushed again.

Richard started coming toward me, hands out in front of him like he was approaching a rabid animal. "I need you to listen to me, Violet."

I stepped away, my entire body trembling with rejection. "You did this to her. You did this, didn't you? Oh my god."

He tried to grab me. "Please, just fuckin' listen to me. Told you we needed to talk last night, Violet. That I needed you to listen. To *hear* me."

A scream tore out of me, made up of so much disbelief and confusion and hurt and terror for my sister that I started to weep. "Don't touch me! Don't touch me. I can't believe you'd do this.

That you did this. You knew. You knew where she was this whole time, didn't you?"

It all flew out. Sobs of accusation.

I couldn't believe he'd come back here. Touched me. Told me he loved me. And he knew what'd happened to my sister all along.

Had been a part of it.

"Violet," he pleaded.

He kept trying to grab me. Hands reaching.

Panic surged, and my mind spun, and I was sure my heart was gonna completely bleed out.

"Where is she? Tell me where she is!" I screamed.

"I can't do that, Violet. I can't fucking tell you. It's not safe."

"You liar! All you do is lie. Everything out of your mouth is a lie, isn't it?"

He grabbed me by the wrists. "Violet…listen to me. God. Please listen to me."

"Don't touch me, you sick, disgusting monster."

He dropped his hands like I'd burned him. But it was the guilt wracking those sage eyes that confirmed it all.

He'd done this.

"You're a monster. Get out of our lives. Go. Don't ever come back."

The words were haggard.

Frayed and splintering apart.

"Violet, I wouldn't."

"You already did!" I screamed, my focus turning to the evidence strewn out on the table.

Richard's jaw clenched, his hands in fists, and he started to come for me again when the door creaked.

Our attention whipped that way.

Daisy stood in the middle of the doorway, fear and confusion on her face. "Mommy?"

My shattered heart jumped. The one thing I had left. That and getting her mother back.

My sister.

My sister.

Mouth trembling with devastation, I looked at him. "Go. The

police are gonna be comin' for you, and I don't want my daughter to witness it when they do. The private investigator already sent the images. It's done."

Richard's attention swung from me to Daisy and back again. "Viol—"

"Don't talk to me. Not ever again. You disgust me."

Wrecked.

Ruined me.

Was a part of ruinin' my sister.

Oh god.

My head spun again, and my throat throbbed with the bile that just kept comin' and comin'.

Reluctantly, Richard started to back away, the man wearing no shirt or shoes as he edged down the porch steps.

When he got to the bottom, he looked back at me, grief on his face. "I would never hurt her. Never."

God, that stupid, vulnerable part of me wanted to believe. To give him the benefit of the doubt, but I couldn't be so foolish not to believe the blatant proof that had been presented to me.

Should have known with his silence that what he was hiding he'd never wanted revealed.

God.

Did Emily know?

Hurt blazed a path through me.

No.

She couldn't. She wouldn't have kept this from me.

The second Richard got to his truck, I rushed for my daughter and swept her into my arms, held her close, pressed my face into her cheek.

I wouldn't allow her to be collateral damage in this mess.

In this disaster.

In this tragedy.

There was only one flicker of light remaining in this total eclipse.

My sister was alive.

And I was gonna find her.

I slammed the door shut and locked it up tight, breaths shallow and hard as I moved over to the window to peer out the slit in the drape.

"Mommy, what's wrong?" Her fear was palpable. Poison on my tongue. "Are you mad at Mr. Richard?"

I ran my hand over the top of her head and bounced her like a baby that needed to be comforted.

"It's okay. It's okay," I told her, unable to actually answer that question.

Her little face twisted. The child so knowing and astute. She wrapped her arms around me, her cast scraping my skin.

She held on tight. "I've got you, Mommy," she said.

"Oh, my sunshine."

I fought the tears that wouldn't stop falling.

The fear.

The horror.

My guts brawling.

A riot of evidence and intuition.

How could he?

I peered at the outline of his face where he sat in the driver's seat of his truck.

Unmoving.

Gripping the steering wheel.

Torment ripping through the air.

And I didn't want to believe what was staring back at me. Didn't want to believe he could be involved in something so cruel.

In something so depraved and wicked.

I felt the movement from upstairs, and I slowly turned to find my father staring down at us from the landing.

All the dread and worry he'd been holding for years etched in the deep lines of his face and swimming through his eyes.

"Violeta."

It was pain.

"Daisy, go with your papa." I set her onto her feet, and she scampered upstairs.

My daddy looked at me, anxiety whipping around his being. "What's happening?"

"Just...please watch over Daisy right now. I need some time."

I couldn't get his hopes up. Not until I processed. Not until I knew for certain.

His frown deepened, but he relented when Daisy took his hand. He dipped his head in acquiescence. Letting me know he was trusting me and was terrified for me at the same time.

I was terrified for him, too.

For Lily.

For what this meant.

"Come, mi amor. Let's see if Nana is awake."

"Okay," she agreed, and he sent me one more concerned look before he led Daisy down the hall into their room.

I whipped back around.

Richard was still there.

A statue in his truck.

Finally, he started it, the sound of the engine jolting me back, and he whipped around in the dirt and took off down the path.

I could almost feel the disturbance that followed him.

The energy that pulled and pulled.

A taunt.

How could somethin' that had once felt so beautiful, so real, suddenly feel like a threat?

The second he was gone, I ran back out and gathered up the pictures, shoving them into the folder and holding it against my chest. I raced upstairs and locked my bedroom door.

I sat on the floor with the images spread around. Trying to process and make sense of it all. There were more of them than just of my sister.

There were pictures of the house where she'd been kept.

It was this massive, ostentatious thing surrounded by what had to be a twenty-five-foot brick and wrought-iron wall. The foliage was so thick there wasn't much that could be made out from the street views other than the big double gates that swung open to a sweeping drive that led into the estate.

The satellite views showed off rambling grounds, a house that looked like some kind of immaculate fortress surrounded by lawn and backed by a huge rectangular pool. A few smaller buildings were laid out around the property that looked like they might be guest houses.

My guts ached.

The idea of my sister being held there.

How could that even be possible?

It seemed unbelievable.

But the most brutal of atrocities were always that way, weren't they? So grievous and inhumane our minds refused to conjure the intolerable.

Rejecting the possibility that people could be so cruel.

I tried to swallow around the razors of disbelief that cut my insides to shreds.

The evidence of it right there in front of me.

Pictures strewn.

My sister's beautiful face.

My heart staked like a sin right there with them.

How could he?

A shiver of revulsion flashed across my flesh as my mind went to the man who'd attacked me in the workshop. The lashes of what he'd said.

Had Richard known the reason behind that, too? Had he stood and said he would protect me while he knew firsthand my sister was in danger?

Grief clamped down on my spirit.

"You mean...like what happened to Emily? I saw, Richard, on the news. That somethin' bad happened to her. It's horrible. I can't..."

"Like that. Even worse."

I buried the gutting pain that made me want to curl into a ball on the floor and tried to focus. Because there were more important things than worrying about my broken heart right then.

I'd have plenty of time for that later.

Still on my knees, I dug for the scrap of paper crumbled inside my pocket, hands shaking as I smoothed it out, then I fumbled to dial the number.

After two rings, a wary voice answered, clearly not sure whether they wanted to accept the call or not.

"Mr. Baronson?" His name hitched on a sob.

"Yes?"

"My name is Violet Marin." I couldn't bear to use my married name. Not knowing what Richard had been involved in.

Those pictures emblazoned in my mind. Scored and scarred and never going to heal.

"I'm the one who'd hired the private investigator, David Jacobs, who has been looking for my sister. I understand you might have a daughter who is in the same position? Someone who's been missin' as long as my sister has?"

Silence stretched thin, and he finally cleared his throat. "I have to admit, I wasn't sure of his intentions. He showed up at my door, saying he'd gotten a tip."

I sniffled. "I understand that. I...I'm sorry I waited so long. My mama...she's at the end of her life, and I came to the point that I knew I had to do everything I could to find her since the police hadn't been able to do it. I gave him all the information that I could."

"I'm sorry to hear that."

I tried to keep another sob from busting free, but it got loose.

"You heard from your daughter?"

I couldn't help but beg it.

Sure if he verified it that would be validation enough that my sister was alive.

He sighed. Hesitated. I could tell that he was warring.

"Please, I need to find my sister."

He blew out a sigh. "Yes. I've heard from her. Several times."

"Oh god," I whimpered with the relief.

He cleared the thickness from his throat and began to explain, "She left home at eighteen with stars in her eyes. Wanting to be famous. She got caught up in the lifestyle. We lost her to drugs, and then finally we just stopped hearing from her altogether." He sniffled but tried to hide it. "I'd thought we'd lost her forever until she recently made contact to let us know she's still alive. That she's in a safehouse."

A frown pulled to my brow. "A safehouse?"

I could feel his reluctance. "I shouldn't be telling you any of this. Hell, my daughter wasn't supposed to tell me."

"Please...what do you know? Do you know something about

my sister?"

He pushed out a slow sigh before he finally relented. "My daughter had been being held against her will. She owed the wrong people money. Before she knew it, she'd become their property." He choked on that. Not wanting to lay it out but his meaning clear. "She was rescued from it a few months ago and taken to a safe place until she could testify."

My heart started beating faster.

"From a house in Los Angeles?" I rattled the address.

"Yes. That was it."

"Is my sister with her? Her name is Liliana Marin. Oh god, please tell me she's safe."

He wavered and stalled, and I was crying out again, "Please."

God, my heart was gonna falter.

"She is," he finally said, so low like he was terrified someone nefarious was listening in.

I reeled.

"Oh my god."

Relief hit me so hard, my entire body quaked.

"Where is she?" I begged.

He hesitated again, and I knew immediately he had information he hadn't given to Mr. Jacobs. That he was doing everything he could to protect his daughter, too.

"Please, you don't understand. I think my sister is in immediate danger. I've gotten threats."

He blew out a sigh. "I'm not supposed to—"

"Please. The authorities have received new information, but we can't help them unless we know where they are."

A sigh pushed through the line.

"All I can give you is a P.O. box at a facility. You can send her something there. Ask her to contact you."

I gushed out a rush of relief. "Thank you."

He gave it to me for a place somewhere in Kentucky.

"You don't know how grateful I am."

"I just want them safe," he said, his voice a dulled, roughened blade.

"I know. I think we're close to that."

The second we hung up, I jumped up to my desk, flipped the lid to my laptop, and entered the address for the box.

"Oh my god."

It popped up the name of the renter.

I searched his name, my heart in my throat.

And he had a house.

A house in Lexington.

Everything sped and flashed.

My relief and desperation.

My sister. My sister.

I dialed the number as I was flying out the door. "Mr. Jacobs. I found her."

Richard
Six Years Ago

*L*ily: Shawn really wants to see me?

Richard: Yeah.

Lily: Violet's already asleep. Should I wake her to come with me?

His gaze traveled around the raging party, and his guts clenched at the thought of his wife being in the middle of this. Of what she would think. A tickle of awareness pushed into his mind. A warning he didn't heed.

He tapped out a response.

Richard: Nah. Not her scene. Come alone.

Lily: Okay, be there in a few.

He tossed his phone to his lap, stretched back, shot Shawn a grin. "She's on her way, asshole. You're welcome. You'd better treat her right this time. She's a good girl."

Shawn cackled a laugh. "You know I will, brother. You know I will."

"What are you doing?" Richard shouted.

Lily wept, cried where they'd stripped her on the bed. He roared, fought and flailed to get to her while three men pinned his arms behind his back and held him back by the shoulders, forcing him to watch.

Bile rushed.

The high gone as he watched men sink to their lowest low.

As they ravaged her.

One after another.

As she screamed.

As she cried.

Tears streaked nonstop down Richard's face and snot ran from his nose. "Stop. Fuck. Stop. Please."

They shoved him at her when they were finished. "Your turn, pussy."

He fell to his knees, crawled to her, gathered her broken body in his arms. "I'm sorry. I'm sorry. Oh my god, Lily," he wailed, choking on the sobs that ripped from his bleeding lungs.

Lily shrieked the second he touched her. A guttural, unhinged fear. She scrambled back into the corner and curled into a shivering, shaking ball.

"Lily."

"Don't touch me," she whimpered. "Don't touch me. You monster. Don't touch me."

Richard

 uck.

"Fuck. Fuck. Fuck."

I punched the steering wheel like it might be able to dispel some of the rage and disgust pummeling my insides from where I'd pulled off the side of the road. Trying to find a way to get air into my lungs.

Not a chance of that.

Not when every organ in my body had caved. Crushed under the magnitude of the sickened outrage that Violet had looked at me with. Under the weight of the betrayal that she'd finally realized the full immensity of.

Only she'd had it all fuckin' wrong.

I knew what it looked like.

Of course, I knew.

Those pictures that had been all over that table.

How the fuck had that private investigator gotten ahold of them?

Hadn't needed a close-up to know they were copies of the same ones that Karl Fitzgerald had tried to use on me to get me to do his bidding.

Ones that had remained secret all this time. Pictures of me and Lily.

What were missing were the ones of me and Gianna. Ones of me and Danica.

Those were the ones Cory Douglas had shown my sister. The ones he'd manipulated her with.

Terrorized her with.

My sister thinking she was protecting me all while trying to reach me. To get answers. To understand because she couldn't believe I would do something so vile.

I wouldn't.

I fucking wouldn't.

But no matter how true that statement was, those pictures were incriminating.

That was the thing about a picture. Sometimes clear evidence wasn't clear at all because the eye couldn't see what was hidden underneath.

Buried.

My debt going so fuckin' deep.

Pain flayed through my insides with a blunt, dull knife.

Tearing and ripping and cutting me open wide.

Violet.

Could still feel the burn of her on my hands. Could still feel the heat of her touch on my skin.

My wife.

My sweet, innocent wife who'd gotten caught up in these atrocities.

Girl unaware she was a victim of the fallout.

Promised her I wouldn't let her go. That I would protect her. Take care of her.

How the hell was I supposed to drive away?

Needed her to understand. Listen.

But what did I expect? That she would stand there and allow herself to be fed more lies?

I'd wanted to fight her on it.

Force her to hear me out even when I didn't want her to have to hear what I needed to say.

And sure as hell not when that precious little girl was standing there.

Scared and confused.

I had to walk.

I should have just told her. Fuck, I should have just told her.

But what then?

She still would hate me in the end.

When she knew what I'd kept from her.

When she knew what I'd done.

Why I'd kept it from her.

Six fuckin' years, and the whole time, it'd just spiraled and spiraled.

Piled up until it was nothing but a shitstorm.

A car went blazing passed on the narrow road, honking as it swerved around me. I hadn't even realized I was still halfway out in the road.

I jerked two fistfuls of hair.

Trying to get myself the hell together.

I eased back onto the road, glancing in the rearview mirror like I might still have a view of her farm. Last thing I wanted to do was drive away.

Let her out of my sight.

But I knew she was too raw to allow me within five miles of her right then.

I fumbled to dial the number, anxiety racing through my veins while I listened to it ring and ring. Doubted Royce was gonna be all that excited to get this wake-up call from me on the morning after his wedding.

Finally, his voicemail came on.

"Royce, man. We've got a complication." My voice cracked on it.

Complication?

It was a fucking travesty.

And I was the fool who'd come to hope for a different outcome.

"The private investigator Violet hired somehow dug deep enough to find the photos. The ones of Liliana and me. She lost it, man. Lost it. Didn't want to hear a word I had to say."

Couldn't blame her.

"She kicked me off her property. Said the authorities had already been notified."

Which was just fine. I'd always known I'd burn for this. Their safety was well worth the cost. But the one person I didn't want to pay for it was Violet.

"Know you guys are supposed to be leaving for your honeymoon this afternoon, but I need you to go over to the farm. Watch out for her. Talk her down and let her know we're trying to keep Lily safe. Think that's what she needs most right now. I'll stay with Emily and Maggie until we see this thing through."

Unease shivered through my senses.

Praying those pictures were as deep as the guy had gotten. That the trail had ended there. At that ridiculous mansion that was nothing less than a prison.

A slew of women kept in the upper rooms. A few men, too. Some who'd stumbled in unaware and were caught up in it before they knew what was happening. Others that had been ripped off the streets. Some lured from other countries, convinced by coming here, they'd have a better life.

Poison pumped into their veins. Their minds and their bodies no longer their own.

"Call me as soon as you get this."

I ended the call and tossed my phone to the passenger seat, my body shaking in a riot of trepidation as I sped the rest of the way to my parents' house.

Every molecule in my body pulsed and fired.

Screaming at me to turn the fuck around and go to her.

Ten minutes later, I pulled to a stop in front of my childhood home, heart ramming against my ribs, breaths so hard and shallow

I was getting lightheaded.

Knew I'd lose her.

Should have known it all along.

But what I couldn't stand was driving away.

Leaving them vulnerable.

Not when I could feel it.

Destruction on the horizon.

I dropped my head to the steering wheel in an attempt to get myself together before I went inside when my phone started ringing. I scrambled to get it when I saw Royce's name lighting up the screen.

"Hey, man, sorry to wake you like this." Didn't get the apology out before he cut me off.

"Richard." His voice was grim, straight terror in my name. "Where are you?"

"Just got to my parents'."

"Turn around and go back to Violet's. Right now," he shouted.

Without asking for a reason, I threw the truck into reverse and gunned it, dust flying as I whipped around, shifting into drive before I'd made the half rotation. Tires skidding on the gravel, truck fishtailing, I pushed the pedal to the floor while I could feel Royce breathing his panic through the line.

"What the fuck is goin' on?" I said when I righted my truck and blew down the narrow lane.

"I just got off the phone with the prosecutor. Both Karl Fitzgerald and Cory Douglas were found dead in their cells this morning."

Motherfuck.

Air rocketed from my lungs.

Entire being slamming forward with the impact of the news.

With what this meant.

Not that I was going to mourn the bastards.

But this was so much bigger than them.

"First the two witnesses. Now the two on trial. It's clear they're systematically silencing anyone who has an inside on this." Royce's words thinned on the end.

Knowing what that meant for him. For Emily. For his sister.

Falling into You

For all of us.

"Where's Emily?" I demanded.

"Right beside me. I'm going to your parents' where Maggie is. No one is leaving until this is done."

Just wasn't sure how we were gonna end it.

No question, the rules of the game had just been changed.

"It's time to bring in Detective Casile. I know they wanted to wait until they could testify, but that's not gonna work when there is no one left to testify against," Royce said.

"I know. Make the call. I'll call Kade."

"Done. Get back to Violet. Don't give a shit if her father meets you on the front porch with a shotgun. You make them understand, and you don't let them out of your sight."

Sweat gathered at my nape and dripped down my back.

"I'm already on my way."

"Stay safe, brother."

Affection pulled tight across my chest. "You, too. Take care of my sister. Of Maggie."

"Promised you I would."

The second he hung up, I punched in another number.

Kade answered on the first ring. "Richard."

I heaved out a strained breath. "We're on high alert, man. Double down your efforts."

"What happened?" he grated.

"Karl Fitzgerald and Cory Douglas are dead."

"Shit," he wheezed.

"Getting them to trial is no longer the focus. The detective is being contacted. Backup should be there soon. For now, stand guard and don't stand down."

Lily had made me promise the authorities wouldn't be brought in.

She'd convinced me it was too dangerous.

Wasn't like she was off base. Someone tried to leave? Expose what was going down in that house and those who visited it? Go to the police?

They ended up gone.

Permanently.

Just like the two women who had agreed to Royce and Detective Casile that they would testify. Even under police protection, they'd disappeared.

It was better the rest of them were thought dispersed into the streets before the raid than as a threat.

Clearly, we were passed that.

"Will let you know as soon as I hear anything," I told him.

By the time I ended the call, I was coming up fast on the curve that brought the Marin house into view.

My spirit clanged. My guts in knots. They twisted a thousand times tighter when I saw Violet's truck was no longer parked in the spot it'd been when I'd left.

I raced up the drive, truck jostling like mad. I barely skidded to a stop before I was flying out the door and sprinting up the steps, banging on the door that whipped open a second later.

"Haven't you done enough?" Mr. Marin spat, words close to a plea.

Not quite.

Because it was time for this all to end.

Violet

I didn't know how I made it to the library parking lot through the tears that kept fallin'. Didn't know how I was functioning at all with the sheer, utter devastation that singed and burned and ate me alive.

My ribs feeling like they'd been cracked wide open and my heart ripped out.

I was running on adrenaline alone.

The bit of hope that my sister was comin' home, even when I didn't know what that was goin' to mean. Knowing I was wholly unprepared for the things she'd been through. That I was gonna learn things that I didn't want to know.

And then there was Daisy.

Daisy. Daisy. Daisy.

The vacancy in my chest howled with the grievance.

That outright fear.

But I just kept reminding myself this wasn't about me. *It wasn't about me.*

I fumbled out of my truck when the sedan whipped into the parking spot beside me, and I jerked open his door and slipped inside.

Unable to breathe.

Unable to see.

Knowing I had to fight for this one purpose. I could fall apart later.

"You've got the address?" David Jacobs asked, peering over at me.

"Yes. I think so. I talked with Mr. Baronson. He gave me the address for a P.O. box so I could attempt to contact my sister. I…I think I traced the renter of the box to a house in Lexington."

"May I see?" he asked.

Hand shaking, I passed over my phone. He looked at the address and then was making a call with his.

"We got them," he said. I guessed that was when his demeanor shifted from concerned P.I. to something else entirely.

When the mood whipped into something cruel.

And those three little words.

They danced and shivered and spun through my mind.

A moment held.

And then it hit me from all sides.

All at once.

A vat of ice-cold water was dumped over me.

The realization of what I'd done.

That voice.

Oh my god. That voice.

How hadn't I made the connection?

"You shouldn't go diggin' up graves. You never know when you might fall in."

I swung around to get to the door handle at the same second the locks engaged.

The car whipped out of the spot, and I fought the lock that wouldn't give, yanking at the handle, trying to escape. "No. Let me out. Don't do this. Oh, god. Please don't do this."

Despair and fear and terror.

They spiraled and curled and shackled.

Leaving me in chains.

I came to the quick, gutting realization. I'd let my despair over seeing Richard in those pictures with Lily overshadow the truth. What had been hidden in Richard's eyes and in his cryptic words. What he'd been trying to convey.

Hot tears streamed down my face when I realized what I'd done.

The car accelerated like a bullet down the street.

And I knew I was a prisoner.

Nowhere to run. No chance of savin' my sister.

The only thing I'd accomplished was leading the wolves to the den.

David Jacobs glanced over at me with a smug grin on his face. "You know, I thought you were going to be a complication when we first intercepted that hit that you were actively looking for Liliana Marin. Turns out you did my job for me. Maybe I should be the one paying you. I guess Richard Ramsey couldn't help himself, could he? You are awful pretty. I'll call that a bonus."

He smirked a disgusting smile.

And I knew, I'd just made the biggest mistake of my life.

Richard
Six Years Ago

"I warned you that you needed to prove how much you wanted this," the sinister voice mocked in Richard's ear before he was met with another barrage of fists and feet. Pain splintered through his body, ribs cracking, skin tearing.

Soul shearing.

Richard climbed to his hands and knees, and blood gushed from his mouth and pooled on the floor. "Never."

They'd tossed him at Lily and told him to "prove it". He'd spat in Martin Jennings face.

He'd rather die.

He was pretty sure he was halfway to it.

Consciousness coming in and out. A darkness sucking him under where he'd never emerge.

A booted foot came at him with a swift kick to the stomach.

Agony bolted through his insides.

Blinding.

Vomit spilled from his mouth while Shawn laughed with the blow he'd inflicted. "Told you he wasn't gonna be game. That he was gonna have to go."

"I own you," Martin Jennings leaned in to say again, "Shawn here gets it."

Richard shook his head, trying to see through the disorder. Trying to find a way to climb out of hell. "Shawn can suck a bag of dicks," he wheezed.

Motherfucker.

Richard knew there was something seedy about him. Knew he couldn't be trusted.

Another kick to the gut.

Richard grunted and slumped to the floor. No longer able to keep himself upright. But he fought it. Fought to climb back to his hands and knees. "You're not getting away with this."

Martin's voice was back in Richard's ear, whispering his wickedness, "That's cute, Richard. But we own you, and I'm not just talking about Mylton Records. You have no idea who we are. How far our reach goes. We own this city. This country. The entire fucking world. Go ahead. Go to the cops. See what happens to that cute little wife of yours."

They sat in the back of the cab in front of the hotel where they'd been staying, the first rays of the morning edging the sky in a vapid gray.

It rose like a slow illumination of horrors.

Like they were waking up from a nightmare to forever live in a bad dream.

Lily was curled up against the door as far away from Richard as she could get. No words said since they'd tossed them into the car and warned they'd, "Be in touch."

Richard's voice was held so the driver couldn't hear. "Lily…let's go to the police. Don't give a fuck what they say. We need to get you help. Need to get you to the hospital."

He reached for her like it would give her comfort.

She whimpered and pushed away, but she turned those eyes on him. So much like her sister's, only they'd faded from the liveliness they'd always exuded. Her voice was haggard. Hushed and hard. "I'm getting out of this car right now, Richard. I'm going inside with my sister, and I'm going to fly home with her this afternoon. Then I'm going to pack up and leave. Start a new life. Leave what happened last night behind."

She kept looking at him. Something fierce on her quivering jaw. "And you're not coming with us. You're leaving right now. You're going to stay away from her. Far, far away."

Torment ripped him in two. "Lily. Please."

"You don't deserve her, and I won't let you wreck her, too."

His spirit screamed in misery because he knew it was true. But he couldn't…he couldn't walk away. "Lily. Please let me help you."

She choked out a disbelieving laugh that was mostly a cry. "Help me? You did this. You. Did. This."

Guilt wracked his body, every inch writhing in agony, broken bones and a broken soul and shattered belief.

What had he done?

What had he done?

Lily's voice scratched through the cab, her fingers flexing on the door handle. "If you ever come near her again, I will tell her what you did. I'll show the texts of how you lured me there. They have pictures, Richard. Pictures of you. Of me. They'll destroy her, but I'll make sure she sees them if that's what it takes to keep you away from her."

"Lily, oh god. Please. I didn't know what was going to happen. I swear to you."

"It doesn't matter, Richard. It did happen. This is your fault. Your fault. If you really love her, if you care about her, if you regret what happened to me at all—if you have an ounce of a soul—you will walk away and you won't look back. You won't mention what you saw last night. Never."

"Lily." Richard choked on a sob. Didn't even care he was sniveling. He had been all night.

Unable to process.

Unable to grasp something so sick.

The pink veil of goodness he'd watched the world with stripped away to reveal the true wickedness that lurked underneath.

How could she fuckin' ask this of him? To ignore what she'd been through?

"Promise me," she gritted on a subdued, emphatic shout. "Promise me."

Richard looked over at her and saw his world go dim.

Just like he deserved.

Guilt and shame cleaved him in half.

Nothing left but the one promise he could give her.

Richard gave her a tight nod. "I promise."

Without saying anything else, she opened the door, whimpering as she got out, and she hobbled toward the entrance of the glitzy hotel, wearing heels and hugging herself to cover the spot where her dress was ripped.

Or maybe she was just trying to hold herself together.

While Richard splintered apart.

It only took one moment.

One fucking mistake.

One misstep to ruin it all. To start a spiral that you couldn't stop.

Richard knew his. The one moment he'd told Martin Jennings he would do whatever it took to make it.

Flashes of last night burned through his mind.

The cruelness and atrocities.

Lily. Lily. Lily.

A guttural cry tore from his throat.

He was the one who'd set it in motion.

The one responsible.

He'd done this.

And there was no way of taking it back.

It'd been almost six years since Richard had seen Liliana Marin. Six fucking years since he'd watched her climb out of that cab and disappear inside and take his heart with her.

Six years since he'd written that letter to Violet.

Six years since his world had gone dim.

And there Lily stood at the end of the hallway at the swanky hotel in Hollywood where the band was staying after they had played earlier that night at a dive bar about a mile away.

Her face frozen in horror and her body rocking back with shock.

She wore this super short glitzy gold dress and super high heels. A ton of makeup. Jewelry.

But there was death in her eyes.

Hopelessness.

Despair.

And with the fear that blanched her entire face, Richard knew immediately she hadn't started a new life.

He just...felt it.

Sure of it in an instant.

Six years of torment flashed through his mind.

She started to turn and run.

"Lily," Richard shouted behind her, racing down the hall to get to her. In those sky-high heels, it only took a few sprinted strides for him to catch up. "Stop, Lily."

She heaved out in desperation, pushing herself faster, turning a corner and dashing down another hall.

Richard snatched her by the wrist.

She cried out when he turned her to face him, the girl backing against the wall. Those eyes were wild. Feral.

"Lily, I'm not gonna hurt you."

Her entire face pinched in grief.

"Fuck. Lily. What happened to you? Tell me what happened."

She looked both ways down the deserted hall. "You can't be here. Someone's gonna see you."

"Who?" He was asking it, his stomach already sinking to the floor.

Awareness right there.

Though it didn't quite make sense. Didn't add up.

"Please tell me, Lily, and don't fuckin' lie. I see you. I see you're hurting. I see you're terrified."

Her chin trembled, and she was looking both ways again, her voice dropped to the lowest whisper when she looked back at him, "Richard. I can't talk to you. Can't be seen with you."

"Why?" he demanded.

"Because I no longer belong to myself," she wheezed.

Rage.

It was instant.

He edged in closer like he could shroud her in protection.

He never should have let her get out of that cab. Never.

"What are you saying?"

The words started to spill from her mouth, "It was Martin Jennings that wanted me, Richard. That night when he took us out to dinner, he took one look at me, and decided he was going to keep me. He used Shawn to get me there."

"But that fucker is rotting in jail."

Her head shook. "It didn't matter. I became his, which meant I became Lester Ford's property, because everybody belongs to him." Her voice dropped even lower on that.

"Lester Ford?"

Richard knew the name instantly.

He was one of the richest men in the world.

Politics.

Oil.

It was well known his hands were in just about everything.

And Richard had always thought he was about as seedy as they came.

Currently, he was a senator from California who was throwing in a bid for presidency.

"Mylton Records has always been a front for him. When Martin went down years ago? That was Lester throwing him under the bus. He made Martin take the fall when one of their trafficking routes was discovered. Lester got off, absolved of any connection, and Martin went down. When he did, Karl took his place."

Richard knew that part, at least. In the mayhem of Martin being arrested right after that fateful night, Carolina George had slipped through the cracks. Their contract stalled.

They'd used the bad press as an excuse to pass on the offer. On top of that, they'd "lost" their drummer and the band was in transition. It'd been easy to convince Emily and Rhys that Shawn had dumped them for bigger and better things.

"I don't understand how you ended up back here?" Richard pressed, trying to piece together the fragments of that time.

Resigned sadness shook her head. "They wanted me, Richard. Don't you get it? They told me if I didn't come back, they'd take my sister instead. That they would make you pay, too."

His insides splintered apart.

Christ.

She'd been protecting Violet that morning. When she'd told him to leave. When she'd made up some lie about restarting her life, she was condemning herself to hell.

Scared for those who she loved most.

Manipulated into taking on this life.

Sorrow collided with the rage.

He should have known when he found out she'd left Daisy with Violet all those years ago. Should have read it for what it was. He should have known. Fuck, he should have known.

"Come with me."

Fear blanketed her face. "I can't."

"Yes, you can. Let's go, right now."

A door opened somewhere down the hall. Horror rushed through her body. This palpable, emanating fear that ate through her being. "You don't understand what will happen to me if I leave. They'll find me, and my fate will be much worse than it is now. I've got to go."

"Where are you staying? Where are they keeping you?" he demanded.

She choked out a whimpered cry. "At the same house."

Footsteps echoed from afar, and she wrangled away from him.

She started heading back in the direction she'd come, and he took her by the hand again.

She looked at him from over her shoulder.

"I'll find a way. I'll find a way to get you out. I promise."

It didn't take all that much to show a change of heart.

Crawling on his knees to Karl Fitzgerald and kissing his scummy-ass feet and telling him that he was interested in signing.

That he realized Carolina George was nothing without him.

A lie the glutton ate up like a feast.

They'd been gaining in popularity as it was. He wanted them. But Richard had stalled. He'd told Fitzgerald he needed time to convince the rest of the band, that they weren't sure since it'd fallen through the last time.

Shawn was still in LA drumming for another band.

The piece of shit smirked when he saw Richard back at that house with Lily on his lap.

When he saw Richard playing it up with other girls.

Lily's friends who were as desperate as her to get out.

Ones who Richard was whispering plans into their ears while he made it look like another depraved, disgusting act.

He knew they were being photographed. It didn't matter. He'd take any chance, risk it all, to get her out.

It was dangerous.

Of course, it was.

But he'd die to save her.

To save them.

He just had to find the right opportunity. Get enough information to take Lester Ford down because you couldn't topple an empire without killing its king.

Pray to God he could keep his family safe in the middle of it.

What Richard hadn't expected was for Royce Reilly to come on the scene. Didn't anticipate his goal.

The night of Karl Fitzgerald's shakedown, Richard made the

split-second decision to make his move.

It was probably the most foolish, reckless thing he'd ever done.

But he had to take advantage of the moment's weakness.

Richard chartered a private jet and flew through the night. Kade was already in LA where he'd been for the last three months.

Ready.

Waiting for direction.

Desperate to get his daughter out.

Game the second Richard had contacted him and told him he'd located his missing daughter.

They went in through a third-story window while chaos ensued through the bottom floors of the massive house.

As Lester Ford's men rushed through the offices to get rid of any evidence of his connection to Karl Fitzgerald, they got six women out.

Risky.

Yeah.

But worth it.

No matter the cost.

Richard

$\mathcal{F}$rantic, I pounded on the front door. My heart was lodged

somewhere in my throat, fully cutting off airflow. I banged again, ready to kick the fucker in when it finally whipped open to Mr. Marin shaking his head in disbelief. "Haven't you done enough? She isn't here, and you are not welcome."

"I know you don't trust me, but I need you to right now. I need to know where she went. She could be in danger."

"She's been in danger since the moment you came back. Do you not see the connection? What has happened since you came back to this town? You've hurt her enough."

Agitation blazed, and I angled closer to Violet's father. "There are people out there who are far more dangerous than me."

His face blanched.

"Listen to me, Mr. Marin. Lily…"

Could see the shock of it punch through his expression. "Lily?" Her name wheezed from his lungs.

"Lily got involved in some stuff years ago. Out in LA. I've been trying to help her."

All the blood drained from his face. The man rocked.

"My Lily is alive? You are certain?"

"Yes. She's alive, and I'm doing everything I can to keep her that way."

"You knew?" Hurt slashed and curled, and his head shook as he struggled to process.

"Please. We don't have time. I need to know where Violet is. I've called twenty times and she's not answering."

Mr. Marin shifted on his feet, looking to the wall before he spoke toward the ground. "She said she had to go meet someone. That she would be right back."

"When?"

"She left thirty minutes ago."

Fuck.

"Call her. See if she'll answer."

He hesitated for a moment before he gave a wary nod, and he dug his phone out of his pocket and made the call.

My nerves ratcheted higher and higher with each ring that went unanswered.

With each second that passed that warned she was already in harm's way.

I knew Violet well enough to be sure that she wouldn't put off a call from her father. Not when Daisy was in his care. She would interrupt anything if she thought it interfered with the well-being of that kid.

That sweet, adorable kid who was standing on the last stair of the staircase.

"She's not answering," Mr. Marin said, pulling the phone from his ear and looking at it like it were coded in affliction. Like he was coming to awareness, too.

Fear crackled in the air.

Daisy stared across at me in her sweet worry. Those eyes too keen. That energy zapping. All the devotion I had for her twisting me in two.

"I want my mommy to come back."

I couldn't stop myself from edging inside. From moving her way. My fucking shredded heart throbbing and moaning and bringing me to my knees. I dropped in front of her and pulled her into my arms. "I will bring her back. I will. I promise you."

Both of them.

Tension bound the cab of my truck. Anxiety rode high. Nothing but fuel to feed the fire that burned and ravaged and became this violent aggression that raged through our veins.

Royce sat in the front seat of my truck. Rhys in the back.

Lincoln and my father had taken Emily, Maggie, Anna, and my mother to Violet's farm so they could all be together.

Safety in numbers.

Detective Casile was on a flight out. Working on putting together a team he could trust.

After what happened last night with Fitzgerald and Douglas?

With this piece-of-shit crooked private investigator?

We knew this had reached a head.

I should have known it the second I saw those pictures that the investigator was not who he'd pretended to be. Should have known exactly how he'd had access to them.

Should have known Lester Ford could get to anyone.

He was the master of that fucked-up universe.

And Lily knew all of it. Had all the details. Had borne witness to it throughout the years of her captivity. She was the one person who could bring his entire empire down.

And I knew he'd stop at nothing to silence her.

I picked up my phone and glanced at it again in the vain hope that I might have missed a call or text from Violet.

Praying for a miracle and knowing it wasn't gonna happen.

Knowing she was in trouble.

Felt it all the way to my soul. That connection blared in the deepest parts of me, shouting of alarm and distress.

I threw my phone back to the console and roughed a hand over my face. I was going to lose my shit.

Felt my skin crawling with desperation.

Desperate to get to her. To find her.

Couldn't let something happen to her.

Couldn't.

"She's going to be fine," Royce rumbled, his jaw clenched. Dude wasn't close to being immune to the turmoil that radiated from my skin.

His fingers beat on the windowsill like he could tap out the anxiety.

"Hell, yeah, she is. She's probably all good and just doesn't want to talk to this jackass. I mean, I wouldn't want to talk to you, either." I watched Rhys' brow lift with the consequence of what I'd done as he looked at me through the rearview mirror, injecting the truth of it with a shot of humor.

It was kind of fucked up that I hoped the asshole was right.

That she'd disappeared because she couldn't handle the truth of what she'd seen.

Fact I'd known where her sister was. Had kept it from her in this skewed, distorted sense of loyalty.

That devotion real.

But at what cost?

In the end, what had it done?

Even if he was right, I definitely didn't need his shit right then.

He'd actually fuckin' shoved me to the ground when I'd told him what was going down, unable to believe what I'd kept from him.

What I'd unknowingly gotten Lily involved in.

How I'd come so close to getting Violet condemned.

Royce had grabbed hold of him. Told him to save the anger for those who deserved it. That we didn't have time right then. More important matters were at hand.

Because Rhys might be spouting it now—that Violet was just pissed and giving me the cold shoulder and was focused on trying to find her sister—but the three of us knew that wasn't the case.

Our spirits wouldn't let us rest with that.

Besides, Kade hadn't heard a peep from her, and I knew if she had the address, she would have shown. He'd kept us updated, letting us know the neighborhood where he lived had remained completely still.

It'd been almost three hours since anyone had heard from Violet. That would have given her plenty of time to get there.

I glanced at the clock.

Counting down.

My foot to the floor as the truck sped down the two-lane country road.

It was the only place we knew to go.

Trees whipping by. Bright rays of sunlight strobing through the branches as we blazed underneath.

Royce wiped the sweat that was gathering on his temple, dude antsy as fuck.

Me feeding him, him feeding me. "When I set out to take down my stepfather, had no clue how far this bullshit went."

"Evil has no bounds." The words were grit.

He grunted an incredulous laugh. "Funny how that bastard had acted like he was the king. That everyone bowed to him. And it turned out he was nothing but a puppet."

"Never meant for you to get in this deep," I said as I swung a glance his way.

"Always have been in this deep. I just didn't know it."

I gave him a tight nod, and I glanced at Rhys who shouldn't have even been there. Asshole had jumped in the fucking truck when we were getting ready to take off.

"Don't give me that look, bro. I know what you're thinking. You two are in deep? You can bet your asses I am, too. That's just the way it is. If I were in something, would you turn a blind eye? Let me go it alone?"

I didn't say anything.

He jutted his chin. "That's what I thought."

We fell into silence as we blew down the road, the anxiety shouting so loud it drowned out everything else. My heart roared and thundered as we finally made it into the small city that was about two and a half hours outside Dalton that we'd made in two.

I barely slowed as we drove beneath the underpass of the freeway and the two-lane road opened to four lanes. The endless green fields gave rise to buildings on each side.

Stores and offices.

Apprehension lighting me up, I tried to keep myself in check as I followed the directions on my phone, considering I'd only been there once and it'd been in the dead of night.

We took the first turn into the family neighborhood.

Quaint and quiet.

Lawns fronting each modest house with kids playing on the street.

That only ratcheted my anxiety ten times higher.

Royce itched.

"Hate this bullshit," he rumbled. "Needs to end."

I made another right and came to a stop at the curb in front of the small house.

Silence took us over while we sat on the street and stared at the stilled structure.

Innocuous.

White bricks with a gray shingle roof.

A sidewalk cut right through the middle of the manicured lawn and led up two steps to the front door that was painted black.

Two planters on either side spilled over with pink flowers.

If you didn't know any better, you'd think a little old lady lived there.

So Kade might be in his 50s, but he was straight 'don't-fuck-with-me' ex-military.

When we'd set into motion the plan to get the girls out, Danica had known her father would step up and keep them safe.

My eyes scanned for anything amiss.

Pulse thumping so hard I could feel it beating in my ears and battering my chest.

Nothing seemed out of place, but that didn't mean I didn't *feel* it. That I couldn't sense this wickedness that rode in on the breeze.

Royce exhaled a harsh breath.

Dude felt it, too.

"Her truck's still not here," I said, stating the obvious. The one hope I'd had was she'd show.

I cranked open the door and stepped out under the Kentucky sky. Sweat slicked my flesh, this anxiousness that ripped through my senses, every single one of them on overdrive.

I tucked my gun in the waist of my jeans as I let my attention skate over the lot.

Birds sang in the full trees and the drone of cars echoed from the main streets in the distance.

Royce stepped out, too, same as Rhys, and the three of us slowly started up the small sidewalk.

Stomach tight.

Everything feeling…off.

Intuition told me we were walking straight into a trap.

But I'd walk into a thousand of them if it meant getting Violet back. If it meant protecting these women.

Decoys.

Distractions.

Whatever the fuck we had to be, that's who we'd be.

Royce's phone bleeped, and he pulled it out before he gave me a nod. "Casile has secured a team. They are coordinating now. He'll be here by three himself. Warrants are being issued as we speak."

"Thank fuck."

I knocked on the door, two times fast and three times slow.

On the other side, there was movement, the rustle of a drape at the window before metal scraped as locks were disengaged. Then the door cracked open an inch, two chains still keeping it secure as Kade peered out to take us in.

His gray eyes were hard and fierce, dude worn and burly. He jutted his chin. "You clear?"

"We're clear."

He looked behind us again before he worked through the rest of the locks and edged the door open a fraction.

The second we stepped inside the gloomy house, he worked back through the locks and then turned to look at us. Could almost see the weight of a thousand lives riding on his shoulders.

"She hasn't shown?" The question grunted from my throat on a vicious plea.

His head shook. "No, Richard. I'm sorry. She hasn't."

I scrubbed a palm over my face, and I started to pace, only to stall when I felt the movement in the hall.

Horror and misery.

It bound and shook and filled the room with dread.

Slowly, I shifted around.

Liliana Marin stood in the archway.

Stringy black hair tied in a twist.

Face still thin but so much healthier than the night I'd brought her here.

Eyes the same color as Violet's staring me down. Though they'd been dimmed. The hope and joy drained from the depths that had once sang of mischief and playfulness.

My fault.

My fault.

That old agonized guilt wailed and screamed.

Knowing there was nothing I could ever do to take it back.

No way to erase her scars.

Only thing I could do was give her this.

Freedom.

Pray to God in it would be a future.

"Have you heard anything?" she begged.

My lips trembled at the side. "No."

She pressed a hand over her mouth, and she dropped her head, trying to subdue the sob that ripped up her throat. "Oh god. Richard, I can't—"

I surged forward. "We're getting her back."

She looked up at me. "What if we don't?"

My spirit howled, refusing to even contemplate the idea, and those nerves were scattering over me again when my phone buzzed. I hurried to check it.

Unknown: Told you I was gonna end you, bitch. That I was gonna end you and all your friends.

Panic seized me when I read the words, and my widened eyes flew to Royce and then to Kade before I rushed for Lily, shouting, "Get down!"

I dove at her, wrapping my arms around her waist.

We toppled to the floor, and I scrambled around to create a shield.

The window at the front of the house shattered as a spray of bullets flew through, same as the one in the kitchen in the next room.

I reached around to rip out my gun.

I was wrong.

We hadn't been walking into a trap. It was an ambush.

A crash banged against the front door. Wood splintered and the chains creaked. Kade whipped around with his rifle drawn.

Royce pushed his back up against the wall, his gun drawn as he started to angle down the hall. "Where are the rest of the girls?" he hissed.

"Back room," Kade growled.

Rhys was behind him, both of them heading toward the back room to protect what we'd always wanted to save.

These innocent women who'd been stripped of it.

The front door busted open at the same second a man burst through the window.

Gunshots rang out.

Deafening.

Me pulling the trigger and fucking hating it, but still knowing this was the duty I'd promised myself to.

The promise that I would stand up and fight.

That I would protect.

No matter the cost.

The guy went down in front of me, falling face-first to the floor. Blood pooled around him, saturating the white carpet.

Lily screamed.

Horror and fear.

"I've got you, Lily. I've got you. Just stay down. Don't move."

I looked to Kade who'd taken down the man who'd kicked in the door, and he angled his head that way and pressed himself tight to the wall as he peeked out, clearly anticipating there would be more.

Two guys came rushing in just as I was climbing to my feet.

Kade fired.

Once.

Twice.

Three times.

They fell.

And I was gasping, trying to see through the storm of agony and chaos that filtered through the air.

But all that air was gone when the dust cleared, and Violet was suddenly there.

Her body pinned against the monster who dragged her inside with a gun pushed up under her chin. An arm locked around her chest as she struggled to find footing. Her hands clawing at his arm.

Thunderbolt eyes found me in the turmoil.

Terror.

Sheer, absolute terror.

So gutting that I felt it stab through the middle of me.

The girl whimpered, and then she choked back a sob when she saw Lily behind me on the floor.

I'm sorry, she mouthed.

My head slowly shook.

In caution.

In encouragement.

In this stunning determination that we were going to overcome this.

Our love was too big for those who wanted to steal it.

Two more men entered through the window, and I could feel another approaching from where he'd come in through the kitchen.

I straightened, gun drawn, turning slow, and Kade was doing the same as we were surrounded on all sides.

"You see what happens when you make the wrong choices, Richard Ramsey?" the bastard sneered, wrenching Violet closer to him, glaring at me from over her shoulder. "You were offered the world. Everything you could ever want. Money. Fame. Fortune. Your every fantasy."

I wanted to spit.

Curse that fucking twisted thought-process. These sick bastards who used and abused and debased.

He huffed the air from his nose like I was the one who disgusted him. "And you had to go and make a mockery of it. Now we're going to have to take it from you."

Violence skated across my flesh.

Singeing.

My hand trembled on the trigger, and I gulped, trying to keep aim, Kade tracking behind me.

He kept glancing at me, and I wondered just how many of these motherfuckers he could take out if I made a move.

If I just started running straight for them.

A decoy.

A distraction.

As long as Violet and Lily got to safety it would be a small price to pay.

He gave me a slight shake of his head.

A warning.

It was too risky.

"And then there's the small matter of your brother-in-law. He started this entire shitshow by staging his ridiculous coup on Fitzgerald. He should have stayed in his lane. Shouldn't have rocked the boat. But I guess he didn't know how high those waves he was making were going to go. He was never going to get away with this. Just like you weren't."

I scoffed out a laugh. Biding time. Praying for backup. "You think it's not already done? You think the records aren't already sitting on the prosecutor's desk? Right this second, there's a warrant being issued for every fuckin' one of you scumbags. Every asshole who took part in those parties. Every person who participated in getting those women and men to that house and everyone who kept them there. The dealers. The traffickers. The lowlifes on the street all the way to that piece-of-shit, Lester Ford, sitting at the top thinking he's the ruler of the world. Know he owns those ships. Ones that come into port. Know how deep his affiliations go."

Every crime.

Every atrocity.

Stretching across the globe.

I kept my voice even. Knowing one misstep and it was over. Any one of these cocksuckers could fire and it was done. Only thing that stopped it from happening was Kade who kept his aim trained between the assholes on either side of me.

Apparently the three guys lying on the floor were proof enough that he might just be a better aim than them.

Could hear the rustle of something at the back of the house. Wanted to cover it. Cover it for Royce and Rhys who I knew were getting the other five women to safety.

"Everyone in between. Including you." I let the taunt roll out with that, wanting his anger directed at me.

He laughed a menacing sound. "You think we don't own every judge? Every prosecutor? Every cop? You are nothing. Just like Karl Fitzgerald and Cory Douglas were nothing. This is so much bigger than you. Now tell me where the rest of the girls are, and I won't have to shoot."

He shoved the barrel of his gun deeper under Violet's jaw, making her head rock back and the air rasp from her lungs.

Toes barely touching the ground, she whimpered and squeezed those eyes closed like she could shield herself from the deranged depravity that dripped from this monster.

My wife.

My wife.

My heart banged at my chest.

Wanting to get to her.

To erase the space.

Wrap her up and take her out of here.

That energy whipped through the room and banged against the walls.

Begging to be filled.

To be heard.

"If we're nothing, then just go."

Except I knew every person in this house was a threat to them. Possessing too much information for them to let a single one of us walk.

Knew if he didn't put a bullet in Violet's head, he thought he was taking her with him, and that was not going to happen.

"Where the fuck are the rest of the girls and your little boyfriend, Royce? Boss wants him, too. Prick cost him over twenty million. He's got quite the debt to pay. It's not going to be pretty."

That was right when a dog started barking from a neighboring yard and the sound of a helicopter echoed in the distance.

Coming closer.

Closer and closer until it was so loud there was no mistaking it was low and hovering overhead.

The asshole's attention snapped toward the window. The rest of the bastards surrounding us did the same.

A frisson of nerves and uncertainty.

It gave us one second.

One second to our advantage.

I looked for a clear shot when Lily was suddenly on her feet and running around me.

"Lily, no! Get down. Get down." I shouted it. Fucking begged it.

Violet wailed, those eyes going round in stark, utter terror. David Jacobs shifted Violet to his side, holding her around the neck, while he stretched out his arm and fired.

In an instant, the house was nothing but pops and cracks. A blister of bullets and shells. Shattering glass and splintering wood.

Lily rocked back before she stumbled forward. The momentum fully knocked Violet free of David's hold.

I pulled the trigger.

What felt like a hundred times.

Same as his was being pulled with his gun aimed at me.

Crack. Crack. Crack.

Shock. Shock. Shock.

He went down.

So did I.

I dropped to my knees.

Too fucking stunned to feel the agony.

My hands went to my abdomen, fingers covered in blood.

Footsteps rushed and pounded, chaos and dust and debris.

Smoke.

A haze.

Thunderbolt eyes staring down at me. Tears streaming down that gorgeous face. Desperate hands searching. Pleading. The girl weeping over me.

And I was swamped in it.

Violets and grace and the good.

My fairy girl.

Her hands were on my face.

Magic.

Magic.

Safe and whole.

The one thing in this world that ever mattered.

My moonflower.

My wife.

Every lyric.

The song of my heart.

Violet

*T*he monitor beeped quietly. Steady and unending. A drone that

lulled through the darkened room and pushed time into eternity. I held his warm hand in mine, the pad of my thumb caressing over the violet tattooed on the inside of his wrist.

Prayin' and prayin'.

I touched his pallid face.

The man far, far away, while I sat in the seat next to him begging him to come back to me.

"Don't leave me, Richard. Don't you dare. I'm gonna need you now more than ever. Besides, you owe me a really big explanation."

The last hitched on a breathy laugh.

On a plea.

On desperation.

Except Lily had told me everything.

I didn't think I had even needed to hear it.

I'd seen everything I needed to know go down right in front of my eyes.

The protectiveness.

The selflessness.

The willingness to give.

I saw the goodness.

I saw it.

Amor. Amor. Amor.

"Do you feel me, Richard? Do you feel me falling with you? I've always been floating in your eclipse. Please, find me in it. I'm right here, calling for you."

"Hi," I whispered.

He blinked, sage eyes staring up at me in confusion, like he was wonderin' if it were a dream.

If I were real.

If this feeling that lulled and lapped and swam around us was just a figment of the afterlife.

It'd been close.

So close.

We'd lost him twice.

Two times he'd coded.

His body rejecting the attempts the doctors made at savin' his life.

Two times I'd begged him to come back to me. To find me in the darkness where I'd forever been falling for him.

His thick throat bobbed as he swallowed around the dryness. "Violet."

I edged forward and brushed back the hair from his face. "I'm right here. I'm here. I'm not going anywhere."

Richard breathed out in relief before he was lost to torment again. "Lily?" he begged.

"She's safe. She was injured, but it wasn't life-threatening."

"The rest of the girls?"

"Safe. They're all safe. Because of you."

His head minutely shook. "I—I never wanted to leave you. Not once. But Lily was right…I couldn't risk getting you involved in that life. I had to walk. Stay as far away as possible. And then once I found Lily again…everything changed, Violet. The focus. My reason. I think the whole time, I felt myself on the way back to you."

"Shh. I know, Richard. I know. Lily told me everything."

"I'm sorry. So fuckin' sorry."

The corner of my mouth trembled. Emotion this ball that bubbled and grew and grasped for what we were.

"I'm sorry I didn't believe you. That I didn't listen."

Richard attempted to sit up.

"Try not to move. You still have a lot of healing to do."

Two gunshot wounds.

One to his abdomen. One to his left shoulder.

The man my miracle.

He grappled for my hand. "All of it was on me. My fault. I wanted the band's success so fuckin' bad that I missed it. Missed every warning before it was too late. A fool to trust who clearly shouldn't be trusted. I started it, and I never knew how to stop it."

"But you risked it all. For her. For them."

"Freeing them was all I had left to give."

My fingers traced the shape of his unforgettable face. "Because you're a good, good man who got lost somewhere along the way."

"And you still found me in the darkness."

"I just had to listen with my heart."

Joy and sorrow.

They bustled through the atmosphere, throbbing in time with the beat of the heart monitor. Most of the machines that had surrounded us for the last week had been disconnected. No longer needed to sustain his life because he'd come back to me.

"Where is Lily?"

"In protective custody. Until they know for sure it's safe." I kept brushing my fingertips along the scruff of his jaw, unwilling to let go of the connection. "More than two-hundred-fifty arrests have been made."

Anger huffed from his nose.

"They found two more houses, Richard. A total of forty captives were freed."

Moisture clouded his eyes, and god, I loved and I loved.

This beautiful, broken man.

"Lester Ford?" he pushed out.

I nodded. "They finally got him, too. He tried to disappear, but he was arrested in South America two days ago. He's being extradited as we speak."

"It's over."

My smile wobbled. "It's over."

Late afternoon light filtered through our childhood home. Drenching it in love and warmth and hope. I wanted to cling to it. To let love whisper its faith into my spirit.

But all of this was one of the hardest things I'd ever done.

But with it came joy.

A juxtaposition that thrashed and banged and calmed.

Maybe it was hers that was crashing into mine, the trembling that reverberated from her body and flooded the room with uncertainty.

As if she no longer knew where she belonged or where she stood.

I could only let her know where I did.

I reached out and squeezed the hand of her arm that was casted. It was where she had sustained the gunshot that had shattered her upper arm. An external injury that would heal. I just prayed all the scars littered inside could one day do the same.

Liliana squeezed back. "I'm not sure I can do this," she wheezed through a stuttered breath of pain, staring up at the staircase like it was going to swallow her.

"It's the one thing she wanted. She needs this."

My big sister sniffled, and my heart jerked in time.

"Just...stay with me, okay?"

"I've always been with you, even when you weren't standing right next to me," I told her, wishing she would have understood that from the beginning.

That she would have fought for herself as hard as she'd fought for me. If she would have sacrificed for herself what she'd sacrificed for the rest of us.

I still couldn't bear it—the truth of what she'd endured.

She nodded as tears coursed down her face.

We started up the stairs.

One step joy.

Another devastation.

Another echoing with the memory of us stampeding up them when we were little, our mama yelling from the living room to be careful in her gentle way, chuckling under her breath that we might as well have been boys with the way we roughhoused.

Another ricocheting with the loss. The loss of laughter. The loss of years.

We made it to the landing, and Lily slowed, trying to find her breaths and slow her heart and keep herself from dropping to her knees.

I squeezed her hand again. "She is happy, Lily. Not just for the moment or because something turned out right. But because her heart knows the true meaning of it. Seeing her sick is the hardest thing in the world, but don't look at her body. Look in her eyes, and you'll see it."

Inhaling deeply, she let go of my hand, finding that massive well of strength that she once was, and she edged forward.

A second later, she stood in the doorway of our mama's room. Staring on the woman who had loved us with all that she was.

The one who had instilled our belief. Who had taught us kindness. Who'd whispered fierceness into our souls.

Lily was the epitome of it.

A fighter.

A survivor.

The second they locked eyes, Lily rushed to her side and

dropped to her knees, edged up high enough that she could bury her face in our mama's belly. "Mama."

Mama choked on the relief.

"Liliana. My sweet child. Liliana."

Pain and joy danced.

Mama tipped her head back and stared down at the daughter she'd been terrified she would never see again.

And those eyes said it all.

Amor. Amor. Amor.

I didn't know how I was supposed to stand aside and watch this happen.

My entire body shook.

An earthquake.

A landslide.

That selfishness that I tried to shuck from my consciousness. To rid from my spirit.

I searched for the kind of strength my big sister had mustered for the last six years, knowing I didn't have an idea, that I'd never come close, praying I could find a modicum of that bravery.

That I'd possess a shred of the type of self-sacrifice Lily had made.

"You should go and say hi," I whispered, running my hand through Daisy's hair where she stood next to me looking at Lily who stood rigid with her arms crossed over her chest about twenty feet away.

The late afternoon sky was chilled, my entire body shivering like it was gonna succumb to the cold.

Daisy danced over to her, stared up into Lily's eyes with one of those grins that could shatter the earth.

Bright.

Brilliant.

Sunshine.

"Hi. I'm Daisy."

Lily knelt down in front of her and tipped up her chin. "Hi, Daisy," she whispered on a tortured breath.

I nearly crumbled.

Daisy giggled and held up her casted arm. "Look, we match."

Lily brushed her knuckles down Daisy's cheek. "We do, don't we?"

"Yup! Did you know I'm a bird? I fly so high. Come and watch me."

Daisy grabbed Lily's hand and dragged her down the sloping lawn to her swing set in the middle of the yard.

A sob wrenched out of my throat.

Strong, strong arms wrapped around me from behind, even though one was in a sling. His voice came as a whisper in my ear, "It's okay. It's okay. I've got you."

"I'm falling, Richard. Falling apart."

His head shook against mine, and he just held me tighter. "It's okay. You can fall. I'll be right here to catch you."

"She's my life."

"And you're mine. We've got this, baby. Whatever life throws at us, we've got this."

Daisy's laughter billowed through the air.

Richard held me tighter. "She's so beautiful."

"All I've ever wanted is her joy."

"And you've given it to her."

Lily caught her at the bottom of the slide. "Wow, you did it!" she sang.

"I'm way big, didn't you know that? And a Tomfoolery, but I'm working on that."

Lily choked on a laugh.

Sorrow and joy.

Sorrow and joy.

It curled through the air like wisps of clouds.

"Mommy and Mr. Richard! Come play with us!" Daisy waved her unbroken arm in the air.

A haggard sound crawled my throat, and my gaze clawed toward my sister's.

Agony. Agony.

Richard held me with his hands pressed over my chest. Keeping me upright.

Liliana smiled. This soft, knowing smile. She gestured with her head for us to join them.

Richard took my hand, weaving our fingers together as he moved to my side. Energy sparked. Alive in the air. His dark aura washing through the encroaching night.

In it was warmth.

His ferocity.

His soul.

The man towered beside me where I stood in his eclipse.

"You can do this," Richard said with soft, soft belief.

I forced myself to walk their way on unstable feet.

The ground rumbled beneath. I thought I could physically feel it getting ready to be ripped out from under me.

"Mr. Richard! Mr. Richard! Are you all better now? Can you go on the slide? My mommy said I've got to be so super careful because she can't take no one else she loves getting hurt. Lords knows I'm a disaster."

A rough chuckle rolled through my aching chest.

Richard squeezed my hand tighter. "Give me a few days, flower girl, and I'll be good as new."

She grinned at the nickname he'd given her, her sweet face glowing, his love flooding out.

"How about I push you on the swing, instead?"

"Oh, yes, that's a great idea. But you gotta do it high. I'm a bird, not a chicken."

Lily and I both choked on shocked, consumed laughter.

Both of us on unsteady ground.

Tiptoeing around this meetin'.

My sister looked at me, took my hand where we watched Richard and Daisy play.

The child laughing and laughing.

Her joy filling the air as the day faded away.

"Sit with me?" Lily asked.

I gave her a nod, and we moved over to the back-porch steps that overlooked Daisy's swing set.

Silence stretched on.

Strung up on the questions.

On the unsurety.

Finally, her voice cracked through the dense, suffocating air.

"I blamed him for so long, Violet. I knew deep down in my soul that he didn't know. I could never erase his screams that night—when he'd pleaded for them to let me go. But I clung to the hatred for so long, desperate to keep him from you, fearing it would lead you to the same place as I'd been condemned."

Misery stung the back of my throat, and a tear slipped from my eye.

I could feel her shift to look at me. "I'm sorry for that. For taking him from you. For putting that burden on his shoulders. I didn't realize what I was doing at the time."

"That's not your fault. I just wish you would have relied on one of us. That you would have left with him that morning."

She laughed out a wistful, sorrowful sound. "So many nights I'd lie awake and wish it, too. Knowing it was too late. That I couldn't go back. Over those nights, I slowly forgave him, Violet, slowly realized he was just as much a victim that night as me. Used. Manipulated. He would have given anything for me. I see that now."

I glanced at her. "I would have given anything, too."

"You gave me exactly what I needed, Violet. Being the best momma that little girl could have. I knew you'd be. All the nights I spent dreaming of her. Loving her. Missing her. And the comfort I had was she had you. That you were her mommy."

I gasped around the shards of glass lodged in my throat, and the words wrenched through my tears, "It's been my absolute honor."

We hadn't talked about her and Daisy yet other than Lily asking a few things about her.

What she was like.

Her favorites.

Her fears.

I could see the longing swimming in her forlorn eyes.

I'd known it was coming.

Her head shook, and she bit down on her trembling bottom lip. "You know…I imagined what it might be like. When Richard found me, when he gave me a hope I'd long since stopped hoping for, when he'd promised he was going to get me out of there, I'd imagined coming back here, imagined what it would feel like to be her mother. To be reunited with this vacancy that has lived inside of me. But I know, Violet…I know looking at you two…hell, I knew from the second I saw you when David pulled you through that door. I knew that little girl was yours. Through and through. Wholly. And I would never steal that from you, and I would never steal that from her."

"Lily." It was a wheeze. A haggard breath of disbelief.

She squeezed my hand. "I mean it. This isn't me taking the high road. This is me loving my child the best way that I can."

"She knows she didn't grow of me, Lily. Ever since she was a baby, I told her about my sister who loved her so much that she wanted to share her with me."

I knew we'd have much more serious talks as she got older. But I'd needed Daisy to understand the love I was certain my sister had for her even though I didn't know why she'd abandoned her.

Before I'd understood it'd been forced.

A tear streaked down her cheek. It glinted and glimmered in the last brilliant rays of the day.

"She's our heart, Violet. And I won't split her little heart in two. I'm going to be right here. Loving her as her aunt. As long as that's okay with you?"

"Are you sure that's what you want?"

Sniffling, she nodded. "I am."

I looked at her through bleary eyes. "I missed you. Missed you so much."

"I missed you, too."

Lily grinned.

The tiniest flash of mischief in her eyes as she reached over and tugged at a lock of my hair.

"Hey," I cried, laughing through the tears.

"Tell me you're not still an old fuddy-duddy."

"Fuddy-duddy? I'm pretty sure it's you we need to be worried about."

I grinned.

She smiled.

Soft and full of adoration. She sniffled and stood, looking at Richard who was pushing Daisy high. "She couldn't ask for better parents."

I gave her a fumbling nod of understanding.

She reached out. "Come on, no more crying. I'm ready to live."

I let her help me to standing. I hugged her tight. Held on for dear life. "I can't wait to see it."

She nodded, squeezing tighter before she stepped back and wiped away her tears with the back of her hand. Then she turned to the beautiful sight that glowed beneath the rising moon. "Hey, Daisy. Why don't you come with Auntie Lily and color a picture for Nana with me? I think she needs another one for her wall, don't you?"

"Yes!" Daisy shouted. "That's a great idea. I got new colors. You wanna see?"

"I sure do."

Sensing she was getting ready to hop out of the swing like the daredevil she was, Richard slowed her, saying, "Whoa, there, flower girl. Slow your roll, wild child."

Curling her nose, she tipped her head back to look at him where she still swayed on the swing. "Are you my boss?"

I thought it was some kind of tease.

He brushed his fingers through her hair. "What do you think?"

"Well, you gave my mommy a ring. I think that means you must be my dad."

Richard looked over at Lily and me.

Lily smiled and she stepped away like she was departing from the scene.

Richard wavered before he dipped down and kissed Daisy's head, and my heart nearly tripped out of my chest. "I'll protect you with my whole life, Daisy. Love you. Warn you if you're doin' something that's not safe and be there to encourage you through all the adventures you have in this amazing life."

"That's what daddies do, right?" She tipped back farther,

squinting up at him.

He nodded. "Yeah, my sweet flower girl, that's what daddies do."

They stared for the longest time, me caught up in their moment.

Lost to it.

Swept away.

Forever falling.

Richard looked up at me like he felt me staring.

Daisy giggled. "Hey, Mommy, you better get over here, I think my daddy wants to give you one of those sloppy kind of kisses. The private kind," she mock whispered to my sister.

She hopped off the swing and came barreling our way.

"Can we have popcorn, too, Auntie?"

Lily caught my eyes, gave me another soft smile, before she took Daisy's hand. "I would love that. How about a movie so your mommy and daddy can talk for a little bit?"

"You mean kiss? You know they got all the *amor, amor, amor.*"

She waved an indulgent hand.

Spinning it.

Stirring it.

The love going round and round.

Shimmering in the air and filling our lungs.

Lily sent me a wink and they started up the porch steps, Daisy prattling on as they went inside.

Richard took a step forward.

"Come with me."

I eased down the slope until he was taking my hand and leading me down the trail as darkness crept across the heavens.

He weaved us through the rows of flowers.

Roses and lilacs and lilies.

A field of violets.

A thicket of roses.

The crickets came to life and the soft sounds of the night began to sing.

Peace.

Hope.

Love.

Richard turned around, stopping to bring us face-to-face where flowering bushes grew up all around us.

"What are we doing?" I whispered.

Richard smirked and wrapped me in the strength of his strong arms. "I want to dance with the prettiest girl in the place."

The smallest grin teased at the corner of my mouth. "I'd better not."

"And why's that?" he said with the slightest laugh.

He'd already started us into a slow sway.

"Because then you're gonna think you can take me home, and I'd have to go and disappoint you because that's not going to happen."

I gave him the same line I'd given him that first night.

The night he'd made a liar out of me.

The night he'd stolen my breath and my body.

When he'd kissed me and pillaged my heart.

Thank God, it'd listened.

His smile softened, and he brushed his fingers through my hair, angling my head back as he gazed down at me. He cupped my face. "Moonflower," he whispered, his nose tracking my cheek, his mouth moving for my ear. "We're already home. Exactly where you know we've always belonged."

Violet

*S*unlight teased through the brand-new leaves adorning the branches of the soaring trees that danced in the late spring breeze. The sun casting its rays down to the earth, touching our skin in a kiss of warmth.

Comfort and sorrow.

Comfort and sorrow.

They spun and billowed and blew.

Bittersweet.

We surrounded my daddy, Lily and me, each of us clinging to one of his hands, and Richard and Daisy stood off to the side of us.

Mama had left us four months ago, on the second day of January. Like she'd stayed for one last holiday. To fill our souls and hearts and our minds with the last of her wisdom. With the true, untarnished joy of who she was. With so much love that it would last us for the rest of our days.

My daddy trembled with the grief, with the massive amount of devotion that would hold him forever.

Daisy came skipping up to her grave with the bouquet of flowers she and I had picked this morning.

"Do you like these ones, Nana?" she said. "Mommy and I picked 'em special because they remind us of you. The most beautiful in all the world."

Then she stood up and started to sing with her arms stretched toward the heavens, her beautiful little voice off-key. "You are my sunshine, my only sunshine, you make me happy, when skies are gray…"

Daisy giggled and spun, reaching for the small yellow bird that flitted and dashed overhead. "Look it, Mommy! She heard me! She heard me! Just like she said she would."

I stifled a sob, and Lily and I squeezed our daddy's hands tighter when he couldn't keep his at bay.

We flanked him, holding him up.

It was such a strange thing to stand in the sadness and the joy.

To miss her but not to despair.

I glanced at Richard who was watching us. Sage eyes soft and knowing.

Fierce and sure and secure.

Daddy edged forward and knelt at her grave, whispered his fingers over her stone, set the single yellow rose on top of the ones that Daisy had left, and he murmured, "I hear you, too."

Richard paced out the line where we were on the opposite hill from my childhood home. He grinned back at us where the rest of us stood huddled together in the fading rays of the day as he carried the roll of architectural plans around like a prize.

"The wraparound porch will extend out to here." He paced the next line, his voice nothing but excitement. "All the way out to here."

My gaze traveled to the right. Over the rolling hills and acres of flowers that blossomed and flourished across our land. The magnificent tree sat in the distance. Standing beneath the sun that sagged low in the sky and lit it up in the most awestriking sort of beauty.

Pinks and purples and reds wisped with the melting blue.

That joy filled me to overflowing.

Sometimes I feared it would be too much. That I was gonna burst from it.

Impossible to fathom the depths of what I'd been given until I'd lost it and it'd been reclaimed.

That hole in the perfect shape of Richard filled, but when it'd been filled, he'd pushed deeper into those crevices, carving out more space, taking me whole in a way I hadn't before grasped or understood.

Not until I was given a full picture of his devotion.

The measure of his loyalty and the span of his love.

"Can you see it?" Richard said, waving those hands again high above his head. "Two stories with a pitched roof. Five bedrooms."

He cut me a smirky glance at that, his gaze drifting to my belly that was barely beginning to swell with our child.

Daisy went dancing his way, flailing her arms, too. "And my room's gonna be right here, right, Daddy?"

He swept her up and tossed her into the air. "Yep, right here!"

"And my baby brother's gonna be right next to me, right? And I'll get up and get a bottle for him and everything. I'm awesome like that, you know."

I barked out a laugh.

Yeah.

She was pretty awesome like that.

Daddy wrapped his arms around mine and Lily's waists, pulling us closer. He planted a kiss to Lily's temple and then turned to do the same to mine. We both settled our heads on his shoulders.

"My beautiful daughters. I am so thankful." He stared out across at Richard and he muttered, "El dador de alegría."

The giver of joy.

No longer the thief.

No longer misunderstood.

"Now you're gonna have to put up with my messes," Lily teased, looking up at him. "Once we finally kick Violet here out, and I get her room permanently."

"I'll take it," he said with a grin.

"Yeah, Daddy, me, too. I'll take it." Her voice was laced with a raw, tentative happiness. My sister was healing slowly, her hope growing like the flowers that bloomed around us.

The light dimming so we could all stand under the stars and the rising moon.

And we rejoiced in it.

This joy.

This peace.

In the faith that we'd fallen and landed exactly where we were supposed to be.

Richard

"What are you grinnin' about?"

From the doorway, I stared down at my wife who sat on the edge of our bed in just a tank and underwear. That black hair tied up high on her head.

So fuckin' pretty I felt her like a straight shot to the heart.

Those eyes holding me snared.

Enraptured.

Thunderstruck.

"Sometimes I still can't believe you're standin' there," she whispered into the swimming darkness that lapped in her old bedroom, the moonlight pouring in illuminating her silky skin.

I clicked the door shut behind me after I'd just tucked Daisy in.

Our daughter.

Our world.

This life more than I'd assumed or dared.

"And where else do you think I would be?"

The flicker of a smile lit at the corner of her delicious mouth. "Well, I'd think you could be a bit closer," she teased.

"Hmm...that so?" I rumbled as I moved her way, pulling off my shirt as I went, because fuck, I was done wasting time.

Second I got to her, I cupped a hand on her cheek, glancing at the suitcases sitting against the wall. "Are you ready for this?"

Tomorrow, Violet, Daisy, and I would be leaving for Savannah, Georgia where Carolina George would be recording out at the Stone Industries studio on Tybee Island. We'd be spending the summer at the mansion they used to house their artists.

Our house built right here on this same property while we were gone.

We'd been lying low for the last six months.

Giving Violet time to grieve.

To be there for her father.

For Lily to adjust.

For Lester's trial to come and pass.

The threat gone.

Put to rest.

Emily had given birth four weeks ago, and it was time to get back to work.

But we were doing it on our terms.

The entire band and their families would be staying at that house on the island, and we were treating it like an extended summer vacation.

Leif and his wife, Mia, and their kids.

Emily and Royce and my gorgeous baby niece, Amelia.

Of course, Maggie would be coming along, too.

Not to mention Rhys, the crazy bastard.

A Riot of Roses was scheduled to record in the middle of our session, since Royce was going to be there, anyway.

It was gonna be wild.

Promised chaos.

Was still a little reticent to rip Violet and myself from this peace. The hedge of healing we'd been surrounded by for so many months.

We'd been so far removed from the glitz and the limelight, the roads and the shows and the life I still desperately wanted but worried would still be a shock.

"More than ready," she said, assuaging the lingering fear of what that hunger had cost. "I can't wait to see you in your element. To see you shine. *Superstar.*" She mouthed the last.

My heart trembled.

"Things are about to change for us in a big, big way. Once that album comes out, all bets are off."

"And that's exactly what you all deserve. Where Carolina George has been headed all along."

"Never wanted to get there unless I could take you with me," I admitted as I crawled over her and pushed her back onto the bed.

That energy surged.

A flash of heat.

A seal of perfection.

"Then let's fly there together," Violet whispered.

I straddled her, both of my knees on the bed as I peeled up her tank.

She lifted her hands and helped me to free it, a sigh leaving her sweet, sweet mouth.

I hissed when I tossed it to the floor.

Girl laid out.

Those tits peaked and pebbled.

Shivers raced her flesh. So soft and right.

"Stunning," I said.

She scooted up until she was in the middle of the bed, and my hand was going out to splay across that miraculous little swell. The evidence of our son just beginning to show.

"Still can't believe it," I murmured, words so low as they rumbled into her childhood room.

I'd thought I'd been sentenced to desolation.

A lifetime of solitary confinement.

And somehow, I'd been given *this.*

I gazed down at her, and Violet lifted her hand and set it on my cheek, those eyes shouting so many things.

Awe.

Love.

Life.

"I'm so happy. I never knew I could feel a joy like this."

"You are the meaning of it."

She yelped, then giggled when I suddenly whipped her around until she was straddling me.

The girl made quick work of my jeans, and I edged up so she could pull them free.

Two of us like this.

Constantly tied.

Connected.

This insatiable need consuming us with a perfect-sort of greed.

A flawless give and take.

She pushed up to standing on her bed, and she wiggled out of her panties, and I nearly died right there.

Miles of lean legs.

Girl magic where she stood over me.

Carved of glass.

Fragile and fierce.

My fairy girl.

"Ride me, baby." I sent her a smirk.

She grinned as she climbed back down to straddle me and took me in a swift stroke that stole our breaths.

Her hands flew out to balance herself on my abdomen, my muscles flexing and bunching and firing.

I reached up and wound a hand in her lush hair as she worked her spell on me. "I love you, Violet."

Thunderbolt eyes gazed down at me.

"My wife. My moonflower in the darkest night. You will always be the song of soul."

"My husband. My sun that ushers in the day. You will always be the beat of my heart."

And our spirits sang together. Our bodies one. Our love abounding.

Breath to breath.
Soul to soul.
Where she fell into my darkness, and where I would forever stand in her moonlight.

the end

Thank you for reading *Falling into You!*

I hope you fell in love with Richard and Violet's story of second chances, forgiveness, and love!

Want more from the Caroline George crew?

Start with their drummer, Leif, in *Kiss the Stars*

https://geni.us/KTSAmzn

Did you love the men and women of Sunder? Start where it all began with Shea and Sebastian in *A Stone in the Sea*

https://geni.us/ASITSAmzn

New to me and want more? I recommend starting with my favorite small town alphas!

Start with *Show Me the Way*

https://geni.us/SMTWAmzn

Text "aljackson" to 33222 to get your LIVE release mobile alert (US Only)

or

Sign up for my newsletter
https://geni.us/NewsFromALJackson

More from A.L. Jackson

ABOUT THE AUTHOR

A.L. Jackson is the New York Times & USA Today Bestselling author of contemporary romance. She writes emotional, sexy, heart-filled stories about boys who usually like to be a little bit bad.

Her bestselling series include THE REGRET SERIES, CLOSER TO YOU, BLEEDING STARS, FIGHT FOR ME, CONFESSIONS OF THE HEART, FALLING STARS and REDEMPTION HILLS.

If she's not writing, you can find her hanging out by the pool with her family, sipping cocktails with her friends, or of course with her nose buried in a book.

Be sure not to miss new releases and sales from A.L. Jackson - Sign up to receive her newsletter http://smarturl.it/NewsFromALJackson or text "aljackson" to 33222 to receive short but sweet updates on all the important news.

Connect with A.L. Jackson online:

FB Page **https://geni.us/ALJacksonFB**
Newsletter **https://geni.us/NewsFromALJackson**
Angels **https://geni.us/AmysAngels**
Amazon **https://geni.us/ALJacksonAmzn**
Book Bub **https://geni.us/ALJacksonBookbub**
Text "aljackson" to 33222 to receive short but sweet updates on all the important news.

Made in the USA
Columbia, SC
16 September 2023

22963418R10274